FATEFUL FORTUNES AWAIT YOU—
in these all-original tales of people whose
futures are forever changed by the
drawing of the cards:

"The Court of the Invisible"—The tarot
had become her life—and she would
learn to interpret the fortune that the cards
held for her even if it killed her. . . .

"New Beginner's Luck"—It wasn't the
cards *in* the tarot deck but the ones that
were missing from it which held the
answers she didn't even realize she was
seeking. . . .

"Articles of Faith"—The deck had been in
her family for a very long time, and
though it did speak to everyone, Brooke
could suddenly hear its message loud
and clear. . . .

"Solo in the Spotlight"—Would the
President allow the fate of nations to rest
on an extremely unorthodox tarot deck?

TAROT
FANTASTIC

More Imagination-Clutching Anthologies Brought to You by DAW:

THE SECRET PROPHECIES OF NOSTRADAMUS
Edited by Cynthia Sternau and Martin H. Greenberg.
From one woman's encounter with a Revelation that is out of this world to a centuries-old international society dedicated to minimalizing the devastating effects of true predictions to a future where people have finally found the way to achieve "peace," here are truly provocative, innovative stories created especially for this volume, each of which breathes new life into the ancient art of prophecy.

WEIRD TALES FROM SHAKESPEARE *Edited by Katharine Kerr and Martin H. Greenberg.* From a computer-peopled "King Lear" to a vampiric Romeo, here are twenty-three bold new tales about the Bard himself and his many memorable creations.

MISKATONIC UNIVERSITY *Edited by Martin H. Greenberg and Robert Weinberg.* For anyone who has ever been caught in Lovecraft's spell, and everyone who loves a good horror tale, here are thirteen original stories that will introduce you to the dark side of education, and prove once and for all that a little arcane knowledge can be a dangerous thing.

TAROT FANTASTIC

Edited by
Martin H. Greenberg
and Lawrence Schimel

DAW BOOKS, INC.
DONALD A. WOLLHEIM, FOUNDER
375 Hudson Street, New York, NY 10014

ELIZABETH R. WOLLHEIM
SHEILA E. GILBERT
PUBLISHERS

First Printing, February 1997
1 2 3 4 5 6 7 8 9

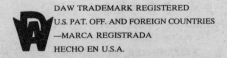

ACKNOWLEDGMENTS

For Michelle Sagara West

CONTENTS

ix

SHUFFLING THROUGH HISTORY: A BRIEF INTRODUCTION

by Lawrence Schimel

Few oracles have so captured the public imagination—and for as long—as has the tarot. Even those who actively disbelieve in the possibility of any sort of divination, who have never had their cards read or turned the cards themselves, can often name part of the Major Arcana.

But what, exactly, is the tarot?

For most people, the tarot is a deck of cards used most often for a parlor trick of fortune-telling, a legerdemain for the gullible.

For others, the tarot is a symbolic language which allows them to discuss matters of the psyche and to delve within themselves for Truth.

And for some, it holds the Future.

Historically, the tarot is thought to originate in the fourteenth century, although not in the format we know today. At that time, playing cards began to appear, scattered throughout Europe, as gambling devices. There were no standards governing the number of cards in these decks, or the suits and designs used. The Church condemned all these decks as instruments of the Devil, and they quickly earned the moniker

"The Devil's Bible" or sometimes "The Devil's Picturebook" because of the painted court cards.

While some believe that the tarot is the ancestor of the modern fifty-two-card deck of playing cards, it is more commonly thought that the Major Arcana originated concurrently but separately with the precursor to the traditional deck of playing cards, and that these two decks converged at some untraceable and unrecorded point in time to give us the tarot as it is known today with its two-decks-in-one hierarchy, the Major and Minor Arcanas.

It is thought by some that the original intention of the tarot, with its allegorical symbols of virtue, may have been to educate children. An Italian deck dating to the fifteenth century is comprised of fifty cards arranged in five groups of ten, including The States of Man (Beggar, Servant, Artisan, Merchant, Gentleman, Knight, Doge, King, Emperor, Pope); Cosmic Principles (Temperance, Fortitude, Charity, Faith, Hope, Justice, Prudence, Genius of the Sun, Genius of Time, Genius of the World); Apollo and the Muses; Liberal Arts; and Systems of Heaven. A handful of the cards overlaps with the Major Arcana of the tarot deck, although Arthur Edward Waite, among others, found tarot symbolism wanting in this deck.

Despite the Church's disapproval of any sort of cards, Europe's nobility continued to commission special hand-painted decks of cards to be created for them. And by the late fifteenth century, tarot decks (with some variation) had evolved in Italy, France, and elsewhere in Europe. The invention of the printing press in the mid-fifteenth century helped the proliferation of cards, which could be printed from wooden blocks instead of painted individually.

It was not until the eighteenth century, however, that tarot cards became considered and were studied as an esoteric art. Tarot had fallen out of favor by

1781, when a deck was rediscovered and misattributed by Antoine Court de Gébelin as part of an Egyptian book of wisdom, the BOOK OF THOTH. The idea that the tarot derived from Egypt was mysterious and alluring, and it quickly spread in popularity as the origin and purpose of the strange cards.

The gypsies, who were also thought to have come out of Egypt (although as we now know their origins lie in India), were quickly linked with the cards, and were instrumental in increasing the popularity of the cards by adopting the tarot as one of their methods of fortunetelling. The link remains strong to this day, although not in a complimentary fashion to either gypsies or the tarot.

In the early twentieth century, the tarot underwent perhaps its most radical reinterpretation, resulting in the decks most familiar today. Arthur Edward Waite, a member of the Hermetic Order of the Golden Dawn, debunked the Egyptian link in his book THE PICTORIAL KEY TO THE TAROT, and reinterpreted the tarot deck according to what he thought were its lost mystical meanings. Waite wrote:

> *The true tarot is symbolism; it speaks no other language and offers no other signs. Given the inward meaning of its emblems, they do become a kind of alphabet which is capable of indefinite combinations and makes true sense in all. On the highest plane it offers a key to the Mysteries, in a manner which is not arbitrary and has not been read in. But the wrong symbolic stories have been told concerning it, and the wrong history has been given in every published work which so far has dealt with the subject . . .*

Published by Rider and Company in 1910, Waite's deck, executed by American artist Pamela Colman Smith from his designs, was the first to fully illustrate the pip cards, and remains one of the most popular decks to this day. He relied heavily on the "Secret Doctrines" of the Hermetic Order of the Golden Dawn in his interpretations, and revealed as much as he felt he could to noninitiates of their way of studying the occult and magic. This aura of forbidden knowledge is part of the tarot's strong allure as a device for fortunetelling, that separation of those few who have the key to understanding the Mysteries and the masses who do not. This aura is so powerful—as archetypic in its way as the symbols of the tarot itself—that even charlatans versed in a partial tradition can draw upon it and seem to know Answers to the Mysteries.

Not everyone accepted Waite's interpretation, of course, although it is now considered the standard deck by which all other tarot decks are measured. Aleister Crowley, for instance, a fellow member of the Golden Dawn, notorious for his extreme behavior and his use of sex and drugs for magical pursuits, disagreed with Waite's mystical focus, believing that the tarot were living entities, and created his own Thoth deck. Today, there are many different variant decks, ranging from the fanciful and fantastic Tarot of the Cat People to the feminist Motherpeace deck of circular cards.

The tarot, however, exists as a separate entity from the cards by which it is best known. The tarot is, instead, an imaginative system, a glyphic language like the Egyptian hieroglyphs it was thought to represent, a road map to the psyche. The images of the tarot provide a visual externalization for emotion, that allows one to then look inside oneself for the mirror of what is represented on the cards. Once the tarot is manifested physically, in the form of cards or paintings, the images can be contemplated singly, allowing for a greater focus, familiar landmarks on a spiritual journey. In physical form, the images of the tarot begin to have spatial relations with other cards and their archetypes.

In this collection, sixteen writers return to the realm of the imagination and engage the archetypes of the tarot. Their stories range from the comic to the sober, as they question and interpret and reinterpret the images of the tarot, our human responses to the tarot and its meanings, and our yearnings for what the tarot might be: a magical, mystical link to the Future.

SONG OF THE CARDS
by Jane Yolen

Jane Yolen, referred to as "America's Hans Christian Andersen" (*Newsweek*), has published more than 170 books, including *The Devil's Arithmetic, Briar Rose, Owl Moon,* and *Cards of Grief.* She is a winner of the World Fantasy Award, the Christopher Medal, The Regina Medal, The Kerlan Award, and many other honors. She divides her time between Massachusetts and St. Andrews, Scotland.

Yolen's "Song of the Cards" is a lyric invocation of the tarot and its potential, making it the perfect frontispoem to set the tone of this collection, in that time-honored tradition of invoking the muse at the beginning of a Work.

Major Arcana: The Triumphal March

For you tellers of fate,
You fortuneers,
You players of change,
You ringers of years,
You gamers of chance,
You cultists of cards,
You prophets of numen,
You mystical guards.

You do not fright me
with the divine deck.

For I am the hanging man,
I am the fool,
I am the Tower and Star.
I am the Lover,
I am the Moon,
I am all the cards
there are.

Minor Arcana: A Small Suit(e)

Give me your sword,
the tip just sharp enough
to puncture alter egos.
And the wand
to wave in the face
of adversity.
Hand me the cup,
fortune's bright codpiece.
And the pentacle,
for a fiver
makes a nice tip
for the driver.
We have many miles to go,
a rough riding,
in a slouch of a coach.
Cards, like stories,
will make destinies come sooner.

SYMBOLS ARE A PERCUSSION INSTRUMENT

by Tanya Huff

Tanya Huff is the author of five novels about investigator Vicki Nelson and her vampire sidekick, Henry Fitzroy—*Blood Price, Blood Trail, Blood Lines, Blood Pact,* and *Blood Debt;* as well as the novels of Crystal—*Child of the Grove* and *The Last Wizard;* the Quarters trilogy—*Sing the Four Quarters, Fifth Quarter,* and *No Quarter;* and two stand-alone fantasies, *The Fire's Stone* and *Gate of Darkness, Circle of Light.* She lives in Ontario.

"Symbols Are a Percussion Instrument" is a delightful romp of a story in which certain forces feel the need to be somewhat heavy-handed to make their point clear.

Her cel phone rang just as they were passing through the gates. As the imperious trill rose over the noise of the fair and people began turning to look, David Franklin put one hand over his eyes and sighed. "Cyn, why didn't you leave it in the car?"

"Are you nuts? Do you know how much this thing cost me?"

"Then why not leave it at home?"

"Because I feel naked without it."

"Naked might do you good."

"Don't start," she warned him as they made their

way out of the stream of pedestrian traffic to the relative quiet by the chain link fence. "This'll only take a minute."

David watched her flick the phone open and muttered, "Beam me up, Scotty," under his breath.

"Augustine Textiles, Cynthia Augustine speaking."

Turning to watch a group of shrieking children race toward the merry-go-round, David grinned as their mother—Babysitter? Teacher?—yelled that Stuart was to keep hold of his little brother. The little brother in question was about four, wearing the remains of a candy apple, and swinging from the reins of a turquoise stallion. Stuart, his own Power Rangers T-shirt none too clean, solved the problem by simply sitting on the smaller child and ignoring all protests.

"Cute kids."

"Where?" Cynthia glanced toward the merry-go-round and frowned. "I wonder who does those banners. We could prob- . . .." The phone rang again before she finished. "Augustine Textiles, Cynthia Augustine speaking."

Not even remotely surprised that she'd seen the banners and not the kids, David waited until she disconnected, then held out his hand.

"Aha." Triumphant, she passed the cel phone over. "You complain until you suddenly need to make a call and— What are you doing?"

He stuffed the battery into one of the outside pockets on his black leather knapsack and handed back the rest. "This is our day off. And that means, we don't work."

Her eyes narrowed. "This is a recession. If the company goes under, that means you don't work."

"You have so little faith in your business that you can't leave it for a few hours?"

"Faith has nothing to do with business." She looked down at the useless plastic in her hand, then up at the man who was not only the company's entire design department but also her best friend. "All right. For you. Two hours, then you give me back my battery."

David checked his watch. "Three and I'll drive home so you can talk."

"Deal."

The fair mixed traditional agriculture and current trends. Ten feet from the ring where yearling beef cattle stood placidly beside their young handlers, a sign proclaimed that for a small fee attendees could have their picture and comments added to the fair's web page.

Farmers in co-op baseball hats watched the circulating crowds of wide-eyed city tourists with amusement or disdain, depending on their natures. The tourists, in turn, considered the farmers part of the ambience and, when they weren't taking pictures, ignored them.

"Ridiculous leash laws in this part of the country," Cynthia murmured as the cattle left the ring, each dragging a child dressed head to toe in white.

"I think it's wonderful these kids have a chance to be part of the whole farming experience."

"Oh, yeah, great experience. Today a beloved pet wins a ribbon, tomorrow it's in the freezer, wrapped in brown paper and labeled hamburger."

David winced. "Do you have to?"

"I call 'em like I see 'em." She tucked her hand in his elbow and propelled him toward the open doors of the hockey arena. "Come on, this was your idea. Let's go see the rest of it."

The arena had been equally divided between tables of produce brought in to be judged and commercial booths. With the fair only a two-hour drive from Toronto, most venders were pushing variations on the country chic theme.

Throwing himself into the experience, David examined every fruit, vegetable, and flower, comparing those that wore ribbons with those that didn't, asking questions of anyone who seemed like they might have an answer. By the time he reached *five tomatoes on a plate,* he'd charmed an honor guard of little old ladies.

Cynthia lost interest by *two ripe cucumbers over nine inches,* and followed blindly, wondering if she could get her phone back in time to call one of their eastern suppliers. Her wandering attention returned with a snap as David stopped in front of a commercial booth selling decorative door stops.

"David, put that down."

"Don't you like it?"

"No."

"I think it's cute."

"For chrissakes, David, it's a cow in a dress!"

He grinned impishly at her. "Drew wouldn't let me have it in the house, but I could always use it at the office."

"Over my dead body."

Tucking it back in with the rest of the sartorial herd, he pulled her back outside. "Come on, let's try the midway."

A few moments later, Cynthia stared up at the double ferris wheel and then down at David. "I was kidding about that over my dead body thing."

"It's perfectly safe. Look, people are letting their kids ride."

"These people have kids to spare. I'm *not* getting on that death trap."

From the top of the ferris wheel, it was possible to see not only the entire fairground but a good piece of the surrounding town as well.

"They've got a scrambler!" The basket rocked as David leaned forward and pointed. "It's been years since I've been on one!"

Cynthia tried to work out the tensile strength of the pair of steel pins that seemed to be all that were holding the basket to the ride. "I wonder how often they check for stress fractures," she muttered as they circled around again.

"Hey! There's a fortuneteller!"

"David, if you don't stop rocking this thing, I'm going to do something violent."

"I think the sign says she's a card reader."

"Great, maybe we can find a fourth for bridge, now SIT STILL!"

Under normal circumstances, Cynthia wouldn't have gone within a hundred feet of a fortuneteller, but with a ride on the scrambler—something she clearly remembered as being nauseating and mildly painful—as the immediate alternative, having cards read—whatever that meant in the real world—became the lesser of two evils.

"So, what do you get when you cross a travel agent with an ophthalmologist?" she asked as they approached the tent. Pointing at the sign, she answered her own question. "Let Madame Zora Help You See the World Through New Eyes. David, you know I don't deal well with this New Age crystal-wearing crap."

"Then you're in luck because tarot cards aren't New Age. They're derived from the oldest book in the world; the Egyptian Book of Thoth by Hermes Trismegistus, councillor of Osiris, King of Egypt."

She turned to stare at him in amazement. "I don't *believe* you know all that stuff."

"I don't; it's in the small print on the sign, but I consider myself open to extreme possibilities."

"I get it." Cynthia's voice rose in exaggerated outrage. "This is an *X-File*." She began to turn. "I'm out of here."

David blocked the path. "Oh, no you're not. You

agreed to have your cards read, and a promise is a promise."

"Don't," Cynthia snarled, "quote Disney at me."

The tent was army surplus. An unsuccessful attempt had been made to dress up the drab canvas by stringing lines of plastic pennants along the guy wires.

Her hands stuffed in the front pockets of her jeans, Cynthia glanced down at the crushed grass path leading under the flap, then around at the fair. They stood in a pocket of quiet; the music from the midway seemed muffled and the crowds parted well in advance of the tent. "Now what? Do we wait to be seated?"

"You enter."

The speaker was not visible, but the tent flap folded back as they watched.

"Here goes nothing," Cynthia murmured, adding to David's back as he hurried past her, "And I mean that literally by the way."

Inside, plastic yard lights pushed into the ground between the patterned carpets and the billowing walls created alternating bands of light and shadow. It would have been a more successful effect had the burning incense been able to overcome the musty smell of canvas stored too long in a damp basement.

A rectangular table with three high-backed chairs lined up behind it stood under the center peak of the tent. The figure in the middle chair had a familiar, if not clichéd, silhouette.

"Come closer, seekers."

As they stepped forward, a pair of hanging lights came on over the table, banishing shadows and throwing Madame Zora into hard-edged relief.

David made a small noise of appreciation.

Hundred-watt floods, Cynthia thought as the fortune-teller lifted a beringed hand and beckoned them closer still.

"Have you a question for Madame Zora?" Somewhere past forty, she looked exactly as a fortuneteller should look, from the shawls to the jewelry to the heavily kohled eyes.

David gave her his best smile. "Only those questions that every seeker has," he said, matching her dramatics.

Madame Zora responded to the smile and nodded toward the chair to her right. "Then come, sit."

"Wait a minute," Cynthia grabbed David's arm as he started to move away. "I have a question. Do you actually believe that pieces of cardboard can tell the future?"

Dark eyes lifted and met hers. "No. That's not what they're for. The value of the tarot is to make people think, to weigh the pros and cons of a situation." Her voice picked up a new cadence. " 'The true tarot is symbolism. It speaks no other language and presents no other signs.' A. E Waite."

Cynthia's lip curled. " 'What you see is what you get.' Yacko Warner."

"Symbols are the picture forms of hidden thought, the door leading to the hidden chambers of the mind."

"Give me a break! What hidden chambers?"

"If you want . . ." Madame Zora indicated the chair on her left. ". . . I'll let the cards answer your question when I'm finished with your friend."

"I don't believe in fortunetelling."

"You don't have to. Your belief or disbelief makes as little difference to the cards as it would to the weather."

"My friend doesn't believe either."

Grabbing her arm, David hauled her around the corner of the table. "Just sit," he hissed. "You're embarrassing me."

As he pushed her into her chair and went to take his own, Cynthia locked the rest of her opinions behind her teeth. She saw the whole old-as-new-spirituality, Mother Goddess, tofu, wheat germ, candle burning sort of thing as a last refuge for those who couldn't cut it in the real world, but if her apparent compliance in this charade made David happy, then she supposed it wouldn't hurt her to play a . . .

Which was when she became aware of the denomination of the bill changing hands. "Twenty bucks!"

The money disappeared into a definitively real world cash box. "I have a sliding scale," Madame Zora explained, snapping the lid closed.

"Sliding from where? What makes you think he can afford twenty bucks to have his fortune told?"

"His two-hundred-and-fifty-dollar, leather backpack."

Behind the curve of Madame's broad back, David shot her a look that clearly said, *Any other objections*?

She glanced from him to the pack now on the floor behind his chair, sighed, and shook her head.

"First, we will remove your significator card." Madame Zora flipped the deck and deftly fanned it. "I would say, the Knight of Cups; a young man with light brown hair and hazel eyes, emotional, imaginative, and skilled in the arts. If you will shuffle the deck . . ."

Leaning to her right, as though she wanted a better view of the pattern being laid out on the table, Cynthia slowly stretched her arm behind Madame Zora's chair and hooked one finger through a leather loop. If she could just get her hands on her battery . . .

"You have a high proportion of cups showing. That indicates good news. Here, in the first position . . ."

The pack slid noiselessly over the short nap of the carpet. Surreptitiously patting each outside pocket, she finally felt a familiar lump.

". . . and the happy conclusion of a task. The Six of Wands, in the fifth position symbolizes what will happen—victory will be achieved and success will be obtained through labor. These two cards obviously support each . . ."

It wasn't easy opening the buckle one-handed, but Cynthia eventually worked the battery free. Dropping it into her lap, she returned the pack to its original position.

". . . symbolizing your own hopes and ideals on the matter. It's interesting that this is your only pentacle . . ."

Under the cover of the table, the battery slid into her phone with a gratifying ease. She sagged back against her chair, feeling the tension leave her shoulders.

When David's reading ended, Madame Zora pulled out a second deck of cards. "To allow the others to clear," she explained. "I never use the same deck twice in a row.

"Normally," she continued, fanning the cards, "the significator for a blonde woman with gray eyes would be the Queen of Wands, but in this instance I think the Devil might be more suitable."

Cynthia frowned down at the card lying alone on the table. "I don't think I like that."

"It has nothing to do with the devil as you perceive him, nothing to do with the evil of the Christian religion. The card symbolizes the domination of matter over spirit. Apt enough, I think? Shuffle, please."

Amazed she was actually going through with it, actually giving implied approval to occult psychology, Cynthia shuffled and split the deck as instructed.

Madame Zora laid out cards with firm, no nonsense movements of her hands, the rings flashing in the light. "Oh. My. Four of the Major Arcana. There are powerful outside forces at work here. Look at the pattern, please, and tell me what you see."

"Words," Cynthia muttered. "Words. Words. Words."

"I beg your pardon?"

"Polonius asked Hamlet what he was reading and Hamlet answered, '*Words*.'" She waved a hand over the cards. "In this instance, however, '*Pictures*' might be more appropriate."

Cocking her head slightly, Madame Zora kept her gaze on the cards. "That's all that you see?" she asked, her tone so explicitly neutral it lifted David's brows. "Pictures?"

Cynthia studied the pattern for a moment before she answered. "There isn't anything else," she said at last. "Pretty pictures that don't symbolize anything but a way for you to make a living which, I assure you, I'm not against, but *I* believe in what I can see and . . ."

The phone cut her off.

"Cynthia!" David could've managed more outrage if he hadn't been so relieved to have the impending rant cut short.

"Augustine Textiles, Cynthia Augustine speaking. What's that? I'm sorry, could you hang on a moment until I get outside?" Scrabbling to her feet she headed for the tent flap. "I'm sorry, but I've got to take this call."

David closed his eyes in embarrassment. When he opened them again, Madame Zora was watching him, her expression unreadable.

"I'm so sorry," he began but she cut him off.

"No need. *I* am sorry for your friend." Her gesture bracketed the pattern. "I see transformation in these cards."

"By powerful outside forces?"

"By, because of, for; who can say? If they feel it necessary, certain *things* will go to extremes to attract attention."

"But you said they were just symbols."

"Symbols," said Madame Zora with ponderous emphasis, "are shortcuts to more complicated meanings."

"I *cannot* believe you did that!"

Looking like the cat who swallowed the canary, Cynthia slipped her phone back in its pouch. "Did what?"

"Broke our agreement, went through my stuff, stole your battery back, *and* interrupted the reading!"

"We got the hotel job."

David choked as he attempted to change responses in mid-word. Cheerfully thumping him on the back, Cynthia reassured a number of anxious bystanders that he was fine, just a little overcome with the afternoon's excitement. Several mothers of small children nodded in weary understanding.

"This is just like Madame Zora said," he gasped, grabbing Cynthia's arm. "Victory will be achieved and success will be obtained through labor."

"Coincidence." She tucked her hand in the crook of his elbow and propelled him toward the parking lot. "Come on, we've got a lot to do."

Digging in his heels, he dragged her to a stop. "I really think you ought to go back and let Madame Zora interpret your cards. Remember those powerful outside forces, Cyn." He repeated his final conversation with the fortuneteller. As he'd expected, it had no effect.

"David, there's nothing to interpret."

"You've got to admit, she did a fine reading for me."

"Well, considering she started with a knight instead of a queen . . ." Placing her hand in the small of his back, Cynthia shoved him forward, moving him another four feet toward the exit. "Now, can we go?"

She managed to keep him moving until a small crowd stopped them both just inside the perimeter fence. In front of an artificial pond, two men, in a mix of medieval armor and hockey equipment, were beating on each other with rattan swords. On a bench to one side, sat a young woman, blindfolded and holding a pair of swords aloft.

Separated from David and caught up in the crowd, Cynthia found herself beside the bench without really understanding how she got there. She staggered, stretched out a hand, and managed to stop herself at the last minute from grabbing one of the two swords.

"You may have a well-developed sense of balance, but you're definitely in need of direction."

"I beg your pardon."

"No need. I'm here to help." Lifting the blindfold with an extended thumb, the girl peered up at Cynthia with dark eyes. "Would you mind holding one of these for a moment?"

There didn't seem to be a polite way to refuse so Cynthia gingerly took the closer of the two swords. It was much heavier than she expected.

"Thanks." Reaching into a side pocket, the girl pulled out a familiar white rectangle. "My card. For later."

"For later," Cynthia repeated, habit extending her free hand. She'd barely returned the sword when the crowd surged past, caught her up again, and deposited her back by David's side. "Is there a reason you've got your mouth open?"

"That girl!"

"What about her?" She shoved the business card in her back pocket without looking at it.

"Two swords! The pond! The rocks! The bench! The moon!"

Cynthia glanced up at the crescent moon barely visible in the afternoon sky and shrugged. "So?"

"The tarot!"

"A verb, David. Try a verb."

He grabbed her shoulders and shook her. "That's the second card in your tarot reading! The Two of Swords!"

"Do you have any idea how ridiculous that sounds?"

"Yes!" He paused. His cheeks flushed as he released her. "Really ridiculous. I think, I think I got too much sun."

"I think you're right." She tucked her arm into the bend of his elbow. "Come on. Let's go home."

Augustine Textiles was in the lower, not quite basement, level of an old red brick building on King Street West, a neighborhood working toward trendy—by the time the higher rents arrived, Cynthia planned on being able to afford them. Over the years they'd seen a number of spectacular accidents from their vantage point a sidewalk's width from the street but nothing like the accident the morning after the trip to the fair.

"I didn't know there was a circus in town," David declared, his ears ringing in the post-crash quiet.

"I don't think there is." Cynthia found it impossible not to tilt her head to try to bring the view into a normal perspective.

A tractor trailer, its sides open ironwork, had jackknifed making the turn off Spadina. When the far wheels hit the curb, it had flipped over onto its back.

"Maybe it's a publicity stunt for 'Beauty and the Beast.' "

In the trailer, a woman in a long white dress with flowers in her hair and around her waist held closed the mouth of a male lion. Both woman and lion were, at the moment, suspended upside down.

The moment ended. Neither appeared too badly hurt by the fall.

Using language totally at odds with her appearance, the woman untangled herself from her skirts and got, somewhat shakily, to her feet. The lion shook itself, squeezed between two twisted bars and took off down the street. Approaching sirens became quickly overlaid with startled screaming.

Fully aware that the most helpful thing she could do was to stay put, Cynthia yanked open the door and raced out onto street. "Are you all right?" She rocked to a halt when she saw that the woman, taking the lion's route out of the destroyed truck, was fine—which left her nothing to do but stand and feel embarrassed.

The woman reached back through the hole to pick up a bronze figure eight, then turned and smiled kindly at her. "Never fear passion," she said. "Now, if you'll excuse me." Pushing a crushed bloom up off her face, she strode purposefully toward the corner where a half dozen police officers had the lion more-or-less cornered. "Here, let me. Brute force will get you nowhere with him."

"Well?" David demanded when Cynthia came back inside.

"She's fine. And, although several members of Toronto's finest are going to need to have their trousers dry-cleaned, the lion's fine. Let's get back to work."

"That's it?"

"There's nothing we can do out there, and there's plenty we can do in here."

David stood a while longer, staring out the window, watching a pair of tow trucks try and pull the trailer away. All at once, he paled. "Cyn?"

"Um."

"What did she say to you?"

Deep in a new database, it took Cynthia a moment to realize what David was talking about. "Something about never fearing passion. Why?"

"That was the third card in your reading. Strength, reversed."

"Strength *reversed?*" Both brows lifted. "You're out of your mind."

"Oh, yeah? How many times have you seen a woman and a lion upside down in the fashion district? Remember what Madame Zora said. Certain *things* will go to extremes to attract attention."

"What things?"

"Well, we'd know if you'd finished the reading, wouldn't we!"

"David, you're getting hysterical."

"No, not yet." He crossed the room and leaned over her desk. "You haven't seen hysterical yet. The tarot is coming to life, forcing you to recognize it the only way it can. Do you remember what your last card was?"

"Of course I don't. And neither do you."

"Oh, yes, I do. I may not remember the middle of the pattern but I remember that last card. It was a Ten of Swords, Cynthia. And you *know* what that means!"

She rolled her eyes and sat back. "No, David, what does that mean?"

"It means that sooner or later you're going to be explaining a dead body with ten swords in it to the police."

"If you don't go back to your desk," she reminded him pointedly, "we're going to lose the best contract we've ever had, and it's going to be your body."

"Cynthia, please. You know I'm right."

"And what am I, chopped liver?"

"Well, no, you're right, too, but . . ."

"Then please, get back to work." She watched him cross back to his desk and shook her head. His sudden obsession with a not-terribly-successful midway attraction was beginning to worry her.

Out on the street, the lion roared.

* * *

"David? Cynthia. Sorry I woke you, but I've got a problem."

"Problem. Right. It's two in the morning. It'll keep."

"David, don't hang up!" Pulling back her kitchen curtains, she took another look out the window. "What was the next card in that tarot reading?" The silence on the other end of the phone was so complete she figured he'd gone back to sleep. "David?"

He hadn't. "The next card?"

"Did it look like a dog and a wolf—although it's probably a coyote—bracketed by a pair of upright things—in this particular case the old bridge abutments—howling at a full moon with some real weird shadow patterns on it while a lobster crawls up out of the water?"

"Uh, hang on a minute."

She flinched as the howling began again. "Don't take too long." One of the Garibaldis in the apartment upstairs, yelled for quiet and threw a boot out the window toward the river. The lobster turned toward the noise, but the howling continued.

"Cyn? The card's called the Moon. It stands for influence just passed away. And Cyn, it's the card of the psychic."

Madame Zora. Damn. "How the hell do you know?"

"I bought a book on the way home. You'd better come over." Sleepy protests in the background were quickly hushed. "Just out of curiosity, what convinced you I was right?"

Sighing, she let the curtain drop. "David, I can rationalize upside-down lions, but trust me, there's no way a lobster could survive in the Humber."

David answered the door to the condo with a slim paperback in one hand and a finger over his lips. "Shhh. Drew's gone back to sleep. We can talk in the den." Ushering her in front of him, he closed the door and relaxed. "How was the trip over?"

Cynthia snorted. "Weird. I stopped at the bottom of the Casa Loma Hill to untie a young woman standing blindfolded surrounded by eight swords. She thanked me, picked up her swords, and said she'd have done it herself except she was afraid of moving out of a situation of bondage." She dropped onto one end of a leather couch. "They, whoever they are, are not very subtle."

"We knew that; they dropped a lion on its head to make a point." Sinking down onto the other end of the couch, David flipped through the book. "The Eight of Swords. Your fifth card. Something that may happen in the future."

"David, pay attention please. It already happened."

"It symbolizes what may happen to *you*."

Her lips pressed into a thin line. "If somebody tries that on me . . ."

David sighed. "Symbolizes. You may be bound by indecision."

"The only thing I can't decide is whether or not I should look up Madame Zora and slap her with a lawsuit."

"For what?"

It was Cynthia's turn to sigh. "Good point. So what comes next?"

"I don't remember."

"You're a lot of help." He looked so hurt she flushed and gripped his shoulder. "I'm sorry I'm being such a bitch. This has got me a little shaken."

One corner of his mouth hooked up. "Cyn, you're always a bitch, I've gotten used to it. Now, let's go over what we know. Madame Zora said it was a pattern of transformation and, counting the significator, you've seen the first five cards. You've got four to go and then the Ten of Swords—The Final Outcome."

"I wish you wouldn't say it like that," Cynthia muttered, sinking down into the cushions. "It makes me think that I might be the body under the swords—my reading, my Final Outcome."

"We're not even going to think that." But they both were. "Don't put your feet on the coffee table."

"Sorry."

"According to this book, the Ten of Swords symbolizes sudden misfortune . . ."

"Well, duh."

". . . and in spiritual matters, the end of delusion."

She straightened. "I am *not* deluded. I'm practical. I've kept a small business afloat in a lingering recession and . . . business . . ." Reaching into her back pocket, she pulled out a creased card. "The girl with the swords said she was here to help and gave me this for later."

The card was blank except for a phone number; a 555 number, an exchange used only by long distance directory assistance and the screen writers' guild. After two rings, an answering machine clicked on and a familiar voice declared, "A changed concept of self automatically alters our future. All outer change takes place in consciousness. If you leave a message after the tone, you'll be wasting your time."

It wasn't so much a tone as the theme from "Close Encounters."

"Well, I think the solution's obvious."

Cynthia stared at him in wide-eyed disbelief. "Obvious?"

"You've got to learn to see the symbolism before the reality kills you. You've got to get in touch with your spiritual side."

"With my what?"

"You'd better stay here tonight. We can get started in the morning."

*   *   *

She felt each of the ten swords as they pierced her body, nailing her to the floor. Closing her eyes against the pain, she muttered, "The stains are never going to come out of this carpet."

From far away, she heard a familiar voice intone, "Look beyond to the symbolism."

"Symbolism? David, this carpet was hand-tied in Morocco!"

When she opened her eyes, it was morning.

"What is this?"

"Granola."

Cynthia poked at the whole wheat, dried dates, and who-knew-what-else in the hand-thrown pottery bowl. "I never realized roughage was spiritual."

Before David could offer reassurance, Drew yelled from the next room that they should look out the window. "Some idiot's gone bungee jumping off his balcony."

"He probably jumped rather than eat tree bark for breakfast," Cynthia muttered as she peered over David's shoulder at the building across the courtyard.

The jumper had anchored his cable on one of the trees that crowded the edge of the penthouse garden. As the bounce wore off, he swung by one leg, hands folded behind his back, free leg crossed back behind the other knee.

"He must've threaded fiber optics through his hair. Look at the way his head's glowing."

"Seems perfectly content though, doesn't he." As David moved out of the way, Cynthia pressed against the window and frowned. "You know, physics was never my strong suit, but shouldn't he have swung back and hit the building?" When she heard pages turning behind her, she sighed and closed her eyes. "Don't tell me . . ."

"The Hanged Man. Representing things that are before you; self-surrender to a higher wisdom."

"Higher wisdom?" Pivoting on one heel, she stared

at David in astonishment. "So far they've created a major traffic hazard, turned a lion loose downtown, tossed a crustacean into a hostile environment, tied someone up in the middle of the night surrounded by illegal weapons, and jumped off a balcony! That doesn't sound like a higher wisdom to me!"

"The cards aren't the wisdom, they're pointing the way."

"Oh, puh-leez."

"Just eat the cereal. We've got a lot to do."

David felt that bicycling to work would've been more spiritual, but they ended up taking Cynthia's car. Fortunately, it had a tape deck.

"What's that?"

"It's a tape called Distant Angels; New Age instrumental music. According to the box, it's the music of transformation and it's supposed to break through your inner resistance, leaving a state of relaxation and attunement."

As the sound of a single flute filled the car, Cynthia's scowl softened. "Very pretty. Very relaxing." She slumped behind the wheel only to jerk erect as a transport nearly ran them off the road. "But do you really think I should be listening to it during morning rush hour?"

There were no surprises waiting for them at the office.

"I'm just glad The Devil was out of the pack," David declared, standing a safe distance away as Cynthia unlocked the door. "That would've made life interesting."

They ate lunch in a tiny park off Spadina. Except for a small disagreement over the burning of some incense—"And what exactly is oxygen deprivation supposed to symbolize?"—the morning had been an

uneventful, and unsuccessful attempt to help Cynthia
see beyond the obvious.

*"All right, look at this deep, rich red. What does this
red symbolize to you?"*

*"It's a color, David. And I think it's too dark for
the hotel."*

"Are you doing this on purpose?"

"Doing what?"

A number of other people were also out enjoying
the sunshine. Mothers with small children, junior exec-
utives with oxford-cloth sleeves rolled up, teenagers
grouped defensively by the fountain, and the ubiqui-
tous variety of buskers.

David pointed out that the buskers could symbolize
artistic freedom, unwilling to be confined by a nine-
to-five world.

"Unable to be confined, you mean." Cynthia winced
as a young woman with yards of orange hair delivered
an extraordinarily off-key performance of Joni Mitch-
ell's "Big Yellow Taxi." "I'm not throttling her. That
must count for something."

"But *why* aren't you throttling her? Because her
music touched you?"

"Because I don't want to face an assault charge."

David sighed and stood. "Close. But not quite."

Dropping empty juice bottles into the recycling bar-
rels, they started back to the office.

Removing his high-crowned hat, one of the buskers
balanced carefully on his head and began performing
a complicated juggling act with two disks and a piece
of hose tied into a figure eight.

As they passed, Cynthia's cel phone rang, the shrill
twitter cutting through the ambient noise.

The busker jerked and one of the disks went flying
into traffic.

Closest to the curb, and feeling a bit guilty, Cynthia
ran out after it, half her attention on the phone—

"Augustine Textiles, Cynthia Augustine speaking."—
half on the disk.

David grabbed her shirt and yanked her back just
as the Spadina bus roared by in a cloud of blue exhaust. When the smoke had cleared, the disk lay in
pieces. Checking carefully up the street before he bent
forward, David picked up the largest shard. Silently,
he held it out to the young busker who sighed and
shook his head.

"Man, I was afraid that was going to happen. That's
no use to me now. You can keep it if you want it."

"No, thanks, I . . ." Then he took a good look at
what he held. As the busker headed off, he waved the
shard in Cynthia's face.

". . . get back to you tomorrow. That's right. Thanks
for calling. David, that was a business call and . . . is
that part of a broken pentacle?"

He nodded and pulled the slender book out of his
back pocket. "Two of Pentacles. Reversed. Your sev-
enth card representing your fears. Oh, gee, big surprise—you're afraid you're having difficulty handling
your problems."

"There's no need to be sarcastic."

Ignoring her, he went on. "And it seems like you
got a double whammy because they also just reminded
you that your fears can kill you."

"I think you're reading too much into it."

"The Ten of Swords. The Final Outcome."

She had a sudden memory of the way the carpet
felt pressed warm and sticky against her cheek. Dry-
cleaning was not going to be enough. "Okay, okay,
you win. What now?"

"I don't know but I'll think of something. There're
only two cards to go, and they seem to be coming
closer together."

"That's not very reassuring."

"I know." David glanced around and suddenly

smiled. "I've got it. This is an easy one." Grabbing Cynthia's shoulders he turned her toward the waterfront. "What does the CN Tower symbolize to you?"

She squinted at the familiar landmark and shrugged. "Radio towers?"

"No, that's what it is. Try again."

"Revolving restaurants?"

"Cynthia!"

"I don't know!" Her voice had picked up a slightly desperate tone. "What?"

"It's the world's tallest, freestanding, phallic symbol."

"But they're not shaped anything like that."

David sighed and considered giving up the fight. "Maybe we're going about this the wrong way. Let's go back to work, I'll put on the Benedictine monks, and while you try to step beyond reality, I'll try to think up a new angle."

"I think we've been beyond reality since we talked to Madame Zora," Cynthia muttered. The thought of falling swords made the skin between her shoulder blades itch.

"I haven't been inside a church for years."

"Nothing does symbolism better." David pushed open the heavy wooden door of St. Michael's Cathedral. "Come on."

"We can't just *wander* in."

"We're not just wandering. Now, come on."

It was cool and quiet inside the church. Aside from a few elderly women praying in the first couple of rows, they had the place to themselves. In a low voice, David began pointing out the various symbols of his faith.

"I know all this stuff, David. I haven't spent my life in a closet, if you'll pardon the expression."

"You know it here." He touched her forehead, then

tapped on her sternum. "But not here. You have to believe that some things stand for things that are bigger than they are."

"Would now be a good time to tell you *why* I stopped going to church?"

They were turning to leave when a figure leaned out of one of the alcoves and beckoned.

Cynthia frowned. "Okay, it was a long time ago and it *was* a United Church, but isn't that guy just a little overdressed?"

The alcove held a low dais, a throne, and two pillars. A pair of monks in robes embroidered with roses and lilies knelt before the throne. Between them, was a pair of crossed keys. Seated on the throne, was a priest.

"What's with the Carmen Miranda hat?"

"It's not a hat," David hissed looking up from the book. "It's a three-tiered crown."

"Don't tell me . . ."

"It's The Hierophant. Your eighth card. The seeker's environment or the fears of your family and friends."

"If you don't mind, young man," the priest said snippily, "I can speak for myself."

"Sorry."

"I should think so." He cleared his throat. "Your family and friends, my dear, are afraid you're overly concerned with a need to conform. That you are bound too tightly to convention."

Cynthia's lip curled. "First, I'm not your *dear.* Second, you're wrong. Tell him he's wrong, David."

"Uh . . ."

"So who says I have to be wild and crazy," she snarled. She glared down at the monks. "Do you two have anything to add?"

"No," said the monk on the left.

"We're just here for effect," added the monk on the right.

Absolutely furious, Cynthia stomped out of the church—modifying her step when she heard the slap of her shoes echoing against the stone. When David caught up with her on the sidewalk outside, she whirled around to face him.

"Why me, that's what I want to know? Why put all this effort into changing me? Am I such a horrible person?"

"No. You're not. You're just . . ." He searched for a polite way to put it. ". . . a little narrowly focused."

"Is that such a bad thing? I'm not hurting anyone!"

His voice gentled. "Except maybe yourself."

The anger left her as suddenly as it had appeared. She clutched at David's arm. "We haven't much time, have we? One more card and then . . ."

"We'll beat it, Cyn, you'll see. But maybe you should stay home until you've made a breakthrough; that way no one can drop swords on you."

"No, but my building will collapse in an unexpected earthquake and I'll be found in the rubble wearing Mr. Garabaldi's collection of medieval weaponry."

"Mr. G. has a collection of swords?"

"Not that I know of *now*. Anyway, I can't be responsible for that. Think of what an earthquake would do to the property values in my neighborhood." When she caught his expression, she almost grinned. "Kidding." The grin slipped. "Mostly."

They came out onto Yonge Street in the midst of a crowd of street vendors. Forward progress meant carefully picking a path through merchandise stacked precariously on rickety tables and spread out on the sidewalk. Her mind replaying the dream of the swords, over and over, Cynthia moved blindly toward disaster.

Her foot struck something hard and cold. Which

struck something else. Which struck something else. Metal rang against concrete.

When she looked down, she realized she'd kicked over three brass goblets, spilling their contents. The vendor, his skinny form, wrapped head to toe in a black cloak, stared down at them in despair as other pedestrians stepped fastidiously over the spreading liquid.

"I'm so sorry."

"Accidents happen," he allowed mournfully.

"I'll pay you for what I spilled."

He sighed deeply. "No point. What's done, is done."

Done.

Done.

Done.

Cynthia suddenly needed to outrun the word echoing in her head, suddenly needed to get out of the crowds. David found her two blocks away, leaning up against a store window, staring at but not seeing the display.

"There were two cups still standing," he said.

"Doesn't matter. That was the ninth card."

"How do you know?"

"Oh, come on, David. Cups. A guy in a full cloak making enigmatic statements—what else could it be. You might want to stand back; you'll never get bloodstains out of that shirt, it's silk."

Flipping through the book, David ignored the suggestion. "Okay, if it was your ninth card, then it represents your hopes and fears."

"I think the fears part is pretty damned obvious!"

"But there were two cups still full! You can break through this, Cyn, if you just try!"

"I *am* trying, but face it, it's not working!" Her words had picked up a panicked cadence. "So something wants to broaden my viewpoint. Suppose I don't want my viewpoint broadened!"

"I don't think you have a choice."

"There's always a choice, David. I can choose to stand here and become some sort of symbolic pincushion!" The look on his face stopped her cold. "All right. No, I can't. But only because it would upset you." She took a deep breath and let it out slowly. "We're almost out of time. What do we do?"

They were standing in front of a shoe store. David peered through the glass and, unexpectedly, he smiled. "Let's buy you some sandals."

"Sandals?" She blinked. "That's your solution?"

"When I was younger, I took riding lessons. When I started I didn't have the right clothes because they were expensive and I couldn't see how they'd make a difference. When I finally broke down and bought a pair of breeches and some boots, my riding improved. What you're wearing can affect your state of mind. Sandals can be very spiritual. Christ wore sandals. Come on."

Shaking her head, but with no better idea, Cynthia followed him into the store.

The pattern of the carpet looked familiar.

Eyes locked on the loops and swirls, she heard nothing of what either the salesman or David said as they picked and fitted and boxed her cowboy boots. Moving numbly to the counter on the unfamiliar slabs of cork, she pulled out her wallet and muttered, "How much?" A moment later she repeated the question considerably louder. "HOW MUCH?"

"Cyn, they're made in Germany . . ."

"So what! I'm not taking them on the autobahn!"

"Think of it as an investment in your state of mind!"

She looked down at her toes, pale and naked, and past them to the carpet. "Oh, well, I probably won't have to wear them for long." Handing over her gold card, she signed where indicated, picked up the piece of plastic . . .

. . . and froze, credit card clutched in one hand.

"Cyn?"

"This isn't money!"

"No, but . . ."

"But it symbolizes money! In a way, it symbolizes a standard of living I couldn't achieve on cash alone! Do you hear music?" Without waiting for an answer, she whirled around. "Those shoes with the three-inch heels, they not only symbolize the patriarchy's effort to keep women helpless but also women taking charge of and flaunting their own sexuality!"

David felt a little the way Henry Higgins must have when the rain finally fell on Spain.

"And red!" Grabbing his shoulders, she shook him back and forth. "Red symbolizes blood and blood symbolizes sacrifice and sacrifice symbolizes passion, so red symbolizes passion!" Releasing him, she spun away, eyes gleaming.

The salesman leaned over the counter. "Is she all right?"

"She's having an epiphany." Trust Cynthia to have an epiphany with a credit card.

"These shoes symbolize a dream of playing like Michael Jordan!"

"Is it going to make a mess on the carpet?"

"I don't think so." He was smiling so broadly his cheeks hurt. She'd done it, she'd managed to acknowledge a greater reality. There would be no tenth card. No swords. No body. It would be enough to know what the meaning was.

"Symbols, symbols tap into the collective unconscious! All of a sudden, poetry makes sense, although," she added throwing herself back into one of the chairs, "I still don't understand Shirley

MacLaine." The chair, made for more sedate landings, tipped backward. "Oh, shit!"

Watching her hit the floor, head down and feet in the air, David had an epiphany of his own. As the chair landed solidly on top of her, he wondered if he should say anything. The Ten of Swords had been reversed. Realistically, there wasn't a lot of difference between being stabbed and being impaled, but symbolically . . .

He checked the new meaning as the salesman—torn between laughter and fear of being sued—helped her up.

The Ten of Swords, reversed. In spiritual matters, the Seeker may now turn to higher powers for help.

He closed the book before Cynthia turned to face him. Higher powers. It was out of his hands. And, thank God, ghod, gods, or whoever for that.

Rubbing one buttock, Cynthia limped over to the counter. "I think," she said, enthusiasm muted slightly, "I'll consider that a warning. The spiritual must be balanced with the practical."

Before David could agree, the cel phone rang.

"Augustine Textiles, Cynthia Augustine speaking."

Eyes locked on her face, David searched for an outward manifestation of the inner change. He couldn't see one and, as she frowned, his heart started to pound uncomfortably hard. Perhaps it *wasn't* over.

"That," Cynthia said as she tucked the phone back in the belt pouch, "was Madame Zora."

David started breathing again. "She wants to congratulate you on reaching enlightenment?"

"Not exactly. She wants her twenty bucks."

THE COURT
OF THE INVISIBLE
by *Billie Sue Mosiman*

Billie Sue Mosiman is the author of eight novels including *Nightcruise, Widow, Stilletto,* and *Pure and
Uncut*, which have garnered her nominations for both
the Edgar and the Stoker Awards. She has written
over one hundred stories which appear in numerous
periodicals and anthologies, and writes a column for
DEATHREALM. She lives in Houston, Texas.
  "The Court of the Invisible" is a story about the
power of determination, as a woman must finally ac-
cede to knowledge and change she does not want
to accept.

I've been spinning like a ball of twine across a polished floor, unwinding as I go. It's the reason Johnny
left me, not that I blame him. He woke this morning to find me still poring over the tarot cards, my
brow furrowed, my right fingers drumming the small
tabletop, and he said in a perfectly reasonable voice,
"Mel? I'm going, Mel. I'm really sorry, but I can't
take this anymore. I think you need some help, but
I'm not the person to give it to you."

I heard him but there was nothing to say, was there?
So I said nothing. I studied The Wheel of Fortune
card, as I had been doing half the night, and waited
for him to change his mind or to get the hell out.

"Mel? Do you hear me? You're sick, you know

47

that, don't you? This obsession with the tarot is . . .
it's crazy!"

I know I'm coming apart and that's one of the odd-
est feelings. It's always been said the insane are protected from knowing they are insane. If you can ask
yourself if you are sane or not, you are, by definition,
still sane. But what they say is wrong, as usual. No
one ever bothered to ask the insane woman if she
ever knew her sanity was slipping.

"I'll be all right," I said to Johnny standing over
me, hovering like a mother hen in his shorts, his hair
still disheveled from sleep.

When was the last night I spent in bed with him?
It might have been as long ago as a month. The Wheel
of Fortune had been my focus for quite some time
now. Hadn't we, Johnny and I, had a good time while
it lasted, though? It was all we could ask of a love
affair, but now it was over and he should not prolong
the leave-taking. Out, out, brown spot, he needed to
just get the hell out.

"You're not going to be all right," he said now,
reaching out to stroke my hair. "You're going to be
alone. You're going to be all alone, Mel. You understand that, don't you? I won't be here to make sure
you eat something, that you rest, that you . . . bathe."

I sighed deeply, pulled the Wheel toward me and
covered it with my right hand in an unconscious gesture to shield it from prying eyes. I looked up at
Johnny. He had been my passion for a long while. I
had turned the cards to find him when I went on a
foray into the night clubs of New Orleans, a predator
of love. I had then turned the cards for advice on how
to keep him, and now it was strange to see him leaving
while I felt nothing at all. All that effort for not much
good reason.

He was handsome in a rugged, wiry sort of way: a
shock of black hair curling down over a broad fore-

head, clear brown expressive eyes that showed too much of his soul. He was a healer, a Page of Wands type of person; he ought to go into medicine. "Don't worry about me," I said. "When the body needs food, I'll eat. When it needs rest, I'll sleep, if only here at the table." I thumped the Wheel of Fortune card with my fist. It made the other cards in the Celtic Cross layout leap and scatter.

Johnny winced as if he had been pinched and stepped back from me.

I rose from the table, pulling the Wheel with me and palming it. I advanced on Johnny as he moved back, away from me and what violence I represented. "When the body is filthy, it will be cleaned! When the body wants sex, it will find a partner or relieve itself with fantasies. When the body feels danger, it will hide. When it finds itself under pressure, it will . . . it will . . ." I inhaled and knew my voice had risen to a shout, but I could not control myself now. "It will EXPLODE!"

"Oh, God, Mel. Let me call someone, please. You're in trouble."

I raised my hand and stared deep into the Wheel. "Just go," I said, "and please leave me alone. I have to figure something out, and I can't be bothered with you." I turned my back on him and returned to the table. I carefully straightened the silk cloth and re-arranged the cards. I replaced the Wheel at the top of the four cards in its place where it stood for the outcome of the spread.

The outcome.

The Wheel of Fortune.

I had been turning up the Wheel as the outcome for weeks now. The probability of that happening in shuffled spreads seemed quite impossible. Out of seventy-eight minor and major arcana cards, how could that occur? Yet my eyes were not failing me, even if my sanity was on the line. There it lay, in each new spread as the top card: the outcome, the Wheel of Fortune.

At the periphery of my attention I heard Johnny scuffling in the master bedroom closet for his things. I heard him in the bathroom riffling through the medicine chest. I heard him enter the living room and say, "I'm going." I ignored him. He said again, "I'm gone, Mel. I'm not coming back." I ignored him. What else could I do when I was in the middle of another spread, trying to lay out the cards? He knew how much concentration it took. He had not always been as courteous as I preferred.

I heard the door close, and finally silence settled around me, a warm, comforting cloak. He was gone at last! Why were men so disruptive in a woman's life? I was better off alone. I had money, an inheritance. The cards had promised I'd get it eventually and I did. Enough that I would never have to earn my bread by the sweat of my brow, a very lucky stroke of good fortune.

I suspected that's what lured many of the young men who shared my bed—the money. Johnny might have been different, not caring for the luxury my money afforded him, but he was still around too much, always needing me to respond to him as if I were a monkey and he played the accordion that signaled I must dance.

These days men and relationships made me weary. Too complicated. Too time-consuming. I had to find out what the Wheel meant, didn't they know that?

The card lay in my hand, and I brought my face close to it until my eyes unfocused and the image swam before me. It was almost as if the items on the card had come alive and were swirling across the cardboard face. Pleased, I moved in ever closer, increment by increment.

The card was made by a company in Dobbs Ferry,

New York, some strange off-brand pack of aquarian tarot that had caught my fancy. I'd tried Ryder-Waite and many of the New Age packs, but none of them felt right to me—until I found this particular deck. The wheel was colored red with a black background. Above the wheel rose a bearded knight's head. He had flowing brown hair that touched the top of the wheel and hid behind it. On each side of the wheel rose two serpents. Below the wheel were winged beasts facing each other. One of a horned horse, the other a black figure, rather like a man-horse creature. With my eyes nearly crossed and the figures vague and floating, it seemed that the knight slipped from behind the wheel and lifted one hand in a come-hither gesture.

I suddenly sat back, focusing on the far wall in order to relax my eye muscles. Surely I had not seen the knight do that. I was overtaxed, emotionally and physically. I had been without sleep now for two days. I had been trying too hard for understanding. I was hallucinating, no other explanation for it.

I glanced down at the Wheel to be sure all the objects in the graphic were in place, nothing sneaking out of balance. It was steady again. Nothing but a rectangular card, paper and ink and color.

I supposed the knight's movement was warning that the body needed rest. I would go into the bedroom and see if Johnny had left behind a warm place for me. It was the least he could do.

I dreamed of the solemn knight from the Wheel of Fortune. I stood in a temple with Corinthian columns rising three stories to a white marble roof. Guards dressed in red and black regalia stood at the exit, sabers drawn and crossed on their chests. Narrow windows high on the walls let in pale lemon light that cut across the room, dust motes drifting lazily in the spears. Everything was so distinct and real it made me catch my breath.

The knight sat on a carved teakwood throne. His hands rested on the arms of the chair, his fingers brushing just the tops of fierce scowling heads of demons fashioned there.

He blinked slowly at me and said, "Here is the Eternal Return. I have been waiting for you."

"I am only dreaming," I said, feeling a spike of fear shooting from the middle of my person straight into the cortex of my brain. "I've been overtired."

The knight smiled as if he knew more than I did and my statement was foolish, though expected. "That which is above is as that which is below," he said.

"I've always considered that a riddle. Riddles bore me." I walked nearer and found myself trembling. He was not a king, not royalty; why did I feel so unsure, so inferior, in his presence?

"You dispute the veracity of your experience and put it down to exhaustion. That is understandable, and human, but to mock wisdom as merely a riddle is hazardous."

"Tell me what it means, 'That which is above is as that which is below.' "

The knight, who had stiffened at my flippancy, relaxed into his chair now. "What you bring into your reality in the world you wander now, the below, is a reflection, merely, of what exists in the above."

"I'm afraid that I am dense. Could you explain further?"

Exasperated, the knight raised his right hand and from purple curtains at his back stepped Johnny. A confused, possibly dumbfounded Johnny. He looked at me and then at the seated knight before glancing anxiously around the temple. "Where am I?" he asked plaintively. "Oh, God, where am I?"

"This person you dismissed on Earth?" the knight said.

"Yes?"

"Exists here, too. Along with every man, every woman, child, and creature you've ever come into contact with in your lifetime."

"What good is it to have two places that are alike in every respect? Is that duplication some kind of backup creation plan?"

Johnny stepped down from the dais where he stood near the knight and approached me. He held out his hands, "Mel, why am I here? How did I get here? What's going on?"

"Go away, Johnny, you're in the way again." I didn't mean to be abrupt, but as soon as I'd requested his absence, he disappeared. Not like a ghost, not slowly dispersing into thin air, but immediately. One second there, the next not.

I glanced about the temple to be sure he was gone. "Did I do that?" I asked.

"You most certainly did."

"Too bad it's not that easy to make pests vanish when I'm awake."

The knight smiled a little to show he found me amusing, though I suspected I amused him in a primitive way like a naive court jester with not too many tricks up his sleeves.

"To answer your question . . ."

I tried to remember what I'd asked. Of course. What did the duplication mean?

". . . there is no real duplication, as you call it. The above is not exactly the same as the below in all respects, and yet in another way it is. All possible choices exist here. In the below, where you are now, each choice cancels all others."

"In other words, Johnny is here, but so are a

thousand . . . a million other men I might have chosen
for a companion. Is that right?"

"Exactly so."

"Why do you keep coming to me? Why do I always
turn up the Wheel as the outcome card in my Celtic
Cross spread? What is your significance?"

"That is a mystery for you to unravel, young
friend."

"Then what good are you, if not to explain these
things to me? Riddles, always riddles!"

The knight and his throne disappeared just as
Johnny had. I turned to look for him, and the guards
at the door were gone. I looked up at the doomed
ceiling of marble, and it shifted ever so slightly until
it resembled nothing more than the smooth ivory ceiling of my bedroom.

"Mel? Mel, wake up!"

I looked to my left and saw Bridget's face too close
to me, all rounded planes of rosy cheeks and full wine
lips, long permed hair tumbling and crawling like spi-
ders on my face. "What is it?" I asked. "What the
hell is it?"

Bridget receded and I sat up, pulling a pillow behind
my back. I rubbed down my face and felt a thick coat
of something metallic on my tongue. A good dose of
mouthwash would take care of that, I hoped.

Bridget had pulled the linen-covered easy chair near
my bedside and sat in it now. She looked worried. I
wondered how many states of being Bridget possessed
and if she could possibly find another one to share
with me. Worry from my lovers and friends was something I had grown weary of long ago. If I had some
power over choice in this "below" world, then why
couldn't I choose Bridget with Smiley-face? Or
Bridget with Fawning Gaze? Or Bridget with Fierce
Intelligence and All the Answers?

The reason, of course, was that Bridget made her

own choices, too. And here I was stuck with her Worry-Wart face.

"Johnny told me he left, he had to. He said you'd been strange for more than a month. You've lost weight, a lot of weight. You have circles under your eyes. He said someone should see about you."

I punched the pillow at my back and kicked the sheets from my feet. Did they look dirty? Maybe I should take a shower, maybe I should paint my toenails, maybe I should tell Bridget to get the hell out. "Johnny's got a bad case of overreaction. I'm fine. You can see for yourself that I'm fine."

"You look a mess."

"Why, thank you, Miss Diplomacy of the Year."

"Don't be that way. I'm trying to help."

"Are you? When's the last time I saw you, Bridget? Three months ago? Four? Saw you in that club where Johnny and I went one night, what was it . . . The Corsair? You said hi and good-bye and not a peep from you since."

"You're right, I'm sorry," she said. "It's been too long. I was a little busy, and . . ."

"Hah! So busy you can't give me a call, so busy you can't invite me over, so busy you couldn't care if your best friend is alive or dead?"

"I didn't come to argue with you, Mel. What's this about the tarot? Johnny said . . ."

"Johnny has no right running to you with my personal life. Why don't we drop it. You want a cup of tea? Raspberry Zinger? A good hot cup of hibiscus flowers will mellow you out if it doesn't give you the runs first."

"The tarot, Mel. You've been turning the cards night and day for weeks. What's going on?"

"You want tea or not? I'm getting a cup. I feel a little constipated, to tell you the unvarnished truth."

I pushed from bed, slipping past her before she could reach out to hold me.

In the kitchen I poured water through the coffee maker to heat and set out the teapot and three bags of Raspberry Zinger.

"Are you going to talk to me or am I wasting my time?" Bridget asked.

"You're wasting your time."

"Fine, I guess I should leave, then."

"Wait." I reached out and caught her hand. "Wait, let me show you, then you'll understand."

She followed me to the living room, and I noticed for the first time that it needed a thorough cleaning. I hadn't allowed the cleaning service a chance to come for a very long time. They got on my nerves when I was trying to concentrate. Running vacuums, flushing toilets, vigorously washing mirrors and windows. But I saw the room now the way Bridget saw it. Clothes and papers and books piled willy-nilly; dust bunnies, dishes and glasses with dried and caked contents. A regular pigsty.

"Sorry about the place. I've been busy." I laughed when I used her lame excuse. Never waste a chance to be sarcastic, that had become my motto. It seemed the only communication people really connected with.

I took her to the table and carefully gathered all the tarot cards. "Watch this," I said. I straightened the deck, shuffled them, shuffled them again, turning and showing Bridget that they were indeed not being manipulated in any conscious way by my hands.

"Sit down across from me," I said, taking my chair. When she was seated, she put her elbows on the table. I paused, the deck in my hands and said, "Don't touch the table, please. It changes the vibrations." She removed her arms, but looked hurt.

"Nothing personal, Bridget. It's just the rules, okay?"

She nodded and I set the shuffled deck on the table. "Now I'll cut them, just to make sure they're really not stacked, no hanky-panky going on here." I cut the deck and took them up again.

"I'm using the Celtic Cross spread, the traditional one for telling fortunes. I put this here to signify me. I put this card on top crossing me to signify the obstacle." I explained each placement's meaning as I turned the spread. When I got to the outcome card, the last one, I flipped it over quickly.

I smiled. "The Wheel of Fortune. See that?"

"Yes," she said softly, watching me with a puzzled expression.

"Well, the Wheel of Fortune lands in that spot every single time. Every single spread I make. It started about a month ago and it's always there."

"That's not really possible, is it?"

"No, Bridget, it's not possible at all. It's passed the probability factor and moved right into the unbelievable. But watch, I'll do it again." I picked up the spread, shuffled twice, cut the cards, and methodically laid out the spread. When I got to the outcome card, even Bridget was breathless. I turned it over.

The Wheel.

"Well? Do you believe me now?"

Bridget raised her gaze to my face from where she'd been staring at the last card. "It happens every time? Every single time?"

"Yes. It does. I'm perfectly willing to reshuffle these cards until Doomsday and you'll see that every time that same card comes up in that spot."

"Well, it's . . . odd. It's sort of . . . weird. But Mel, it's making you sick. You have to stop it now."

"No, don't you see? I have to understand it. There's a message here, but I have to fathom it. It's like running into a wall accidentally and finding it conceals a hidden door; could you not open it? Or a gift under the Christmas tree; could you not unwrap it? I'm not crazy, Bridget. Yeah, I'm pretty obsessed with this, but who wouldn't be? Here, you deal. Let's see what cards you turn up." I handed the deck to her.

She scooted back from the table as if I'd offered her a Gila monster. "No," she said, "I don't like fooling with that stuff."

"All right then, how about that tea? Want a cup?"

We had our tea and Bridget left, but not before one more admonition to seek help on "my problem." I saw her out and this time locked the door. I didn't want any other helpful friends dropping in to waste my time.

I had a spread to lay.

Another month passed, or it might have been two, I had no calendar to tell me what day it was. I thought I might have the dream again so that I could consult face-to-face with the knight on the Wheel. However, my sleeping stints were dreamless and I usually woke feeling hung over and as fatigued as when I fell asleep. Sometimes it took hours before my circulation was working and I felt myself.

I called bookstores and ordered a copy of every book on the tarot they had. I spent what hours I had free from turning the cards reading up on the Wheel.

"A change is about to happen."

"Change is the invariable order of the world."

"This card is a symbol of evolution."

"The soul comes from the deep, is briefly on the zenith and then goes down again."

"That which will happen is inevitable since it corresponds to the way of things."

Riddles, riddles, some of them couched in medieval language, some in ridiculous New Age mutterings, but all of them little less than riddles.

What did it all mean to my life? What was the message? What change was coming, what evolution, what zenith and fading away, what inevitability?

I slept less and hardly ate. My stomach shrunk so that I could keep down no more than a few mouthfuls at a time. My eyes gave me trouble, my vision fading in and out as if I were suffering from a brain tumor. My thoughts grew erratic and I had difficulty keeping my mind on what I was doing. I might turn the cards and find I'd only turned half of the cross and sat in a static trance with the cards in my hands, staring across the room into the middle distance at nothing, thinking . . . nothing.

Finally it came to me that if I were to keep my health and what sanity I had left, I must seek out a seer. It had been a long time since I'd left the house. I lived in the French Quarter in an old mansion with a courtyard locked to sidewalk traffic. I'd been insulated inside the house from the noise and stink of the rest of humanity for longer than I'd realized. Once I'd bathed, dressed, and stepped outside, the world struck me as a cacophonous and perverted simulacrum of a madhouse. The crazy horse-and-carriages for the willing tourists rolled by like thunder through the lamplit night. The hordes of partyseekers with their riotous laughter clogged the avenues swilling Hurricanes from paper cups. Thieves, mainly pickpockets, beggars, and even the occasional killer swirled through the crowds like amoebas swallowed by the larger organism, and I could smell the noxious odors of the deranged.

It was as if life outside my doors had been given a clarity usually reserved for angels and wizards. I smelled, distinctly, all the rich scents. Vanilla perfume. Chocolate-pecan pie. Fog from the river. Rat and horse droppings. Sweat, sex, foot powder, hair cream, flowers, cooking food, blood, urine, and stale puddles of water left over from a recent shower. I saw individuals, not the mass. Every face, every gesture, every

moue as if I were a camera recording each nuance. I
felt the tremor of mankind pulsing as with an electrical
charge. It was enough to cause me to stumble on my
step and hold onto the black wrought iron rail for
strength.

As above, so below? Was that other place so populated by chaos as was this one? But multiplied by un-
told numbers so that other place was millions of times
more so, a chaos that could unhinge reality? What hell
that had to be. And did it not follow then that my
knight from the Wheel was mad, completely and absolutely lunatic if he belonged in such a world as that?

I hurried down the walk through the courtyard and
unlocked the gate to the sidewalk, locking it again
behind me. I saw a petty burglar watching me and
stepped quickly to his side to murmur, "I'll send the
knight of chaos after you if your feet take one step
on the stones leading to my home. Beware."

I felt his eyes on me as I moved into the crowd. He
would not venture forth to my house tonight, I was
sure of it.

In a little street off the main course of Bourbon
Street I found what I was looking for. It was an unpre-
tentious occult shop where I had bought all my different decks of tarot. I stepped over the threshold, the
jangle of the doorbell loud in my ears. The shop, by
happenstance or perhaps not, was thankfully empty of
customers. From the rear the proprietor entered
through a curtained doorway. She was dressed in the
gay garb of a fortuneteller, even to the scarf turbaned
around her head, but I knew instantly that this woman
normally dressed in satin suits and had her hair done
at the most stylish salon in New Orleans. Who did she
figure to fool with this pretense?

"You live in a four-hundred-thousand-dollar home,
employ four full-time servants, and have enough

stocks to retire twice over. Why do you pretend this fake gypsy shit?"

The woman halted and gave me a long appraising stare. "You've come a long way since the first time you bought a deck of tarot from me."

"Too far," I said, moving toward her. "Tell me what's wrong with these cards." I pulled the box of cards from my purse and thrust them toward her. "Are they bewitched? Cursed? Tell me what's wrong with them."

She took the box and glided to the front door, turning the closed sign to face outward, then fastened the lock. "Come with me to the back," she said, passing me by.

Beyond the curtained doorway, where I had never been admitted, was a small cramped room set up for telling fortunes. A round table, two chairs, a crystal ball. Muted orchid light and the spiraling smoke of stick incense. I really hated this sort of fakery. "I don't want my fortune told," I said.

"Don't you?" She was close to me and smelled of sandalwood, as if her burnished tan skin had been saturated with the oil.

"No. I want to know why these cards, no matter how many spreads I do, end up with the Wheel of Fortune."

I saw her eyes widen. "Every time? The outcome card?"

"Yes. Exactly. What does it mean? I've tried to figure it out on my own, but except for one solitary dream sequence, I am still in the dark. It's driving me batty."

"Sit down. Tell me about the dream."

And so for the next few minutes I talked and she listened, her hooded eyes hardly blinking. She reminded me of no less than a snake, a large stealthy anaconda, a jungle plunderer.

I finished and sat waiting. She took her time before speaking. I stared at her fixedly, firm in my resolution to find out the meaning of the card.

"You've crossed over," she said finally. "I can't help you."

"What the hell do you mean I've crossed over? Crossed over where, to what? I have to tell you that I find riddles highly inappropriate in my situation, and on general principle I despise the hell out of them."

"I am afraid, madam, that you are dead."

I started to laugh, to guffaw, to throw my head back in a hysterical spasm, but just as I was about to let go, to let the laughter bubble up and out, her raised hand stopped me.

"I am serious. I am not making a bad joke. I suspected it when you walked in the door, but now that you've told me the dream and your problem with the cards, I am certain. You've left this world, sometime during the hours and weeks and months you've spent working with the tarot to find the secret meanings, and now you linger only because you don't know that you've passed on. You're stuck here. You must leave."

"I'm not dead. That's the most ridiculous, asinine . . ."

She reached across the table and grabbed my wrist tightly.

She held it a moment and then said, "Feel this."

I put my hand on my wrist where she'd had her hand and felt for my pulse.

I dropped my wrist and pressed my hand over my heart. Then I rested my head on my arms on the table, my face turned to the side.

"I'm sorry, but you have to go now," she said. "The longer you stay, the more trouble you'll have getting . . . loose."

"I died," I whispered. "I didn't even notice it and

I died. When did I die? Why am I still walking around?"

"Because until now you didn't know. That's what the dream was trying to tell you. That's why you kept getting the card of change, the card of evolution. Now, please, you must go home and lie down and seek your peace."

"But I thought the Death card meant death. Or even the Tower. Why would it be the Wheel for me?"

"You will have to seek that answer elsewhere. In the beyond. With your knight. I cannot help you. Really, I cannot."

I stood shakily and aimed myself toward the curtain. I stumbled from the shop and down the streets toward home. I no longer was bothered by the brilliance of the colors, the intense scents, the strident voices and sounds.

I was dead. I was dead.

I had been dead for some time and just had not stopped walking around. Had I been dead before Johnny left? When Bridget came to see me? How could one die without knowing? Tears came down my cheeks, and I didn't bother to wipe them away. It is a sad thing to die, but sadder still to run through time as if it were endless when, in fact, the body has ceased functioning and is, in fact, decaying.

I managed to get the gate unlocked and made it into the house. I dropped the box of tarot onto the table, the top coming off and the cards spilling across the tabletop and to the floor. The Wheel of Fortune landed on my shoe, and I shook it off as if it were a blob of something nasty. "I know, I know," I sobbed. "I know what you mean now!"

I made my way to the sofa by holding onto the backs of chairs. Now that I knew the truth my strength was running out like sand from an hourglass. My legs wobbled, my muscles hung loose and weak from the bones, my eyesight was dimming, my hearing all but gone. Even my fingers and toes were numb, useless digits that I could not move, not even a wiggle or twitch.

I sat down heavily and then lay back, bringing my legs with great effort onto the cushions. I closed my eyes. I placed my hands folded on my chest. I must look properly dead. I must present the living world with a corpse.

It was true I had not eaten, I had not slept, I had not had any interest in the world other than the cards. I had fallen into death the way a stone falls into a pond, dropping silently and twirling a bit with the last of life as it makes for the bottom and oblivion in the mud and gently swaying undergrowth.

I sought the dream. It was not long in coming.

"Hello," I said. He sat in the teakwood throne before me. I knew that at my back were the guards and that this time I would not be allowed to exit.

"Here is the Eternal Return," he said kindly.

"Yes. Yes, I suppose that it is."

"That which is above is as that which is below."

"Yes," I said. "Yes, I suppose you are right." I must be resigned. I had no argument to defeat death.

He stood and came to me, taking my arm delicately. "Will you come with me?"

"Are there more choices to make? Endless choices?"

"And riddles," he said.

"Endless?" I asked.

He smiled enigmatically and led me behind the purple curtains into the darkness.

NEW BEGINNER'S LUCK

by Mark A. Garland

Mark A. Garland is the author of *Dorella, Demon Blade*, and *The Sword of the Prophets*, as well as two *Star Trek* novels. His short fiction and poetry has appeared in *Cricket* and *Analog*, and in the anthologies *Xanadu III, Chronicles of The Holy Grail, Bruce Coville's Book of Magic, Monster Brigade 3000*, and others.

Garland's "New Beginner's Luck" is a sweet story of love's second blooming, complete with a cat and a tarot deck and a little help from some friends that doesn't always turn out the way it's intended . . .

"It's been like this ever since David died," Linda said, turning away from Darlene, gazing out the window. Everything in the front yard reminded her of him, the green hedges, the little bench beside the walk, spring flowers blooming all around it, the car parked in the driveway—everything except the FOR SALE sign. She couldn't afford to keep the house on just her salary, much as she wanted to.

"You shouldn't make it sound worse than it is," Darlene said. "You're only twenty-seven, you're attractive, you're smart. In short, you're everything I wish I was."

That wasn't true. Darlene was bright and attractive, and dating an ophthalmologist who gave her free contacts, just for beginners. But she was a good friend, too.

Linda had spent the morning cleaning out the backs of closets, and finding more of David's things. She was feeling sorry for herself, and she thought she had a right. For lots of reasons.

"It's just that everything seems to go wrong all the time," she said, glancing at the pile on the sofa. The biggest item was David's folk guitar, which he'd never played. Some clothes, a small and tacky collection of empty wine bottles, back issues of *Popular Mechanics,* an Oktoberfest beer stein and a few small boxes of she-didn't-know-what lay piled on top of the guitar case. He'd been gone for nearly a year. It was time to move on. At least that's what everyone said.

And everyone was right, of course. But it was more than that. It seemed her luck had died with her husband.

"You've got to stop pouting," Darlene said.

Linda stuck out her tongue. George lay curled up on top of a small wooden box near the guitar case. He'd been David's, too, a very large, fat, fluffy brown cat that had barely left Linda's side in—well, in months. Linda got up and moved toward him. George looked up and began to purr. She scratched him gently behind his ears.

"See, even animals love you," Darlene said.

"George loves everybody."

Darlene leaned off the edge of her chair and started rubbing George's side as if to test that assertion. George proceeded to uncurl and role over onto his back, exposing his tummy. He slid right off the box, landing on his feet on the floor. The box came next, and hit the floor right next to him. Unshaken, he immediately began to rub his cheek against Linda's leg.

"Meow!" George said loudly.

"I love you, too," Linda said, which seemed to please the cat no end.

"You need to get out more, do things, meet people," Darlene said, bending down and picking up the box. "All you do is go to work or sit around here."

"Not so!" Linda said. "I've tried going out. The last time I went out to dinner I got so sick—my insides were on fire. I sat on the toilet for days. They closed the restaurant just after that, remember?"

"Well, yes, but—"

"And what about that guy, Cordwayne something, the one you tried to fix me up with?"

"Corey Wayne," Darlene said, looking at her shoes."

"Whatever. Anyway, drool is very unbecoming."

"I told you, he was a friend of a friend, and—"

"The last time I went to a movie some kid pulled the fire alarm, and we all ended up out in the street, which was precisely when it started to rain. Of course. I felt like it was all my fault."

Darlene frowned. "Now you're being ridiculous."

Linda frowned back. "I don't have much choice."

Silence prevailed for a time.

"Anyway," Linda said, considering, "I like work." She'd been doing layouts for the local PennyWise ad paper for six years. It was a small staff, she did every job there at times, or so it seemed, and they didn't pay enough—in fact she hadn't had a raise in almost two years—but she enjoyed composing and photographing the ads, and there was usually some overtime . . . which was fine.

"Work is work," Darlene said, making a face. "Maybe you just don't know any better." She worked for a big advertising company, an executive secretary, a great job, as far as Linda could tell.

"Maybe," Linda said.

Darlene was still holding the wooden box George

had toppled, examining the latch. She pulled at it, and the cover came up." "What's this?"

Linda shrugged. "What?"

"Tarot," Darlene said then, eyes wide as she removed an oversized deck of cards from the box. "I didn't know David was into tarot."

"Neither did I. You want them, they're yours."

She looked through the entire deck, laying cards in little piles on her lap, then on the arms of the chair. Finally she shook her head. "There are three cards missing, and the rest are all pretty beat up. Anyway, I've got my own deck."

"I suppose I could just keep them, you know, as a remembrance."

"If you ask me, you've got enough remembrances," Darlene scolded. "You need to—"

"I know. And I will."

"Promise."

"I promise." *Did I just say that,* Linda thought, as Darlene handed everything over. Linda put the cards back in the box, set the box on an end table. "Tell you what." She got up and went out into the kitchen, then came back stuffing a bottle of Maalox into her purse. "Let's try going out to lunch."

"That's more like it. I'll get you your favorite. Salmon steak, isn't it?"

Linda nodded. Salmon was absolutely her favorite, but she hadn't had it in months, and she already felt a knot forming in her stomach.

Linda touched the remote and shut off the TV. She had to get up for work tomorrow, and it was already past her bedtime. And she was tired. She'd spent the whole afternoon shopping with Darlene, using credit cards to spend money she didn't have, but she had begun to feel a little better. About everything. And lunch had been . . . nice. She went around and checked the locks and lights, then set up the coffee maker so she could just throw the switch in the morning. Finally she went to collect George, who usually slept at the foot of the bed, something Linda especially liked these days. She found him curled up on top of the wooden box containing the tarot cards again. When she picked him up, she saw one of the cards underneath him, lying on the lid.

"How did this get here?" she asked George, more or less.

"Meow!" George said, and sounded quite serious, Linda thought. She put the card in the box, on top of the deck, then she took it back out again. On its face were two interlocking half circles, each divided into four lines, and each marked by the Roman numeral VIII. "Strange," she said out loud.

"Meow!"

She sat staring at the colors, red and blue, black and yellow. She'd never put any stock in anything the least little bit mumbo jumbo, really. A lot of people did, though, including David. And Darlene. But she felt a subtle curiosity tugging at her now, as she held the card in her hand; or perhaps it was just a kind of loneliness. . . .

She wasn't sure. And she had no idea what the card meant. She checked her watch. Ten-thirty. "Oh, hell," she said. She picked up the phone and touched one of the speed dial pads. She got the answering machine, but halfway through the message Darlene picked up.

"Hello?"

"I've got a silly question."

"I'll think of a silly answer," Darlene said.

"Do you know how to read those tarot cards you were looking at earlier?"

"Well, pretty much. It's an art, you know, like reading horoscopes or bumpy heads. Why?"

Linda described the card in her hand.

"Okay," Darlene said right away. "It's the Eight of Swords. I've got a book. I can look it up exactly." She came back a moment later. "Got it. It has to do with frustration and confusion due to problems. It means hesitation and self-doubt are impeding your progress." She paused. "Boy, is that ever your card," Darlene added after a moment.

"Yeah, I guess."

"You know what, though? That's one of the three cards that was missing from that deck of yours. Where did you find it?"

"You're sure it was missing?"

"Absolutely."

Linda didn't know what to say.

"Listen," Darlene started, "there's this new technician starting at work tomorrow, and I heard he's cute. If he is, you want me to work on him for you?"

Linda sat looking at the card. "Hesitation and self-doubt impede your progress?" she repeated.

"That's right."

She could hear Darlene smiling through the phone. She'd probably put the card there in the first place. "I'll think about it," Linda said. "Good night."

"We're starting a softball team," Bob, the assistant editor, said about noon, when Linda was getting her bag lunch out of her drawer. He was a nice guy, not long out of college, sweet, good-looking. She'd taken a slight interest in him a couple of months back. In fact, he was the first guy she'd really noticed since losing David. Bob, it had turned out, was quite gay.

"We're having our first practice tonight. You're probably not interested, but I felt I should ask."

Hesitation, she thought. *Self-doubt.* "No," she said. "I'll be there." She finished her lunch feeling rather good.

She found herself growing more anxious and,

strangely, less apprehensive as the afternoon wore slowly on. By five o'clock she was positively charged.

"Ready?" Bob asked, passing her desk on the way out.

"Absolutely," Linda declared, and followed him out.

She went home and ate light, a yogurt and some wheat toast, then changed into jeans and a loose T-shirt. The field was only a mile from her house. She was one of the first ones there.

As the others arrived, Linda chatted with them, asking questions; she really knew very little about the game. Then they chose sides, a pitcher took the mound, and she wound up first in line to bat!

"Am I holding it right?" she asked Bob, waving the bat around.

He was all smiles. "Well enough!" he shouted.

The pitcher tossed one in, she swung, and connected! The ball went sailing. *I don't believe it!* she thought, as she realized everyone was telling her to run. She threw the bat away and took off, charging for first base with all her might—and lost her footing. She landed on her left arm, and knew right away it was a very bad thing.

"It'll heal," Darlene insisted. "It's not the end of the world. You can't keep doing this to yourself. You were lucky!"

It was a bad sprain. The arm was in a sling. Linda didn't feel very lucky. She'd said so. "I just don't know what I was thinking."

"Linda, shit happens, that's all; we'll have to get you one of those bumper stickers. Listen, how about, this weekend, you and I—"

"I think I'll just stay home this weekend and watch TV. It's for the best."

"Well," Darlene scoffed, "you won't convince me."

Linda turned away, found herself looking at George, who was curled up on the same wooden box, the one containing the tarot cards, which was still on the end table. All cats ever did was eat and sleep, which sounded pretty good, actually.

"Did you ever figure out where that card came from?" Darlene asked, apparently following Linda's gaze.

"No, not a clue." Linda got up and paused next to George, petting his wide, soft head. George rolled a little, stretched, then stood up, pressing his noggin into her hand.

"Is that the one?" Darlene asked, pointing. A tarot card lay on the top of the box, directly under the cat.

"No," Linda said, tipping her head to look. "It's different."

Darlene tugged it out from under George's paws and took a look. "It's another one of the missing cards," she said, raising both eyebrows. "The Six of Cups. It has to do with dynamic attractions, like the possibility of a new love affair, and infatuation, and happiness. It's a very good card."

"Probably nothing to do with me."

"Stop it! Look, do you know what this means? It means you've really got to meet that new guy, that technician I was telling you about. He really *is* cute, and so far he seems nice enough. I got into a quick conversation with him, and kinda asked if he needed anyone to show him around town. He just moved here, from out west, I think. He's got the most delicious accent. Anyway, he said he'd like that. I told him I wasn't available, but a friend of mine might be."

"You are completely insane, do you know that!" Linda stalked across the living room, then stalked back, fuming the whole way.

"We could make it a double date," Darlene suggested.

Linda didn't know what to say, or what to do; she just wanted to be left alone. She stood pat just a meter from Darlene and shook her right index finger at her. "If you weren't my best friend, I'd tell you to take a hike! If I didn't live here, I'd stomp straight out the door!"

Darlene held up the card, grinning. "So, what do you say?"

Okay, fine, Linda thought, *so he is really cute.* His name was Miller, his first name, and he picked her up in a very used, but very nice black Porsche. And he seemed easy to talk to, which was something Linda was already enjoying by the time they got to the restaurant, where Darlene and her ophthalmologist were meeting them. They went into the lounge to wait, and Linda ordered a wine cooler. Miller ordered a Bud.

"You seem a little edgy," Miller said, sipping, smiling warmly.

"I'm sorry. I haven't dated much in the last year or so. It's nothing personal."

"Perfectly all right. I understand. Darlene tells me you wouldn't mind showing me around."

Linda nodded. "She did say something about that."

"Good." He leaned closer—very close, in fact. "But you know, I've got all I want to see for now right here."

Oh, brother, Linda thought. *You really aren't ready for this.* "That so?" she said. She picked up the wine cooler and gulped. Twice.

"Indeed," Miller said. "I think I know exactly how you feel, and believe me, you couldn't have picked a better partner. And I'd say I did all right myself."

She looked at him. He winked at her. "How's that?" she asked.

"I figure a beautiful woman like you, she gets used to a lot of attention along the way, right? Then something happens, and there's no one there for her, for months. No guys, I mean. But you still have needs, right?"

Linda didn't like the sound of all that—

"So," Miller put his hand on her arm, "I'm here for you. I'm all yours!"

—didn't like it one bit. *Have to turn this around somehow,* she told herself. *Try to smile.* "Okay, what if I do need something, maybe, but I don't know exactly what it is? Can you work with that?"

Miller got a very strange look on his face, like the machinery was breaking down, then he seemed to come to something. He leaned close again, right up to her ear. "You mean you want . . . kinky?"

"This in unbelievable," Linda moaned.

"Not really," Miller said. "I'm just a good guesser."

"Oh, God."

Miller downed the rest of his beer, then he shook his head and grinned. "Boy, my wife would rather divorce me than try anything different. Get you another round?"

"Hi!" Darlene said, swooping up to the bar, smiling at everyone. "How are we doing?"

"We're leaving!" Linda said, grabbing Darlene by the arm and hauling her straight back out again.

"This is the last time I listen to you, or to any tarot cards, or to myself if I'm smart!" Linda groused as she fished in her purse for the keys to her front door. "Did he actually tell you he wasn't married, or didn't you bother to ask him?"

"I thought I did, honestly, and I thought—anyway, I'm sorry. He seemed so nice."

"He's slime."

Darlene frowned deeply. "Well, I know that now."

Linda opened the door and went inside. She flopped

down on one end of the sofa, and Darlene flopped down next to her. "Can you ever forgive me?"

"No," Linda said. "But I will anyway."

"Meow!"

Linda glanced at the end table. George was lying on top of the tarot box again, yawning at her. "Good kitty," she said. "Come here." He got up and crossed the sofa arm, then stepped gingerly onto her lap.

"You won't believe this," Darlene said. Linda was afraid to look. She already knew. She looked just the same. Darlene reached in front of her and picked a card up off the top of the box, where the cat had been.

Linda closed her eyes. "It's the third missing card, right?"

"Exactly," Darlene said with a little too much awe, at least as far as Linda was concerned.

"Personally, I've had enough."

"It's the Seven of Wands."

Darlene didn't say another thing. After about a minute and a half Linda caved in. "Fine, what the hell is it supposed to mean?"

"Success. It means the risks you took are beginning to pay off, or they will, if you take the initiative. And it means you can gain a strong position in spite of rivals. How are things going at work? Any big changes you aren't tell me about? A promotion maybe?"

"No, but I hope this one's right," Linda said.

Darlene grinned conspiratorially. "And why's that?"

"I'm getting so far behind around here," Linda said, staying serious, "and the house isn't selling, so I've got an appointment with Mr. Sedholm tomorrow to ask him for a raise."

"Ah, well, that's good, then. Very good!"

"Meow!"

George got down and sauntered off toward the kitchen.

"He agrees," Darlene said, still beaming. Linda withheld her opinion.

"I already know why you're here," Mr. Sedholm said, running one thin hand through his short, graying hair. She'd hardly ever seen him in the seven years she had worked at PennyWise Press, and she'd only spoken to him a handful of times. He had a reputation for being difficult to approach, and not very generous, but he left everyone alone to do their jobs, which she appreciated. He would never retire, Linda thought, noticing how old he looked these days. *He'll be here till he dies.* But that at least meant job security for the foreseeable future, if not financial.

"It's my expenses, Mr. Sedholm. I have to have a little more money, or I don't know what I'll do. I'd probably have to look for another job or something. I'm just getting farther behind every week, even with the overtime."

"I understand," Mr. Sedholm said, "and I am sorry to hear about your predicament. But life goes on, does it not? Of course I wish you well in whatever new employment you find. Good day."

With that he picked up the phone and dialed, then started talking. Linda sat there, stunned, until Mr. Sedholm paused to wave four fingers at her, shoo-fly style. "Go, you can go!" he said. So she did.

"I'm never going to leave this house again," Linda said. "They'll have to carry me out of here."

"You've been holed up here for a week!" Darlene argued, growling today, more so than yesterday. "They *will* carry you out of here pretty soon. You have to snap out of it. Listen, you're going out to lunch with me, and that's that. I'm buying, okay?"

She did have to do something, she knew that, and maybe going out to lunch was a start. She hadn't even gone down to sign up for unemployment yet. "I appreciate what you're trying to do," she told Darlene.

"I know that. Now come on."

She let Darlene drag her out to the car. When they stopped, she let Darlene drag her out of the car again and into a popular downtown café. They walked right through, then out onto a street-side patio. As they approached what was apparently their table, Linda saw a man already sitting there. He was in his early thirties, well dressed, neat, a solid chin, and eyes as dark as David's had been. He was nothing short of gorgeous, in fact. But that wasn't the point.

"What the hell is going on?" she snarled in Darlene's ear, stopping on the spot.

"I got you an interview with *my* boss. He's head of advertising, and a really decent guy, too. We've had someone leave recently. I told him you were very creative, the best design and layout person in the city, and that I thought he could steal you away from your current position. He even believes me!" She craned her neck so that they were facing each other. "This is real, Linda, I swear. No mix-ups, no fooling, and no cards. All you have to do is sit down, smile, and you're in!"

"All I have to do is sit down and I'm doomed." It sounded too good to be true, especially the "no cards" part. Darlene had tried to convince her that they ought to do a full reading with the tarot cards, now that they had the whole deck, that you couldn't really tell anything looking at just one card. There was no way.

"Does he drool?"

"Nope."

"Do I have to sleep with him?"

"Only if you want to. He's not like that. Now keep walking. You've got to do this. You've got to!"

Linda felt Darlene nudge her in the back with one

fist. She stepped forward, then kept going. He stood up and Darlene introduced everyone. His name was Nathan. It was a beautiful day. They sat and talked about the weather. He seemed politely enthusiastic. More than that, he seemed . . . genuine. The waiter came and Nathan ordered the wine.

"We can't pay you what you're probably worth," he said, getting down to business after that. He scribbled something on a notepad. "How would this be?" He slid the notepad toward her. The figure was two hundred a week more than she had been making at the PennyWise. Linda put her open hand on her chest, staying a gasp. "And benefits, of course," he added. "We offer a very attractive package."

Linda wanted to tell him she had already noticed hat, but she didn't. She just sat there, blinking.

"Say something," Darlene prodded.

That helped bring her around. "Okay, I mean, yes," Linda said.

Nathan extended one arm toward Linda, and they shook hands. "It takes guts to come out like this, give up your old job, then take a chance on someone you don't know," he said, as the wine arrived. "A lot of people would hesitate, let doubt rule their minds. You're every bit the person Darlene says you are."

Oh, if only, Linda gasped in silence. She drank her wine, then sat there, quiet. She found Nathan looking at her, smiling.

"I'm sorry, I didn't mean to stare," he said, and he stopped.

"It's . . . it's all right, if I can stare back," Linda kidded, wondering at once if her own mouth had actually said that. But he was smiling.

"Did I mention that Nathan is single, just like you," Darlene said, raising her refilled glass, embarrassing everyone else. Linda glared at Darlene. Nathan glared at Darlene right along with her.

"No," Linda said after a moment, "you didn't."

Nathan looked away, then he nodded. "I lost my wife a little over a year ago, and nothing has been quite the same. I haven't really started dating again. I've been kind of working up to it."

The waiter returned to take their orders.

"You know, I'm awfully sorry, but suddenly I'm not feeling very well," Darlene said. "I think I'll just go home and lie down. That is, if you think you could give Linda a lift, Nathan? I hate to impose, but she doesn't live very far, and I thought—"

"No, I think I could do that," Nathan said. "If it's all right with her."

Linda just looked at him, then she remembered the correct procedure, and nodded. Darlene practically vanished into thin air.

"She's good people," Nathan said of Darlene.

"Yes, I know."

The waiter seemed impatient. Linda only glanced at the menu. She ordered the salmon steaks. "My favorite," Nathan said, adding a complimentary nod. He ordered the same thing.

"Tell me, are you this friendly with everyone who works for you?" Linda asked.

He chuckled. "Probably not."

"Good."

Cars passed on the street, a dish fell, children giggled at the next table, Nathan started talking about himself. Linda wasn't sure through all of that, but somewhere very near to her she thought she heard a cat's meow.

HOUSE OF CARDS
by Don Webb

Don Webb is the author of two quirky collections,
Uncle Ovid's Exercise Book and *A Spell for the Fulfillment of Desire*, and numerous stories which have
appeared in *Isaac Asimov's SF Magazine, Fiction Review, Atticus Review*, and other journals and 'zines.
He lives in Austin, Texas.

In "House of Cards," Webb explores the idea that
the tarot is not merely a way for us to better understand ourselves, but in some cases what we ulti-
mately become—among a baker's half dozen other
ideas and notions.

I smiled when I saw the address on the little package.
I hadn't had a delivery to Rosa Mackenzie in about a
year. I loved her occult shop, the Nine of Disks, full
of jars and jars of sweet smelling herbs, crystals, and
jewelry. I never had my cards read there, I don't go
in for that kind of stuff, but I supposed that if anyone
did have the ability to peer into the hidden, it was
Rosa. She often explained to me that the cards didn't
reveal the future, but states of self that were coming
into being now—moods and ideas that would affect
the future depending on the matrix of their manifestation.

I pulled my brown truck up in front of the Nine of
Disks, and I wondered why I hadn't brought any packages here in a long time. Rosa used to get things every
week. Sometimes twice.

The shop was closed, there were weeds in the yard, the beautiful painting of the Nine of Disks card was faded, the bright green doorway had a piece of typing paper over it with the word closed written in brown-red magic marker. The porch swing had lost one of its chains and dragged on the concrete porch with an annoying grating sound. I walked up to the door. The sweet smell of the amber and frankincense still hung in the air, mixing with the sharp scent of the weeds.

"She's closed!" a woman yelled at me from across the street. It was Juno Remphan, who used to work as a reader in the Nine of Disks. Tall, red-haired, sea-green eyes, an interesting treat for the eyes of an enervated UPS delivery man. Dumb name, though. There was nothing breezelike about her; she was a storm from the get go. She was standing on the porch of a similar small Southern brick house across the street. It, too, had been made into a business. the House of Cards.

"She's closed!"

I walked across the street. Sure I've got a girlfriend, but I'm no idiot. Besides I'd need to start the paperwork on the package.

"Hey, Dave, I haven't seen you in a while—all my deliveries are RPS. How's it hangin'?"

"I can't complain, wouldn't help if I did. What happened to Rosa?"

"Got tired of it. You know I think we've only got so many readings in us, and when the cosmic counter goes—it's gone. That last reading probably tells you too much. What you got?"

I showed her the little package.

"Is that from Adi Tattva Cards in St. Louis?"

"Yes."

"Damn, that's for me. I tried to get those bastards on the phone when I set up my business. It's the first set of a deck I designed. Damn, what will I need to do to get it?"

"It doesn't have your name on it."

"I know. I dealt with them from Nine of Disks, so they kept putting Rosa's name on it. Can you put a note on it or something when you send it back? I want to get them started on making the decks. Maybe I'll make a buck or two."

I started to write a slip, and then she invited me inside for a glass of red hibiscus tea, and asked about my girlfriend, and batted her pretty eyes at me. She even said I looked tense and gave me a backrub, hitting that special spot below the neck that I carry my tension in. Then she told me what herb tea I needed to drink. Juno knew her herbs very well, or at least she had always said that was the one area she was more knowledgeable in than Rosa.

Since Rosa was out of the business anyway, I gave her the deck. Okay, that's not what we're supposed to do—but if we followed all the rules all the time, nobody would get their packages.

A couple of hours later I picked up Sheila and we had dinner at the Double Dip, a famous hamburger dive near campus. Sheila was blonde and muscular and had the biggest brown eyes. She fenced. I met her at the fencing club; there aren't many girls who fence, and all the ones who do are very, very pretty. But not as pretty as Sheila.

Nor half as cuddlesome.

Or a third as bright.

While we drank our Dreamsicle smoothies, I said, "You used to get your cards read at the Nine of Disks, didn't you?"

"Well, back when it was open, why?"

"I had a delivery there today, and I just saw it was closed."

The rest of it, especially being flirted with by Juno, seemed an unwise story at this point. Sheila and I have an open relationship, but not a combatively open relationship.

"That's strange, I bet it's been closed for a while. Let me see . . . it's July, so it's been three or four months."

"Do you shop at the House of Cards?"

"I got my cards read there, and that's where I bought my Thoth deck. But I haven't been into divination for a while."

"Getting into something else?"

"Well, I'm starting a new business, and I'm doing a pottery class, so this isn't the time for divination. Divination is good for one thing—it can give you a sense of wonder about your life, let you know that there's so much more going on than you think there is. Of course you know that as a delivery person."

"Beg pardon?"

"You're always telling me about weird coincidences in names, running into people again, little scenes of love and hate you see played out. I think you've got a really neat job."

The nice thing about Sheila is she really did think this way. She thrived on richness.

"Well, thanks. But I don't know if I'm following this."

"Divination can remind you of many hidden wonders in your own life, and if you apply that energy— that sense of wonder—to the cyclic dynamism of your life, you can jump-start things."

"You mean get high from a happy reading, and then you start a company?"

"I'm not talking about just happy readings, I'm talking about good readings—ones that're accurate. Rosa used to talk about this all the time. She said that she got a lot more business if she gave the happy, fortune-teller crap that fills the world. She said it was better for people to do the best job you could. Most people wouldn't like it, they might feel belittled, but a true reading inspired the few, and the few who faced the unknown and were energized and inspired by it, could do more for the good of the world than the many."

"Well, that's inspiring sounding and all, but it doesn't seem like good business."

"Rosa wasn't much good at business. She'd been rich sometime in the past, she used to say when Teddy Roosevelt was president, but it had worn away. She just liked to play with the world, and the cards were the best medium for that. 'People forget,' she'd say, 'that these things are for games, too. People are too uptight.' "

"A phrase dating to Teddy's administration."

"Yeah, I know, but she was a lot wiser than she pretended to be."

"So what happened? Where is she now?"

Over the course of the evening, Sheila told me the story. We had wine and cuddling, and candles. We talked about our Fourth of July plans, and the weather, and some very naughty things. When the story came to its conclusion, we had to leave Sheila's house quickly, so we didn't get to do those naughty things for a few nights.

Some months ago, Rosa announced that she was in the middle of an important project, so that she would need more help at the store. Sheila had toyed with the idea of giving up her job at the city council and going to work there for the experience, but decided against it. Rosa had hired Juno. Juno came from a weird family that was big into the occult revival, hence her name

and her generally witchy persona. Rosa had semire-
tired to a cottage behind the shop. It had originally
been built as a wedding cottage in a now shabbily
genteel section of Amarillo, Texas. It had been in the
Mackenzie family since the 1890s.

Rosa stopped seeing most people, and even cut out
the symphonies and the operas which were her main
passion. She let Juno do whatever she wanted in the
shop. Some evil-minded folk suggested that Juno was
stealing both from the till and the shop itself, but evil-
minded folk can suggest anything.

Sheila came by the shop one rainy day, and happened to catch Rosa inside. Rosa talked to her about
her new vision of the tarot. The tarot told a story—
not just as most people thought, the universal tale of
cyclic dynamism of manifestation, being, dismanifesta-
tion, remanifestation; but it told a personal story of
the deck designer—in the art, in the mathematical
form, in the names for the trumps and suites. Someone
could live on in such a story, if it was told well enough.
You could hide your own life in the cards—and then
you'd continue to play with others and the world as
they used the deck. You could do your good or evil
as long as the deck was shuffled. Rosa went on to say
any game, maybe Monopoly or chess, might have the
spirit of its creator playing through each and every
board, changing the world bit by bit. A wonderfully
spooky thought that the world is filled with thousands
of haunted chessboards. Rosa likened the process to
the thousand eyes of unsleeping Argus.

Sheila joked with her that Rosa didn't need immortality since she knew Teddy Roosevelt. Rosa
said that just showed she paid attention to her girlish figure.

The problems began soon thereafter. Rosa's once
vast wealth had apparently run its course. One day

while Sheila was shopping, the power was cut off. Juno fumed, but lit some candles and kept the shop open.

Juno told her that Rosa had gone crazy, wasn't paying her bills, and was spending all her time in the cottage in the back. Sheila sympathized and talked with Juno about Rosa's theories.

Sheila's retelling of the story sort of went awry here, and I gathered that Sheila showed a bit more sympathy to Juno's problems than the average customer would have. Like I said, we have an open relationship but not combatively open. I have to admit a sneaking admiration for Juno at that moment, and I thought of some interesting games which three people could play.

The upshot of the candle-lit encounter was that Juno had never heard of any of Rosa's theories of immortality, and decided it was time to end her employment with the Nine of Disks. She hadn't been paid in a couple of months anyway.

Juno quit town for a month, and then showed up with her pockets full of money. The house across from the Nine of Disks was for sale, and the N.O.D. wasn't doing so hot since Rosa was in the depths of her "research." So Juno bought the house and opened up the House of Cards.

Now some people said that all of her inventory had been stolen from the N.O.D. and kept in a self-storage warehouse on Amarillo Blvd. But some people will say anything. Evil to him who thinks it.

Sheila went to the Grand Opening. There were prizes and cakes and a smoky cauldron (lime Kool-aid with dry ice). She won a packet of Egyptian blend resin, which was mainly frankincense from Ethiopia. Juno brought out some Lone Star beer, and everyone partied and had a good time; although many people would occasionally look across the street in a spasm of guilt. There were toasts to the goddess and toasts

to Juno and toasts to Juno's aunt who had died of
cirrhosis—and whose piece of the rock the House of
Cards was founded on.

Juno's old customers came, and then anyone who
dropped by the Nine of Disks came, and then Juno
laid out some big bucks advertising in the local free
paper and the like—and suddenly there was a going
business. Most days you couldn't even park in front
of the Nine of Disks, since the overflow from across
the street parked there.

Sheila visited Rosa one of the few days the Nine of
Disks was open. Rosa looked old. She had always
been a pale dark beauty who looked like a very well-
preserved fifty, but now she had new wrinkles, circles
under her eyes, and those once-so-bright eyes had a
yellowish cast. Rosa said she needed to work faster
now, clearly her herb tea had come to the end of
its effectiveness.

Sheila had asked about the shop across the way.

"Oh, poor Juno, she'll play a part in things since
she was here when they started. She's so interested in
temporary things, that her part will be like this world:
nasty, brutish, and short. I wish you had come to work
for me instead."

The House of Cards began a price war soon after
that. Sheila admitted that she had bought her Thoth
deck then, something that she felt guilty about. N.O.D.
tried to duke it out by slashing its own prices, but the
momentum was already with the new shop.

Juno finally bought the merchandise of the other
shop.

A few days later, Sheila heard that an ambulance
had stopped in front of the Nine of Disks, and carried
out Rosa's body. There was a rumor that her skin was
as yellow as a lemon and that she had died of liver
failure, but Sheila disbelieved that since she knew that
Rosa never drank.

Rosa used to joke about it, saying that she could drink anyone under the table before Prohibition, but that had been a good time to quit. Now, whatever her project had been, it was over.

I thought about it for a minute and said, "Well, maybe it's not."

I told her about the small package I had delivered. Juno had said it was a pack of cards. I suppose it could be a pack of cards that she had designed, but what if Rosa had been working on a deck?

"Well," said Sheila, "she never said she was working on a deck. But that could've been in it. That would be pretty cold-blooded of Juno to just take it like that."

"Not any more cold-blooded than starting a shop to take all of Rosa's business."

"I don't think so, she's always been so friendly."

"Friendly?"

"All right," Sheila said with a little bit of a blush that stabbed me with the sharp dagger called lust. "All right, touchy-feely and cute. I don't want to think that someone I found attractive has a greedy side."

"Maybe worse than greedy. You said her aunt—and Rosa—died of liver problems?"

"Now wait a minute, you're getting into bad territory here. Greedy is one thing, but you're suggesting murder."

"I'm not thrilled with the idea, but I wonder what it would take to poison Rosa's tea."

"This is really morbid," said Sheila.

I knew that tone which meant no more lovin' tonight. I didn't really know what to do with the suspicions that filled my mind, but I did feel really bad about leaving that little packet at the House of Cards.

"I think I'll go down to the House of Cards. I'm not happy at having left that packet there, but I'm probably just projecting my bad feelings. I'll ask Juno for the package back, fill out the proper forms, and we'll forget about it," I said. "You want to come along?"

Sheila thought long and hard. I knew she was putting together the same facts I had, and wanting to deny them. "Sure," she said, but she sounded anything but.

It was nine in the evening, which was gloaming for Amarillo, Texas, in July. The House of Cards would just be closing if I remembered the hours right. The town baked, the sky was light blue, and clouds of a deep salmon color floated by, telling us not to bother hoping for rain. By the time we had driven south, the clouds had become an angry red-black, the sky a dark blue-purple, and folks were just beginning to turn on the lights of their cars as they drove.

The OPEN sign still beckoned customers, but when we went in, no one was evident.

We called out after a few minutes. No answer.

"Maybe she's in the reading room."

We knocked at the door of the room where clients could get their cards read, and then I tried the door.

Juno sat in the endless shock from her last reading at the reading table, a half-finished spread and a small opened cardboard box in front of her. It was the package I had delivered five hours before. I think it had only been opened a few moments before we had come in, though. Probably just after her last customer had left.

I surmised that because the blood on her throat was still wet.

The police and the paper had many theories about how some madman had broken in and threw or otherwise forced a card into her neck. I have my own theories, of course.

It was a beautiful card, the Trump called Judgment of the now-quite-popular Mackenzie deck. The blood ruined the illustration on the front of the card, but the peacock design on the back, the symbol of the thousand eyes of Argus, was exceptionally beautiful.

(For all the people who called me "Gypsy")

ARTICLES OF FAITH
by Nina Kiriki Hoffman

Nina Kiriki Hoffman is the author of the fantasy novels, *The Thread That Binds the Bones*, for which she
won the Bram Stoker Award, and *The Silent Strength
of Stones*, among others. Her excellent short stories
appear in innumerable magazines and anthologies,
and some have been collected *Courting Disaster* and
Legacy of Fire. She lives in Oregon.

In Hoffman's "Articles of Faith" a young girl finds a
reason to believe in the future in her grandmother's
deck of tarot cards.

Brooke stood on the threshold of her older sister's
bedroom for a moment, listening to the house. No one
else disturbed its quiet. She was alone.

She wasn't supposed to go into her sister's room
without asking.

It was Brooke's thirteenth birthday, and she was
pretty sure no one had remembered. No one had
asked her what she wanted in the past week. No one
had said anything at breakfast this morning. No birthday card had waited at her place at the table. There
weren't any suspicious wrapped parcels in her parents'
closet. No reminder note magneted to the refrigerator
to pick up something at the bakery, no ice cream in
the freezer compartment, and Mom hadn't even said
anything to Dad about making a special effort to get
home for dinner on time tonight for once.

So Brooke had gone to school as she always did,

and come home to an empty house. Brooke's sister Susie—no, Brooke was supposed to call her Star now—was off somewhere protesting the Vietnam war with her long-haired, hippie boyfriend. Dad was at work, and Mom had gone out. Brooke wasn't sure where, she only knew that she would recognize the sound of Mom's car when it came back in plenty of time for Brooke to get out of whatever she shouldn't be into.

This was a good time to snoop.

She parted the amber-beaded curtain with her hand and stepped into her sister's room.

The air smelled of incense and musk. A lit lamp on the floor was draped in a pink shawl, staining the light so that the room looked like something in a dream. Brooke's sister had papered over the windowpanes with black construction paper. Black light posters crowded the walls, windows into garish worlds full of giant multicolored flowers, stained-glass butterflies, bulbous mushrooms, and balloon letters Brooke couldn't read without a struggle.

Brooke glanced around, looking for changes. Changes gave clues, and Brooke needed all the clues she could find these days. For the past three years the family had been falling apart one brick at a time, and Brooke didn't want any more bricks to slip away. She couldn't stop what she didn't know about, so she wanted to know everything.

Not that that helped much either.

Most of Susie's room looked the same way it had the last three times Brooke had peeked in. Except . . . scattered across her sister's purple Indian print bedspread lay some large cards.

Brooke remembered seeing these cards once before. Where?

When she was six, before her mother started taking

those pills that made her spacy, and going to one psychiatrist after another.

Seven years ago.

One night . . .

One night, when Daddy had missed supper again and was still at work, and Susie was at a friend's house for a sleepover . . .

One night Mom had brought a lunchbox-sized wooden chest into the living room. The chest had faces carved on it, people Brooke had never seen walking around, men with beards of leaves, women with snakes for hair, and even a little child with wings instead of ears. "This was your grandmother's box," Mom had said, setting it on the coffee table. "Your grandmother, my mother. The one I named you after."

Grandma Brooke. Brooke remembered a stern, wrinkled face, a wide soft lap, arms that had held her, a little buzzing voice that had sung her songs about little horses and mockingbirds. It seemed like a long time ago.

"What's inside the box?" Brooke asked her mother.

"Let's find out." Mom worked at the bolt—it was rusty and resistant. "I hope it's serenity," Mom muttered, tugging on the bolt. "I sure could use some, and Ma always seemed so calm. . . ."

The bolt snicked open and Mom sat back, sucking on her finger which was bleeding.

"What happened?" Brooke asked.

"Scraped myself, damnit."

Brooke sat on her heels, waiting. It wasn't smart to ask Mom questions when she was in a cussing mood.

Presently Mom wrapped the scrape in a handkerchief and looked at the box again. "Well, shall we see what's in here?" She sounded friendly again.

"Yes, please."

Mom lifted the lid. Red velvet on the inside of it,

and in the box's cavity, something wrapped in shiny green cloth.

"Oh, no," said Mom.

"What is it?"

"The cards," whispered Mom. "The damned cards."

Brooke pretended she was invisible. It worked pretty well most times. She waited, keeping her breath quiet, and presently Mom lifted the green-wrapped thing out of the wooden box and untied a little cord around it. The cloth slid away and showed a stack of big cards.

Cards. Bigger than the ones Brooke and Susie used to play War. They looked old, brown around the edges. A smell came from them like dried and crumbled flowers, crushed weeds. Brooke was afraid to touch them. Mom never liked her to touch anything without asking, anyway. These cards looked like something she would have to wash her hands five times after touching, worse than doorknobs, almost as bad as toilet seats.

Brooke waited.

Mom set the cards on the coffee table, turned them over, and pushed them into a fan.

Pictures, so many pictures, so many colors—not like playing cards that were usually just black and red, or if you were lucky, maybe the face cards had a little yellow and blue on them.

Every card had a picture. People dancing, people hanging upside down, devils, angels, dogs, lions, stars, sun, moon. The cards called to Brooke, the colors bright even though the paper they were printed on had yellowed.

"Can I look?" Brooke had asked at last, wanting to study each picture as though it were the best kind of book. She leaned forward, staring at the nearest card: a fierce-looking man with a bandage around his head held a tall stick, with a bunch more sticks standing behind him. All the sticks had leaves sprouting from them.

The man turned his head and looked up out of the card at Brooke.

Her mouth dropped open. She had never seen anything on a card move before.

Because Brooke had spoken, Mom remembered she was there. "No," Mom said. "You mustn't look. What was I thinking?" She grabbed the cards, shoved them square, and twisted them into the green scarf again. She dropped them in the chest and closed it.

Here they were, those cards, all spread out, and Brooke was alone in the house. She hardly dared breathe. She leaned over and looked at the closest card.

A man stood by a table, holding a rod up in the air and pointing toward the Earth with his other hand. Flowers grew from the ceiling and the floor. The table had things on it. The card had a name: the Magician.

The magician winked at Brooke.

She jumped back, wondering if she had really seen it.

She remembered the man looking at her from the card when she was six, but when she was six, she had thought cats could talk, and monsters lived under her bed.

She was still afraid to touch the cards all these years later, though she no longer washed her hands so much they bled. Her mother had sent her to a child psychiatrist about the hand-washing, and she had learned not to do it, even though she still wanted to. There were so many things she wished she could wash off.

Should she look again?

What if another card changed expression?

A spark danced across one of the cards.

Brooke wondered if her sister had put anything

funny in the banana bread Brooke had eaten for an after-school snack. After that time with the brownies, though, Susie—oops, Star!—was much more careful about all that hippie stuff.

Brooke thought about those brownies. She was glad she had never like chocolate much. Mom had eaten three of the brownies, and then she had wandered down the street without a shirt on, laughing and singing.

The Chapins next door still wouldn't talk to any of them.

Brooke edged forward and peeked at the card the spark had flared on. A boy in a yellow outfit covered with lizards stared at the top of a stick he was holding. The boy had a feathered hat. Or maybe it wasn't a feather—maybe it was a flame.

It was a flame, all right. It burned right up off the card, brilliant and yellow and smelling like a match head. Only the card didn't burn.

Brooke fell back on her rear. What the heck was going on here? A boy with his head on fire! And for a second, the boy's face had looked . . .

. . . had looked like hers in that picture Daddy took three years ago at the lake. Mom, Susie, and Brooke in their swimsuits, standing on the beach. Brooke had glanced sideways at Mom, wondering if this was going to be a quiet vacation or one where Mom yelled a lot.

Susie and Mom had been smiling and squinting into the sun and waving to Daddy, playing dress-up: We are a happy family.

A foot from her sister's bed, Brooke waited a moment to see if anything else would rise up from the cards. They lay there looking flat and quiet. Brooke closed her eyes and thought herself into her body to check if she felt sick. She had a hard time connecting with herself. Usually it was a bad idea. Too many things hurt.

She didn't feel hot. Her stomach wasn't heaving. The inside of her mouth tasted like nothing special, and she didn't have a headache.

She inched back to look at the cards.

Golden light shone up from one. She leaned closer and looked at it. The light came from a stained-glass window with a tree of stars in it. Below the window walked a starving woman and a man on crutches. The woman was barefoot in the snow. The man had a bell around his neck.

Brooke blinked. The crippled man looked up at her with her father's face, and the starving woman who looked away had the face of her mother.

Brooke edged away from the bed, stood up, and ran from the room.

Mom came home later, but her eyes looked elsewhere as she walked through the kitchen making dinner. Pork chops simmered in cream-of-mushroom soup; frozen peas boiled to a pale yellow-green; Mom made a salad of lettuce and tomatoes, with too much dressing on it. Brooke, setting the dining room table for four, walked silently past her mother with the silverware and napkins. It was just as well that Mom wasn't at home in her head. Often enough Star skipped dinner without even calling, and Dad didn't seem to make it home in time for dinner more than twice a week, though he rarely called to mention he'd be late.

Brooke and her mother ate silently between the two empty chairs. Brooke practiced invisibility, even though Mom wasn't looking.

I'm thirteen today, Brooke thought. *It's my first day as a teenager. This is my birthday dinner? This is the worst birthday yet.*

And then, *I don't want it to go on like this. I don't*

*want to always be quiet and wait. I keep waiting, and
it doesn't get better.*

What have I got to lose?

Mom was deep in her own haze, which made her
less dangerous than when she was alert. She rarely got
angry in this state.

"Mom?"

"What."

"You know those cards of Grandma's?"

"What? What are you talking about?" Mom blinked
and struggled to focus.

"The cards in the green cloth."

"The cards. The cards?"

"The cards that were in Grandma's chest. What
kind of cards are those?"

"The damned cards," Mom said slowly. "The
damned cards."

"That's what they are? Damned?" Maybe Mom
meant this literally. Which would be weird—Mom had
never been religious that Brooke could remember.

"The tarot cards. The damned tarot cards." Mom
stared at the wall beyond Brooke, and Brooke sat
very still.

After a little while, Mom began to speak. "She kept
'em in a kitchen cupboard on the very top shelf where
none of us kids could get hold of 'em. At least not
until Henry got tall enough and figured out how to
drag a chair over and grab 'em. She tanned his hide
all right for touching her things. He couldn't sit down
for a week. Rest of us were too scared to try it after
that."

Brooke set her fork down and waited.

"She had those cards as long as I can remember.
Times were hard. It was the Depression. We never
had enough to eat. Six kids, and Pa out of work; Ma
took in laundry and mending, and we were always out
scrounging for food or little bit jobs.

"Every night she'd get those damned cards down and lay them out on the kitchen table and study them. She was always looking at the cards and never at us. She'd talk about them while she looked at them, but not in any language we could understand. One time Pa said she was probably bringing bad luck to the house with that heathen trash, maybe that was why he couldn't get a job. He went as if to grab at the cards, but she gave him a look that stopped him in his tracks. I never saw such a look. Like her eyes could shoot fire.

"She would look at those damned cards for a while, and then she would look at Pa, and tell him, if you do this and this and this, you'll find a job. He never did pay any attention to her. She stopped telling him after a while. She was never out of work, though in those days a woman couldn't make the kind of money a man could.

"So one night after months of this, she says she sees a job waiting for him if he'll get on over to the corner of Third and Main the next morning before eight. 'Listen to me this time,' she says. 'Aren't you ashamed your children don't have shoes?' So the next morning he gets up and goes to wait on that corner, and sure enough someone drives up in a truck and asks if he wants some farm work. Pa never did like that kind of hard work, but he took the job anyway.

"Our lives started getting better then. The war came along pretty soon after that and Pa and the oldest three kids got factory work and we all got comfortable."

Mom paused. She stared down at her plate, then mashed her peas flat with her fork, leaving crosshatch patterns on the yellow-green mush. She studied the ruined food. Brooke sat still. Eventually Mom spoke again in a low voice.

"Ma used those cards to wish me up a husband,

too. Your dad was fresh off the boat from the war when she found him for me, and full of promise. It was just like with Pa. 'The man you want will be coming down the dock tomorrow evening just after five,' she told me. 'Stop him and ask him for a cigarette.' I told her I didn't ever want to be poor again. Find me somebody so that wouldn't happen. Wish I had asked her for somebody who would never sleep with his secretary instead."

Brooke sucked in a breath, then sat holding the air inside her, afraid to make a sound. She had known, but she hadn't let herself know. All those late nights of Dad's.

Mom swallowed and blinked awake. She glared at Brooke. "What did you ask me, young lady?"

"I was just wondering about those old cards," Brooke whispered.

Mom glared a moment longer. Then she leaned back in her chair. She closed her eyes and sighed. "Those cards caused a lot of trouble. Offer you a future, but when you get there, it's full of worms. They can just stay locked up in that chest for the next hundred years, far as I'm concerned."

Brooke looked down at her plate. She ate a forkful of mushy peas. If she kept her eyes down, maybe Mom would stop looking at her.

"They're not coming home," Mom said after a little while. "They're just not." It was the first time Brooke remembered Mom mentioning Dad's and Star's absence out loud. Most of these missing-people dinners, Mom just pretended she had planned all along to cook for four and feed two. Sometimes she left the unused place settings at the table until the next night, and the next. "It's just you and me," she said. She stared at Brooke. The corners of her mouth drooped.

Then she laid her head on the table. "What am I going to do with my life?" she moaned. "What am I going to do? My kids hate me, my husband cheats on me, I have no place to go home to." She started crying.

Brooke really wanted to wash her hands. Instead she tiptoed out of the room and went upstairs.

She pushed through the beaded curtain again and knelt beside Star's bed in the sandalwood-scented room.

One of the cards pulsed with red light. She stared down at it, hearing a distant drum bang slowly. A heart, pierced with three swords. Behind it, clouds letting down rain.

Brooke pressed her hand to her chest. She could feel her own heart beat against her fingertips in time to the light pulsing from the card. For a long moment she sat listening to her heart and watching the heart on the card. Was this how you wished up a future? What kind of future was she going to get from such a spooky picture?

Maybe it was a picture of Mom's heart. How could you tell?

The heart had three swords going right through it, but it still beat.

"Grandma," Brooke whispered. She touched the heart in the card and felt warmth under her fingertip. "Are you here?"

A scent of roses came to her. Brooke looked at another card. An armored skeleton rode a white horse and held up a black flag with a big white rose on it. DEATH. The horse was trampling right over some people, or about to. None of the people looked like anyone Brooke knew.

"What?" Brooke asked. "You're dead, Grandma? I know you're dead. *I'm* going to die? Mom's going to die? What?" Maybe Death would be a relief. It would be better than watching her mother turn into that starving woman in the card, angry and abandoned and despairing. Better than watching Daddy limp along on those crutches in the snow.

Brooke reached toward Death's face. Before she had quite touched the card, she heard footsteps in the hall. She jerked her hand back.

"What are you talking to?" Star swept into the room, the beads of the curtain clicking against each other behind her. "What are you doing in here?" She smelled like marijuana, a smoky burned tea-leaf smell, with an overlay of Sen-Sen.

"Where'd you get these cards?" Brooke asked. *I'm thirteen now. I don't want to be quiet the rest of my life. I want some answers!*

"Found 'em way up in the back of Mom's closet in a really psychedelic box. Aren't they neat?" She flopped down on the bed, sitting on top of some of the cards, shoving the others into a loose stack.

"They used to be Grandma's," Brooke said. Star had sat on Death, and her smoky odor eclipsed the odor of roses."

"Cool," said Star. She had on a blue dress with fringes around the neck and big glass beads on the fringes. She wore a beaded headband around her forehead, her thick curly dark hair spilling out below it. Her pupils were wide. "They're so trippy I never would have thought Grandma owned them. She was so uptight." She grabbed a card. "Look. See this hand coming out of the cloud holding out this yellow thing? The yellow thing is acid! It's, like, saying, 'Here's this cool life experience just waiting for you. Have some.' " Star laughed. "Can you imagine Grandma ever figuring out there's a card in her deck that says it's a good idea to drop acid?"

Brooke looked at the card, saw a glowing white hand holding a golden circle with a star in it. "It's money," she said. "Not acid."

"Get with it," Star said, dropping the card on the bed. "You are such a square."

"Can I have these?" Brooke asked. She wanted them more than she had ever wanted anything in memory. So what if Death was there, if the outlook was bleak for Mom and Dad? At least the cards looked at her, winked at her, burned at her. At least the cards responded to her.

"Are you kidding?"

"No."

"Of course you can't have 'em. I found 'em first."

Brooke licked her lips. Used to be, when Star was Susie, Susie would never give Brooke anything—they'd fight over things they were supposed to share; but this new Susie, this Star, she was a hippie, and hippies believed in sharing. "It's my birthday," Brooke said.

"It is? Oh, man, I'm sorry, kid. I completely forgot. I am such a jerk. Why didn't you say something?"

To her embarrassment, Brooke began to cry.

"Oh. Hey. Don't do that, kiddo. Stop it. You're bringing me down. Here." Star squashed all the cards together in a ragged heap. "Pick a card, any card." She tried to fan the cards, succeeded only in spreading out the chaos.

Brooke pulled a card out of the middle of the mess. She licked a tear off her lip and turned the card over.

THE HIGH PRIESTESS, it said. It showed a seated woman in a flowing blue-and-white dress, with a horned hat on her head. A big white disk was in the middle of the hat. After a second Brooke saw that it was a pearl. The woman had a crescent moon at her feet and pillars to either side of her, one black, and one white. Behind her a veil stretched between the two pillars. She was holding a scroll on her lap, half-hidden under her cape. She had a big cross on her chest.

Or maybe the thing on her head wasn't a pearl. Silver light shone from it. Brooke laid her finger against the white circle and felt a breath of cool air coming from the picture. She smelled water and ripe fruit, some kind of fruit she had never tasted.

"Happy birthday, kiddo," said Star, dropping the rest of the cards on the bed. "You can have that one."

Brooke swallowed and sniffed. She tried to smile. "Thanks, Star," she said. One card was better than none.

She went to her own room. She had no posters up. Her furniture looked so plain, wooden and boring. Her bedspread was white with fuzzy chenille outlines of flowers on it. Her schoolbooks sat in a stack on her desk; everything else was neat and empty.

She thought about all the decorations in Star's room. She thought about Grandma, wishing up a job or a future with the cards. She put the Priestess card on her desk and got out a sketch pad and some colored pencils, then sat down to draw and color a copy of her card.

"Is there a future where Mom and Dad love each other and Star goes back to being Susie?" she asked the Priestess as she drew a picture of two pillars.

"No," whispered the Priestess.

"What good's a future if you can't make it do what you want?" Brooke said. She threw her pencil on the floor.

"The future is full of astonishing things," whispered the Priestess. "Don't you want to see them?"

"Not if I'll still feel like I feel right now," Brooke said.

"You won't. Not always."

Brooke stared at the painted face of the Priestess. For a brief, flickering second she saw the soft, wrinkled face of her grandmother in the card. She had only known her grandmother a little while; Grandma died when Brooke was four.

"I'll stay with you," whispered the Priestess, "whatever else happens."

Brooke slid the card under her pillow when she went to bed.

In her dreams she heard strange music, saw people dancing and giving each other ripe fruit and cups full of something good. A woman in a flowing dress gave Brooke a handful of red grapes, and Brooke ate them. Their taste was strong and sweet and satisfying.

The High Priestess and the Magician were under the trees. He played a flute and she played a drum.

"Dance with us," a man said.

"I don't dance," said Brooke.

"You may now."

Oh, why not? Brooke danced. Later she laughed. When she woke up, she was smiling, and she couldn't remember why.

WILD HORSES
by Charles de Lint

Charles de Lint's urban-fantasy novels have won him legions of fans and helped create a popular sub-genre. His more than two dozen books include *Moonheart, The Riddle of the Wren, Yarrow, Memory and Dream, Spiritwalk, The Ivory and the Horn*, and *The Little Country*, among others. He operates a small press, Triskell Press, and lives with his wife, Mary-Ann, in Ottawa, Ontario, where they are both musicians.

In "Wild Horses," de Lint shows us the power of the tarot as we want it to be, the magic that so many of us wish the cards actually posessed and the responsibility of controlling such power.

> *Chance is always powerful. Let your hook be always cast; in the pool where you least expect it, there will be a fish.*
>
> —OVID

1

The horses run the empty length of the lakeshore, strung out like a long ragged necklace, perfect in their beauty. They run wild. They run like whitecaps in choppy water, their unshod hooves kicking up sand and spray. The muffled sound of their galloping is a rough music, pure rhythm. Palominos. Six, seven . . .

maybe a dozen of them. Their white manes and tails
flash, golden coats catch the sunlight and hold it under
the skin the way mine holds a drug.

The city is gone. Except for me, transfixed by the
sight of them, gaze snared by the powerful motion of
their muscles propelling them forward, the city is
gone, skyline and dirty streets and dealers and the
horse that comes in a needle instead of running free
along a beach. All gone.

And for a moment, I'm free, too.

I run after them, but they're too fast for me, these
wild horses, can't be tamed, can't be caught. I run
until I'm out of breath and stumble and fall and when
I come to, I'm lying under the overpass where the
freeway cuts through Squatland, my works lying on
my coat beside me, empty now. I look out across a
landscape of sad tenements and long-abandoned factories and the only thing I can think is, I need another
hit to take me back. Another hit, and this time I'll
catch up to them.

I know I will. I have to.

There's nothing for me here.

But the drugs don't take me anywhere.

2

Cassie watched the young woman approach. She
was something, sleek and pretty, newly shed of her
baby-fat. Nineteen, maybe; twenty-one, twenty-two,
tops. Wearing an old sweater, raggedy jeans and
sneakers—nothing fancy, but she looked like a million
dollars. Bottle that up, Cassie thought, along with the
long spill of her dark curly hair, the fresh-faced, perfect complexion, and you'd be on easy street. Only
the eyes hinted at what must have brought her here,
the lost, hopeful look in their dark depths. Something

haunted her. You didn't need the cards to tell you that.

She was out of place—not a tourist, not part of the Bohemian coterie of fortunetellers, buskers, and craftspeople who were set up along this section of the Pier either. Cassie tracked her gaze as it went from one card table to the next, past the palmist, the other card readers, the Gypsy, the lovely Scottish boy with his Weirdin disks, watched until that gaze met her own and the woman started to walk across the boards, aimed straight for her.

Somebody was playing a harp, over by one of the weavers' tables. A sweet melody, like a lullaby, rose above the conversation around the tables and the sound of the water lapping against the wooden footings below. It made no obvious impression on the approaching woman, but Cassie took the music in, letting it swell inside her, a piece of beauty stolen from the heart of commerce. The open-air market and sideshow that sprawled along this section of the Pier might look alternative, but it was still about money. The harper was out to make a buck and so was Cassie.

She had her small collapsible table set up with a stool for her on one side, its twin directly across the table for a customer. A tablecloth was spread over the table, hand-embroidered with ornate hermetic designs. On top of the cloth, a small brass change bowl and her cards, wrapped in silk and boxed in teak.

The woman stood behind the vacant stool, hesitating before she finally sat down. She pulled her knapsack from her back and held it on her lap, arms hugging it close to her chest. The smile she gave Cassie was uncertain.

Cassie gave her a friendly smile back. "No reason to be nervous, girl. We're all friends here. What's your name?"

"Laura."

"And I'm Cassandra. Now what sort of a reading were you looking for?"

Laura reached out her hand, not quite touching the box with its cards. "Are they real?" she asked.

"How do you mean, real?"

"Magic. Can you work magic with them?"

"Well, now . . ."

Cassie didn't like to lie, but there was magic and there was magic. One lay in the heart of the world and was as much a natural part of how things were as it was deep mystery. The other was the thing people were looking for to solve their problems with and it never quite worked the way they felt it should.

"Magic's all about perception," she said. "Do you know what I mean?"

Laura shook her head. She'd drawn her hand back from the cards and was hugging her knapsack again. Cassie picked up the wooden box and put it to one side. From the inside pocket of her matador's jacket, she pulled out another set of cards. These were tattered around the edges, held together by an elastic band. When she placed them on the tablecloth, the woman's gaze went to the top card and was immediately caught by the curious image on it. The card showed the same open-air market they were sitting in, the crowds of tourists and vendors, the Pier, the lake behind.

"Those . . . are those regular cards?" Laura asked.

"Do I look like a regular reader?"

The question was academic. Cassie didn't look like a regular anything, not even on the Pier. She was in her early thirties, a dark-eyed woman with coffee-colored skin and hair that hung in a hundred tiny beaded braids. Today she wore tight purple jeans and yellow combat boots; under her black matador's jacket was a white T-shirt with the words "Don't! Buy! Thai!" emblazoned on it. Her ears were festooned with studs, dangling earrings, and simple hoops. On each wrist she had a dozen or so plastic bracelets in a rainbow palette of day-glo colors.

"I guess not," the woman said. She leaned a little closer. "What does your T-shirt mean? I've seen that slogan all over town, on T-shirts, spray-painted on walls, but I don't know what it means."

"It's a boycott to try to stop the child-sex industry in Thailand."

"Are you collecting signatures for a petition or something?"

Cassie shook her head. "You just do like the words say. Check out what you're buying and if it's made in Thailand, don't buy it and explain why."

"Do you really think it'll help?"

"Well, it's like magic," Cassie said, bringing the conversation back to what she knew Laura really wanted to talk about. "And like I said, magic's about perception, that's all. It means anything is possible. It means taking the way we usually look at a thing and making people see it differently. Or, depending on your viewpoint, making them see it properly for the first time."

"But—"

"For instance, I could be a crow, sitting on this stool talking to you, but I've convinced everybody here that I'm Cassandra Washington, card reader, so that's what you all see."

Laura gave her an uneasy look that Cassie had no trouble reading: pretty sure she was being put on, but not entirely sure.

Cassie smiled. "The operative word here is *could*. But that's how magic works. It's all about how we perceive things to be. A good magician can make anything seem possible and pretty soon you've got seven-league boots and people turning invisible or changing into wolves or flying—all sorts of fun stuff."

"You're serious, aren't you?"

"Oh, yeah. Now fortunetelling—that's all about perception, too, except it's looking inside yourself. It works best with a ritual because that allows you to concentrate better—same reason religion and church work so well for some people. Makes them all pay attention and focus, and the next thing you know they're either looking inside themselves and working out their problems, or making a piece of magic."

She picked up the cards and removed the elastic band. Shuffled them. "Think of these as a mirror. Pay enough attention to them, and they'll lay out a pattern that'll take you deep inside yourself."

Laura appeared disappointed. But they always did, when it was put out in front of them like this. They thought you'd pulled back the curtain and shown the Wizard of Oz, working all the levers of his machine, not realizing that you'd let them into a deeper piece of magic than something they might buy for a few dollars in a place like the Pier.

"I . . . I thought it might be different," Laura said.

"You wanted it all laid out for you, simple, right? Do this, and this'll happen. Do this, and it'll go like this. Like reading the sun signs in the newspaper, except personal."

Laura shook her head. "It wasn't about me. It was about my brother."

"You brother?"

"I was hoping you could, you know, use your cards to tell me where he is."

Cassie stopped shuffling her pack and laid it face-down on the table.

"Your brother's missing?" she said.

Laura nodded. "It's been two years now."

Cassie was willing to give people a show, willing to give them more than what they were asking for, sometimes, or rather what they were really asking for but weren't articulating, but she wasn't in the business of selling false hopes or pretences. Some people could do it, but not her. Not and sleep at night.

"Laura," she said. "Girl. You've come to the wrong place. You want to talk to the police. They're the ones who deal with missing persons."

And you'll have wanted to talk to them a lot sooner than now, she thought, but she left that unsaid.

"I did," Laura told her.

Cassie waited. "And what?" she asked finally. "They told you to come here?"

"No. Of course not. They—a Sergeant Riley. He's been really nice, but I guess there's not much they can do. They say it's been so long and the city's so big and Dan could have moved away months ago. . . ."

Her eyes filled with tears, and her voice trailed off. She swallowed, tried again.

"I brought everything I could think of," she said, holding up her knapsack for a moment before clutching it tightly to her chest again. "Pictures. His dental records. The last couple of postcards I got from him. I . . ." She had to swallow again. "They have all these pictures of . . . of unidentified bodies and I . . . I had to look at them all. And they sent off copies of the stuff I brought—sent it off all over the country. But it's been over a month, and I know Dan's not dead. . . ."

She looked up, her eyes still shiny with unshed tears. Cassie nodded sympathetically.

"Can I see one of the pictures?" she said.

A college-aged boy looked back at her from the small snapshot Laura took out of her knapsack. Not handsome, but there was a lot of character in his features. Short brown hair, high cheekbones, strong jawline. Something in his eyes reflected the same mix of loss and hopefulness that was now in his sister's. What had *he* been looking for?

"You say he's been missing for two years?" Cassie asked.

Laura nodded. Showing the picture seemed to have helped steady her.

"Your parents didn't try to find him?"

"They never really got along. It's—I don't know why. They were always fighting, arguing. He left the house when he was sixteen—as soon as he could get out. We live—we *lived* just outside of Boston. He moved into Cambridge, then maybe four years ago, he moved out here. When I was in college, he'd call me sometimes and always send me postcards."

Cassie waited. "And then he stopped?" she said finally.

"Two years ago. That's when I got the last card. I saw him a couple of months before that."

"Do you get along with your parents?"

"They've always treated me just the opposite from how they treated him. Dan couldn't do anything right, and I can't do anything wrong."

"Why did you wait so long?"

"I . . ." Her features fell. "I just kept expecting to hear from him. I was finishing up my Masters and working part-time at a restaurant and . . . I don't know. I was just so busy, and I didn't realize how long it had really been until all of a sudden two years have gone by since he wrote."

She kept looking at the table as she spoke, glancing up as though to make sure Cassie was still listening, then back down again. When she looked up now, she straightened her back.

"I guess it was pretty crazy of me to think you could help," she said.

No, Cassie thought. *More like a little sad.* But she understood need and how it could make you consider avenues you'd never normally take a walk down.

"Didn't say I wouldn't try," she told Laura. "What do you know about what he was doing here?"

"The last time I saw him, all he could talk about

were these horses, wild horses running along the shore of the lake.''

Cassie nodded encouragingly when Laura's voice trailed off once more.

"But there aren't any, are there?" Laura said. "It's all . . ." She waved her hand, encompassing the Pier, the big hotels, the Williamson Street Mall farther up the beach. "It's all like this."

"Pretty much. A little farther west there's the Beaches, but that's all private waterfront and pretty upscale. And even if someone would let him onto their land, I've never heard of any wild horses out there."

Laura nodded. "I showed his picture around at the racetrack and every riding stable I could find listed in the phone book, but no one recognized him."

"Anything else?" Cassie asked.

She hesitated for a long moment before replying. "I think he was getting into drugs again." Her gaze lifted from the card table to meet Cassie's. "He was pretty bad off for a few years, right after he got out of the house, but he'd cleaned up his act before he moved out here."

"What makes you think he got back into them?"

"I don't know. Just a feeling—the last time I saw him. The way he was all fidgety again, something in his eyes . . ."

Maybe that was what she'd seen in his picture, Cassie thought. That need in his eyes.

"What kind of drugs?" she asked.

"Heroin."

"A different kind of horse."

Laura sighed. "That's what Sergeant Riley said."

Cassie tapped a fingernail, painted the same purple as her jeans, on the pack of cards that lay between them.

"Where are you staying?" she asked.

"The Y. It's all I can afford. I'm getting kind of low on money, and I haven't had much luck getting a job."

Cassie nodded. "Leave me that picture," she said. "I'll ask around for you, see what I can find out."

"But . . ."

She was looking at the cards. Cassie laid her hand over them and shook her head.

"Let me do this my way," Cassie said. "You know the pay phone by the front desk? I'll give you a call there tomorrow, around three, say, and then we can talk some more."

She put out her hand and Laura looked confused.

"Um," she began. "How much do you want?"

Cassie smiled. "The picture, girl. I'll do the looking as a favor."

"But I'm putting you to so much trouble—"

"I've been where you are," Cassie said. "If you want to pay me back, do a good turn for someone else."

"Oh."

She didn't seem either confident or happy with the arrangement, but she left the picture and stood up. Cassie watched her make her way back through the other vendors, then slowly turned over three cards from the top of the deck. The first showed a set of works lying on worn blue denim. A jacket, Cassie decided. The second had a picture of an overpass in the Tombs. The last showed a long length of beach, empty except for a small herd of palominos cantering down the wet sand. In the background, out in the water, was the familiar shape of Wolf Island, outlined against the horizon.

Cassie lifted her head and turned to look at the lake. Beyond the end of the Pier she could see Wolf Island, the ferry on a return trip, halfway between the island and the mainland. The image on her card didn't show the city, didn't show docking facilities on the island, the museum and gift shop that used to be somebody's summer place. The image on her card was of another time, before the city got here. Or of another place that you could only reach with your imagination.

Or with magic.

3

Cassie and Joe had made arrangements to meet at The Rusty Lion that night. He'd been sitting outside on the patio waiting for her when she arrived, a handsome Native man in jeans and a plain white T-shirt, long black braid hanging down his back, a look in his dark eyes that was usually half solemn, half tomfool Trickster. Right now it was concerned.

"You don't look so good," he said as she sat down.

She tried to make a joke of it. "People ask me why I stay with you," she said, "and I always tell them, you just know how to make a girl feel special."

But Joe would have none of it.

"You've got trouble," he told her, "and that means we have trouble. Tell me about it."

So she did.

Joe knew why she was helping this woman she'd never seen before. That was one of the reasons it was so good between them: Lots of things didn't need to be explained, they were simply understood.

" 'Cause you found Angie too late," he said.

He reached across the table and took her hand, wanting to ease the sting of his words. She nodded and took what comfort she could from the touch of his rough palm and fingers. There was never any comfort in thinking about Angie.

"It might be too late for Laura's brother, too," she said.

Joe shrugged. "Depends. The cops could be right. He could be long gone from here, headed off to some junkie heaven like Seattle. I hear they've got one of the best needle exchange programs in the country and you know the dope's cheap. Twenty bucks'll buy you a thirty piece."

Cassie nodded. "Except the cards . . ."

"Oh, yeah. The cards."

The three cards lay on the table between them, still holding the images she'd found in them after Laura walked away. Joe had recognized the place where the horses were running the same as she had.

"Except I never heard of dope taking someone into the spiritworld before," he said.

"So what does it mean?" Cassie asked.

He put into words what she'd only been thinking. "Either he's clean, or he's dead."

She nodded. "And if he's clean, then why hasn't he called her, or sent another postcard? They were close."

"She says."

"You don't think so?"

Joe shrugged. "I wasn't the one who met her. But she waited two years."

"I waited longer to go looking for Angie."

There was nothing Joe could say to that.

4

It was a long time ago now.

Cassie shows them all, the white kids who wouldn't give her the time of day and the kids from the projects that she grew up with. She makes top of her graduating class, valedictorian, stands there at the commencement exercises, out in front of everybody, speech in hand. But when she looks out across the sea of mostly-white faces, she realizes they still don't respect her and there's nobody she cares about sitting out there. The one person who ever meant something to her is noticeably absent.

Angie dropped out in grade nine and they really haven't seen each other since. Somewhere between Angie dropping out and Cassie resolving to prove herself, she and her childhood best friend have become more than strangers. They might as well never have known each other, they're so different.

So Cassie's looking out at the crowd. She wants to blow them off, but that's like giving in, so she follows through, reads her speech, pretends she's a part of the celebration. She skips the bullshit parties that follow, doesn't listen to the phony praise for her speech, and won't talk to her teachers who want to know what she plans to do next. She goes home and takes off that pretty new dress that cost her two months' pay working after school and weekends at McDonald's. Puts on sweats and hightops. Washes the makeup from her face and looks in the mirror. The face that looks back at her is soft, that of a little girl. The only steel is in the eyes.

Then she goes out looking for Angie, but Angie's not around anymore. Word on the street is she went the junkie route, mixing crack and horse, selling herself to pay for her jones, long gone now or dead, and why would Cassie care anyway? It's like school, only in reverse. She's got no street smarts, no one takes her seriously, no one respects her.

She finds herself walking out of the projects, still looking for Angie, but keeping to herself now, walking all over the city, looking into faces but finding only strangers. Her need to find Angie is maybe as strong as Angie's was for the drugs, everything's focused on it, looking not only for Angie but for herself—the girl she was before she let other people's opinions become more important than her best friend. She's not ready to say that her turning her back on Angie pushed her friend toward the street life, but it couldn't have helped either. But she does know that Angie had a need that Cassie filled, and the drugs took its place. Now Cassie has a need, and she doesn't know what's going to fill it, but something has to, or she feels like she's just going to dry up and blow away.

She keeps walking farther and farther until one day that jones of hers takes her to an old white clapboard house just north of the city, front yard's got a bottle tree growing in the weeds and dirt, an old juju woman sitting on the porch looking at her with dark eyes, skin so black Cassie feels white. Cassie doesn't know which is scarier, the old woman or her saying, " 'Bout time you showed up, girl. I'd just about given up on you."

All Cassie can do is stand there, can't walk away, snared by the old woman's gaze. A breeze comes up and those bottles hanging in the tree clink against each other. The old woman beckons to her with a crooked finger, and the next thing Cassie knows she's walking up to the porch, climbing the rickety stairs, standing right in front of the woman.

"I've been keeping these for someone like you," she says and pulls a pack of tattered cards out of the pocket of her black dress.

Cassie doesn't want to take them, but she reaches for them all the same. They're held together with an elastic band. When the old woman puts them in her hand, something like a static charge jumps between them. She gets a dizzy feeling that makes her sway, almost lose her balance. She closes her hand, fingers tight around the cards, and the feeling goes away.

The old woman's grinning. "You felt that, didn't you, girl?"

"I . . . I felt something."

"Aren't you a caution."

None of this feels real, none of it makes sense. The old woman, the house, the bottle tree. Cassie tries to remember how she got here, when the strip malls and fast food outlets suddenly gave way to a dirt road and this place. Is this how it happened to Angie? All of a sudden she looks at herself one day and she's a junkie?

Cassie gaze goes down to the cards the old woman gave her. She removes the elastic and fans a few of them out. They have a design on one side; the other side is blank. She lifts her head to find the old woman still grinning at her.

"What are these?" she asks.

"What do they look like, girl? They're cards. Older than Egypt, older than China, older than when the first mama woke up in Africa and got to making babies so that we could all be here."

"But . . ." It's hard to think straight. "What are they for?"

"Fortunes, girl. Help you find yourself. Let you help other people find themselves."

"But . . ."

She was valedictorian, she thinks. She has more of a vocabulary than her whole family put together, and all she can say is, "But."

"But there's nothing on them."

She doesn't know much about white people's magic, but she's heard of telling fortunes with cards—playing cards, tarot cards. She doesn't know much about her own people's magic either.

The old juju woman laughs. "Oh, girl. 'Course there isn't. There won't be nothing on them until you need something to be there."

None of this is making sense. It's only making her dizzy again. There's a stool beside the woman's chair and she sits on it, closes her eyes, still holding the cards. She takes a few deep breaths, steadies herself. But when she opens her eyes again, she's sitting on a concrete block in the middle of a traffic median. There's no house, no bottle tree. No old woman. Only the traffic going by on either side of her. A discount clothing store across the street. A factory outlet selling stereos and computers on the other side.

There's only the cards in her hands and at her feet, lying on the pavement of the median, an elastic band.

She's scared. But she bends down, picks up the elastic. She turns over the top card, looks at it. There's a picture now, where before it was blank. It shows an abandoned tenement in the Tombs, one of the places where the homeless people squat. She's never been in it, but she recognizes the building. She's passed it a hundred times on the bus, going from school to the MacDonald's where she worked. She turns another card and now she's looking at a picture of the inside of a building—probably the same one. The windows are broken, there's garbage all over, a heap of rags in one corner. A third card takes her closer to the rags. Now she can see there's somebody lying under those rags, somebody so thin and wasted there's only bone covered with skin.

She doesn't turn a fourth card.

She returns the cards to the pack, puts the elastic around them, sticks the pack in her pocket. Her mouth feels baked and dry. She waits for a break in the traffic and goes across to the discount clothing store to ask for a drink of water, but they tell her the restroom is only for staff. She has to walk four blocks before a man at a service station gives a sympathetic look when she repeats her request and hands her the key to the women's room.

She drinks long and deep, then feels sick and has to throw up. When she returns to the sink, she rinses her mouth, washes her face. The man's busy with a customer, so she hangs the key on the appropriate hook by the door in the office and thanks him as she goes by, walking back toward downtown.

Normal people don't walk through the Tombs, not even along well-trafficked streets like Williamson or Flood. It's too dangerous, a no man's land of deserted tenements and abandoned factories. But she doesn't see she has a choice. She walks until she sees the tenement that was on the card, swallows hard, then crosses an empty lot overgrown with weeds and refuse until she's standing in front of it. It takes her a while to work up her nerve, but finally she steps into its foyer.

It smells of urine and garbage. Something stirs in a corner, sits up. Her pulse jumps into overtime, even when she sees it's only a raggedy boy, skinny, hollow-eyed.

"Gimme something," he says. "I don't need to get high, man. I just need to feel well again."

"I . . . I don't have anything."

She's surprised she can find her voice. She's surprised that he only nods and lies back down in his nest of newspapers and rags.

It doesn't take her long to find the room she saw on the second card. Something pulls her down a long hall. The doors are all broken down. Things stir in some of the rooms. People. Rats. Roaches. She doesn't know and doesn't investigate. She just keeps walking until she's in the room, steps around the garbage littering the floor to the heap of rags in the corner.

A half hour later she's at a pay phone on Gracie Street, phoning the police, telling them about the dead body she found in the tenement.

"Her name's Angie," she says. "Angie Moore."

She hangs up and starts to walk again, not looking for anything now, hardly able to see because of the tears that swell in her eyes.

She doesn't go home again. She can't exactly explain why. Meeting the old woman, the cards she carries, finding Angie, it all gets mixed up in her head with how hard she tried to do well and still nobody really cared about her except for the friend she turned her back on. Her parents were happy to brag about her marks, but there was no warmth there. She's eighteen and can't remember ever being embraced. Her brothers and sisters were like the other kids in the projects, ragging on her for trying to do well. The white kids didn't care about anything except for the color of her skin.

It all came down to no one respecting her except for Angie, and she'd turned her back on Angie because Angie couldn't keep up.

But the cards mean something. She knows that.

She's still working at the McDonald's, only now she saves her money and lives in a squat in the Tombs. Nobody comes to find out why she hasn't returned home. Not her family, not her teachers. Some of the kids from school stop by, filling up on Big Macs and fries and soft drinks, and she can hear them snickering at their tables, studiously not looking at her.

She takes to going to the library and reading about cards and fortunetelling, gets to be a bit of an expert. She buys a set of tarot cards in The Occult Shop and sometimes talks to the people who work there, some of the customers. She never reads or hears anything about the kind of cards the old woman gave her.

Then one day she meets Joseph Crazy Dog in the Tombs, just down from the Kickaha res, wild and reckless and a little scary, but kind, too, if you took the time to get to know him. Some people say he's not all there, supposed to be on medication, but won't take it. Others say he's got his feet in two worlds, this one and another place where people have animal faces and only spirits can stay for more than a few days, the kind of place you come back from either a poet or mad. First thing he tells her is he can't rhyme worth a damn.

Everybody calls him Bones because of how he tells fortunes with a handful of small animal and bird bones, reading auguries in the way they fall upon the buckskin when he throws them. But she calls him Joe, and something good happens between them because he respects her, right away he respects her. He's the first person she tells about the old juju woman, and she knows she was right to wait because straight away he can tell her where she went that day and what it means.

5

It was almost dark by the time Cassie and Joe reached the overpass in the Tombs that was pictured on the card. At one time it had been a hobo camp, but now it was one more junkie landmark, a place where you could score and shoot without being hassled. The cops didn't bother coming by much. They had bigger fish to fry.

"A lot of hard times bundled up in a place like this," Joe said.

Cassie nodded.

Some of the kids they walked by were so young. Most of them were already high. Those that weren't, were looking to score. It wasn't the sort of place you could ask questions, but neither Cassie nor Joe were strangers to the Tombs. They still squatted themselves and most people knew of them, if they'd never actually met. They could get away with showing around a picture, asking questions.

"When did heroin get so popular again?" Cassie said.

Joe shrugged. "Never got unpopular—not when it's so easy to score. You know the drill. The only reason solvents and alcohol are so popular up on the rez is no one's bringing in this kind of shit. That's the way it works everywhere—supply and demand. Here the supply's good."

And nobody believed it could hurt them, Cassie thought. Because it wouldn't happen to them and sure people got addicted, but everybody knew somebody who'd used and hadn't got strung out on it. Nobody set out to become an addict. Like most bad things, it just snuck up on you when you weren't paying attention. But the biggest problem was that kids got lied to about so much, it was hard for them to accept this warning as a truth.

They made a slow pass of the three or four blocks where most of the users congregated, showing the photo of Laura's brother when it seemed appropriate, but without much luck. From there they headed back downtown, following Williamson Street down Gracie. It was on the gay bar strip on Gracie Street that they finally found someone who could help.

"I like the hair, Tommy" Cassie said.

It was like a close-cut Afro, the corkscrew curls so purple they had to come from a bottle. Tommy grinned, but his good humor vanished when Joe showed him the picture.

"Yeah, I know him," Tommy said. "Danny Packer, right? Though he sure doesn't look like that now. How come you're looking for him?"

"We're not. His sister is and we're just helping her out. Any idea where we could find him?"

"Ask at the clinic."

Cassie and Joe exchanged glances.

"He's working there?" Cassie asked.

Tommy shook his head.

6

"What is this place?" Laura asked.

They were standing in front of an old yellow brick house on McKennitt Street in Lower Crowsea. Cassie had picked her up outside the Y a little after four and Joe drove them across town in a cab he'd borrowed from a friend.

"It's a hospice," Cassie said. "It was founded by a writer who died of AIDS a few years ago—Ennis Thompson."

"I've read him. He was a wonderful writer."

Cassie nodded. "His royalties are what keeps it running."

The house was on a quiet stretch of McKennitt, shaded by a pair of the tall, stately oaks that flourished in Crowsea. There wasn't much lawn. Geraniums grew in terra cotta planters going up the steps to the front door, adding a splash of color and filling the air with their distinctive scent. They didn't seem to make much of an impression on Laura. She was too busy studying the three-storied building, a small frown furrowing the skin between her eyebrows.

"Why did Dan want me to meet him here?" she asked.

Cassie hesitated. When they'd come to see him last night, Laura's brother had asked them to let him break the news to her. She understood, but it left her in the awkward position of having to be far too enigmatic in response to Laura's delight that her brother had been found. She'd been fending off Laura's questions ever since they'd spoken on the phone earlier and arranged to drive out here.

"Why don't we let him tell you himself," Cassie said.

Joe held the door for them. He nodded a greeting to the young woman stationed at a reception desk in what would once have been a front parlor.

"Go ahead," she told them. "He's expecting you."

"Thanks," Joe said.

He led the way down the hall to Dan's room. Rapping softly on the door, he opened it when a weak voice called out, "It's open."

Laura stopped and wouldn't go on.

"Come on," Cassie said, her voice gentle.

But Laura could only shake her head. "Oh, God, how could I have been so stupid? He's a patient here, isn't he?"

Cassie put a hand on her arm and found it trembling. "He's still your brother."

"I know. It's not that. It's just—"

"Laura?"

The voice pulled her to the door and through it, into the room. Cassie had been planning to allow them some privacy for this meeting, but now she followed in after Laura to lend her moral support in case it was needed.

Dan was in bad shape. She only knew him from the picture that Laura had lent her yesterday, but he bore no resemblance to the young man in that photograph. Not anymore. No doubt he had already changed somewhat in the years since the picture had been taken, but now he was skeletal, the skin hanging from his bones, features hollow and sunken. Sores discolored his skin in great blotches and his hair was wispy and thin.

But Laura knew him.

Whatever had stopped her outside the room was

gone. She crossed the room quickly now, sat down on the edge of the bed, carefully took his scrawny hands in her own, leaned forward and kissed his brow.

"Oh, Danny. What have you done to yourself?"

He gave her a weak smile. "Screwed things up as usual."

"But this . . ."

"I want you to know—it wasn't from a needle."

Laura threw a glance over her shoulder at Cassie, then returned her attention to her brother.

"I always knew," she said.

"You never said anything."

"I was waiting for you to tell me."

He shook his head slowly. "I could never put one past you."

"When were you going to tell me?" Laura asked.

"That's why I came back the last time. But I lost my nerve. And then when I got back to the city, I wasn't just HIV-positive anymore. I had full-blown AIDS and . . ."

His voice, already weak, trailed off.

"Oh, Danny, why? What did you think—that I wouldn't love you anymore?"

"I didn't know what to think. I just didn't want to be a bother."

"That's the last thing you are," Laura assured him. "I know . . ." She had to swallow and start again. "I know you won't be getting better, but you've got to at least have your family with you. Come home with me."

"No."

"Why not? Mom and Dad will want to—"

Dan cut her off, anger giving his voice some strength. "They won't want anything to do with me."

"But—"

"You never understood, did you? We lived in the same house, but it was two different worlds. I lived in

one, and the rest of you lived in the other. I don't
know why things worked out that way, but you've got
to accept that it's never going to change. That not
even something like this could change it."

Laura didn't say anything for a long moment. She
simply sat there, holding his hands, looking at him.

"It was so awful for you," she said finally.
"Wasn't it?"

He nodded. "Everything, except for you."

That seemed to be too much for her, knowing that
on top of his dying, how hard his life had been, right
from when he was a child. She bowed down over him,
holding him, shoulders shaking as she wept.

Cassie backed out of the room to join Joe where
he was waiting in the hall.

"It's got to be tough," he said.

Cassie nodded, not trusting her voice. Her own gaze
was blurry with tears.

7

"You never told her how you found me," Dan
said later.

When Laura had gone to get tea, Cassie and Joe
came back into the room, sitting on hardbacked chairs
beside the bed. It was still hours until dusk, but an
overcast sky cast a gloomy light into the room.

"And you won't, will you?" he added.

Cassie shook her head.

"Why not?"

"It's hard to explain," she said. "I guess I just don't
want her to get the wrong idea about the cards. You
don't use them or any oracular device to find answers;
you use them to ask questions. Some people don't
get that."

He nodded slowly. "Laura wouldn't. She was always

looking for miracles to solve everything. Like the way it was for me back home."

"Her heart was in the right place," Joe said.

Dan glanced at him. "Still is." He returned his attention to Cassie. "But those cards aren't normal tarot cards."

Cassie had shown him the cards the night before, the three images that had taken her and Joe up into the Tombs and eventually to Dan's room here in the hospice.

"No," she said. "They're real magic."

"Where did you get them? I mean, can I ask you that?"

Cassie smiled. "Of course you can. They come from the same place where your wild horses are running."

"They . . . they're real?"

"Depends on how you translate real," Joe said.

Cassie gave him a light tap on his shoulder with a closed fist. "Don't start with that."

"What place are you talking about?" Dan asked.

For once, Joe was more forthcoming than he usually was with a stranger.

"The spiritworld," he said. "It's a lot closer than most people think. Open yourself up to it and it comes in close, so close it's like it's right at hand, no farther away than what's out there on the other side of that window." He paused a moment, then added, "Dangerous place to visit, outside of a dream."

"It wasn't a dream that took me there," Dan said.

"Wasn't the drugs either," Joe told him.

"But—"

"Listen to me, what took you there is the same thing that called Cassie to the old juju woman who gave her those cards. You had a need. Doesn't happen often, but sometimes that's enough to take you across."

"I still have that need."

Joe nodded. "But first the drugs you kept taking got in the way. And now you're dying and your body knows better than to let your spirit go visiting. It wants to hang on and the only thing that's keeping you going is spirit."

"What about Laura's need when she was looking for me?" Dan asked. "Why didn't the spiritworld touch her?"

"It brought her to me, didn't it?" Cassie said.

"That's true."

Dan looked away, out the window. The view he had through it was filled with the boughs of one of those big oak trees. Cassie didn't think he was seeing them.

"You know," he said after a moment, not looking away from the window. "Before all of this, I wouldn't have believed you for a moment. Wouldn't have even listened to you. But you start thinking about spiritual things at a time like this. When you *know* you're going to die, it's hard not to." His gaze returned to them, moving slowly from one to the other. "I'd like to see them again . . . those horses."

Cassie glanced at Joe and he nodded.

"When you're ready to leave," he said, "give me a call."

"You mean that? You can do that?"

"Sure."

Dan started to reach for the pen and paper that was on the table beside his bed. "What's your number?"

"We don't have a phone," Joe said. "You just think about me and those horses hard enough and I'll come take you to them."

"But—"

"He can do it," Cassie said. "Even at the best of times, he's walking with one foot in either world. He'll know when you're ready, and he'll take you there."

Dan studied Joe for a moment, and Cassie knew what he was seeing—the dark Coyote eyes, the crow's head sitting just under his human skin. There was something solemn and laughing wild about him, all at once, as though he knew a joke no one else did that wrapped him in a feral kind of wisdom that could scare you silly. But Dan was past fear.

"That's something else you discover when you're this close to the edge," he said. "You get this ability to cut away the bullshit and look right into a person, see them exactly as they are."

"So what are you seeing?" Joe asked.

Dan smiled. "Damned if I know. But I know I can trust you."

Cassie knew exactly what he meant.

8

Summer gave way to fall. On a cold October night, Cassie woke near dawn to find Joe sitting on the edge of the bed, pulling on his boots. He came over to the bed and kissed her cheek.

"Go to sleep," he said. "I might be a while."

They'd been up late that night, and she fell back asleep before she could think to ask where he was going.

9

Dan's funeral was two days later. It was a small service with few in attendance. Laura. Cassie. A few of the caregivers from the hospice. After the service, Cassie took Laura down to the lakefront. They sat on a bench at the end of the Pier where they'd first met, looking out at Wolf Island. A cold wind blew in off the lake and they sat close to each other for warmth.

"Where's Joe?" Laura asked.

"He had to go out of town."

Laura looked different to Cassie, more sure of herself, less haunted for all her sadness. She'd been working as a bartender for the past few months—"See, I knew that MA would be useful for something," she'd joked—spending her afternoons with Dan.

"It's been really hard," she said. "Especially the last couple of weeks."

Cassie put her arm around Laura's shoulders. "Probably the hardest thing you'll ever do."

"But I wouldn't give up any of it. What Dan had to go through, yes, but not my being with him."

"He was lucky you found him in time."

"It wasn't luck," Laura said.

Cassie raised her eyebrows.

"He told me about the cards." She shook her head before Cassie could say anything. "No, it's okay. I understand. I know it would be so tempting to use something like that to make all your decisions for you. I'm not asking for that." She hesitated a moment, then added, "But I was wondering . . . can they show me Dan one last time? Just so I can know if he finally caught up with those horses? Just so I can know he's okay?"

"I don't know," Cassie said. "I think the only way we ever find out where we go in the end, is when we make the journey ourselves."

Laura gave a slow nod, unable to hide her disappointment. "I . . . I guess I understand."

"But that doesn't mean we can't look."

She took her arm away from Laura's shoulders and brought out the set of cards the old juju woman had given her, sitting there on her porch with the bottle tree clinking on the lawn. Removing the elastic, she gave the cards a shuffle, then offered the pack to Laura.

"Pick one," she said.

"Don't you have to lay them out in some kind of pattern?"

"Ordinary tarot cards, yes. But you're looking to see into some place they can't take you now."

Laura placed her fingers on the top of the deck. She held off for a long moment, then finally took the card and turned it over. There were horses running along the lakeshore on it, golden horses with white manes and tails. The image was too small to make out details, but they could see a figure on the back of one of them, head thrown back. Laughing, perhaps. Finally free.

Smiling, Laura returned the card to the pack.

"Where he goes," she said, "I hope he'll always be that happy."

Cassie wound the elastic back around the cards and returned them to her pocket.

"Maybe if we believe it strongly enough, it'll be true," she said.

Laura turned to look at her. Her eyes were shiny with tears, but that lost, haunted look Cassie had seen in them that first time they met was gone.

"Then I'll believe it," Laura said.

They leaned back against the bench, looking out across the water. The sound of the ferry's horn echoed faintly across the water, signaling its return from the island.

THE INTERSECTION OF ANASTASIA YEOMAN AND LIGHT

by *Rosemary Edghill*

Rosemary Edghill is the author of more than a dozen novels, including *Speak Daggers to Her*, *The Book of Moons*, *The Sword of Maiden's Tears*, *The Cup of Morning Shadows*, *The Cloak of Night and Daggers*, and *Fleeting Fancy*, among others. She has worked in publishing and lives in Poughkeepsie, where she writes full-time.

Edghill's "The Intersection of Anastasia Yeoman and Light" is about the crossroads we face at each contemplation of the future, such as during a reading of one's cards, and the ramifications of our choices.

The Five of Cups: water, the senses, change after completion. Under the tutelage of the moon, a seeker abandons the possible to focus on the impossible.

I first met Aldith Lector at an SF convention several years ago, which wouldn't be anything much to shout about, except for the fact that *I* am Aldith Lector. Or, at least, I was.

The room is dark; hotel lighting is never enough, and half of it is broken anyway. The sinks are full of ice and beer, the bathtub filled with ice and bottles; there are M&Ms and liquor bottles everywhere. Hot and filled with noise, she imagines the room as filled with water; a turbid and echolalic sea in which every thought, every perception, is exposed to any who wish to look. It is a familiar venue, but no less threatening for all of that. She sees them at the border of perception, circling to their necessities like feeding sharks. Like icons, their form is pure information. She uses their information to define herself, but to define herself is to swim with sharks.

Focusing on the impossible.

There's an old saying that the only two random things in the universe are spree killers and writers who've finished a book. Add to this "writers who have finished a book with no prospect of selling another one" and you'd pretty much have an idea of my state of mind that night at the party.

Or so I infer; I don't really remember, memory being the remarkable editor that it is. Which will bring us to editing, eventually.

And to Anastasia Yeoman.

I first heard of her when I first heard of *everybody,* at the moment when I made my first book sale and went from that tenuous link to ultra-reality onward to the convention circuit. Nominally, the SF convention in all of its apparitions is a celebration of our mutual genre. Practically, it's an end in itself—Elf Hill, the party that never ends, a lost weekend where the invited writers are a cross between the main course and the sideshow for an entire continuum of people who self-define as writers, possibly without ever having written one entire paragraph in the third person.

We call them fans—for fanciers—they call us pros—for professionals—and there isn't a lot of truth in either label. And the way that some of them look at us is an uncomfortable mirror of the way some of us look at each other.

Case in point.

Anastasia Yeoman was one of those odd social hermaphrodites you find in our genre: a professional anthologist who was almost better known as an essayist and critic for those "little" magazines that pay in copies, a traveler from an antique land when to be civilized meant to be witty and literate on three continents and to have mastered the forgotten art of the essay. As soon as I knew who she was, I went and looked up her writings—how could I not; she was an editor, and one must know one's enemy, right?

I would have done a lot better not to drink from that cup. I fell instantly, shatteringly, in love. How else should a writer—that species of awkward, solitary gawk—be seduced, except by the word? She wrote poetry, too—that was the *coup de foudre*.

And so I doted, in one of those random savage limerences that are only superable when the object of desire is far, far separate from one's self on the random roads of causality and one has not even a social class in common with the object. The more I discovered, the more I was dazzled: She was such a *suitable* object. She'd been around forever and was on the most intimate terms with everybody—everybody who was likewise a legend, that is. I doubt she distinguished me from those wanton star-collectors who hang around the fringes of those pretend-exclusive parties you'll find yourself invited to when your name's on the guest list of the convention and you've sold a book or two—or three, or four, in genre. As I had, somewhere between the benchmarks of discovering who Anastasia was and being introduced to her by someone well-meaning or at least indifferent.

Unfortunately, while my passions had remained the same, I had become socially mutable; not fluid enough, you understand, for the I-and-Thou-ness of it all to disappear, but visible to the point where I moved, however speciously, on the fringes of the same world; a condition that caused moments of acute embarrassment, like living with an invisible chimpanzee.

The Five of Cups: choices, or rather, the art of choice. The loss of opportunity is an illusion; pathways that appear closed are discovered to be open. The seeker will see that he has the ability to make the impossible, possible.

She walks in as though she has a right to be there, knowing that she does, unsatisfied with that and spinning her illusions. The best available dress becomes inappropriate, what made her blend in before makes her stand out—subjectively—now. She weaves an internal tale of her own particularity, needing the shape of it to let her stay in a place she feels so unwelcome.

No, not even that. Irrelevant is what she feels; that neither her presence nor absence would matter to anyone here beyond perfunctory courtesy. And that would be all right, would be the tenor of modern life, numbing water that she can slip fish-freely through. Except that she has made all the choices in her life so that she can be someone—

—be someone special—

—someone *in particular*—

—and secretly she feels—never more than tonight— that for her to be special would take some kind of miracle, a disordering of the way things are for Aldith Lector (real name Edith Lector, but don't you like Aldith better?) that is flatly impossible.

Are the books really that midlist? Is the dress really that middle-class? Is declassé better than no class at all? *Miracleworx: We make the impossible, possible.*

I won't say, back in those dim, dead Eighties days, that I'd scaled the heights of my chosen profession.

More like entered the foothills, but like the man says, "you can *see* the Himalayas from there." By this particular party night I'd published half a dozen books, and I knew that I could plug along and sell at least another dozen at about the same advance—meaning that if I worked seven-day, eighty-hour weeks, I could probably pull in about $15,000 a year, gross income with no benefits—before the market closed up and shut me out. It does that, periodically: publishing, like the cat who walks by himself, turning around and devouring its young—i.e., midlist genre writers without a breakout book in sight.

In short, I'd had about enough success to be depressed about it, and *just* enough to think I saw a way out of the trap.

Which party was it? It doesn't matter. Publishers throw them for the publicity and the tax write-off; writers and editors and well-placed fans come. I was there, feeling—as usual—like the Little Matchgirl, a disease for which time-in-grade is the only cure. It's just too bad that Impatience isn't one of the Deadlies, because it screws up more lives than any of the Seven. They call them Deadly Sins because they kill, and Envy is the worst. With Pride, you never feel the killing blow; Envy, like Prometheus, is reborn with every situation. To see Anastasia, gypsy-dight, in douce colloquy with Wynton Marchand and two other editors plus a writer so cool he preferred to be known as an *English professor*, was to feel social displacement like a silver dagger to the heart, and I thought, not for the first time, that I could be perfectly happy and perfectly empowered if somehow I could *become* Anastasia; stepping into her life and leaving my own behind like an outworn garment.

It was not a new thought. In my saner moments I realized this was sheerest idiocy. I imagined she had a life very much like my own, at least in spots, and my own life wasn't that beguiling. I was not even completely certain what it was about her that I coveted. Her flair with an English sentence? Her vast circle of acquaintance? She was neither pretty nor kind—the literary realm, like Elfland, is not a resort for the pretty or the kind. What Elfland respects is glibness, and savagery, and a lack of past. The ability to choose, if not wisely, then well.

As I chose. I said I was in the foothills of the genre. The foothills are a place from which to elect the path to a number of different peaks. I'd finished a book, I was out of contract. And someone had brought a deck of cards to the party.

The Five of Cups: emotional subjectivity; a card belonging to the Moon. The ascent of rationality, which does not yet triumph. Willingness to embrace rebirth.

The faces are familiar but not friendly. She gets a drink, confining herself to seltzer. People greet her; Aldith is gracious-by-the-numbers, knowing that some people would be doing themselves some good here, knowing she does not know how to work a room and never will. The fact that there are others here who are more outside than she is, who regard her as farther advanced along the path they wish to tread, is a matter of distant amusement. That's who they think she is, not who she is.

Perhaps it would not matter so much to her that she hover, motionless, her career caught suspended like a bright fish in the shallows, but for the fact that Aldith is one of the clever ones and knows that if you don't move, you die, though maybe not this year.

Forward motion is rebirth: She'll do anything for that.

Then she sees the cards.

*   *   *

It is necessary here to digress. That the cards were tarot cards goes without saying. A tarot deck is the hallmark of First Tier Coolth; for it to be a poker deck used for poker is Second Tier. Further subarctic rarifications can be had if it is a tarot deck from which 26 cards have been removed so that poker can be played with it, or if fortunes are told with a 52-card deck. You will understand the sort of party it was if I tell you that it was a tarot deck being used for its appointed purpose: to tell fortunes. It is perhaps even more to the point to mention that I used to tell fortunes.

This was in the bad old days before I had reinvented my ambitions. It was still the Seventies, before New Age was crystal power and drumming in the woods. I was managing the only occult bookstore in Minneapolis, Minnesota. The owner was the wife of a building contractor, and she was as crazy and he was as shady as you got in the Upper Midwest in the Seventies. The previous manager—who handed me the keys and left in the middle of my job interview—told me Carolyn ran the shop as expiation for her particular deadlies. I leave it to you to decide what sins receive their atonement through the sale of Madame Blavatsky and Carlos Castenada; suffice it to say that Carolyn was crazy, the shop paid its bills and my wages, and had, as all shops of this sort seem to, a back room in which people, from time to time, met.

It was there that I learned to read the cards, in that peculiar dishonest fashion of people providing a service for money. After a while I began to see a parallel truth to the one I told. It whispered in my ear like a serpent, promising me a special grace: Isn't Pride the loveliest of sins? The truth became too insistent; I stopped reading entirely. It was a conflict between intellectual honesty and the commercial instinct, and honesty won.

By the time I signed my second book contract I'd
learned not to make that particular mistake, and could
probably have gone back and made a pretty good living as a reader, but I still believed that partial purity
was possible; that you could be a conditional pander.
I only read for my friends; I only told the truth. But
the truth isn't in the cards, it's in the information—
give me anything information-dense enough and I
could decode the presence of something else inside it,
if only the way the story was supposed to go before
the writer got distracted from what they'd originally
meant. I didn't tell that truth, but I knew it.

Someone she knows slightly—Gail, an editor who
writes—lays them out on a table cleared of Triscuit
and dried cheese morsels. The bright, four-color pasteboard is archaically gaudy, souvenir of an outmoded
time when the colors used for the insistent conveyance
of information *were* this sweetly blatant and oblivi-
ously coarse. Tarot cards; the suit of what would ordi-
narily be the pip cards (it is the Waite deck) buried
in a splendor of disquisitive ornament and testifying
line. Aldith knows the suits by the tales they tell.
Swords: the betrayal of friendship, murder, flight.
Wands: the hero seeks fame, does battle, gains home
and kingship. Coins: the miser amasses wealth obsessively; his heir, caring nothing for coin, makes abun-
dance. And Cups: emotion, illusion, loss.
    Truth.
    Everybody gathers around—not for truth (she
knows that much at thirty-two) but for whatever thing
they expect from a sheaf of pasteboard prophecies.
Maybe authority. Maybe validation. Maybe a directive
they can flout. Gail laughs, laying them out all wrong,
as though she's playing a hand of Solitaire. Does anyone know how to read these? (She asks as if they are
printed in Japanese.) They were a present.

To know the truth is not a good gift. To keep silent about it is the beginning of wisdom. Aldith steps forward. She used to be a fortuneteller, everyone knows that about her. It's a harmless truth to confide to official biographies. Gail stands up, Aldith sits down, preparing in her mind the list of concordances, harmless substitutions for the truth. Suicide, alcoholism, debt, unemployment—it's all in the cards, along with the quieter betrayals. Aldith oils, not her traps, but her releases.

And Anastasia Yeoman sits down in the other chair.

She smiles at me; I've seen her smile that way at a thousand others. It's the smile she reserves for the *nyetkulturny;* those who aren't in on the joke. As befits something intended to insulate, it isn't particularly cruel. She knows my name, but to her, I'm no one special. We've met before without embarrassment; inside myself—to whom?—I justify her now. Anastasia is brilliant; she worships talent. Both of us do—we have that in common, a commonality guaranteed to keep us facing away from each other for the rest of our natural lives, sun and moon. She's an anthologist; she feeds upon the special, spinning gold into more golden yet. There's nothing personal in her impersonality, it's just that I have nothing to give her.

I shuffle, she cuts, I turn up the face card—Five of Cups—and lay out the rest. Celtic Cross, they call this spread, though it's far from Celtic and not much of a cross either. You read it right to left, bottom to top; the top card on the right-hand side is the final outcome. What I call the Wish Fulfillment card; it's something far enough in the future that the querent will have forgotten all about today by the time it happens.

It's the Five of Cups again.

Laughter and disturbance at this blunder that smacks of magic; I lift the cards off her significator

and check, just to be sure it's the same. It is. There
are two of the Five of Cups in this deck. It's a mistake
made at the factory; it happens. If I'd been laying out
my own deck for the first time I would have checked
and pulled the duplicate; I wonder if there's a missing
card to match, and what it is. I meet her eyes; do you
want to go on? Hazel eyes, with a gold star in the
center—worldly-wise, amused, Anastasia plays to the
gallery just as the gallery preys on me.

She votes to read them as they lie—this is only a
game, remember?—and I slide in among the symbols,
to winnow out the innocuous from the socially lethal.
Cups, wands—the Queen of Wands with her black cat;
Aradia, Queen of the Witches. Swords, the Chariot,
the Tower. Car stereos and coworkers, intellectual
puzzles (I read that as work-related and the way she
shifts in her seat tells me I'm right). And sitting right
in the middle of it:

She's going to be fired.

Even anthologists have day jobs; Anastasia's is
something boring and unlikely—editing textbooks
someplace; one fact about her I haven't been able to
memorize, or possibly it changes, as the cards say it's
about to. Not immediately, but soon—Coins tell me
she's fired without warning, Wands that there's a lot
of hostility involved. That one's easy to candy—job
change, you say, new opportunities. But that isn't the
way it works in Publishing—even I know that. Job
changes are dark secrets, until The Day.

Five of Cups. Despair, hidden opportunity. The card
of sweet unreason, of paying damn-all attention to
conventional wisdom.

But fired is as fired does, so I stay away from that
and stick to the meanings you'll find in any book. It
makes what I tell come out flat and false, without even
a storyteller's vigor. The party has a life of its own; it
eddies elsewhere—I feel it shift while I'm shuffling the

cards again—and after another reading or two (they aren't concentrating so I can't), I can abandon the deck and mingle. My unshared secret obsesses me: Just how geeklike would it be to corner her, break in uninvited on whatever more-interesting conversation she's having, and tell her what the cards tell me?

I switch to bourbon for an hour or so and do it.

She looks past me, mapping escape routes—I've cornered her coming out of the bathroom, not elegant, but sure—as she acknowledges me. The name of this game is to get in and out of the conversation before the other person expresses any opinion; I deliver my abjured news flash from the collective unconscious, suitably veiled in the outlook for new job opportunities, and prepare to let her go. I am not facile enough to feign another conversation to join. The best I can manage is to release her cleanly, as though I'm lofting a hawk into the wind.

But job has led to day-job in the way these exchanges do, and, in a dispensation of gossip to cover her retreat, she tells me Dave's looking for an Editorial Assistant.

Dave is evident from context; I know all the players in this masque, or anyway, she assumes I know them. She wanders purposefully away in gypsy scarves. Do I know anyone who'd be good for the job?

It's an entry-level job that any English-speaking masochist can master, but is it true?

Gail knows Dave. I check. She didn't think I'd be interested, but then, the torpid and only vaguely exciting proposal for my next book isn't sitting on her desk.

The Five of Cups: Night. Between a mountain range and a stream stands a Seeker, whose back is to us. He sees two Cups overturned upon the ground, spilling their contents into the stream. He prepares to leave, not realizing that three more Cups are behind him, still full.

*   *   *

Time is a river.

It is a truth universally acknowledged that we name them, hold their hands, make them what they are, and occasionally bury them, but writers are the ones in the big type on the program ads and editors are the ones who hover in the background like bridesmaids.

On the other hand, we don't have to fantasize a bankable capital out of infinitesimal royalty checks and tomorrow's conjectural inspiration. We have steady (if small) paychecks—until Corporate decides we're redundant. Irrelevant. Or just old and familiar, and a new hired gun would suit the company image better. I got my first promotion that way. For the second I left the company and went elsewhere. New doors, new desks, same slush pile. And Elf Hill, of course, where past and future blur—only now it's the feeding pool where lifesaving gossip is acquired, authors charmed, and agents seduced.

If you want to forget, don't bother trying to join the French Foreign Legion. It's been disbanded anyway, and publishing is a much better place to court an abiding intersession of the ego. The job can expand to occupy every waking moment, and your definition of self is rewritten in endless interoffice memos and the tiny petty wars over who is going to be funded to buy what. The only writing I've done in fourteen years is the occasional short story and a couple of hundred pages on a novel I confidently expect never to finish. I see the truth in the manuscript palimpsest, and I still don't tell it: "Rethink this" is as close as I have any intention of coming, with the sure and certain knowledge that if I'm any more incisive, the author will be on the phone to his agent, screaming like a violated nun—and that *she* has a client list esoteric enough to warrant lunch dates with the publisher, during which my name will probably come up. Edie Lector, it is now, and damn few people, including the authors on my list, remember Aldith's books. They got me here to the start of this particular road, and after that I buried them and her deep; I'm finished with the truth at last, in any incarnation. Nobody wants it, not from priests, writers, politicians, or cops: All anyone wants here at the end of the century is for his particular fantasy to continue uninterrupted until he dies. And with a good enough daydream, somehow he may be able also to finesse that.

I'm finished with Anastasia Yeoman, too. It didn't end badly; she died last year "after a long illness" as the obits tactfully say. Long before that I'd become her in-house editor for that anthology series that scoops the awards with such boring regularity (boring to everyone but our Sales Department, which has trouble grasping the distinction between "award" and "merit," for which I'm duly grateful). For the last few years we had lunch any time she was back on this coast. She was, as a matter of fact, fired my second week on the job as Dave's assistant. I don't know whether she remembered my warning, or recognized it for what it was. She went on. So do we all.

And familiar repetition was at last the universal solvent that loosened her all-unintended death grip on my adulation. I'd never wanted to have her, or, really, to be her. No, what I'd always wanted was to be the Anastasia I saw when I read her essays, and fortunately I had the wit—even at the time—to realize that the person I created out of the words on the page and the person who had written them were grossly different. In fact, I already was the person I saw in the essays; the woman I met there was created by the intersection of the words on the page with my junk-heap memory and corseted imagination. Like the rainbow, that isn't really there until light collides with a prism. But in another way, the rainbow is there all along.

And Aldith? A trick of the light, I'd like to think, and then again, maybe I wouldn't. I hit all the major stations on the convention circuit these days, logging frequent flyer miles in and out of Elf Hill until it gets hard to remember which part of the country I'm going to see outside my hotel window. The World Science Fiction Convention is always the worst—five thousand of your dearest friends colliding with unsuspecting hoteliers and every year the dear souls who have been chosen (in the fashion a sacrificial lamb is chosen, I imagine) to run it discover something new and interesting to do with function space layout.

I saw her there; a brief nonencounter between engagements. She was wearing an old outfit of mine in a way I'd never worn it—defiantly—making the skewball fashion ten years out of date a thing she meant to do. Her hair was a disordered halo, she'd put on a few pounds—solitary rooms being less conductive to one-yogurt lunches than an office along Editorial Row that you have to fight to convince Management you're young enough to occupy—and she glowed.

Not actually, but internally—Aldith was happy; you can feel that across a crowded room, just as you can feel what lies behind the *rictus sardonicus* of mute endurance. She was standing just outside one of the function rooms—I was on my way to another, and good luck trying to find it in a hotel this size—and had just gotten off a panel to judge by the cluster around her. I passed by close enough to see her nametag—Aldith Lector—and her name above the title on the cover of a book someone was holding out to her. Foil and embossing, very nice, and cover art that might not win a Chesley but sure as hell said "A New Installment in the Big Bucks Series," which is all that Sales and Marketing ask of the Art Department.

That was the first time I saw her. I put it down to the migraine I got later that day. It wasn't the last— I'm relieved to report that Aldith doesn't always come with headaches; I can't afford them. But I see her— writers and editors attend the same parties here in Elf Hill. Not often. Often enough.

Even if I can't sign her, I like to keep a maternal eye on her career. She seems to be doing very well for herself in whatever alternate reality has an imprint called Blyman Books. Or is hers the real reality, and mine the alternate? Does she even remember the night she read tarot for Anastasia Yeoman? I don't read tarot any more, even for fun; I'm not that frivolous a person, or maybe I like to keep my dead buried deep.

Two Five of Cups, two choices—meant for the reader, this time, and not the querent. Choices, and who's to say which one was the right one to make? Or is right, like truth, just another inconvenient concept, ashcanned to serve you better in the fast-food franchise of the soul? Is every choice the right one? If that were true, choices wouldn't be hard. I think that when we choose we murder all the might have beens—I am Aldith's executioner, and she is the ghost that haunts me.

"Beware of a journey over water," the gypsy says. "In the mirror you will meet a dark stranger, at the intersection of Anastasia Yeoman and light."

CHATTEL
by Lucy Taylor

Lucy Taylor won the Bram Stoker award for her first
novel, *The Safety of Unknown Cities*. She has devel-
oped a cult following for her short stories, many of
which are collected in the volumes *Unnatural Acts,
Close the Bone*, and *The Flesh Artist*. She lives in
Colorado.

Taylor's "Chattel" journeys through an inner realm
of the tarot to question our human desire for posses-
sion in our relationships.

It was one of the eccentricities of Thorne's personality
that he not only flourished in, but actually relished,
the brutal poverty and hardship that characterized life
in Berkana in the first few months after the end of
the war. He had no family and no real friends, so
there was no one whose death he could lament, and
his avocation—being thievery and gambling and
grift—thrived in an atmosphere of desperation and the
kind of want that provokes people to take risks and
consent willingly, even gratefully, to debasement.

Truly, his rogue's life had never been easier nor—
with the absence of any real law—any safer.

Only one thing disrupted the comfort of his vast
self-absorption, and that was the loss of his concubine
and mistress and slave. The only name he knew her
by was Chattel, although he supposed she must have
had another name from her previous life. No matter.
Whatever that life had been, it was over now. He had

won her in a game of chance and kept her with him
for the duration of the war. For Thorne, Chattel was
magic. A talisman. A badge. Into her, he could release
all the maladies that seared his soul, his hatreds and
resentments, and the niggling, deeply buried suspicion
that he was a creature crippled and despicable, incapa-
ble of loving or receiving love.

Her flesh was the palette on which he expressed the
greed and want and isolation of his life, the mirror in
which all his faults and shortcomings were magically
erased.

Without her, he was thwarted and insatiable. No
other woman came close to satisfying him. No other
woman absorbed his lust and loathing and aroused
him to greater passion the more that he degraded and
despised her.

She had escaped from him soon after the war
ended. It was his own fault, Thorne acknowledged.
He'd grown careless with her, mistaking her submis-
sion for real subservience when her compliance was
merely a facsimile with which she saved her life on
a daily basis. In his folly, he had come to believe
that she was actually a willing captive, devoted to
him, grateful for her bondage. The half-healed scar
above his temple where she had smashed him in the
head with a wooden stave bore witness to the truer
nature of her feelings.

Whether she was alive or dead he didn't know, but
his search for her was relentless.

So it was for that reason that, in early April, he
traveled south to the once embattled town of Ansuz
to consult the Witch of Isa. Even prior to the outbreak
of the war, the Witch was known to use her powers
to hide fugitives. Many men and women, hunted by
those who pursued and persecuted them, had seemingly vanished from the earth after the Witch agreed

to aid them. Thorne suspected it was to her that Chattel might have fled.

He reached the city on the edge of evening, delaying his visit to the Witch only long enough to break into and pilfer a cottage that he found unoccupied. Then, having had his fill of food and drink, he continued into the town.

The war had left Ansuz a pestilential rubble. Now scruffy children roamed the alleyways, one hand held out for coins, the other clutching a knife or brick behind their backs. Corpses moldered and putrefied, pawed over by dogs.

The Witch lived in a tin-roofed shack as colorful and cluttered as the inside of a sewing box. She was young and stick-thin with long yellow hair spun through with gray and a dry, steady voice lacking any accent or inflection that reminded Thorne of long nails clicking on a tabletop.

At first, he tried to flirt with her, taking off his jacket to show off his tanned, muscled arms and the lush mat of black hair revealed by his open shirt collar, but the Witch was not to be seduced. She dismissed his attempts at coy banter and told him to be still.

While Thorne sat cross-legged on the rug, the Witch removed a deck of tarot cards from a mahogany box inlaid with malachite and onyx. Before Thorne could tell her what he wanted, she fixed him with a scathing glare, drew a deep breath, and said, "You come too late. The woman you search for has journeyed far away."

Annoyed, Thorne growled, "And I have journeyed far to find her and will go as far as need be to get her back."

"As your property, you mean?"

"That's what she is."

"You do not love her?"

"What has love to do with this? I own her, and I

have my rights," Thorne blustered as he threw down two heaping fistfuls of currency.

The Witch stared at the money as though counting it with her eyes, then cradled the deck of cards in her sinewy hands. "She came to me some weeks ago, desperate to be hidden. She says that you abused her terribly."

"She tells outlandish lies," said Thorne. "Her head is full of twisted fancy and perverted notions. I suspect she may even be mad."

"She loves you," said the bony crone. "She would help you, if you would let her."

"Enough of this!" yelled Thorne and made as if to sweep the notes back into his purse. The Witch stopped him by placing her blanched, skeletal hand upon the loot.

Silently she handed the cards to Thorne, who shuffled them and cut. Then cut again. The cards were large and varnished and glossy. They reminded Thorne of the stained-glass windows, a few still intact, the others cast about the ground in brilliant shards, that he'd glimpsed in his wanderings through what remained of the city of Teiwaz.

The Witch took back the cards and laid out the first half dozen in the deck. Thorne was not a learned man; the mysteries of the tarot were unknown to him, but he recognized a few of the cards from a brief dalliance he'd enjoyed with a gypsy wench: the Queen of Wands and Five of Swords, the Hermit and the Eight of Pentacles. Thorne shivered when he saw the Hermit in his hooded cowl, clutching his staff, bent and brittle and bitter with age. In the Hermit's utter solitude lurked something sinister and furtive that he found inexplicably terrifying.

"The cards are doors," said the Witch "and the woman you seek has already passed through one of them. To find her, you must follow where she leads."

"No woman leads me," grumbled Thorne.

The Witch tilted one white eyebrow and laid out another row of cards to make the pattern of a cross. One by one, she turned them over. The last card was the Seven of Cups. She handed it to Thorne. "This is the first portal."

Thorne stared at the card. "But how—?"

"Go!" commanded the Witch, sweeping up the rest of the cards. Furious, embarrassed at his inability to comprehend, Thorne slipped the card into his knapsack and rushed from the house.

He spent the night in Ansuz, then traveled on to the town of Hagalaz near Lake Laguz. There was little to steal and few people with enough money to be interested in taking part in any of Thorne's dubious wagers. Frustrated and weary, he found himself peering in the window of one of the few still prosperous-looking houses, looking for whatever booty he might find.

Inside, on display upon a mantel, he saw a row of seven golden chalices, each brimming with some rarity or treasure: one overflowed with coins, another with a splendid cache of jewels, from one a crown of laurel seemed to sprout, and in another, what seemed to be a serpent made entirely of gold coiled languidly around the lip of the cup.

Galvanized by greed, Thorne kicked the door open and entered with the aplomb and swagger of a master returning home after a long journey. But what he found inside the house bore little correspondence to what he'd seen while looking in the window. The chalices, he now discovered, were simple earthen mugs, some holding beans and trinkets, another full of worthless half-penny coins.

The transformation unnerved Thorne. He tried to retreat, but found the door he'd just booted open was now sealed shut—in fact, it was not a door at all, but a faux portal carved into the plaster wall.

Searching for another means of escape, he made his way through an elaborate hallway where each door he discovered led into another corridor and other lavishly appointed rooms, but he could find no windows nor a single door that would allow him to leave. He was trapped inside a nightmare palace, a labyrinth impossibly huge and convoluted, a hundred times greater and grander than the house he'd broken into.

A shadow flitted along the edge of what, from Thorne's vantage point, appeared to be an opulent dining hall.

He heard the swish of clothing, a sigh of indrawn breath.

Chattel stood in the doorway beyond him. Her hair was loose and fell around her shoulders. On her wrists she wore black circlets. Black pearls encircled her neck and her gown was a diaphanous mix of ebony and gray.

She was so close he knew that he could catch her easily. Contempt and sarcasm edged his voice as he said, "Who are you in mourning for?"

"For you," she said. "For us. It didn't have to be this way. Why did you have to have a slave when you might have had a lover? Why did you have to ruin it?"

Her words smacked of blame, and Thorne avoided blame the way most people avoid digging at a sore. Fury and desire wedded in a lethal union in his heart. He knew only that he wanted her—to possess and to have and to hurt her—but as he came to claim her, she retreated back into the room beyond. He arrived in the doorway in time to see another door in still another room open up to take her and then another and another until she became a black, receding speck at the center of an endless proliferation of doors.

Bellowing with thwarted spite, Thorne charged after

her. He passed through rooms of opulence and splendor and others whose furnishing were impoverished and plain. In one he saw a slain knight laid out for burial. Three swords hung on the wall behind him, a fourth lay on the floor. In another, a hanged man dangled by his ankles from a makeshift gallows. Thorne glanced at him and shuddered, then hurried on.

But as fast as he ran, he caught no glimpse of Chattel nor did he succeed in finding a door that led back outside the mazelike palace.

At length he came upon an atrium filled with flowering trees—oranges and tamarinds and figs. Although it was bright daylight, stars glittered overhead like flecks of foam on a turquoise sea. A blonde woman was leaning over an oval pool, drawing water up into two pitchers. Thorne's throat was blistered with thirst. He snatched one of the pitchers from the woman, drank from it, then bent to fill it again. In doing so, he looked down through the clear water, into the pool.

Chattel gazed up at him from deep below the water. She seemed alive and calm, and yet she made no move to swim toward the surface. She stared at Thorne with a primitive longing, a mix of desire and despair. It occurred to him, with something of a shock, that he had not been so wrong in his estimation of her feelings for him, after all. She did want him. Perhaps she craved her freedom more, but she hungered for him, too. He could feel her wanting him like she must want the air and yet so fearful of him that she held her breath, willing to drown rather than risk pulling the air—pulling *him*—back inside her.

Thorne didn't hesitate. He dove headfirst into the water.

And an unseen door, one just below the pristine surface, was penetrated by his falling form. A blackness more profound than any thieves' night Thorne had known engulfed him like a giant maw. He would have screamed, but terror snatched his breath. Then his head erupted above the surface of cold, brackish water covered over with algae and weeds. He was no longer in the sunlit pond, but floating in a vast, forbidding lake.

The water chilled him, the weeds clung to his clothes as he swam. Far away, he could see the outline of turreted palaces against dark, fog-shrouded hills. Once ashore, he built a fire to warm himself, glancing about nervously now and then, wondering if Chattel spied upon him.

The next morning, he set off again. As he proceeded, he came upon a wedding, the bride and bridegroom sipping wine from golden cups, and lingered long enough to sample from the banquet spread and to enrich his purse with the contents of a few of the guests' pockets.

Thus fortified, he headed onward and came, near nightfall, to the remnants of a village, in the center of which stood a huge, impressive bell tower. From the neglect of its brick walls and the grounds surrounding it, he guessed it to be unoccupied and lost no time in smashing in a ground-level window and slipping inside.

Almost at once, he heard a female voice cry out from above him in fear and desolation. Her pain was palpable, her suffering a balm to his own misery. With renewed energy, he climbed the circular stone stairs until he reached the bell tower. The cries were very near now, but the beating of his heart was almost as loud.

Creeping closer, he peered around an upright beam and saw a woman bound tightly, a filthy rag across her eyes. Eight swords surrounded her. Even without seeing her face, he knew that it was Chattel.

Before he could act, however, she spoke to him. "Thorne, I know it's you. If you free me now, you free us both. Let us be lovers, able to give ourselves without duress or degradation."

But the concept of such love was alien to Thorne, and the sight of Chattel bound quickened his blood and spurred his heart to a riotous gallop. He felt an exaltation of vengeance and joy, a sweet surge of vindictive elation.

"Be silent," he commanded. "You have no choice in this matter."

He seized Chattel and untied her hands, then ripped the rag away, eager that she see him and witness everything he did to her. Beneath the soiled cloth, a death's head leered up at him, wormed through and maggoty. The black robes became a tattered burial gown and slithered to the ground, revealing rotted flesh and ivory bone. He tried to fling the hideous thing away, but it wrapped its bony limbs around him, professing love for him in Chattel's honeyed voice.

With a scream, Thorne flung himself headfirst over the tower wall. The dead thing clinging to him fell away, but he smashed into the earth below with stunning impact.

Slowly Thorne came to his senses. The tower, if it was still there, was now eclipsed by fog. He was in a field where, all around him, the dead were rising from the ground, sprouting like rows of corn. Their arms were raised beseechingly, their eyes upcast with hope and trepidation. A dark shiver flitted through Thorne's soul. He knew the dead were being judged, that the fate of their souls now rested on lives well-lived or misspent.

Scrambling to his feet, he tried to flee, but found he, too, was rooted in the field's dark earth, that the force of his fall had driven his feet into the ground as if he were a stave.

He struggled, crying out in distress and fury and, in

his panic, he allowed himself to call out Chattel's name.

Almost at once, she came to him, all tenderness and consolation. Her touch made Thorne feel lighter. The earth no longer held him and he wriggled free. Vindicated by what he perceived as her surrender, he clutched her roughly to him. She moaned and folded herself into his arms like a cloak, molding herself to the hard angles and contours of his body. He could smell her perfume, which was a mix of all the subtle tangs of desire and yearning and want, so powerful in its intensity that it terrified him as much as the smell of his own spilled blood. In her voluntary yielding, he seemed to lose his power and sensed the frightful paltriness of his own masculine dominion.

"You've never understood," she said. "There was no need to hold me prisoner. I wanted you as much as you wanted me. I told the Witch that you would follow and to send you after me. To search for me in the Inner Realms of the Arcanas. I cannot be your Chattel here, but I can be your Love, your Heart, your Life."

She moved against him, penetrating his flesh with her lust and permeating his blood with her heat, and he was terrified and captivated in a way he could neither accept nor understand.

"Enough of this," he said and put his hands up to her throat, thinking to exert his mastery in the most extreme way possible, by killing her and ending her infuriating game.

"I own you," he said. "I will do what I want with you."

She closed her eyes. Her lips moved and she spoke in the language of the land where he'd obtained her, a lilting tongue of trills and hums and soft, low moans, that were not words at all, he realized, but the primitive, despairing sound of unquenched and unutterable physical desire.

"You sad fool," she said, "I could have belonged to you for all eternity. And you, to me, if only you would have seen it. I am the door you have been seeking all your life."

Behind Thorne, the dark earth split and fissured.

Chattel spread her arms, her lips, her thighs, but Thorne, reaching out for her, could no longer make contact. He teetered backward, plunged, and dropped into the vastness of a new and terrifying firmament. He plummeted through an ocean of stars where constellations pulsed and gleamed, the pathway to all experience and lifetimes: the High Priestess and the Devil and the Chariot, each outlined in the pulsing light of Pentacles whose fiery tails resembled Wands. He clutched out for something solid, but there was nothing but the darkened sky, empty now of stars and moons and planets, and he fell, backward and downward, into the bleak land of his own barren heart.

Thorne found himself in a wilderness as blistered and raw as a wintry moon. He shouldered his pack and went in search of others like himself, outcasts from the world of men, prisoners of their own self-constructed hells. At times, he shouted out for help. At other times, so parched for the sound of another human voice was he that he invented dialogues with himself. He spoke at length about the long war, about the carefully plotted cons he had devised, about the woman he had not dared love and so designated slave before he ever asked her given name.

At length he came upon a pond and, lowering himself to drink, was shocked to see the countenance of an old man looking back, a scowling misanthrope with hooded eyes and bitter mouth, an ancient Hermit with the wild sheen of lunacy in his eyes.

In the claustrophobic confines of his madness, in the

landscape of isolation and grief, Thorne lay upon his back and searched the sky. At night, when the moon slid out from behind the clouds like a luminous, blind eyeball, he fancied he could hear the trilling, birdlike sounds that Chattel made, as she roamed among the brilliant firmaments, looking for him.

As she searched the sky and peered behind the moon and tipped the stars askew.

Bereft of him and in eternal mourning.

ELVIS LIVES
by Nancy Springer

Nancy Springer's more than thirty books include *Fair Peril, The White Hart, The Sable Moon, The Silver Sun, The Black Beast, Larque on the Wing, Metal Angel, Toughing It, The Boy on a Black Horse, A Horse to Love, Looking For Jamie Bridger, Colt, Wings of Flame, Chains of Gold,* and *The Hex Witch of Seldom,* among others. Her stories have appeared in many magazines and anthologies, and she has won the Fassler Award, the Tiptree Award, and twice the Edgar Award. She lives in Pennsylvania with her family.

In "Elvis Lives," Springer examines the awkwardness of human relationships, especially in a small-town setting, and the ultimate universal power of love. She also shows how certain musicians, through devotion and adoration, have become powerful archetypes for today akin to those of the tarot.

The night I walked out, the night I finally got it through my head that Howard honest to God really just did not love me, was the night I saw the Elvis impersonator.

"Elvis Emulator" was what he called himself on the sign. There was this hole-in-the-pavement basement bar, and this sign on the easel, ELVIS LIVES, and I was strolling along, admiring the night—if I must tell the truth, I was crying; no idea where I was gonna go or what I was gonna do now, Howard had called me a fat ugly cow. He'd said no man was ever gonna want

me—and then I heard "Heartbreak Hotel" floating to
me like a black butterfly, and it was like I, Giddy
Stump, was a dog under the table of fate and they'd
thrown me a bone. Like love and Elvis were dead, so
they were giving me a scrap of what was left, but I
didn't have enough pride to say no thank you. So I
went on in.

I don't want you thinking that I *worship* Elvis. The
last thing I want to be is one of those sincere big-
haired polyester cowgirls in tight jeans and high heels
with a light-up black velvet Elvis shrine in the rec
room. I've never teased my hair in my life and I've
only been to Graceland twice and I only have a few
Elvis things around the house, like a porcelain statuette of Elvis riding a unicorn on the living room man-
telpiece—well, I did have it, until Howard smashed it.
What I want to say is, I am not freaky about Elvis.
But if you want to think that I *adore* Elvis, that's all
right, because I do. Not some of the things he did; I
just adore *him*. That bruised-looking mouth and those
bedroom eyes. That little-boy shyness. The sweet way
he treated his mama. The shiver in his voice. The way
he let the music whip him crazy. Everything.

The impersonator wasn't wearing a white sequined
jumpsuit or a cape or silver sunglasses or gobs of rings.
I stared at him for a minute when I walked in—let
me tell you, he knew how to emulate Elvis with his
hips—then I sat as close as I could get, which was
pretty close; it wasn't that big of a bar. He wasn't
wearing gobs of Brut either. He was dressed like the
early Elvis, in chinos and a sport coat and white socks
and penny loafers.

And then he began to sing, and I had to close my
eyes to hold back the tears. His voice—it was Elvis.

His face wasn't quite right—not enough bone. He
had the shadowy eyes and that sweet roundness in the
cheeks, he even had that curling mouth, like one of

them old pagan gods, but there was something not
quite Elvis about the chin and nose—but heck, it
didn't matter. When I closed my eyes, it was like
magic. Like Elvis, the real Elvis, was right there and
he was singing straight to me. No so-called emulator
should ever have been that good.

"Are you lonesome tonight. . . ."

Yes, damn it, yes, I was lonesome.

Nearly fifty years old. Only us old women care
about Elvis anymore. Nearly fifty, and who the heck
was ever going to give a damn about me? Not Elvis.
I'd never even seen him in real life. I'd picked what
might have been one of his toenail clippings out of
the shag rug in the Jungle Room in Graceland, but
Harold had sold it to some collector for seven hundred dollars.

"Love me tender. . . ."

Tears ran down my face. I did, I loved him, but he
was dead—I'm not one of those Elvis wackos, I knew
he was dead—and who was ever going to love me?

"I'm caught in a trap, I can't get out. . . ."

It was when Harold threw my porcelain Elvis to the
floor and smashed it that I walked out. He could keep
me penned in the house, he could cut me off so I
didn't have no friends, he could bust on me—in fact
he did most of the time. He had smashed my face a
time or two, and I could deal with it. But he better
not smash my dreams.

"Thankyou. Thankyou ver' much," the fake Elvis
mumbled into the mike. "Thankyou. G'night." Hardly
anybody applauded except me. Elvis had left the audi-
torium. But they didn't care.

I left, too, because if anybody tried to pick me up,
I was likely to bawl on their shoulder. No, that's a lie.
I left because I knew nobody would try.

I strode out onto the dark, empty street, trying to
look like I was going somewhere.

Somebody else was striding along ahead of me. Elvis.

Carrying a purse.

At that moment things started happening so fast that I didn't have no chance to think, Huh? A purse? There were shadows moving. Two guys lunged out of an alley. One of them hit the Elvis emulator on the back of the head with a brick. The other one tried to grab the purse. Elvis fell, but he held onto his handbag, he was wrestling the guy for it, and the guy with the brick lifted it to smash him in the face—

I screeched like a steam whistle and ran toward them, and I pulled my can of pepper spray out of my own purse and let the guy with the brick have it right in the face.

More like the ear, actually. But he howled anyway, dropped the brick, and ran. The other guy kicked Elvis, then ran before I could blast him.

"Are you all right?" I got down on my knees beside the Elvis emulator, who was sitting on the sidewalk holding the back of his head with one hand and his ribs where the guy had kicked him with the other. He still had his purse, but it had come open and his stuff was scattered all over the sidewalk. Typical woman, I started to pick it up.

He had a deck of weird cards in there, and it had gone all over the place. Thick pasteboard cards with lots of gold on them—they glittered in the street lamp light—and pictures of people in fancy clothes. I was gathering them together when it happened.

From one of the cards, Elvis Presley was looking back at me.

Not just a picture of Elvis. It was him. Real.

Stone bone real. Alive. Moving. His blue-black hair lifting back from his forehead, feathering in some breeze I could not feel. He blinked. His coal-dark eyes gazed into my soul.

"Elvis!" I squeaked.

"For God's sake," the impersonator said in her own natural voice, which sounded pissed off and like she wanted to cry, "I am not Elvis, and I'm getting blood all over my suit. Does anybody have a Kleenex?" Like there was anybody there but me, which there was not.

Realizing that the fake Elvis was a woman startled me almost as bad as seeing the real Elvis looking back at me from the card. Plus, like she said, she was getting blood all over her suit. Her head was bleeding like a sonuvabitch, like conked heads always do. Put everything together and I was so rattled that I jammed all the cards back into her purse without thinking about it.

I started digging in my own purse for a hankie. "No," I babbled, "on the card. Elvis was looking at me on the card."

The Elvis-girl who had been mugged just stared at me. I kept babbling. "Um, are you okay, honey? Do you need a doctor?" I gave her a wad of nose tissue. She pressed it to her head and stared at me some more and didn't answer my question.

She said, "You saw Elvis?"

I nodded.

"Which card?"

"One of those cards you got in your purse."

"Yes, but which one?"

I just knelt there like a dummy. Now, maybe you can't believe I got to age almost-fifty and never seen a deck of tarot cards before, but what can I say? I was raised Baptist. Ain't been to church since I met Howard, but the way a person was raised is like a habit they don't even think about. I just never been noplace or around no people where I might see no weird things like them cards.

Ms. Elvis was still staring at me. "Who are you?"

"Um, Giddy." My real name is Gladys, but I hate it. Anyway, I didn't feel like she really cared about my name. The question seemed to mean something else, somehow.

"Where do you live?"

"I—noplace." I thought I was done crying, but my voice came apart, damn it.

She looked at me some more. Then she nodded like she knew all about it. She stood up, threw the bloody wad of Kleenex on the ground, hefted her purse, and said, "C'mon."

"Huh?"

"C'mon."

She took me home with her. She lived in a back-alley, third-floor apartment by herself, her name was Lisa, and when I washed the blood off her head for her, the black hair dye came off with it. Her hair was a nice tawny tabby-cat color. Her head didn't look like it would need stitches, but I put Bactine on it and made her take a couple aspirin. She washed out the rest of the dye and pulled off her fake sideburns while I worked on getting the blood out of her jacket. There's nothing like cold water and ordinary hand soap for lifting bloodstains. I should know.

Lisa watched me. "You're a good mom," she said.

I shook my head; I never had any kids. I watched Lisa. She looked pretty, sitting at the kitchen table in her underwear. She wore one of those sports bras to flatten her breasts, though she didn't have much there to start with. Boyish. I asked her, "Are you a lesbian?"

She just laughed. "Are you going to run for the hills if I am?"

"No." I didn't know much about lesbians, and like I said, I was raised to stay away from anything weird—but no, I was staying. I told myself, what could she do to me that Howard hadn't done already? But the truth was, I looked at her and I kept seeing Elvis.

I slept on her sofa that night.

In the morning while we had our coffee, she laid the four kings from her deck of fancy cards in front of me. "Which one was it?"

I blinked, fuzzy-eyed; it always takes me till noon to wake up in the morning. Which was a good thing, because if I hadn't been so sleepy, the cards would have scared me. Weird. A king in black armor hefted a sword. Another king sat on his throne with a big ugly club tucked between his legs. Another one looked like a drunk carrying a monster goblet. The fourth one was—well, the fourth one had this big gold circle like a gold record, with a star on it like on a dressing room door, and he was moon-walking. It didn't scare me because I didn't care about Michael Jackson one way or another.

"That one's Michael Jackson," I told Lisa, pointing.

"Oh, really?" She looked at him, and I could see her starting to see him, and her lip curled. She didn't like him. "That's just groovy. Which one's *Elvis*?"

"They're your cards. You don't know?"

"Would I be asking *you* if I did? But he's got to be one of the kings." She peered at me with her eyebrows worried. "Doesn't he?"

I shook my head. Michael Jackson was groping himself, but none of the other kings were doing a thing.

"Huh." Lisa pulled out another card and showed it to me. "That's The Boss," I told her. The card said, "The Chariot," but it was a picture of a big old Cadillac and Springsteen was driving it.

"Oh, God, no, I don't want to sing like him." Lisa shoved it to the bottom of the deck and showed me some more. The Emperor was nobody, just a card. The Heirophant was nobody. She was showing me mostly the cards with male royalty on them, but I caught a glimpse of a card that showed a woman in a cone bra patting a lion, and I told her, "That's Madonna."

"Jesus." She blinked at it. "Christ, you're right. You see twice as much as I can." She put Madonna away, and hesitantly she pulled out a card labeled "the Devil."

"Sinatra."

She slapped it to the bottom of the deck. "Damn it! Which one is *Elvis*?"

Right then I started to rebel. The coffee was waking me up. I was getting nervous and next thing Lisa would want me to go through the whole freaky deck with her, and I wanted no part of it. I did want to see Elvis, but not like that. Those cards frightened me. I reared back in my chair. "How come you want to know?"

She cocked her chin up and gave me a hard stare. She didn't look much like Elvis when she did that. *I'm no fool,* that glare said. Whatever it was the Elvis card could give to her, she thought I meant to take it away.

"Who *are* you?" she demanded.

She made me mad, not trusting me. "I am an ugly, overweight, middle-aged woman," I told her, flat and loud, "with bad teeth and no job and nobody—" I stopped short. If I admitted that nobody cared about me, I might as well give up.

Lisa was giving me one of them long, thoughtful looks. You could tell, being around her, that she did a lot of thinking. Maybe too much. "You're a clairvoyant," she said, quiet and gentle now.

"Well, who or what the heck are you?"

She didn't answer. Nothing about her answered to nobody. She wore her tabby-cat hair flopped over her forehead, and she had a gold ring in one nostril. She wore what looked like a man's undershirt dyed black, one of them stiff stick-out ballerina skirts that should have been pink but it was dyed black, black tights, black Army boots. She didn't look a thing like Elvis. She said, "Stay here if you got noplace to go," and she got up and went out. I noticed she took her cards with her.

I stayed.

I did things for Lisa. I sorted through her clothes and mended some torn seams and sewed on some buttons. I cleaned mold off the inside of her refrigerator. She wasn't a slob, just a normal person who didn't have time. Not like me—I got nothing but time. I cleaned her apartment. I made tuna casserole, spaghetti, chicken corn soup.

Lisa did things for me. She listened to me when I talked about Howard and how he'd beat me. She ate the food I fixed and she liked it. She gave me money for clothes and groceries. She took me out for Chinese buffet. She brought me a little statuette of Elvis riding on a unicorn.

She didn't collect Elvis porcelain, but she did have Elvis books. A whole shelf of books about Elvis. I looked at the pictures, but I didn't read them. I don't read much.

"How'd you get such a feeling for Elvis?" I asked her. She was so young. No more than thirty. She never told me much about herself but she did say she didn't have no family. No mama.

Eating the apple crisp I'd made for dessert, she shrugged her bare shoulders. She wore tank tops a lot, and her shoulders were strong, like a boy's. "I dunno. How did you?"

"I fell in love with him, that was all. I was a young girl. I saw him on television. I went to see all his movies."

"I think . . ." She gave me a shadowy sideward look. I could see Elvis in that look. "He's the King, that's the thing. The way he sang—the way he put his heart in his voice—"

"Yes," I said.

"He's the greatest there ever was," Lisa said. "Isn't that what you'd want to be? The greatest ever?"

Days, Lisa worked as a part-time package gorilla at RPS. It kept her in shape, she said. Nights, she did Elvis gigs. I always came along to watch her and listen to her sing. It was magic, the way she could turn herself into Elvis. I closed my eyes and I cried every time. Every single time.

Who can explain why people start to love each other or how it happens?

I didn't say nothing to Lisa about the way I felt. I wasn't no lesbian. Besides, I was too old for anybody to love me. Lisa was just being a nice person, keeping me around.

I began to worry a lot. I knew I ought to get out of there. But I didn't have noplace to go.

"Lisa," I said, "what the heck am I going to do with what's left of my life?"

She was stretched out on the floor with her headphones on, listening to Nirvana—I can't stand Nirvana—but she took the headphones off and rolled her eyes to look at me upside down. Then she got up and said, "C'mere," and when I turned around there she was sitting at the table with the tarot cards.

"C'mere, what?"

"C'mere, I'll do a reading for you."

Lisa always had those tarot cards with her wherever she went. Especially when she went on an Elvis Emulator gig. They helped her sing, she said. They gave her luck. But they didn't feel lucky to me. She had stopped trying to show me the cards and get me to pick out the Elvis one because one time I started screaming, I just started screaming and crying and I couldn't stop. It was because of the Death card, but I didn't know how to explain what I saw.

"C'mon, Giddy."

I sat down across from her and she made me shuffle the cards till I felt like they knew me. Then she made me give her ten cards, and she laid them out face up in a kind of diamond-and-pillar pattern. No Death card, thank goodness.

"*Five* major arcana," she said like that meant something.

I wasn't listening because I knew now which card was Elvis. I saw him—he was looking at me with them shadowy eyes and dancing in his blue suede shoes—it made me hot and bothered just to watch him. But I didn't say a word because I wasn't sure I should tell Lisa. Them cards scared me. And she never would say why she wanted to know which one was the Elvis one.

"And what's not trumps is almost all cups and wands," she added. "You're a very nurturing person." She started at the center card of the diamond. "This card's you," she said. "The Fool." I could see her thinking of something kind to say. Lisa had a mind as sharp as swords, which made it hard for her to be kind, but she tried. "That means, sort of a drifter," she said. "Living for the day. Chasing butterflies. There's a lot of child in you. And see the playful little dog? That means animal nature, like, you're cute and cuddly, like a pet. You're crossed by—" She pointed to the card lying across the Fool. "The Emperor."

"I thought Howard was out of the picture," I grumbled.

"You haven't got him out of your head yet. But

there's love in your future." Her hand moved to the next card. "Two of Cups."

She went on like that. A lot of it I don't remember. My unconscious foundation of being was Ace of Cups, which made me kind of a fertility mother, and my outlook was the Wheel of Fortune, which meant everything was changing for me and I had a great chance to make an ass of myself. This was nothing I did not already know. The way I was perceived by other people was as the Queen of Wands, which was the same as my foundation, fertility mother.

"But I never had any kids." Meanwhile, Elvis was giving me his slow smile, and I was trying to keep my eyes off him.

"Well, maybe you should." Lisa was looking puzzled at the next card. "What's this?"

Page of Coins. My secret desire, Lisa said, but she had no idea what it meant. Then there were a couple of other cards I forget. And then the be-all and end-all of my life was the World. A naked young woman dancing in an oval made of flowers and planets and beasts. Except she wasn't just a young woman. She had broad shoulders like a man. She—I blinked and stared; she was Elvis, doing the jailhouse rock. But no, she wasn't just Elvis. She was Michael Jackson, too. And Jimi Hendrix, dancing like a guitar afire. And Buddy Holly in a plane going down, and John Lennon, and Morrison from the Doors, and even that idiot Kurt Cobain—

Seeing me staring, Lisa demanded, "Is that Elvis? Is that the Elvis card?"

"What would you do if it was?"

"Look, *tell* me. Listen, Giddy, if I could just see— if *all* the cards rocked, then that would be, like, peace on Earth. The end of the world as we know it."

I sat up straight like she'd jabbed me with a pin. I yipped, *"Where* did you *get* these cards?"

But she didn't get to answer me, because at that moment somebody started pounding on the door and yelling, "Gladys!" I knew that voice, and my bowels clenched, and I started to sweat.

"Oh, God," I whimpered, "don't let him get me." It was Howard, of course. I should have known he wouldn't just let me go.

"Go shut yourself in the bedroom." Lisa gave me a shove that way.

"Gladys! I know you're in there. You open this door, or I'll bust it down."

He would, too. Years ago I would have called that love, I would have thought, *Oh, Howie, my Howie, he loves me so much, breaking down doors so he can slap me around.* Now I knew better. I wasn't someone he loved. I was just something he thought he owned.

But old habits are so strong. I felt like I should open the door. There'd be less trouble if I did.

"Giddy," Lisa told me between her teeth, "go in the bedroom and lock the door. *Now.*"

I did what she said. I scuttled toward the bedroom, but I didn't quite make it before Howard kicked down the apartment door. He came toppling in, and he saw me. Lisa stood between him and me. "Out of my way, dyke!" He swore at her and tried to swat her to one side.

She karate-kicked him.

Or maybe it wasn't karate, maybe it was one of them other fancy Oriental ways of fighting, how would I know? I never even knew Lisa was a fighter. If she'd had her combat boots on, she would have broken Howard in half, but she'd been hanging around the apartment, she was barefoot, so all she did was make him howl and make him mad.

And Howard was a big man.

I don't know how many times he hit her. She fought back, she fought hard, brave, God she was brave as I stood there screaming, but he beat her back, and all the time he was swearing about what he was going to do to her and to me, and he beat her down to the floor—

Something snapped or clicked inside my head, and I moved. I grabbed the nearest thing, a lava lamp, and as he crouched over her, I swung it high and hit him on the back of the head just as hard as I could.

The lamp broke all over him and Lisa, and he flattened like cookie dough. I didn't know whether I'd knocked him out or killed him, and I didn't care. I flopped down beside Lisa and pulled her into my arms and cuddled her against my chest and bawled. I cried and cried.

"Hey," she said gently, nestled against my breasts, "I'm okay."

She wasn't okay; her face was all bloody. I lifted her in my arms and kissed her on her bloodied lips. Her bruised eyes widened.

"Okay," she whispered, "so you do love me a little."

I loved her a lot, and my heart was beating like dove wings because she loved me, she loved me, I knew she loved me, the way she sang to me, the way she had fought for me. "The Fool," I told her.

"Hm?"

"The Fool card is Elvis."

"God." She started to grin. "You're right. I am a fool. Nothing but a hound dog." She heaved herself out of my arms and stood up, tottering. I scrambled up to help her, but she was already staggering toward the tarot cards.

Lying on the floor amid broken glass and whatever that gook is they put inside lava lamps, Howard groaned. He wasn't dead, damn it.

"Never mind him." Lisa reached with shaky hands for the tarot deck and started looking for the Fool card. I saw blood in her hair.

"Lisa, honey, put those down, let me see if he hurt your head—"

"Never mind that." Her hands still fumbled with the deck, but her mind started working again and she focused on the Fool, which was lying right in plain sight on the table, where she'd been telling my fortune. "Of course," she whispered. "He's you, Giddy. The male side of you." Her eyes shone, and I could tell she was seeing Elvis. "The way he kind of stumbled backward into being who he was. The way he danced on the edge of the cliff and sang. Of course you're in love with him." A slow, boyish smile turned her hurt face beautiful. She picked up the card. She kissed it, then pressed it against her cheek, wet with blood.

I'll never know whether she intended this to happen or not. My feeling is, maybe not that way, but some way. She knew if she could find the Elvis card, she could find a way to make it happen.

It doesn't matter what she meant to happen. It happened.

The wetness of her blood soaked into the card. And the goldness of the card softened and mingled into her.

Howard, struggling up off the floor, saw the change coming over her, and it freaked him so bad that he yowled and scrambled out of the broken-down door like he might wet his pants. I heard him thudding down the stairs and out of there. Bye bye, Howard.

Me—I couldn't run away. I couldn't run away from anything in my life anymore. "Lisa," I cried, "no!" Tears stung my eyes.

Elvis Presley looked back at me with those coal-dark eyes. "What's the matter, Mama?"

Oh, that love-me-tender voice. That little-boy charm. It should have been the butterflies-and-rainbows moment of my life, right? There he stood in his gold lamé suit, Elvis, blue-black unruly hair that needed to be smoothed, velvet glance resting on me. It was Elvis, I was living with Elvis, his soft mouth flexing into a hint of pout, don't be cruel, his forever-young face not quite sure as he approached me with the respect and affection a good boy shows for his mama.

I stepped back from him. "Lisa," I begged, "you think I love you better this way? You're crazy!"

Why did she want to be someone other than who she was? Because her mother didn't want a dyke for a daughter? Because being Page of Coins wasn't as good as being the King? Why?

But she did want this. Since I'd known her she wanted to be—him.

"Mama, it's all right." Gently he put his arms around me.

His embrace felt like soup; I tore loose from it. "Lisa," I yelled, sobbing. "I want Lisa!" I stamped at him. "Is she in you? Don't you remember her?"

He watched me with sweet bewilderment. Elvis, and he was just a stupid dream, damn it, a fool's dream. In real life he'd fart and belch and get fat like any other man, and hump bimbos, down in the Jungle Room, and—and he wouldn't know a real woman if you hit him over the head with one.

Lisa . . .

The tarot cards—maybe they could somehow help me get her back? But where were they? They should have been right there on the table. Had she—oh, God, had she taken them with her, the way she always did?

On the floor, facedown, lay a single gold-backed card. I picked it up and turned it over.

Smiling, innocent, and covered with Lisa's blood already turning brown, the Fool gazed back at me with sweet shadowy eyes. As I looked, the card crumbled to glittering dust in my hand.

IN THE CARDS
by Barbara Delaplace

Barbara Delaplace was born in Vancouver, British Columbia, and, until lately, had lived and worked there all her life. She worked as a research technician for fourteen years at the Terry Fox Laboratory, a facility specializing in the study of blood cancers. She's also been a sysop for the Science Fiction and Fantasy Forum on CompuServe. Her short stories appear in *Dragon Fantastic, Horse Fantastic, Alternate Warriors, By Any Other Fame, Christmas Ghosts*, and *Aladdin: Master of the Lamp*, among other anthologies. She has been twice nominated for the John W. Campbell Award for Best New Writer and her story "Black Ice" won the HOMer Award for Best Short Story of 1992. Recently married, she lives with her new husband, Jack C. Haldeman II, in Gainesville, Florida where they share three computers, five cats, and too many books to count.

Delaplace's "In the Cards" is about a man's sense of validation from helping people through the tarot—and whether or not he can help himself after helping one person too much.

"No, Mr. Robbins, you don't need to worry. The Ten of Swords is not a card of violent death." The small, pale man smiled reassuringly at his anxious client. "Though I grant you, the image on the card *is* a rather violent one."

It certainly was: a body lying facedown, with ten swords plunged into its back. Mr. Robbins glanced uneasily at the card again, then back to the man doing the reading. "George, you're sure?"

George looked compassionately at Thomas Robbins. *It must be a great challenge,* he thought, *being CEO of a company as large as Industrial Amalgamated. No wonder he shows signs of stress every time he comes for a consultation.* "Believe me, sir, this card is not the bad news it seems. In a tarot reading, the orientation of the card is as important as its position in the layout. When it's reversed—as it is here—the meaning is entirely different. It suggests both wealth and power—at least in the short term."

Mr. Robbins laughed nervously. "Guess I'd better watch that new merger pretty closely, then."

"That would be prudent, yes," said George.

"Good—I never was very enthusiastic about it anyhow. Is there anything else I should pay close attention to?

"No, I'd say that about sums up your reading this time. The many cards from the suit of Pentacles is appropriate, given your profession, of course, since Pentacles are associated with the world of business. But there are a number of Swords as well, and as they represent strife, it suggests that you should use great caution for the next while."

Mr. Robbins had regained his self-assurance. He smiled and said, "I certainly will. Thank you as always, George. I don't know how I'd manage without you." He paused, as if uncomfortable with his admission.

It was so good to be needed. He never tired of seeing the gratitude and respect in the eyes of his clients. But he certainly understood how a man like this, a captain of industry, would be embarrassed admitting he regularly consulted a "common fortuneteller." Never mind that reading the future was such a small part of it all. George quickly spoke to cover the awkward moment. "Now, shall I see you next month?" he asked in a matter-of-fact tone.

"Yes, indeed. The fifteenth at the usual time." Mr. Robbins rose from his chair by the low table that held the cards.

"Excellent." He stood as well, and escorted his client to the door. "Do drive carefully. The freeway traffic always seems to be busy, even at this time of the evening."

There was a pause while Mr. Robbins reached inside his jacket and brought out a long white envelope. "And here's your fee, as usual. Are you sure you don't want more? Considering how valuable I find your advice, I'm quite happy to increase the amount. I'm used to paying for top-quality work."

George took the envelope. "No, thank you, sir. This is sufficient, I promise you. I have a day job, as you know, and that takes care of all my needs." The cards took care of so much more.

"I can't imagine they're paying you what you're truly worth. Why in the world don't you do this full-time?"

"Oh, I'm quite busy enough," George replied easily. "I need time for meditation between clients, for one thing. This isn't the sort of product you can churn out on an assembly line."

"Quite true. Well, good night—until next month."

"Good night, Mr. Robbins."

George closed the door and turned back toward the small sitting room where he did consultations. It was simply furnished with a desk and office chair, and the low table, which had an armchair and sofa arranged around it. All were worn, though cared for. Bookshelves lined the walls.

He went over to the desk and sat down, reaching for a letter opener. Slitting open the envelope, he glanced at the money inside, then put it aside. *They never seem to understand that money isn't what it's about.* No, he realized, that wasn't it. Rather, it was that money was the only way they had of showing their appreciation. If only they could understand that the appreciation was what made it so worthwhile. The cards were the key.

He shuffled through his mail. Letters from clients, of course; George smiled. He was always happy to read those: out-of-town patrons arranging appointments, thank-you notes praising him for guiding the letter writer down a fruitful path, queries about whether he was taking on new clients. The usual bills—ah, well, those were always with him, and he made ends meet. His smile became crooked when he saw the familiar handwriting on the last envelope.

His baby brother, of course. *Though I suppose you shouldn't call a thirty-nine-year-old man a "baby" anything,* he thought to himself. Sammy hadn't really grown up, though. Always full of business schemes that never quite seemed to work out. Sometimes they failed so badly that Sammy was left in debt, and he never hesitated to come to his older brother for help. Somehow, George was always able to scrape together enough money from his modest resources to bail him out.

I wonder what it is this time? Last time it was stock in a gold mine in northern British Columbia. George heard mental alarm bells going off when Sammy told him about it. Even he, unsophisticated in the ways of investment as he was, knew that offerings on the Vancouver Stock Exchange were often highly speculative. Sammy, alas, had brought that lesson home to him.

"But this one is different, George!" Sammy told him excitedly. "Look at Pine Tree Mines—they're making millions! And this is right in the same alluvial fan formation!"

Reflecting to himself that his brother wouldn't know the difference between an alluvial fan and a baseball fan, George had looked into Pine Tree Mines. It had indeed struck the jackpot—after many years of fruitless exploration, changes of ownership, and millions of dollars in investment poured into it. He also looked into past stock offerings in gold mining ventures, and discovered just how many of them had not panned out. But Sammy wouldn't listen to reason.

"They've got sample drillings that show an incredibly high concentration of gold! They've included the analyst's report—here it is!" He brandished a paper covered in figures.

"Sammy, those samples could be 'salted' with extra gold ore to make them look richer than they really are. *That's* happened before, too, you know. Look at Corsair Gold Explorations. That was a scandal that rocked the Stock Exchange for months when it was revealed. And this one you want to invest in is run by the very same people."

"Aw, George, you have no vision. This is the big one—the one that's going to make me a fortune. You'll see." And Sammy had hugged him and gone away to Vancouver to make his fortune. Again.

George reached for the letter opener and slit open the envelope, knowing he shouldn't—not before a reading. It would upset his concentration, make him lose focus. But . . . it was his brother, his only living relative, and he loved him. He took out the letter and began reading.

The stock in the gold mine had collapsed, as George had predicted. Sammy had attempted to recoup his losses by taking out a loan, so he could invest in a new offering—by the same company directors. George sighed. Nothing new in that, unfortunately; and undoubtedly Sammy had figured his older brother wouldn't look kindly on throwing more money down a rathole dug by the same people, no matter how attractive its prospectus seemed.

His jaw tightened as he read further. This was serious. Sammy had been unable to raise capital from any regular source—his past record was starting to catch up with him—so he had gone to a loan shark. Who now wanted his money. In full. With interest. Could George, *would* George help him? This would absolutely be the last time, he promised. He'd learned his lesson for good, truly he had.

George felt a hollow in the pit of his stomach. The total was staggering. Where on earth could he get such a sum? The old grandfather clock in the hallway bonged, and he suddenly realized his next client would be here in fifteen minutes.

She would be the last one for tonight, thank goodness. Mrs. Fuertes. A schoolteacher, she would likely be concerned about a pupil, what was going on in the child's life, how to approach the problems the child would be having. He'd best prepare himself before she arrived.

He stood and went over to the low table, where the cards were laid out in a complex pattern. He sat down and gathered them up, then carefully wrapped them in a blue silk handkerchief before placing them back in their polished wood box. Then he leaned back in the armchair and closed his eyes, focusing himself on that inner serenity that was so important, the calm void where he could empty his mind and let the delicate intuitions about each client take shape and form . . . George drifted away from his earthly chains.

The soft chime of the doorbell broke into his meditations some uncounted minutes later. Mrs. Fuertes, of course. He hurried to the door.

"Mrs. Fuertes, how nice to see you again." He

guided the plump, gray-haired woman inside. "Come into my office."

"Oh, George, I'm so worried about Maria Hernandez. You must help me with her."

"Of course. Now sit down, and we'll get started immediately." She looked at him gratefully. *It was so good to be needed,* he thought.

"Wilson! I said I wanted those results ready by today!"

George tensed. His boss, Phil Cole, had a voice that carried across the entire lab when he thought it was necessary. He thought it necessary quite often—even when, as now, he was standing next to his victim. George looked down at his lab bench as Phil patiently explained how slow George was, how sloppy his sterile technique was, and how easy it would be to replace him.

No, it wouldn't, George thought. *Just try and find someone else willing to do those setups.* Haldenski tests were unpopular because they entailed racking three hundred test tubes and filling each with one of thirty different solutions, all of which had to be freshly prepared the day of the procedure. And that was before the experiment itself was performed. It meant a fourteen-hour workday—if the tech worked fast—and no one wanted the job, particularly since the results added little useful information about the reagents being tested. But Phil was fond of Haldenski tests; they produced satisfying amounts of paperwork to show management. It always seemed to be George who wound up doing the job; the other techs somehow found themselves extremely busy whenever Haldenski tests were assigned.

He clenched his hands as Phil wound up his harangue with ". . . and I expect those results in my office by the end of the day, understand?" He turned away before George had a chance to reply.

George sighed. Another missed lunch hour, no coffee breaks, and his regular work for today postponed until he completed the analysis. Once again, he likely wouldn't get home before nine tonight. *I'll have to reschedule those readings,* he thought. And he needed the readings—Sammy needed the money they'd bring in.

First things first, he thought. *You can make those phone calls later.* During his skipped lunch—surely they wouldn't begrudge him a few minutes' worth of phone calls? He resolutely pushed the other problems out of his mind. *Focus on the job at hand, George.* He reached for the pages of raw data and began punching the first of the endless series of numbers into his calculator.

It was a long way from the microscope to the tarot deck, and George was never sure what had started his journey. He often wondered if it was truly chance that had led him to that used bookstore years ago where he'd found a tarot deck. He'd never seen one before, and found himself fascinated with the mystic designs on the cards. So captivated, in fact, that he found the nerve to ask the clerk, "What kind of cards are these?"

"Tarot cards," she replied. "Says so on the box—can't you read?"

A response like that would discourage someone with more self-confidence than George, and normally it would have deflated him so completely he'd have slunk away. But the odd cards exerted a compelling influence on him. He'd heard of the tarot, and knew they were used for divination, but had assumed that anything of the sort would be garish and childlike.

But there was nothing childish about these cards. The designs were full of mysterious symbolism. Why

was the Hanged Man's face so serene? What was foolish about the Fool, who was depicted as a handsome—
and normal—young man? He found the exotic suits
appealing; Wands and Pentacles were so much more
interesting than Clubs and Diamonds. To his mild surprise, he found he wasn't much concerned with what
the woman thought of him, and actually said, "They're
very interesting. I'll take them. Do you happen to
have some books that explain them?"

She did, and he walked out of the bookstore a few
dollars poorer, but feeling as though he'd just found
the key to a fortune.

The cards were indeed a key. He found that they
spoke to him. When he arranged them for a reading
in the Celtic Cross or the Tree of Life layout, they
formed beautiful, meaningful patterns that he could
interpret as easily as men with other talents could hit
home runs or compose sonatas.

He practiced, first by doing readings for himself,
then—again with that astonishing, newly-found self-
confidence—for his friends and coworkers at the lab.
Some of them found it hilarious that a man with his
scientific training would resort to fortunetelling, and
would tease him. "Your future is in the cards, right,
George? Ha ha ha!"

The laughter didn't bother him at all, he was so
consumed with improving his skills at reading. He simply crossed the wise guys off his mental list and continued doing readings for those who were interested.

There were a lot of them. And they had friends,
relatives, acquaintances who wanted readings as well.
His confidence soared. He was good at this—people
wanted him to do it! It was a heady feeling. Soon there
were so many that he couldn't accommodate them
during lunch hours at work, so he began setting up
appointments at his home in the evening.

Not every client was sincerely looking for guidance. Some came giggling, and asked foolish, trivial questions. This, he felt, was unworthy of the ancient wisdom the cards embodied. He began charging a small fee. The gigglers stopped coming, which gave him more time to devote to those who truly needed his help. His readings became ever more accurate. And the word-of-mouth referrals spread wider and wider.

The inspiration struck him the next morning as he was looking over his appointment calendar. Hairdressers, artists, politicians, construction workers, actors, stockbrokers, they were all there; it had been a busy week. All of them needing reassurance, some guidance, an empathetic listener. *Why not charge more for my readings?*

He immediately pushed the thought away. It wasn't right to do this for mere profit; he'd known that from the very beginning. His gift from the cards was meant to be used as a gift to others.

But the idea wouldn't go away. Sammy needed his help desperately. And quickly— George knew enough about loan sharks to know that the amount owed increased at a horrifying rate of interest. Why, he'd heard about rates of one hundred percent a week or more.

And if Sammy wasn't able to pay . . . George shuddered. They wouldn't kill him—you can't get money from a dead man—but they wouldn't hesitate to put him in the hospital either, especially if they thought it would "encourage" Sammy to come up with the cash.

Would it really matter if he raised his rates? Just for those who could afford it? Mr. Robbins, for instance, wouldn't find it a hardship at all—he offered to pay extra every time he visited. And he had associates who were eager to have readings; George had turned them down because he didn't want to overload himself, dilute the quality of his work. But this would be only temporary.

He really ought to do a reading for himself, he supposed, but he felt reluctant. He glanced at the gleaming wooden box which housed the cards. Surely the ancient powers enthroned there would understand? This was for a good cause—it wasn't as though he was asking for the money for himself. He didn't really have a choice. After all, it was his own brother. . . .

In the end, George ignored the cards and reached for the telephone.

Mr. Robbins was delighted to spread the word among his friends and was very understanding about the rate increase. So were George's other well-to-do clients. Within a few days all his empty appointment slots filled up, and he began doing readings on Sunday, formerly a day of rest that he felt was necessary to recharge his spiritual wells.

But Sammy had telephoned from Vancouver. "George, you've got to hurry." He sounded terrified. "These guys are really eager for their money, if you know what I mean."

"I'm working on it, Sammy. I'll wire you what I've been able to raise so far, okay? It won't be enough, but maybe it'll help convince them that you're working on it."

"Thanks, big brother. I knew I could count on you."

The relief in his voice was balm to George's worried mind, and made up for the weariness he was beginning to feel. All the extra readings were draining. But it was worth it, for his brother.

It was in the middle of a reading for a new client, a graphics artist friend of Mr. Robbins, that it happened. The Queen of Swords—who sat in profile—

ever so slightly turned her head and glanced at him out of the corner of her eye.

He was so shaken he stopped talking and simply stared. The artist, an intense dark-haired, dark-eyed woman, noticed immediately. "Mr. Wilson, are you all right?"

"I . . . yes, I think so." *I couldn't have seen what I just thought I did.* The figure on the card now was in its familiar conformation, staring straight ahead. He glanced up at the woman and realized she was upset. He hastened to reassure her. "Really, I'm quite all right, my dear. Let's continue, shall we?"

"Are you sure, Mr. Wilson?" she asked doubtfully. "You're white as a sheet."

"Absolutely. Now, this one happens to be one of my favorite cards, and I'm always happy to see it turn up in a reading . . ." He resolutely pushed the incident to the back of his mind. It was just his imagination; he was tired. Right now, his client needed him.

After the reading was over and he had escorted the artist out, George wrapped the cards in their silken shroud and put them away immediately. Then he sat down at his desk to open the envelope she had given him. It had never bothered him before, but now he was uncomfortable handling money with the cards out on the table. He felt as though they were watching him with disapproval. It didn't seem to matter that the money wasn't for selfish use; the guilt was there all the same. He shouldn't be doing this for merely worldly reasons.

This is sheer nonsense, he tried to tell himself. *You're working too hard and paying the price—that movement of the queen was just your imagination.* Once he'd earned enough, he'd stop all the extra readings and return to his previous fee levels. Then these feelings would go away.

But a few days later, something happened that proved it *wasn't* just his imagination.

He cried out and awakened himself. Perspiration beaded on his forehead. He'd been dreaming.

The atmosphere in the dream had been foreboding and full of tension. And the driver of the Chariot, one of the twenty-two cards of the Major Arcana, the most powerful part of the tarot, was speaking to him. The image was looking gravely, sorrowfully at him as it spoke. George heard the words but couldn't quite make them out—they didn't seem to be in English. Try as he would, he couldn't communicate with the image or understand what it said. And even when he spoke, the figure from the card didn't appear to be listening, but was intent only on its own words. This seemed to go on for many minutes, to no avail. Frustrated, George turned away.

A mistake—he had forgotten what he was dealing with. One didn't turn one's back on a majestic personage like this, even in a dream. The black sphinx, which drew the chariot in tandem with its white counterpart, suddenly snarled and sprang forward, talons bared. The claws sank into his arm, and he screamed as he felt the pain.

That was when he awoke.

He was still breathing hard after several minutes. *That all seemed so real,* he thought. But what was even more frightening was the idea that somehow, the Chariot was angry with him. He'd always thought of the cards as . . . well, not friends, exactly. One didn't call ancient and powerful images "friends." He was their steward, perhaps, explaining the images to his clients as clearly as his skill permitted. Focused only on helping them, never thinking of gain for himself. Even his efforts to increase his income from readings was for Sammy's sake. If it were only himself, he'd stop right now. But he was needed.

He had always felt the ancient beings symbolized in the cards looked on him with favor, had honored his faithful service to them. He wiped his forehead. To discover that they were displeased with him, as the dream seemed to indicate, came as a shock.

His body ached all over. *I must have clenched every muscle I have,* he thought. He massaged his arm and gasped from the unexpected pain. What on earth was wrong with it? He switched on the bedside lamp, to take a good look.

And screamed in shock.

His arm had been gashed, as if from the talons of a great beast.

Quite possibly a sphinx.

There was no doubt in his mind after that. Doing readings for purely financial gain had been a mistake. The cards had become his enemies. Sammy would have to find his own way out of the mess he had made for himself. He kept phoning to beg for more money, but after emptying his bank account, George had nothing more to send him, and finally, racked with guilt, he had to stop answering the phone. He couldn't bear to sit helplessly, listening to Sammy's pleadings.

He canceled all appointments; he couldn't give proper guidance to clients who came to him seeking help when, at any moment, the figures on the cards might begin moving.

And they *did* move. He found himself shuffling through the deck over and over during the now-empty evenings, studying each card in turn. Kings and queens would look angrily at him. Pages would turn their backs, and knights brandished their weapons at him. He found the rejection frightening.

But the Major Arcana were the most terrifying of all. Like the court cards, the images moved—but unlike them, they seemed to be manifesting themselves physically. Arriving home from work one day, he found the dusty tracks of chariot wheels crossing his living room rug. Another day he found several dark brown eagle feathers on the floor by the hat rack, which had obviously been used as a perch by the great raptor that decorated the card called the Wheel of Fortune.

And what George found the most horrifying of all were the Arcana that had *not* yet manifested themselves. What in heaven's name could he do if Strength, with its huge lion, chose to appear? Or the Devil? Or . . . Death?

He took the only course of action he could think of: he burned his tarot decks—the Aquarian deck, the Tarot of Marseilles, the Thoth deck, the Golden Dawn Tarot. Even the most beautiful of all, the Tarot of the Cloisters. He found it heartbreaking as he consigned one magnificent image after another to the fire. He'd pored over each card so many times, striving to gain new insight into the true meanings of each one. There were tears in his eyes as the flames roared, fueled by the colored pasteboard pictures. "Good-bye," he whispered to the rising smoke.

But there was one deck he couldn't make himself burn: the very first one he'd ever purchased, the classic Rider-Waite pack, designed by Edgar Arthur Waite. More than any other, he'd found this deck to be the one that held the most symbolism for him, had the most to offer in the way of insight because of the complex images on each card. He *couldn't* burn this one!

*   *   *

But then came the night when the fireplace saved his life. It was chilly, and he had kindled a fire. It was comforting in a small way to know that this fire had been built for warmth, rather than for its destructive ability.

He stared into the flames. Fire was such a potent symbol . . . after a while, he roused himself. He would study all the cards that had flames in them. Perhaps a new understanding would come to him, something that would explain this nightmare and let him return to the happy, productive life he had been leading previously. He missed his clients, missed the wonderful feeling of purpose they gave him. He missed his brother.

He had just turned over the Devil and—although the figure held a torch and thus met his criteria— was about to quickly shuffle it back into the pack, when he heard a sudden sound of ponderous breathing coming from the kitchen. The reflection of an intense, flickering light grew brighter and brighter on the glossy painted surface of the kitchen door. And there was a rhythmic clacking noise, as if whoever was in the room was walking on nail-studded soles. The sound drew closer and closer to the passageway leading from the kitchen to the living room.

They weren't nail-covered soles at all. They were claws. The Devil, hairy and leather-winged, stood stoop-shouldered in the doorway, burning torch in one hand, clawed, birdlike toes opening and closing, scratching against the bare kitchen floor. Each movement left grooves in the linoleum. The creature laughed at him, a truly awful sound, and came into the living room.

It was all George could do not to gibber in fear. He backed and backed away, the card still in his hand, until he knocked over the fire screen and felt the heat of the flames on his calves.

The Devil laughed again and moved closer.

Desperately, George flung the cardboard image of the monster into the fire.

The Devil stopped moving and began to waver and flicker, like a television image growing weaker. At first, he thought it was the reflection of the torch it brandished. But then the figure became fainter and the torch went dull, as if a veil had been dropped over it. It grew dimmer and dimmer and eventually vanished.

George's relief couldn't be measured. He had warded off, single-handedly, one of the most terrifying things he had ever seen. *It's over,* he thought to himself. *I made it—I'm okay.*

Then he heard the sound of hoofbeats in the backyard. Many hoofbeats, as if every mounted image in the entire deck had come alive. And then George remembered.

One of the Major Arcana, Death, rode a horse as well.

He didn't have much time to act—the hoofbeats were crossing the yard. He looked at the deck on the table and quickly gathered it up. The fire flared, waiting. If he didn't burn the deck, Death would take him. But if he *did* burn it, a lesser death would take him. He'd already failed his brother. A living death awaited him, of endless days in the lab, performing endless, meaningless tests, listening endlessly to his boss. Endless nights without people to help, no guidance to give. No useful purpose to his existence.

The hooves were crashing at the back door.

His hands were over the fire, holding the cards, ready to fling them into the flames.

Which future? Which death?

*　　*　　*

Like Schroedinger's cat, George Wilson is suspended between two futures, and only he knows which choice he's going to make, which of his realities is the lesser of two evils.

As his friends would say, his fate is in the cards.

TURN OF THE CARD
by Michelle Sagara West

Michelle Sagara West's books include, most recently, *Hunter's Oath* and *Hunter's Death*, and the forthcoming *The Broken Crown* and *The Shining Court*. Her first four novels and numerous short stories earned her a nomination for the Cambell award for best new writer. She writes a column for *The Magazine of Fantasy and Science Fiction* called "Guilty Pleasures." She lives in Toronto, Ontario.

"Turn of the Card" is a dark, complex look at the sometimes overwhelming nature of responsibility—for our actions, and our futures.

1

She made those cards.

Watching them as he turns them and places them precisely into their proper position, she sees their frayed edges, their cracked and worn pictures; Major Arcana now sun-bleached and sweat-damaged beyond all repair. The deck was a naive attempt at a work of art, but as with many a naive attempt, it was the vessel for the whole of her heart while she worked to make a gift.

For him.

It is so hard to look at him.

The cards tell a story as they lay before her, a work in progress, the end of which will be an inverted Celtic

Cross. At fifteen, at sixteen, at seventeen, she would slip into the comfort of her darkened basement, dimming the lights and clearing off the round-edged teak table that had been, like so many things, banished from the upper world when something better could be afforded.

She had a deck of cards, some store-bought affair, the Waite deck that everyone used. A Crowley deck in pristine perfection remained in its box; she couldn't master the reading of it, couldn't quite see how the one card could influence the other, forming a chain, a link of chains.

Younger, then.

The Celtic Cross was easy, and she liked it; she made of it a personal talisman. To it, she would come, shuffling and cutting the cards with care and trepidation, finding the significator, the card that represented either herself, or the heart of her question—as if, at fifteen, she truly understood that heart—and then she would seek Answers.

She remembers the fear and the hope and the self-deception; the way she turned from the answers that she didn't like, reframing the question again and again until it at last satisfied her sense of desire, if it cheated her sense of fate. Mystery. There was mystery then. Profound, unknowable, hallowed by the privacy of a basement in isolation.

And that mystery was as nothing to this one.

This is not the man she married. Not the man she knew. She misses him terribly.

The nurse comes to stand by her elbow. "Mrs. Brentwood?" she says softly. "Dr. Brevin is waiting."

But she cannot rise; her husband has not yet finished his reading. As compulsive, as silent, as he, she waits, bound by more than the stiff arms of the chair, the gleaming edge of the table. She holds her breath, as he does, laying out the cards. She cannot see what he has chosen as the significator, and because she can't, she doesn't know who he thinks he is, or what question he hopes to answer.

But the answer comes. He lays out the first card; the second—one to cover, and one to cross, and then the rest unfolds as naturally, as painfully, as a life.

Hands shaking, he turns the last card. It is Death, of course. Stricken, he folds; he is not the man that she married; hardly a man at all.

It's a card of change, she wants to say. *Death doesn't mean death.* But this once she would be lying, and she's certain he would know it. Even though he never responds to a single thing she says, she knows it's important to offer him nothing but the truth.

And so she often offers him nothing at all.

The nurse frowns and leaves her side; there's a curious screech of rubber as she lifts the brake arm and begins to wheel this man away. His hands flail; his arms shoot out. In one swift motion he gathers the fallen cards in a pile in his lap; the nurse barely waits.

And Shelagh knows that she hasn't really touched him at all.

"I'm sorry, Mrs. Brentwood," Dr. Brevin says. He doesn't smile, and she's grateful for that particular mercy.

She says nothing, waiting.

After a moment, he shifts in his chair, lowering his eyes to the paper on his desk. "We can't be certain when he'll recover from the shock. The damage isn't physical. There is no reason whatever we can discern that prevents him from walking. Or speaking."

Dr. Brevin raises his hands, massages his forehead. Shelagh knows that she's being difficult, but she's beyond caring. "We both know it's guilt," the older man says at last, speaking a "we" not of doctor and patient, but of doctor and patient's wife. "It's the guilt that's killing him."

Her lips are a tight line, a terrible line; thin and sharp. They have to be, to stop the words from coming. She likes Dr. Brevin as much as one can like a doctor, but she will not share her ambivalence with him, and he should know it by now.

"Mrs. Brentwood, if you could bring yourself to—"

Scraping the chair against hardwood that's seen better days, Shelagh Brentwood rises and flees the room, moving deliberately and gracefully through the open door. After all, it's her husband, not her. It's her husband who's trapped here in this terrible, would-be sterile world.

She doesn't remember what the cards mean anymore. Individually, they've blurred and smudged. She doesn't know what pentacles signify, or wands, although she remembers that cups are emotional fonts. If she were to do a reading now—for herself, or for anyone else—she would need a book, some sort of guide to remind her of all that she's lost.

Sitting in the back of a cab whose driver has been forced to surrender his illegal cigarette to the wind, she stares at her left hand, at the two rings that adorn her finger, one on top of the other: the diamond promise and the band without end. Thinking of symbols, of what the symbols mean, of how they can remain, depleted of life, as if they were always merely vessels.

She used to drive, but her license has expired.

They don't own a car anymore.

The summer is hot; she lives in it, thinking that she should have dressed for the weather. Thinking that her arms will burn if she doesn't take care.

Wondering how to care about something so stupid, so petty, as a little blistering of the skin, the glancing kiss of fire.

She hates the car. She hates this cab.

"Driver," she says, "stop here."

And he stops without a single word. Of course he insists on breaking the silence to ask for money; she pays him and leaves. When she can breathe again, she'll find another cab. This is Toronto. They litter the roads.

Robert Brentwood is lifted out of his chair by two able-bodied orderlies and settled into bed. He senses their pity, but they've little enough time for it, which is just as well; he wants them gone.

The night is coming. He lifts his hand, his shaking hand. They've gathered his cards, all but five, and he spreads them across the surface of the table they put his food on. The Moon. The Devil. Death. The Tower.

And the High Priestess. The other four cards he sets aside; he knows them better than he knows himself; he's lived them, lived with them, for the harvest and the cold, cold winter. Spring did not come to the Essex Manor Special Care unit, and although the sun shone high through the glassed-in walls, its light was just that: light. No warmth there. No warmth.

Will she come? Will she return tonight?

In the early evening, Shelagh Brentwood remembers that she is not fifty. Not forty. Not yet thirty. The Essex Manor Special Care unit ages her decades every time she steps through the doors that lead to the wing. As she walks down the asphalt, she lifts her head higher; her hair, which is long and dark, if a bit too fine, swirls down her shoulders at the touch of a brisk breeze. She picks up the remnants of her youth, wraps them about her face, lets the dourness and the grimness bleach away from her expression until she looks like a young woman. Like any other young woman, dressed in reverse-fit jeans and a white turtleneck with no sleeves, who comes alone to the Canadian National Exhibition, the great-grandfather of fairs in the city of Toronto.

What are you doing, Shelagh?

She stops at the gate and then reaches, self-consciously, for her purse; pulls out her wallet, fumbles a moment with the bills, dry and leaflike, as they pass between her hands and the hands of a bored attendant.

And then she is gone, passing through the arch and the stiff turnstile into the moving press of bodies that carries her, like a river, in its own direction. She doesn't have to think. It's easier not to think.

Until she reaches the midway.

This, like the cards, was a magical place less than half her life ago. The dirt and the loud cries of employed summer students were't as obvious as the freedom of a first venture into such a big world without parental interference. Of course it was only a day trip, and of course she had had little money. But neither of these things mattered as much as the sense that she stood on the brink of a world that was so much larger—and so much more wonderful—than the world her parents lived in, and wanted her to live in, for all of their lives.

For just a minute, she is fifteen again.

Just a moment, and that moment, the passing of a cloud over the face of the ever-present summer sun.

It was at the CNE that she first had her fortune told. Or rather, had her cards read. It was one and the same to her then. She'd hoped for magic, the mysterious old gypsy lady in a tent or a wagon, her face painted, ears ringed, face wreathed in smoke that was dear as breath. What she'd got instead was a girl little older than she, standing behind a tall counter, holding a stapled booklet in which she could check off each of the meanings of each of the cards, or their reverse, as she laid them out.

That girl didn't understand what a querent was.
That girl didn't know what significator to choose,
choosing the Fool as a symbol of youth, when in fact
Shelagh's question had been about—what else—the
fate of her heart, and heart's romance.

So the outcome itself should have yielded little, as
it answered nothing clear. Queen of Pentacles.

Reversed.

The stapled booklet was pink; the young woman
had two piles—pink ones for girls and blue ones for
boys. Incongruous and ridiculous, as if fate could be
girdled in modern gender convention. Ridiculous or
no, she'd paid for that booklet, and after the girl had
finished, she'd clutched it tightly to herself, half-afraid
that her friends would see it and know what it meant.

Because she knew. Checked there, in red letters
against the pink background, the one, the telling, passage: *Greatness of soul, a dark woman who is powerful, intelligent, and uses these traits with generosity and
good purpose; if the card is reversed, these traits are
used for selfish, petty, and malicious ends.*

*This is a face card; the court cards imply choice, not
absolute fate.*

Choice. She'd grasped that word for all she was
worth, standing at the tacky counter, her hopes for
greatness dashed. Not one of the Major Arcana appeared in the reading; not a single one. Swords
abounded; the Three of Swords, the Two of Swords,
the Eight, the Nine—she could not honestly remember
the rest. But the memory of the Queen of Pentacles
was enough, even handled as she was by a girl who
just needed the hourly minimum wage that checking
off passages in a preprinted booklet could provide.

Because Shelagh *knew* that she was the Queen of
Pentacles, standing on the edge of an adult life that
she herself—that she *alone*—could define. Power, yes.
But generosity or selfishness? Kindness or cruelty?

Reversed.

The cards had offered her a warning, that day. Unchecked, unhindered, undisciplined, she was to become everything that she had thought, until that moment, she despised. And what was left, once one despised oneself and *knew* it?

The shadow passed, the memory lingered.

Because if cards could do that, could give her that momentary understanding, that knife-sharp, necessary as breath-and-blood clarity of vision, they were better than mirrors. Better than self-help books and the advice of strangers or friends that one couldn't quite trust.

The noise of the midway returned. Thirteen years fled in an instant. A coke spill, half-dried, released the underside of her sandal with the sound of tape being pulled up too quickly. There was no freedom here anymore, just mechanical rides and children who thought they knew everything about the world.

Just as she had, until that day.

2

Robert Brentwood is not a young man. And he is not an old man. He is not a man anymore; he is barely a name. He sits in front of the silvered mirror, thinking these things, knowing them to be true. If he were a man, he could speak. If he were a man, he could walk. If he were a man, he could drive a car.

But he does none of these things.

The moon is in the mirror. It comes through the sheers; he doesn't have the curtains pulled. It's the one thing he can do—keep the curtains open. The nurse thinks that he needs the sun, and she knows that if the curtains are drawn, someone less observant might not notice this, so she leaves them open, always. Because he wants it.

But it's not the sun he needs. The moon, baleful, glares down at him with Her face. It is almost time. Hand trembling, he turns the face of the High Priestess to the window.

And the moon disgorges her whole.

"Robert," she says, as she steps from her throne.

He sits in his, as if he were her equal. It's why she stands; the height gives her the advantage. But she is not displeased; she is never displeased.

That she is never happy has not really occurred to him. Her black hair hidden by the fall of her midnight blue veil, her white shimmering robes concealed, in part, by a cloak, she offers him a benediction.

"I was watching," she tells him softly. "Do you know what Death means?"

He nods.

"You are coming closer to your truth, Robert. The only truth. Are you afraid of it?"

He nods again. There is no point in lying to the High Priestess; she sees beyond the lie, above and beneath it, and she knows how to sting him with the truth she extracts.

"Why?"

He doesn't know. He doesn't know, and because he doesn't know, he can't answer. She speaks for him, as always.

"Death is change," she says. "You have reached the end of this road. You have lost what remained to you in it. She will not speak the words that will free you."

Oh, the High Priestess is perceptive. Stung, he retreats, his face becoming a mask, a thing of flesh that more resembles latex than it does his true self. Buried, his true self winces, because it knows that if he has just five cards, she has the deck.

She will bring the Empress.

And the Empress is cruelty defined to those who have disappointed her.

If he could speak, he would beg. He does not.

"Robert," the High Priestess says, her voice serene, "you must let go of your fear. The Empress hurts you because you wish her to hurt you; she pains you because you fear her. What harm can she do you? What greater harm *can* be done?" But although her words are serene, her eyes are the silver of the moon's light in the mirror, and when she unfurls her left hand, the Empress comes from the shadows.

And he whimpers.

In the morning, he is alone. The scars have healed; they heal, with the passage of the night, but they hurt and they ache and he is growing tired of the pain. It's Wednesday, and Shelagh doesn't come on Wednesdays. Faithful Dr. Brevin does, offering him words and questions, as if they can somehow be of help.

He has all the help he needs, if he can only see his way clear to understanding it; she was always more intuitive than he could ever be. But perhaps she knows this. She brought him the cards, after all, brought them and passed them over the wall where they fell in a fan of perfect, aged color, of memory, of time.

He sorts through the deck in his lap, occasionally pulling out a card or two after he's cut and shuffled, shuffled and cut. None of them catch his attention until one sticks to his hand. In this ward, in this room, at this time, he knows what that means, and he takes the card out, studies it carefully, lays it upon the table his meals grace.

The Nine of Swords. He shows the card to the doctor, and the doctor smiles uneasily.

"That's a very interesting image, Robert."

She made it for him, painting the black too pale and the swords too silver, but catching, perfectly, the

sense of utter loss and desolation. It's one of her better cards. He hates it. He would give it away if he
could, but it clings to him; clings to them both.
Maybe—maybe if the doctor pulled hard enough—

But the doctor doesn't touch the card, and no
surprise.

"I don't know why you brought him those cards,"
Dr. Brevin says, and pauses.

She lets him have his pause, meeting his eyes with
the quiet, perfect composure that he finds—that they
all find—so unnerving. The odd thing is, she would
answer the question he's not quite asking if she knew
the answer herself. But she doesn't.

She just knows that when she was cleaning out the
room, boxing things, putting things that she could no
longer bear to look at—but is still not certain she
could ever bear to part with—into the basement, she
found the cards in their hand-embroidered linen bag,
string half-rotted with time and sweat.

He hadn't spoken a word to her since the night of
the accident. Hadn't spoken a word to anyone, not
even the father that he so respected. Months had
passed, and the hopes of his loved ones had dwindled.

Hope.

She sees the rings around her finger, unbroken, un-
breakable, and wonders, in the bright light, if the alloy
that hardens the gold is iron, or platinum; she knows
nothing at all about the process it takes to make a
band. Remembers little about the process of wearing
one.

"Mrs. Brentwood?"

"I'm sorry; my attention must have wandered."

He is used to this, but worn by it; worn by her, by
the care of her husband, by this place—a mansion of
little rooms, the madwomen and madmen poured free
from their attic confines like ghosts raging and silent

in the face of their pasts, and their helplessness to change or alter them.

"I said, I think your decision to bring those cards was a good one. They seem to be having an effect on Mr. Brentwood." He pauses. "I'm not familiar with the cards themselves, but I was wondering if you could tell me what a few of them mean?"

"Out of context?" She snorts; old habit. "They don't have meaning out of context."

"Then look at them," he says, his voice suddenly thin and sharp, "in the context of your *husband*."

She doesn't like that at all. "Have you forgotten, Dr. Brevin, who the patient is?" And she rises.

"No." He rises, but heavily, pushing himself up by the flat of both hands. "The High Priestess," he says. "The Devil. The Tower. The Moon." He pauses. "Justice."

She shrugs, wondering if the last word is the name of a card, or the doctor's demand. "It's been a long time since I touched those cards. I was a teenager. I don't remember."

But she does.

She takes the subway home; she leaves the Manor behind. She does not stop to speak with her husband because the time for words has long since passed and she doesn't really know how to speak to him anymore.

Doesn't want to see him, mute and stunned and hidden, his hands turning card after card, as if to force the words from her. From her. Why does it always come back to her?

Her home is far too large for her needs, but it's his home as well. Almost a year ago, she thought he would come back to it, but time has passed; he lives in this house in photographs and memory. She has put so much else away.

Twisting the ring around her finger, she thinks about

age, about how he ages her; about how she wants—for just a moment—to be held and to be loved and to be trusted. She is twenty-eight years old, but she feels, as she stands in the arch that leads to the kitchen, that she has a winter heart, a heart as heavy as his mother's heart, as blistered, cracked, broken.

And thinking about his mother always reminds her of herself, and it comes back to this, time and again: She mounts the stairs, wide and bent and cushioned by thick carpet so a fall won't be so dangerous; her hand grips the rail, whiter and whiter with each step she takes; she crests the last step as if it were the unexpected peak of a mountain that has no plateau. Stumbles. Rights herself.

And then she walks to the closed door that no longer has a tacky nameplate. And she thinks as she opens the door, that she is dead.

But she isn't; it's only desire, and the desire is momentary.

He can see her; in the waters at the foot of the woman who holds the Star, he scries like a madman, fascinated, horrified. The High Priestess stands at his side, cloaked in moonlight, a presence not unlike a judgmental mother, one calm and serene in her implacability. She has opened this window to Shelagh's world, and if he could speak, he would tell her to close it. He would beg her to close it.

But he cannot speak.

Wrapping his flannel-draped arms round himself, he rocks back and forth in his chair.

She rocks back and forth in the room.

In the darkness, she can pretend for a moment that she is a mother, like any other mother, come to check on her sleeping child. The bed is there, flat and narrow and low to the ground; the dresser, chipped and damaged by temper and time, stands beside it. There is a small mirror on the wall, a single large picture. Of herself, and her husband, on their wedding day.

Kara loved that picture because her practical mother looked like a princess, wearing a dress that cost far too much for the conceit and the hope of a single bright day. Robert—Robert took it down from their room and put it up in hers, at the foot of her bed. So that, he said, she would know they would always watch over her.

She walks to the picture and stares at it; it is dark in the room; she is a pale white shape within the confines of the ornate frame, and he is almost invisible. Lifting her hand, she touches the textured surface of the print, her fingers hovering a moment before her hands fall stiffly to her side. Her lips move.

He hears her bitter laughter, her angry laughter, and he cringes. The Empress is better than this, and he turns his face to the High Priestess, but she is remote; her eyes, as his, are caught by his wife. His almost wife.

Till Death do us part.

And it has parted them.

But she will not let go. And he will not. He sees her, for a moment, as she sees herself: a young woman. A lonely woman. Knowing what she suffers, and seeing it, are very, very different.

The bed is empty, of course. The sheets are not her sheets, and the drawers have not held her clothing for two months. Two months ago, she found the courage and the strength to admit that her daughter was never— could never—come back. Not even in her dreams, and she desires those dreams more than she desires the comfort of being loved. Desires the ability to hold, to love, and to comfort more than even the desire to be held. Her arms are empty.

She never understood that phrase until the police came and took her to the hospital. Until she saw her child's body. Her brother had offered to identify it, to spare her the pain of seeing it—but she *had* to see it. She had to know. And, of course, it was what it was: her daughter's death, writ in flesh.

She remembers that the only thing she said to the technician who waited in somber silence was thank you. Just thank you.

After seeing the dead, she went quickly, numbly, to see to the living: her husband, attached to tubes and machines. His clothing was being removed from the corner of the room, and she'd offered to clean it—to *clean it*—as if, somehow, that would give her purpose, function. But it was a terrible mess, torn and bloodied. She'd let them take it, as she let them take her daughter.

She couldn't wait for him, for the funeral.

He would forgive her, she felt certain of that. But she couldn't wait. It wouldn't be right. But she feels, now, that she is still waiting for him, for an ending. He has not come home.

Lying down on the bed, her hair a spill across a cool pillow, she closes her eyes, trying desperately to remember what her daughter smelled like. What she looked like, in motion, not in the flat confines of the photographs that line her walls. Even the sound of her voice.

Nothing returns except loss, and there is no one to share it with.

"Do you see?" The High Priestess says, as she stands in front of the moon and the image of his wife in the darkness gives way to the ripple of water. "You have been here too long."

He nods, holding his tears.

"You are the earth," she tells him softly, "that is laid across her brow." She hands him a scythe, then, swinging it gently; from its crescent the breeze comes to disturb the curtain's fall. He watches the neutral fabric sway in the shadows a moment, and then turns to look at the weight in his hands.

The scythe has become a shovel.

He knows what she is telling him.

3

She has lived in terror of the phone since the day she picked it up a mother, and in a short sentence, became childless and almost-widow both. Its ring is jarring and, no matter what she is doing, it disturbs her stillness, shatters the silence, brings back, for however small a fraction of time, the memory that she is driven by.

During the day it's not so bad; the sun and the sky and the presence of traffic in the road beyond her walls do much to dispel the shadows. No, it's at night, always at night, that the fear is worst; she is waiting for an emergency. Another death.

Because death still has the power to diminish her, to hurt her, where so little else does. Oh, the pain wouldn't be as great, the loss as complete—but loss is loss and pain is pain, and she would feel them both. Her parents are here. Her friends.

But when the phone rings—and it does ring on this night, summer's heat forcing the windows open as surely as if it had possessed her body and moved her hands—it peals, tolling electronically, no depth or grandeur to the sound.

"Mrs. Brentwood?"

The voice is familiar, and it is unwelcome, and she

recognizes both before the last syllable of her name has reached her ears. "Dr. Brevin." Not a question.

He doesn't pause, doesn't wait to hear her greeting; he plunges into the conversation as if—as if it weren't one. "There's been some trouble at Essex Manor," he says. "Your husband has—has injured himself."

She hears herself telling him that she'll come right away. She sees her hand put the receiver back into its cradle. She knows the weight of the phone book as she takes it down from its shelf and flips it open. To call a cab.

But she doesn't feel anything at all.

In the darkness, the road is empty. The driver is smoking; he asked her permission, and she couldn't quite bring herself to say no. Even though she knows it's bad for his health, and for hers. It comes back to that—what she knows, what she's willing to do in spite of it. Because it's easier. Because it will make someone else happy.

Was she always this much of a coward?

She hates the thought; hates the man who brings it to her; hates the cab. She hates cars, and she'll always hate them; it's a truth, and its her truth, and, God knows, she's tried to accept her truths.

All of them.

What else can she do but accept?

The road brings her closer to the Manor, farther from home, but there's no safety in either, so she doesn't resent the journey.

Dr. Brevin is waiting for her on the front steps. He sits; if he stood, she thinks he would be pacing, and pacing offers no comfort. He's a trained professional; he knows how to take control of a situation.

Pity that she doesn't know how to give it up.

Because if she knew how—if she remembered how for even a minute—she would. She would let him tell her what to do, just as she let the cab driver smoke. As she let so many things happen, for so many years, each of them small and insignificant.

But nothing ever went wrong when I did it. Nothing ever went wrong. I knew when to give in.

Oh, she's close to the edge, to think that, to think that here. She pulls herself in, standing stiff and tight, her hands clenched behind her back as if they might, with a will of their own, reach out to touch someone for support.

Even if that someone is Dr. Brevin.

He can read her face; he's good at it, even though it gives so little away. "Mrs. Brentwood," he says, and it seems to be he, and not she, who relaxes.

"Take me," she says quietly, "to him."

He sees her enter his room.

They have taken his chair away; they have removed his table; they have added a strap to his bed. A strap that restrains his arms, that holds him down, that takes away even his minimal choices. The cards, he knows, are in the dresser by the bed; they have left him that.

Arms buried in blankets, straps holding him down, he looks less like a prisoner than a baby. And he knows it; he sees it a moment in the lines of her brow.

How old is he? He can't remember. He has been in this place so long, time must move differently for him; she is so young. His hair is gray, his face lined, his skin whitened by sun's lack.

"Robert," she says, as she crosses the threshold. The first time she's used his name in as long as he can remember. Because all memory that's real starts here, waking up to the short ceilings and blank walls of the Essex Manor. Trapped, just as surely as if death had already brought him to hell.

Does she think he can just answer her? He opens

his mouth, but the words don't come. And he can't lift his arms. They've taken that away.

"Dr. Brevin says—Dr. Brevin says you tried—tried to kill yourself."

Accusation, there.

Anger.

But at what? Failure? Incompetence to do *even that* well enough that it gets the job done?

She is the Empress; he never saw it before, or he might have known better than to marry her. He closes his eyes, accepting the punishment she has to offer, but she withholds even that. Instead, she turns to Dr. Brevin.

"Is he restrained?"

The doctor's reply isn't framed in words, but he knows what the answer is, even though he isn't watching; Dr. Brevin is an honest man.

"At least let him sit up."

Make him sit up.

He sits. Opens his eyes. Watches as she searches his drawers, wondering what she's looking for. Wondering if he can help, if it's important that he help. He nods in the direction of the bedside table. She doesn't notice. He throws his head back, tossing it sideways like an angry horse. Sweating with effort, he repeats the motion; it's always this way, the work and the struggle just to make himself understood.

But she understands, this time, and she circumnavigates the bed, taking great care not to touch him at all, he the landmass, the room the ocean in which he would like to be lost. The drawer squeals open; the cards come up in her hands.

In her hands, in the day, they shine like gold. Or silver. "Where is the table?"

"It's being cleaned."

"Can I have another?"

Dr. Brevin leaves.
Leaves them alone.

She takes the cards in shaking hands and stares at
them because they are brightly colored, vibrant, strong
images—everything that he is not. She can't remember
what she wanted to say anymore. Can't remember if
she wanted to say a thing, although she wouldn't say
it in front of Dr. Brevin in any case.

*What is it? What is it about these goddamned cards
that you can spend your whole life looking at them?*

She made them.

For him.

Her hands are shaking again; she is angry. She has
tried *so hard* not be angry at him. He is injured, he
is crippled, he is driven by his own guilt—by his own
damned guilt—he is weak and she is—

She is strong.

And she will not give in to this impulse.

But she wants to rage. She wants to shout. She
wants to scream, and it's been so long since she
screamed her throat aches at the restriction.

If she had a table, she would seat herself behind it, use
it as a shield wall. She doesn't. She has the cards. The cards
are flimsy, too flimsy for such a task. Or—maybe not.

She sits on the floor by the foot of his bed, crossing
her legs, feeling, beneath her thighs, the coolness of
linoleum tile. Hears his labored breath, and raises her
head, eyes slowly cresting the end-board of fake ve-
neer cut through with metallic handles—three—until
she meets his eyes. They are dark, a brown so deep
they seem black surrounded by white. He tosses his
head to the side like a maddened beast, and she knows
what he's asking.

That she sit on the floor by his side, where he can
see her.

She shuffles the cards again, unexpectedly angry at

the request. Angry at herself for the anger, for the
selfish desire to have privacy when he's trapped here,
and she's free.

Free?

She compromises, choosing to sit where he can see
her but to sit in such a way that he cannot see the
Celtic Cross that she lays out against the pale gray
floor. Because it's hers. Because it might tell him
something that she doesn't want him to know: her
anger, her deep and abiding anger, her grief, her guilt,
her—say it—No. No, she will not say that to him. And
because she cannot even think the words, pronounce
them in the silence of her thoughts, she must hide a
moment, willing them away.

She cuts the deck, left-handed, although she can't
remember if the need to cut the deck left-handed is
founded on superstition, false memory, or truth. The
cards come down in three piles, three obsessively even
piles, spaced a half-tile apart. She picks them up, right
to left, making out of the three a single whole.

And then she remembers that she's forgotten the
significator. The question. The querent. The cards
have to cover something. Have to ask something. But
she doesn't want to reveal herself, put too much of
herself into this task; Dr. Brevin will be back, and her
husband is waiting.

She looks for the Queen of Pentacles, because she
is the Queen of Pentacles—dark-haired, powerful, a
woman past the bloom of youth and in the prime of
experience, of wisdom. Looks for the Queen of Pentacles because she's been trapped once by that card,
changed once by it, forced once to give up the life
that she had been quietly leading—and she's not to
be trapped that way again, in this room, with this man.
If the Queen is the querent, she can't be the result. It
can't come down to her, again. It can't always be her
that's forced to choose, to choose, to choose.

He tried to kill himself.

Card after card falls into her lap as she searches for the Queen of Pentacles. The pile in her hand grows slimmer, the weight in her lap greater. There is no Queen. He's lost it. She made these cards. For him. And there was no card that she put more of herself into than that Queen.

And he's *lost* it.

She would ask him where it was, if she could speak at all, but she can't speak, she won't speak. And she will not rise to face him until she is certain that she can.

So she chooses a different card instead. Something suitably insipid, something that won't tell her anything she doesn't want to know. The Three of Cups. Three happy women holding their golden chalices in union in agreement. Happiness. Fulfillment. No, wait—that's not quite what it meant. She starts to think, the seriousness of the moment takes her in, as if she were fifteen again; anger rescues her. That's what it bloody well *will* mean. There's no one here to judge how well she handles the cards, how good her memory is, how keen her sense of intuition; there's no one here to impress.

Easy question. *When will I be happy again?*

And it's a cheat, and she knows it because she used to cheat all the time, and it doesn't matter anyway because they're just cards, *just* cards, but she needs to have something to do while he watches her.

The light in the room is poor. She could move the lamp across the floor, but she'd have to stand, and she doesn't want to now that she's here.

She turns the first card over. Thinking, remembering that this is the card that covers the question; the atmosphere that pervades it, that holds it. Three of Swords; stark, no matter how it's done; shaft of metal, three

times, through a red heart. It doesn't surprise her at
all.

The card that crosses does: the Four of Wands. Do-
mestic tranquillity. A peaceful home. Home. She tries
to think of what it means, even though she doesn't
want to put that much of herself into the cards. She
shouldn't have started, but like so many things, once
started, she cannot pull back. How does this cross her?
What does it mean? Is she trapped somehow by the
memory of a better time? By the desire for it?

Desire, yes. She looks up, meets her husband's eyes,
and wonders why she hasn't let go of him yet.

The third card, now; her ideal hope, the best that
she might achieve in the future of the question—but
what question? What question lies beneath the formal
words? She lays it down gently and smiles, feels a little
jump. Major Arcana. The Sun. Almost, she feels its
warmth, the passage between this night and that day.

When she lays the fourth card down, she places it
carefully beneath the significator. At the heart of the
question she's asked is the Nine of Swords, a woman,
sitting in bed, weeping against a background of swords
and darkness. She does not need to remember the
cards to understand what this one means; does not
need to look beneath the surface of the picture to see
the heart beneath. It is hers.

But if she doesn't need to look, she can't look away
either, not immediately; the reading of the cards is a
thing that can't be rushed if they are to tell their story.
And why shouldn't they?

The Knight of Wands is the fifth card that comes
off the top of the deck. In armor, he is obviously a
man in flight; he holds a staff of living wood. *He is
leaving,* she thinks, and then, *he tried to kill himself.*

But he is in the past, and the significator looks
toward the future; toward the influences of the future.
She places the sixth card down. Queen of Swords. Did

she draw this woman? Paint her expression? Did she
turn the woman's lips down in that expression of distance and pain? She sees no happiness here, and she
understands well why the Queen wields the sword: It
is for her own protection. She has so little left, she
cannot afford to be careless.

She cannot remember, anymore, what the next three
cards mean; how they relate either to her, or to themselves. But she knows that they lead to the outcome,
to the answer. Self-conscious, she looks up, sees her
husband's eyes and turns away again, all in a single
motion.

Ten of Swords.

Ace of Swords.

The Star.

Loss and desolation. Will and power to conquer.
Hope.

She takes a deep breath, takes the last card from
the deck and holds it a moment, thinking neither too
clearly nor too deeply. Afraid, although why, when
everything she has ever feared has already come and
gone and she has survived it all, she doesn't know.

And as he watches her, the moon grows brighter
through the window; the wind comes in, carrying
within the folds of its breeze an ancient melody, a
song of reeds and brooks and wild, wild water.

It is, he thinks, a lovely song.

So much better than the words that he often hears,
left alone in the dark of the night. So much kinder
than his dreams—the shards of a previous life, the
echoes of past greatness.

She rises from the floor, sliding out from the deck
in silence as his wife lays another card down. Hair the
color of midnight, skin the color of moonlight, the
book held against her chest as if it were a child.

"Let go, Robert."

He doesn't know what she means.

"Don't you? Let go. You cling to this place as if it birthed you." Lifting a hand, she gestures; the straps slide clear of his body, falling into shadow and away. "And perhaps it will, now. *Let go.*"

He remembers, through a haze that never, never clears, that she was tired. That she wanted to ride with Daddy. That her seat was too small and the straps hurt her neck—and they did; she was tall and too slender. He remembers that.

And he remembers that she was crying, and her tears were not the near-tantrum that he so disliked; they were quiet, hurt, bewildered. Her hair was matted to her forehead and the sides of her cheeks, dark curls, fine and soft.

He can feel the key in the ignition; the car thrumming like a live thing beneath him; he can see, if he turns to look at the side mirror, the exhaust rising and drifting in the still evening.

He can think: *It's only fifteen minutes. We aren't going near a highway.*

He can think: *It's late, we're both tired, we don't need a fight right now.*

He can think: *I rode in a car from the time I was born without a seat belt, and nothing ever happened to me.*

Nothing ever happened to me.

Close his eyes and he can see the lights flailing against the windshield in the darkness. He can see the car, the other car, the green light; he can feel the pedal beneath his feet, the weight of his reflexes, the plastic beneath his hands.

He opens his eyes before he can see the rest; he does not want to see the rest.

She turns the card over and lays it down, to have an ending. A poorly proportioned skeleton stares up at her, riding on a red-eyed steed over a field of bodies. In the distance, beyond his implacable form, the sun is rising.

The breath leaves her lungs in a rush, and with it, her heart. She is cold, sitting in the shadows made by poor light and the midnight sky. She starts to gather the cards, her hands almost numb, when she realizes that there's something clinging to Death, something stuck beneath the card's back. With care, she slides her fingernails between the cards and gently levers them apart.

Queen of Pentacles.

Reversed.

She stares at it for a long moment, and then she starts to laugh. It is a quiet laugh, at first. But as it grows louder, she loses it, the laugh becomes a wail, a cry of anger, of the terrible anger that grips her and will not let go.

She gathers her cards in a furious rush, betrayed by them, forced by them to make some choice, any choice—as if there *were* a choice to be made.

And what choice? What bloody choice?

She was not the one who was driving the car.

She was not the one who chose to let Kara sit in the front seat.

She was not the one who *killed their daughter.*

She turns, rising, her hands clenched in fists; she turns to face this half-man, this cringing, terrible *coward,* and she steps across the line that she has drawn for herself, across her life.

"How-could-you-let-her-drive-like-*that*?" She strikes the baseboard with her fist, punctuating each word. Waits a half minute for a reply, some answer, some proof that he's even there at all. "You *killed her,* you selfish bastard, and then you just went into hiding, you crawled off into your own little world, you played guilty, you played hurt—"

Her eyes are full of tears now; she can't even see his face, and she doesn't care if she never sees it again. But she can't stop talking, and the breaths that she needs to throw her words at him come between those words themselves, awkward and poorly timed. "You killed her, and I had to clean up. I had to clean up her death, I had to clean up my life—I had to clean up your life because you couldn't even face me!"

She shakes the baseboard; shakes it as hard as she possibly can with a single hand. "Say something."

Silence, of course.

"Say something."

He won't. She doesn't care if he can't, or he thinks he can't. She doesn't care. She leaves the foot of the bed, throwing the cards behind her in a fan of terrible color.

Touching him isn't hard at all.

She shakes him; he expected that. Worse will follow. And he's grateful for it, for what he no longer sees lurking behind the pale surface of her eyes. It's out now; finally, after a year: Judgment. Truth.

He would offer her anything, if he had it to offer. He had something that she wanted, once. That she even loved. He doesn't remember what it was.

She slaps him; she slaps him twice and then grabs the collar of his nightshirt and yanks him up; her arms are strong enough to bear the weight a moment.

You killed our daughter, she says.

Do you understand? You killed her, and then you left me to deal with it, she says.

I hate *you,* she says.

And this is what he was afraid of; he knows it once he hears it; he feels something click into place.

She hits him again, just once, an open-palmed slap that resounds in the sudden silence. And then, just as suddenly as it came, it is gone. Her eyes widen, her face pales; she looks down at her hands as if they aren't, and can't be, her own.

The cards form an arch above her. She doesn't see them; he can tell by the way she retreats. But they glow like a scintillating rainbow in the mystery of the night.

The High Priestess is waiting for him; her face is impassive, and she, like he, is silent.

I hate you. He sits up. *I hate you.*

And he thinks, as he repeats it, that it doesn't play right. It should have been definitive. It should have been cold and final.

But across the room, Shelagh is weeping as if her heart has been broken. As if she still had a heart that could be broken. She stumbles back until she hits the room's sharp corner, and then her knees give way, she falls.

This is not the way he envisioned her: knees against her chest, body curled against the cradle of wall and floor.

"Robert," the High Priestess says, and her face is luminescent, "this is the only door that you will ever have. Take it, or reject it, but understand it for what it is." And she points to the arch through which his wife has passed.

He is confused; by the night, by the memory, by the Priestess. She wanted him to die.

"Did I?" She smiles again, and he realizes that the luminescence is a haze; she is vanishing, as the night does, to light. "*You* wanted," she tells him. "We are not separate." And the arch, like the Priestess, begins to fade.

He turns, quickly, bringing the dead weight of his legs round. Urgent now, filled with a kind of purpose that he has not had since the night of his daughter's death. For the first time in a year, Robert Brentwood walks. He does not stumble; he knows that tonight he cannot take a single false step.

She rests against wall and floor and her tears are a bridge that he knows he can cross. The only one.

He takes it, becoming, as he crosses the room, Robert Brentwood. Becoming, for a moment, the man that married Shelagh Caverson seven years ago. He reaches out to touch her; touches her; enfolds her in both of his arms. She spins there like a trapped animal, and then snarls in rage.

He doesn't let go.

She hits him, beats at his shoulders and the side of his head with white-edged fists.

He doesn't let go.

She screams at him, almost incoherent, and when that does not shake him, she bites.

He doesn't let go. She is Tam Lin, and he is her lover, and he holds her because he knows, now, that he *must* hold her. That he *can* hold her. He was afraid of her anger, paralyzed by it; he'd forgotten how much of her anger came from a deeper place. Hurt. Loss. Pain.

He holds her until she cannot fight him anymore, and then, when she slumps against his chest, he tightens his arms, and he offers her a place of safety that he'd forgotten—until he saw her curled like a child in the corner—she ever needed.

"I'm sorry," he tells her, his chin in her hair, his hands stroking her back. She hits him again, but feebly, and he continues to speak; he has a year's worth of words to say and he will not stop saying them until she is safe.

"You left me," she tells him, although he can barely hear the words, her voice is so child-soft. Spent, the anger has left her vulnerable. And all vulnerability is a child's vulnerability.

"Yes. I won't leave again."

"Why did you leave?"

"It doesn't matter," he tells her gently. "I'm not going anywhere now."

She doesn't believe him, and she wants to believe him, and he knows that he could spend a life trying to convince her that this time he's speaking the truth. He wonders, as he holds her, if it will work, but he knows he's going to try. Feels almost hallowed by the knowledge.

Looking over her hair, he sees the sun come up across the surface of the cards; shakes his head, thinking of the illusion and the madness by which he's been both trapped—and freed.

He lifts her, knowing how his arms will ache in the afternoon, but wanting, for a few minutes, to carry her. To carry her completely.

Dr. Brevin stands just outside of the doorway, breath held, movement stilled, because otherwise he might disturb this perfect moment. He watches, as Shelagh slowly relaxes in the arms of a Robert Brentwood that he only barely suspected existed at all. That man lays her down, reluctantly, upon the room's single bed. His lips brush her forehead, her cheek; they hover a hair's breadth above her mouth before he pulls back, perhaps unwilling to take what must be offered again, anew. Wise man.

He kisses her sleeping lids instead, brushes her wet hair from her forehead, and then, kneeling in the dawn-touched room, he quietly begins to gather the cards.

SOLO IN THE SPOTLIGHT

by George Alec Effinger

George Alec Effinger, winner of both the Nebula and the Hugo Awards, is the author of many novels, including *When Gravity Fails, A Fire in the Sun*, and *The Exile Kiss*. An obsessive collector—"if I have two of anything it's a collection"—he lives in New Orleans.

Barbie is a curious social phenomenon. She is a powerful symbol, which was quickly adopted by legions and has dominated the mindframes of so many as *the* ideal of femininity and womanhood. Even those who reject her are impacted by her existence, for they use her as a reference and negative example.

On one level a political satire, "Solo in the Spotlight" is Effinger's humorous look at Barbie's pervasive nature, as her influence invades even the tarot and the mystical sciences.

Colonel McNeill leaned down and murmured, "Mr. President, the pilot asked if you want him to turn the plane around and head back to Dulles."

I took off my reading glasses and rubbed the bridge of my nose. "How far are we from Chicago?" I asked.

"We'll be landing in about half an hour, forty-five minutes."

It was a long flight back to Washington. "What does General Paradiz think?" I asked.

Colonel McNeill paused. "Maybe you should ask *him* that, sir."

That wasn't what I wanted to hear. "I asked you, what does General Paradiz think?"

He looked uncomfortable. "The general thinks it's definitely a situation, but it's not a crisis yet, and it's a long way from becoming an emergency. Of course, any situation can turn into a crisis without warning."

This colonel from one of the small states in the Frozen North was telling me—his Commander-in-Chief—something I'd figured out for myself in about the ninth grade. I didn't want to seem impatient, though. You never want to say or do anything to discourage your subordinates from showing what little initiative they have. "We'll just go on to Chicago," I said. "I think we can stay on top of things from here. Please keep me informed."

"Yes, Mr. President. Thank you, sir."

I don't know why he thanked me; they're *always* doing that.

When he'd gone away, the First Daughter turned to me. She had been cruising her favorite Internet sites through the modem in her laptop. She never went anywhere without her laptop. My wife, the First Lady, worried that our daughter was growing up to be a geek rather than a lovely young woman. I told my wife that the girl had plenty of normal teenage interests.

"Is this going to spoil our trip to Chicago, Daddy?" she asked.

I shrugged. "I hope not, sweetheart, but even if things get worse, I've got lots of advisers to help me." I'd been President for only nine or ten weeks, and this was the first troubling situation of my administration. To tell the truth, because it was the first time, I felt more anxiety than conditions warranted.

"Good. I want to see you throw out the first pitch, I want to have cheeseburgers, chips, and Coke at the

Billy Goat Tavern, and I want to see the big dollhouse in the Museum of Science and Industry."

"And we have to shop for your mother, too," I said.

"Frango Mints from Marshall Fields' and—"

"I have her list, honey. Now, I need to do some work. There's a lot of reading every day, and I'd rather not depend entirely on my staff's summaries."

"Okay, Daddy." She went back to her laptop. She's a great kid, and if anybody's daughter could handle the pressures of growing up in the White House, I knew she could. Sometimes her mother worried about her too much.

Colonel McNeill worried too much, too, but he got paid for that. A little while later, while Air Force One was beginning its descent into O'Hare, he was again murmuring into my ear.

"There's been some news, Mr. President, very distressing news. The general thinks we need to have a meeting."

"We'll be on the ground in a few minutes, Colonel," I said.

"Sir, the general thinks we should go back to Washington."

That sounded bad. "What happened?" I asked.

"The Breulen rebels have seized the American Embassy. Some Marines and other embassy personnel have been injured, possibly killed. No confirmation yet on the fatalities, though."

Fatalities—what an empty, distancing word. I felt my stomach tensing. "All right," I said. "How do I order the pilot to head home?"

"The intercom at the table, sir."

I turned to the First Daughter. She hadn't heard any of this. "We're going back to Washington, sweetheart," I said. "Sorry. It's an emergency."

Colonel McNeill cleared his throat. "Mr. President,

the situation is now a *crisis*. It's not an emergency yet."

I turned and gave him a look, but I stopped myself from saying anything. Nobody liked the Colonel; he was an attitude without a person.

The First Daughter sighed. "Well, okay, Daddy, Chicago isn't going anywhere. We'll miss the ballgame, but you've got seven more first pitches to throw out."

"That's my girl." I liked the way she assumed we'd be going to Opening Days during my second term, too.

I stood up, took a deep breath and let it out, straightened my suit jacket, and followed the Colonel to the conference table. Most of my advisers stood up and greeted me with a "Mr. President." General Paradiz didn't. I made a mental note of that.

"Please sit down, gentlemen," I said. "And we can do without ceremony and protocol. Let's just get to work."

"Mr. President," General Paradiz said. He glanced around the table, checking to see if any of the other advisers, military or otherwise, objected to his taking charge. No one did, of course. "Before I begin, do you have any questions?"

"I think I have all the facts of the situation," I said.

"Crisis," Colonel McNeill corrected. We all ignored him.

General Paradiz went on. "It's extremely important to act with speed and confidence, Mr. President. This is the first test of your administration's foreign policies."

"Our first concern is the welfare of the Americans in Breulandy," said Luis, my Secretary of Defense. "But you should remember that there is a political side, as well."

I frowned. "I'm not thinking of politics right now. The safety of our people is not a political issue."

"If you actually mean that," General Paradiz said, "then you'll be the first U.S. president in my experience who did."

He was not a likable guy, either. The best you could say about him was that he was a mammal. The trouble was that if you got more specific, the very next word would have to be "however." I wondered if I, as Commander-in-Chief, could simply reassign him to some Distant Early Warning outpost on the tundra. If we still had the DEW Line.

"How much can we accomplish now?" I asked Luis. "From Air Force One?" He was on the plane only because he'd grown up in Chicago, and the mayor was his boyhood friend. Luis had come along just for the baseball game, but I was grateful to have him with me.

He shrugged. "You don't have to wait until you get back to Washington, Mr. President, if that's what you mean. Anything you can do from the White House, you can do from here. Major Mathias has the football, of course."

"The football" was a large briefcase that contained everything I'd need to commit the country to any sort of action, up to and including Global Thermonuclear War. All the necessary secret codes and commands were in the football, and wherever the President went, Major Mathias or someone very much like him carried it nearby.

"Good," I said.

"Yes, sir," Luis said. "And Master Hsu has the hockey puck."

Okay, that one got by me. I'd known about the football before I took office—I read about it in *Time* years ago; but I'd never even heard of the hockey puck. "Who is Master Hsu?" I asked.

Colonel McNeill indicated a portly, sober-faced man

seated near—but not at—the conference table. "The gentleman with the wooden box." I didn't recall ever seeing the man before.

"He's the President's psychic adviser," Luis explained.

"Psychic adviser?" I said. "I don't have time for that."

"Sir," said Colonel McNeill, "almost every administration since Andrew Jackson has had a psychic adviser. President Jackson himself consulted Marie Laveau, the New Orleans voodoo queen, on several difficult matters. The 'hockey puck' is the code name for the tools of the psychic trade. In the case of this particular adviser, Master Hsu, I understand that means tarot cards."

I looked at Master Hsu for a moment. "I know I didn't appoint him."

"He was selected by someone on your staff, Mr. President," the colonel said.

"Mr. President, sir," said Master Hsu, standing and bowing his head, "I may offer insights not available to your other advisers."

"That remains to be seen, Master Hsu." I turned back to the others at the table, and I put the psychic adviser and his hockey puck out of my mind.

The conference lasted from Chicago to just beyond Toledo, Ohio. Luis and General Paradiz discussed the likely scenarios as they foresaw them, along with the options I'd have for each. I found the procedure upsetting because we were, in effect, completely helpless. We didn't know exactly what had happened; we could only wait for new information, and, in the meantime, prepare for the worst.

After the meeting I went back to my seat. The First Daughter was worried, so I gave her a quick summary of what I knew. She was as surprised as I to learn there was a psychic adviser aboard. "But that's *great*,

Daddy!" she said. "The one thing you're short of now is like *information,* right? So, okay, like this Master Hsu could maybe see things in the cards that won't get reported for *hours* yet."

"The difference between us," I said, "is that you like playing with your tarot cards and your Ouija board and your astrology charts. I'm the President of the United States. I have to base my decisions on more scientific sources. Tarot cards are imprecise, bewildering, and completely nonlogical. That puts them squarely in the Legislative branch, not the Executive."

"Daddy, give him a chance.

"Sweetheart, in your own words, *as if*!"

"Daddy!"

The look of concern on her face was genuine. She was probably afraid I'd make some horrible mistake and go down in history as the worst president of all time. "All right," I said. "I'll have him come over here." I thought if Master Hsu could keep her entertained for half an hour—and take her mind off her anxiety—it would be worth putting up with a little mystical nonsense.

I signaled to Colonel McNeill. "Tell that psychic adviser to join me."

Something flickered in McNeill's eyes; it may have been amusement. "Yes, sir," he said.

He brought Master Hsu, and then McNeill left us alone. The old man bowed again. "Mr. President, sir," he said.

"I don't know if you've met my daughter."

"Mr. President, sir," Master Hsu said, "may I speak of security matters in front of the young lady?"

I shrugged. "Right now, she knows as much as I do about what's happening in Breulandy."

Master Hsu smiled briefly. "In a few minutes the three of us will know much more."

He sat down across from me. On his lap was a small

box made of polished dark wood—the puck, I guessed. He opened it, looked inside, and his expression changed. "Ah," was all he said.

"Is something wrong?"

"My cards," he said, looking up at me. "They're not in the box where they belong. I don't know why."

"My daughter spoke up. "That's cool, 'cause I've got my cards with me."

"I prefer to use my own deck," said Master Hsu.

"You *wish*! But your deck is probably back in Washington, right?"

He looked very unhappy. "Yes. I suppose we'll have to wait."

"Uh-huh," my daughter said, "but the whole *point* is you're supposed to be giving my Dad some advantage from, you know, the *psychic* world. If he has to kill time until we get home again, then you're not being very much help, are you?"

"That's true, young lady."

"So why not use my cards?"

He blinked a couple of times. "All right, I'll use them."

"Great!" She reached under her seat for her backpack, and rummaged around in it for a while. Finally, she pulled out a pink-and-purple cardboard box. "Here you go," she said, handing it to Master Hsu.

He opened the box and slid out the cards, glancing at a few of them. "What are these?" he asked.

"My deck," the First Daughter said. "Well, I guess some of the cards look different to you. It's the Barbie tarot."

Master Hsu stared in disbelief at one of the cards. "Barbie?"

"Here, see that card you've got? Handbags are the suit of love and romance and stuff."

"Handbags?" Master Hsu looked by turns horrified and offended.

"Look at the *card,* okay? In the picture, Barbie's checking out this shop window, and there's all these handbags: blue ones, black ones, a green one, a yellow one, and a clear plastic one with scrunched-up newspapers in it, right? So this is *The Point of No Return,* where you've come down so far from the Spiritual World that you can't get out of the Material World and go back up. It's a decision card, on account of Barbie's got to make a choice. So okay, one of the handbags is the *obvious* one, right? But it really *isn't,* not if you're looking real close. See the silver clasp on the clear handbag? It just won't go with her gold-tone earrings and necklace and stuff. The bird on her shoulder is supposed to be this great knowledge coming from somewhere, but the bird on the sidewalk pecking at the crumbs could be advice coming from some *really faux* person, so like there's a warning to be careful. Hint, hint."

For a few seconds, the loudest sound I could hear was the whoosh of the air nozzle above my head. Then the old man slowly reached out and gave the cards back to the First Daughter. "These are not tarot," he said.

"Tcha! I guess they *are*! You just have to learn how to read them. There are like *hundreds* of different decks around, okay?"

"Yes," said Master Hsu, "and most of them are false friends."

"Oh, *right*," my daughter said. "So it's like you've got this real truth that nobody else knows, huh?"

It was time to stop her, so I reached over and squeezed her shoulder; that was the signal. She glanced at me for a few seconds—you've seen that look they get, they *know* they've met you somewhere before—and then she nodded. "Sorry, Daddy. Maybe that school in Switzerland will teach me to keep my mouth shut some of the time."

As I mentioned before, she's a great kid. "Master Hsu," I said, "what do we do first?"

"If I had my deck, I'd do a reading. The cards would indicate how you should proceed, whether to begin negotiations or use more forceful means. There'd also be information about the people involved in this situation."

"A lot of lives are at stake," I said. "Some people may already have died. I'd like to have that information, if it can be trusted."

Master Hsu's expression didn't change. "It's synchronicity, Mr. President, sir," he said. "We are of the moment, the crisis in Breulandy is of the moment, the way the cards are dealt—that, too, is of the moment. At this time, in this place, the cards can be arranged in only one way. That gives the reading its significance."

"Yes, but—"

He'd been through all this before with other doubters. "Doing the reading changes the moment, so another reading won't produce the same results. Sometimes it's a sign of bad faith to continue." He showed his brief smile again. "The cards have chewed me out plenty over the years."

I liked him. "Why the tarot?" I asked. "Why not the I Ching?"

He spread his hands a little. "Why does one person follow shotokan karate and another practice kendo?"

"Will you do a reading? With my daughter's cards?"

"I don't like them, Mr. President, sir, but if you want me to go ahead, I'll try."

"Please," I said.

Master Hsu looked through the cards for a moment, then gave up with a sigh. "Young lady," he said, "which one of these is the King of Swords?"

"The King of Swords—that's, um, the King of Shoes. I'll find him." She took the deck and searched

through it quickly. "Here he is. Brad, Christie's boyfriend. The kings are all boyfriends of Barbie's
girlfriends."

Master Hsu took the card as if it were his own death
warrant. He put it down on the table between us. Brad
was a handsome young black man. I'd never thought
about black Barbie characters before; many people
haven't.

"Brad's my Dad's card?" she asked. "I don't usually—"

Master Hsu cut her off with a gesture. "Mr. President,
sir, please shuffle the deck and form your question. You
don't have to ask it out loud, you can just concentrate
on it if you like. It's important to be clear and simple.
The tarot may not reply to what you think you've
asked. I mean, sir, the cards will be truthful, but they
may respond to something else in your mind or heart,
something personal and not political."

In law school they called that an elastic clause. It
covered and absolved just about everything. I took the
deck and started to shuffle. "Tell me about the crisis
in Breulandy," I said.

"Now, with your left hand, cut the deck into three
piles and put it together again in a different order."

I did that and gave him back the cards. "This covers
you," he murmured, laying the Nine of Handbags over
Brad. The card showed a plump and happy man surrounded by nine bulging purses. Master Hsu paused.
"Handbags are Cups?" he asked my daughter.

"Uh-huh," she said.

His eyebrows raised a little. "It's a good card to
start with, Mr. President, sir. You're going to get
your wish."

"I didn't wish for anything."

"Yes, you did."

"This is about Breulandy, not me."

Master Hsu shrugged. "Let me finish and we'll see."

He laid another card on Brad and the Nine of Handbags, but turned ninety degrees. "This crosses you," he said; the card was Barbie's pink Classy Corvette. There were eight more cards in the layout: beneath me was Great Shape Barbie, in leotard and leg-warmers; behind me was the Barbie Queen of the Prom boardgame; crowning me was Barbie's Little Sister Stacie; before me was the Five of Shoes; my fears were Malibu Barbie; my environment was the original #850 Ponytail Barbie, blonde, in black-and-white striped swimsuit, NRFB (Never Removed From Box); my hopes were the Three of Handbags; and the final outcome was the Barbie Dream House.

"Mr. President, sir, I don't know what to say."

"Is it bad?" I asked.

Master Hsu shook his head. "No, I mean I don't know what to say. I don't know what most of these cards are."

"I can sort of translate," said the First Daughter.

"I'd appreciate that," he said.

"So okay, Brad and the Nine of Handbags you know. The Corvette is the Chariot. Great Shape Barbie is Strength, and the Barbie game is the Wheel of Fortune. Stacie is the Page of Pentacles. The Five of Shoes is the Five of Swords. Malibu Barbie is the High Priestess, and the original Barbie is the Fool. The Three of Handbags is the Three of Cups, and the Barbie Dream House is the Tower. Got it?"

Master Hsu gave a little shudder. "Well, Mr. President, sir, the first thing I notice is five cards out of ten are Major Arcana. That's unusual and makes for a dramatic reading. Strength and the Wheel of Fortune are good cards, but they're not drawing my attention; neither is the Chariot, although it's a victory card. The Fool and the High Priestess are esoteric but not threatening. Generally speaking, it's a very good layout. Nine of the ten cards range from neutral to great success. Only the last card troubles me."

If he was troubled, so was I. "What does it mean?" I asked.

"If this were my deck, sir, you'd see for yourself. I don't know what the Barbie Dream House is, but in most tarot decks the Tower has been blasted by a lightning bolt, and two people are falling from it into an abyss. It's a card that can mean catastrophe, but not always. It's frightening, but like the Death card it can mean change in a good sense. I think the nine hopeful cards outweigh the Tower, especially the card just before it in the layout, the Three of Cups or Handbags, which often indicates a happy ending."

I don't know what made me think of it, but I wondered what the Washington *Post* would say if they knew I'd replaced the State Department with seventy-eight pieces of cardboard. I took my glasses off and rubbed the bridge of my nose, hoping Colonel McNeill would interrupt soon with some news from Breulandy—good news or bad news, I didn't care.

Master Hsu coughed. It was meant as a question.

I waved at him. "I'm fine," I said. "I'm just a little tired." At the conference table, General Paradiz, Luis, and a couple of the others were playing *Risk*.

My daughter squeezed my shoulder. That was our signal again, coming back at me. "Master Hsu," I said, "would you excuse us for a moment?"

"Certainly, Mr. President, sir." He got up carefully without disturbing the cards and moved toward the front of the plane.

"Daddy, remember the bird on the sidewalk?"

"No, I don't. What are you talking about?"

She heaved the sigh that kids use when they're absolutely disgusted with everything you stand for. "Hellooo? The Five of Handbags, Daddy, okay? The two birds, one of them was like warning you about *this very thing*?"

"I'm sorry," I said. "I'm thinking about hostages with their hands tied behind their backs, and you're talking Barbie cards. We're not on the same wavelength here."

She did the sigh again, this time adding a tongue click. "But like we totally *are*! So, okay, I'm *telling* you, he's wrong about the tarot layout. Things are lots worse than he thinks."

I opened my mouth to argue with her, but I didn't. Fifteen minutes ago, the very idea of a Presidential Psychic Adviser had been just absurd. Now I was about to take the man's side against my own daughter. What did I know?

Nothing. That was part of the problem. The other part of the problem was that I didn't know how much Master Hsu knew either.

"What do you think?" I asked.

"I think he's an okay guy, but like he's *so* wrong. Have him do another reading."

"But he said it wouldn't turn out the same—"

"Ask a different question."

Page One of my screenplay: Interior, Oval Office, Day. JFK is sitting behind the big desk with Caroline on his knee. Pierre Salinger or somebody is just leaving and closes the door behind him.

Caroline: Daddy, call Mr. Khrushchev and tell him you know he's bluffing.

JFK: (worried) I don't know he's bluffing. We could end up in a nuclear war because of what he's doing in Cuba. (He pronounces it "Cuber.")

Caroline: Trust me, Daddy, he's bluffing. My Magic 8-Ball told me.

I see myself in the role of JFK, and I'd like to get Mira Sorvino for Caroline. Maybe it needs a little work. I'll get back to you.

I felt the aircraft start a slow turn to the right, so I guessed we'd run out of continent. Far down below was Philadelphia, a city I've always found dreary. It's not politic for a President to say things like that about a major city; the truth is that Philadelphia *isn't* dull, it just seems that way because it's across the river from glamorous, exciting Camden, New Jersey.

All right, I'd given myself a couple of minutes to calm down; now it was time to get back on the job. I signaled Master Hsu to join us again.

"Mr. President, sir?" he said.

I glanced quickly at the First Daughter; she nodded. "I'd like you to do another reading."

"Yes, sir." He found the Brad card and put it on the table, then handed the rest of the deck to me. "Please shuffle again and form another query."

My daughter and I hadn't talked about the second question, but I had an intuition. I asked, "Who's in charge in Breulandy?"

"This covers you," said Master Hsu in a low voice; he put the Three of Handbags over Brad. His eyes flicked up at me; that was the same happy-ending card he'd been so glad to see in the previous spread. "This crosses you," he said, and damn! if he didn't lay down the Barbie Dream House.

"Son of a bitch," I muttered.

"It still might not predict a calamity, Mr. President, sir. The card's reversed, and that could mean winning freedom for the hostages after a great struggle."

My daughter squeezed my shoulder. I just held my breath and waited to see what came next.

"This is beneath you." It was a card named Allan.

"The Emperor," my daughter said. "Allan is Midge's boyfriend."

Behind me was the Ten of Earrings; crowning me was the Nine of Shoes; before me was the Seven of Hairbrushes; my fears were the Eight of Earrings; my environment was the Ten of Hairbrushes; my hopes were Great Shape Barbie; and the final outcome was the Four of Shoes.

"Only three Major Trumps," said Master Hsu. "There's a very different feeling to this reading."

"Explain it to me," I said.

Master Hsu hesitated. "Keep in mind, sir, that these cards speak of what's happening in Breulandy. I don't believe any of them refer to you personally. The Three of Handbags still points to a successful conclusion, although the card that crosses you warns it may cost a lot, one way or another. Allan is a worldly ruler; let your intellect control your emotions in this situation. Some of the other cards support this, especially the Seven of Hairbrushes, a lone man holding off a number of enemies—grace under pressure, as Hemingway put it. The Ten of Hairbrushes shows someone who's bitten off more than he can chew; that could be you, or it could be the leaders of either side in Breulandy. Great Shape Barbie means the same as it did in the first reading: patience and perseverance. The final result card, the Four of Shoes, is ambiguous; it usually promises important insights after some creative meditation."

"Daddy—"

Colonel McNeill interrupted her. "Mr. President," he said, "we've established a telephone link to our embassy in Breulandy."

That snapped me right back to reality. "Good," I said. "Who do you have there?"

"The Breulen prime minister."

I hadn't heard the latest news yet, but it felt good just to have some movement. "I want a conference call with him and the rebels' head guy."

"We're trying, Mr. President."

"And I want you to get me Jimmy Carter on another line. He had to deal with the first big hostage situation."

The First Daughter grabbed my arm. "It's *real* important—"

"Sweetheart," I said, "I've stopped caring what the tarot says."

Master Hsu frowned. "That's a mistake, Mr. President, sir," he said.

I stood up. "It's the nature of advisers to contradict each other," I said.

I started to move out into the aisle. "Daddy, do you trust me?"

The unfamiliar urgency in her voice made me stop and turn around. "Of course I do."

"Then like it's *totally* a bad idea to do the conference now. You should talk with the prime minister first, and then you should talk with the rebels."

"Why?" Just hearing her opinion, I was giving my teenage daughter a cabinet-level position.

" 'Cause." I *hate* that explanation. " 'Cause Master Hsu's never even *seen* the Barbie tarot before, so like there's no *brainstorm* every time he looks at a card. No offense, Master Hsu."

"There's truth in that," he admitted.

I paused and shook my head. "Thanks, honey," I said, "but we'll be all right."

"No, we *won't*!" she cried. Everyone at the conference table turned to stare. "He's absolutely *wrong* about the Barbie Dream House, okay? It *is* a disaster. I saw it from the first card he turned—it's like the whole world in glowing *ruins* or something!"

What could I tell her? Anything I'd say would be the equivalent of "there, there." And "there, there" isn't much consolation in the middle of a shooting war. Still, I had some of the best minds in the country with me on Air Force One, and I had to trust their judgment over my daughter and Master Hsu.

I took five steps and stopped. "You think so?" I asked her.

"Daddy," she said with tears on her cheeks, "it couldn't be worse if you had ten Low-Fat Diet cards in the layout."

My heart beat maybe six or seven times; I suppose that counted as a period of creative meditation. "Colonel McNeill," I said, "cancel that conference call, but keep the prime minister on the line, I'll be with him in a minute. Keep trying to find Jimmy Carter, too."

"But, sir—" said the colonel.

"Just do what I said. Master Hsu, please stay right there. I may need to consult you again."

He bowed his head. "If you do, Mr. President, sir, I will be guided by the young lady."

"Thank you. Tell me one last thing: where do you study to become a tarot master?"

He looked puzzled. "I'm not a master. That's my name. My mother named me Master."

"Oh." That's all I said.

What happened in Breulandy over the next few months is on record in the Washington *Post* and *Time* magazine. This is the first time the tarot has been mentioned, though, because I never told anyone all the reasons for my decisions. No one else knew what happened between Master Hsu, myself, and the First Daughter. I think it's time they both got a little credit. Especially my kid.

Days later, back home in the White House, I told her she deserved a reward. "What would you like?" I asked.

She pretended to think it over. "So okay, like those famous movie Barbies?"

She owned some of the special collectors' Barbies and Kens, the ones packaged in costumes from *Gone With the Wind, My Fair Lady,* and *The Wizard of Oz.* They cost seventy-five dollars each, but they're very handsome dolls—except the Rhett Butler Ken, which is an abomination in the eyes of the Lord. "Uh-huh," I said, hearing the charges chiming on my Visa card.

"Well, buy me the *Pulp Fiction* series: Foot Massage Barbie and Ken, Pumpkin and Honey Bunny Barbie and Ken, Hypodermic in the Heart Barbie and Ken—"

I believe I went mostly ballistic. "You're *kidding*!"

"Gotcha!" She grinned at me.

Talk about striking down with furious anger. . . .

THE GATES OF JORIUN
by Kate Elliott

Kate Elliott is the author of *Jaran, An Earthly Crown, His Conquering Sword, The Law of Becoming,* and *King's Dragon,* among other novels. In collaboration with Jennifer Roberson and Melanie Rawn, she is the author of *The Golden Key.* Her infrequent short stories can be found in the anthologies *Weird Tales From Shakespeare, Return to Avalon, Enchanted Forests,* and *The Shimmering Door.* She lives with her husband and three children in Pennsylvania.

In "The Gates of Joriun," the tarot helps an imprisoned woman retain her sanity—and hope.

The magicians say the sun rises every morning, and so far I have found that to be true. I depend on the sun; it is how I mark time, by that and by the food the woman brings me twice daily and by the unending cycle of the moon. I have discovered also that the stars move in the sky each night—when they are not obscured by clouds—and that I can trace pictures in them and see those pictures again and again if only I am patient enough at night and through the seasons. I try to sleep during the day, except for the food. During the day it is worst, for then there are people about and all of them eager to abuse me.

The magicians taught about the stars also, but I did not listen to them about those matters. I was a younger woman—how much younger I no longer know—and newly married. My nights did not involve gazing at stars. Now some of what they said has come back to me and I hoard it. I must hoard what scraps I can because as the days run one into the next, I lose more and more of my past; like the moon my memory waxes and wanes.

But I must remember. If I do not remember, then I become nothing, a mindless animal in a cage hung before the gates of Joriun, and then the king wins and my brother loses.

I remember the magicians.

Duncan was gone, ridden out to raise the Alarn clan behind the standard of war. Anyone would have noticed their entrance, but that day, distracted and feeling sorry for myself because my husband of but one month had been sent away on my brother's errand, I was overwhelmed by it.

They entered like moonlight and sunlight and the twilight between.

The first wore a robe of silver fabric so pale that at first I thought I could see through it. Only later did I realize I could see into it, like staring into the heavens at night. Small of stature, no bigger than a woman, he had neat hands, eyes the bleached color of the noonday sky washed in clouds, and a nose too big for his face. But he had power. It rode on him like a second garment.

The woman towered above the others. As big as a warrior and thicker through the middle, she had skin the color of charcoal, burned black, and robes so voluminous and of such a startlingly piercing gold that she seemed like the billowing sun fallen down to Earth, scorching and bright. I almost could not look at her straight on.

But the third entered in their shadow, like a shadow, and this one's gaze sought and found me my own shadowed corner where I spun wool to thr

and waited for my husband to return. Is that not the
lot of women: to wait?

The third waited until I stared, and then beckoned
to me while my brother and his advisers were busy
with the first two magicians, swarming round them as
moths swarm round any bright light—and these lights
brighter than most. King in name only, half his coun-
trymen in league with the usurper and the other half
too poor to do more than scrabble at the dirt of their
farms to save themselves and their kin from starvation,
my brother needed help wheresoever he could find it.
Even from magicians.

I set down my spindle to rise and cross the long hall.
Closer now, I shook off my distraction and studied the
visitors: the small moon man, the big sun woman, and
the other, the third, the twilight between.

Not tall, not short, this one wore robes that were
neither striped yet not of a solid color either, a dusky
gray that held night in it and also the coming of morning. Long-fingered hands cupped a deck of cards as
another might cup a fistful of gold rings or a child's
hand. But it was her face I returned to again and
again. Or perhaps I should say his face. Beardless, I
might have guessed at once that this was a woman,
but upon a second look, despite the lack of beard, I
would have said it was a man. His—her—complexion
was like to that of a lover seen in half-light as day
fades or night lightens.

"You are the sister," he said, her voice so soft I
could barely hear it above the ring of voices in the
hall, my brother and his captains, lords and fighting
men whose loyalty to the rightful heir was greater than
their prudence, for certainly our uncle the king had
usurped my brother's throne because he had the
strength and the riches of the southern lords to back
him up. Our uncle the king was not a foolish man,
nor did he let ambition rule over common sense. But

I was only a girl and my brother an infant in swaddling clothes when first our father died and our mother soon after, poisoned by our uncle so the rumor ran. Made regent, he found it easy enough to take over the duties and privileges of the crown outright and send the poor children—myself and my brother—away to the benighted northcountry; easy enough to put them in the care of a certain ambitious duke who would not be above seeing the two children die of a winter chill or an untimely accident.

But we were stronger than that.

"It is said," remarked the twilight mage, "that you raised your brother. That you led him through dark night and cruel winds to this castle, your safe haven protected through the years by your father's most loyal retainers. Is that true?"

"When he was old enough to walk, we escaped our keepers together," I said, and then added tartly, "though it wasn't in a winter's storm, as some say. Even as a girl I wasn't so foolish as to try such a thing. There was an old woman in the house who pitied us and it was through her offices that we survived as long as we did in the hall of the Duke of Joriun. I waited until a clear warm summer's night, and she gave us bread and cheese and water. She had arranged for a cousin to meet us at a fishing village at the coast, not more than an hour's walk away. The cousin took us north and eventually by one means and another got us to Islamay Castle. I needed only to lead us out of Joriun and out to the village. It was no great journey."

"Nevertheless," said the mage. "Your brother would never have grown to manhood without you."

"Perhaps," I said evasively. I did not like this kind of praise, though I had heard it more than once. My brother was a strong, clean, good man, if rather too fond of pretty young women, and he had to be respected for *his* strength, not for mine. That was the only way he could regain the throne stolen from him.

The mage opened his hands to display the cards. With a deft movement he flipped one over and laid it on the table between two burning candles. The card had a picture on it whose like I had never seen before: a woman, crowned and robed in a simple manner, holding a strong wooden staff in one hand.

"Queen of Staves," the mage said. "She is strong and independent and will gladly fight for that which is rightfully hers."

I snorted, having heard this kind of thing also— before Duncan laid claim to my heart, and my brother, with my approval, granted him my hand in marriage. However desperate my brother's plight, however unlikely his prospects might seem with only a handful of dirt-poor lords as his allies and for his soldiers only common-bred captains and farmers who had but one season in which to march on campaign before they had to return to their farms, there were always a few men who thought to gain my brother's ear through my—well, how shall we say it?—through my favors. I gave them short shrift and had shouted more than one out of Islamay Castle.

"And she is known sometimes to be short-tempered," the mage added with a quicksilver smile that charmed me utterly.

"It's a pretty picture," I said, reaching out to touch the card. But I hesitated before laying my finger on the thin painted card. I felt as strongly as if a voice had shouted in my ear that this was not mine to touch, not without permission.

"You may," the mage said softly. "It is you, after all."

So I did touch her. I felt the film of paint under my finger, touched her stern face and her stout stave that had a single leafing green branch growing from the upraised end.

"We call this card the Significator," the mage continued. "It signifies the person whose fortune we tell with these cards."

I laughed. "Are you going to tell my fortune?"

"Do you have a question you want answered?"

I smiled, thinking of Duncan and of long summer nights. Thinking of our greatest wish, when we whispered together and held each other tight. Was it shameful that, this time, my first thought was not for my brother and our struggle? I don't know. But I was newly wed, and Duncan was, for this summer at least, my world.

"Where will I be next year?" I asked, dreaming of Duncan holding a baby—our baby—while I sat sewing beside him, sewing, perhaps, the child's naming gown or my brother's coronation robes.

The mage's expression turned dour, like a lowering storm. "Very well." I thought the tone disapproving.

I was suddenly apprehensive. "I can ask something else."

"You have already asked," the mage said. And it is true enough, as with my brother, that some enterprises, once begun, must be played out to the bitter end. "If you will, shuffle the deck." He placed the cards in my hands and showed me how to divide them and combine them again, like lords in a dance of evasion and persuasion: Whose side will I come down on this year? When I had finished, shuffling them to her satisfaction, he took them from me again and began to lay out the cards into a strange pattern on the table.

I could not help but watch. There was a hall behind us and people milling there, but they might as well have vanished for all the attention I paid them. All *my* attention was on the cards placed so carefully, so precisely, between the two burning candles.

The first card he laid directly on top of the Queen of Staves. "Placed atop the Significator, it represents the current situation. The Four of Staves," he smiled slightly as he spoke the words, "represents marriage. It is crossed by—"

"Crossed by?"

"Crossed by," he repeated placing a card athwart it, "the King of Swords."

"My uncle," I breathed, for although the card did not portray my uncle's actual face it did indeed represent his aspect: a robed and crowned king, stern of face, armed with a sword.

The king's position was unassailable. Many people said so. Those people had no doubt predicted my brother and I would be dead within the year eighteen years ago when our father and mother died. We had proved them wrong.

The mage continued. "At the base of matters, the Ace of Swords, the beginnings of conflict. What is passing away, the Two of Cups, happiness in romance."

I caught in a laugh, not wanting to show him open disrespect—as if what Duncan and I shared could ever pass away.

"What crowns the matter, how the situation appears now, the Nine of Staves . . . a pause in the midst of battle. What is coming into being, the Three of Swords. Heartbreak."

Now, and only now, the mage paused. He hesitated, and I was suddenly afraid. I felt the crawl of the evil eye on my back even as I heard laughter in the hall behind me. The candles burned evenly. The mage turned a gentle eye to me and smiled sadly. "I must go on," she said, "for once begun, a reading must be ended. That is the way of life itself."

"Of course," I said, refusing to surrender to this sudden crawling fear. "Go on." I would not give in to my weakness. Everyone knew that fortunetelling is for the superstitious and gullible, even in such a guise as this, for he asked no coin of me nor nothing in trade, and they say that is the sign of a true magician.

He laid a card to the right of the cross he had made of the others. "This card represents you," she said, "your inner being. Strength." The card depicted a woman, unafraid, holding a lion. "This next card represents what influences you: the Knight of Swords." A fierce and determined knight rode forward into the fray. "Is this your husband?"

"No," I said wonderingly, not knowing how I knew. "That is my brother."

"Ah," said the mage, and turned another card. "Your wishes and fears. The Hanged Man." I shuddered when he spoke those three words, for our uncle had promised us hanging, an outlaw's death, should he ever catch us. He hated us that much for living and surviving and daring to contest what he had gained through treachery. But this hanged man was not a gruesome sight. He hung upside down with the rope around his ankle, and he seemed utterly calm, a light of wisdom shining behind his head. "The Hanged Man represents waiting," said the mage. "Suspension. And the last card lies here, above and to the right of all else. It signifies the outcome."

"The outcome of what?"

"Of your question: 'Where will I be next year?' " He turned it over slowly and I watched, staring, breath held in. His whisper coincided with my hissed breath. "Eight of Swords."

Eight swords stuck point first into the ground and between them, bound by their sharp steel, stood a woman shackled by ropes.

"Mary!" The voice from the other side of the hall startled me out of my shocked contemplation of the horrible card. My brother's voice rang out, strong and true, as he was strong and true, the rightful heir. "You must come and meet our guests."

Mary. That is my name. I remember it now. The folk who come in and out of the gates of Joriun, about their business, on their way to and from the fields or the market, shout it sometimes, but as a curse. *"Mary,"* they shout. *"Hang that whore Mary."* They call me slut and traitor, bastard and demon, apostate, heretic, cunt, and witch. They shouted it more often at first, when the Duke of Joriun's men built and barred this cage and locked me inside it and winched it up to hang, suspended by rope and supported by wooden pillars, beside the central gates that lead into the town and castle of Joriun. They came in packs, in mobs, to jeer at me, and then I was thankful I hung so high above them. Few of them had strong enough arms that the rotting vegetables, the shit, the dirt, and the hail of wood shavings and nails and stones they threw actually hit me. They would have ripped me to pieces had I come within reach of their hands.

War has been hard on the people who live in Joriun. Some of them are refugees from the north. Perhaps a few pity me. I will never know. I never hear those voices.

Now only a few remember my name, or only a few bother to pause and curse me. They are used to me here. But maybe that is worse. I forget my name sometimes for days on end. They don't remind me of it anymore. I cannot turn their hate into strength for myself, living on it as a dog laps water on a hot day, if they do not remember to hate me.

Even the woman who brings me my porridge each day no longer bothers to spit in it before she hands it over to me.

How many years I have been imprisoned here, in this prison hung out like a songbird's cage? The bars are weathering and gray, the bench on which I sleep, swaying in the night wind, cracked and splintered. Gaps in the floorboards show the ground, littered with my refuse and the refuse thrown at me, far below. Too far to jump, even if I could pry open the locked door that abuts the parapet, even if I could break apart the thick bars. Perhaps it would be better to jump and be done with it.

A songbird is treated gently for the song it may sing for its master. I know the song they wish me to sing for all to see.

God help me. Let me not descend into madness.

Let me not weaken. It is so hard.

How many years? One year? Two? Five? I see my hands are weathered, though whether from age or exposure I do not know. I see my nails grow long; filthy and cracked, they curl at the ends. I break them off when they get in the way of eating, of caring for myself such as I can.

I do not know how many years it has been. The woman who brings my food is my only mirror, and she is a new woman every season so I cannot track my days by watching her age. She never ages, because she is always young. I have no knowledge by which to track the time except the round of stars and the procession of spring into summer, summer into winter, and winter into spring. Three winters I think I have been here, but perhaps it is four. I hang in limbo, suspended in this cage, this purgatory.

How fares my brother?

I pray you, God, watch over him and over my husband.

The watchmen tell me sometimes my brother is dead. They taunt me with it, his death, his dead body eaten by crows. I do not believe them. I cannot believe them. They must be lying.

But I don't know. I know nothing but the opening

of the gates at dawn and their closing at dusk. I know nothing except that the sun rises every morning without fail and that night comes and passes and comes again.

I must not believe them.

Today I hear a horn. At dawn the gates open. This activity I watch each morning, the opening of the gates below; it is one of my talismans. By this means I remember I am alive.

Today no farmers march out to their fields. No peddlers scurry out with bundles on their back; no carts or wagons roll out onto the morning road.

They come instead, the lords and knights and ladies of Joriun Castle, in their bright procession, their fine clothing so painful that I shade my eyes, for I am dressed now in rags though once this gown was what any decent woman would be proud to wear in her brother's hall, entertaining guests, coaxing reluctant allies to throw in their lot with his desperate cause.

The noble folk of Joriun Castle, no greater in rank than I, flood forth in their brilliant procession. They are off to hunt, I think, for they have hounds aplenty romping beside them or taut under leash and their horses are caparisoned as for a gala festival.

They are not alone.

They are led by their master, the young Duke of Joriun. He is, I see, not yet an old man, so must I be not yet an old woman. The master of Joriun and I were of an age once, and I suppose we remain so now although he walks in freedom and I wait, hanging, in this prison.

My lips are unused to smiling. I feel them crack as the corners turn up as I remember what everyone said: his father, the old Duke, died of apoplexy the night after my brother and I escaped from this castle.

How the son hates me, even after so many years.

He looks up though the others ignore me. I am no

longer of interest to them, I am ugly and dirty and
mad and lost and sometimes it seems I am a hundred
years old, but he never neglects to look up. He always
marks me on his comings and goings. He looks, and
he *smiles,* in answer to my smile.

I remember his smile.

The magicians stayed for an entire month while we
wined them and dined them better than we ate ourselves and then they went away. But they left behind
them promises, or so my brother said. I asked him
how one can hold a promise and suggested he would
have been better off asking for a wagonload of spears
and a herd of cattle.

He laughed and agreed. Of course, you see, I could
never be angry with him because he always agreed
with me. That he then went and did as he wished
made no difference to his amiability.

When Duncan rode in empty-handed from the Alarn
clan, my brother decided then and there to journey to
Alarn himself. It is true he needed the Alarn clan to
swell his army, such as it was. He needed their support. He needed the support of every ancient lord and
old retainer who had once sworn fealty to our father,
especially the ill-tempered and independent lords of
the craggy northcountry highlands. If you have not
the riches of the south, then you need the rock-hard
stubbornness of the north. Gold is not harder than
granite.

It was a difficult road into Alarn country. The paths
were the known haunts of bandits. So, despite my irri-
table objections, the ladies were left behind. Even
Duncan protested that it might be too difficult for
women, though he truly did not want to leave me. His
mother and young sister were among the ladies who
lived now for part of the year in Islamay Castle and

for the rest moved to other estates with my brother or some group of his adherents.

"Of course *you* could make the journey, Mary," said my brother sweetly, "but what of the others? What of Widow Agnes and Lady Dey? They are not strong like you. I must leave someone to watch over them."

So I remained behind. We stayed another month, we ladies—twelve of us and our servants. But as autumn laid in its bitter store of cold and the meager harvest was brought to the hearth to be measured and stored, I knew we would have to split up and move south. I sent Widow Agnes and Lady Dey and most of the other ladies to the western estate of Lord Dey, the lady's husband; it had a milder climate but was more vulnerable to raids form the south. Duncan's mother and young sister I kept by me, for I was fond of them—I knew I could love Duncan soon after I first met him not just for himself but because of the care he took of his widowed mother and his dear sister.

We rode east to the fortress of old Lord Craige, an inhospitable setting but rather safer than the valley manor of Lord Dey.

It was not a trap, precisely. It was only that I did not know that in the skirmishes that raged in the border country, Craige fortress had just fallen to the Duke of Joriun. Few riders dared the high roads alone, and it was easy to miss a fleeing messenger on the road. I did not know, as I rode into the courtyard, where peace reigned and some few men whose faces I did not recognize stared at me in surprise, that but three days earlier Lord Craige had been deposed and sent to the tower.

I did not know until they escorted me with all due respect into the hall and I faced the man who sat in the high chair.

And the young Duke of Joriun smiled *that* smile at me.

"So the woman who killed my father walks like a lamb into my hands," he said when they put the chains on my wrists and neck.

How the son hated me, even after so many years.

But like his father before him, he was ambitious. He wanted reward more than revenge, so he took me south with Duncan's mother and young sister to the court of my uncle the king.

The king had mercy on the old and the young. "Let them be placed in a convent," he said, and I was not even allowed to kiss them nor they me before they were led away.

"But you," he said, turning to look on me, "you I have promised a hanging."

"Hang me if you will," I said, smiling. "It will not alter my brother's cause, nor the outcome, for the just shall triumph and the wicked perish."

"It will give him a martyr," he muttered. He twisted the rings on his hands musingly, for he had many rings, gold encrusted with rubies and diamonds, a black opal set in silver, a ring of green malachite and one of turquoise that had once been my mother's but had failed to change color when danger loomed, as turquoise was said to do. Most impressively, the large seal ring of the king's authority half covered the knuckle of his right middle finger. He wore a houppelande sewn of brilliant blue cloth embroidered with small gold crowns, trimmed with ermine at the neck and lined with a heavy cloth of gold. The hem was beaded with pearls. The crown that rested so easily on his brow I had last seen on my father's head.

At last he stilled himself and came to some conclusion. I was not afraid of him, not then, not yet. I knew my cause was just and I knew I was stronger than he was because I was not afraid of death.

And he knew I was not afraid.

But I should have been afraid. Only a man as cunning as he could have stolen the throne and crown and scepter and husbanded it so well. He smiled oddly and crookedly and beckoned to the Duke of Joriun, calling him before the rest.

These words did the king my uncle the usurper speak.

"Hang her in a cage at the gates of Joriun so that all may see and abuse the sister of the traitor. All may see that I hold captive that which gives him strength."

How many years has it been since I was captured?
It is so cold in the winter.

I am so weary of the cold.

But it is not cold now. It is not even autumn, the season for hunting; I see by the green of the fields and the ripening fruit in the orchard beyond the moat that it is summer, the season for war.

They are not hunting at all. Here they come back, so soon, too soon. They are so cheerful, the young lovers gazing at each other, the men boasting and laughing, the women talking sternly of serious matters or giggling over light ones. I do not exist to them. I am nothing.

I am Mary.

They are no longer alone. They have gone out in such festive attire not to hunt but to greet he who has come to Joriun, ridden north at long last. No army that size has ever marched behind my brother's standard. Great clouds of dust mark their coming, and I see the king my uncle's standard at the head of the army long after I see that an army has come to Joriun.

The duke and his company ride at the head of the procession, flanking the king my uncle. I curse him—all the words I have ever heard cursed and spat at me—but he does not even look up. He does not even

seem to know I exist. He does not even glance my
way or at the cage, as if I have become invisible. As
if I no longer matter.

I must matter. I have to matter. Am I not my brother's strength? Isn't that what everyone has always
said?

The nobles enter the town and the gates close behind them. Out, beyond the walls of Joriun, the army
encamps. Their tents cover the fields like locusts.

God help me. I am so weary.

The woman brings porridge that night and this night
she remembers to spit in it first, as if the king's presence has reminded her that she must hate me. Almost
I recoil, too sickened by the gesture to eat, but then
I remember that I must eat and that her hatred is a
spice to make the bland porridge taste better, to be
more nourishing to me in my solitude.

She speaks to me, though this woman has never
spoken to me before. "His Majesty has brought the
whole army, hasn't he?" she says with a coarse grin.
"There's a big battle to be fought, isn't there, and that
will make short work of that traitor of yours."

Is that why the king my uncle did not look at me?
Does he know I am truly nothing now? That he has
pikes and swords and shields enough, soldiers enough,
armor and gold enough, to defeat my brother even
though I still live? Their campfires burn like stars
fallen to earth: I see no end to them as I stare out all
through the long long night.

Let me not weaken. Let me not fall into despair.

At dawn the gates open and the mobs come with
their curses and their stones and their shit and their
rotting meat and fruit. I cower by the bench, arms
flung up to cover my face. An ancient mildewing apple
splatters against my thigh. A stone grazes my elbow.
I have forgotten what their abuse is like. They are
themselves the hammer, beating me down. They are

themselves the hands strangling the breath out of me.
My tattered shawl cannot cover me. I have no armor.
I am weaker than I was in the beginning. I begin to
cry and, seeing that, their clamor increases. I am pep-
pered with stones, each one a nail driven into my skin.

Please, God, let this cease.

The horns call and at last the mob retreats from the
road to let the nobles pass through the gates. They
ride in their glory, the men arrayed for campaign and
the women with their false brave faces to goad on
their menfolk.

He comes, the king my uncle. He draws up his horse
below me and yet by every aspect above me. He wears
a fine white surcoat over his armor, glittering in the
sunlight, magnificent. Gold embroidery traces the symbols of crown and scepter on the surcoat; his sword is
my father's sword, the scabbard plated with gold and
the hilt fixed with jewels. He is an older man now,
silver-haired, and yet by no measure weak.

He raises his gaze to touch me, and it is worse than
the stones and all the rotten things that have ever
been thrown at me. But I must show a brave false
face. He must not sense my weakness and my despair.
I dry my tears and strangle my sobs in my throat.

He speaks.

"Mary, Mary, quite contrary," he taunts. "Are you
still there, hanging? Or is that another woman, another criminal, who hangs there in fitting punishment
for her crime?"

I say nothing. If I speak, I will betray my weakness.
He must never know.

"Do you even know your name?" he demands. "Do
you remember how to talk or who you are?" He
laughs, delighted by this prospect: that I have gone
utterly mad. Dear God, how I wish to speak sharply
to him while all can hear, for the mob and the nobles

and the army all look this way and many can hear his voice.

But I am too weak to answer. My voice will break, if I even have a voice left.

"Do you even know it has been seven years?" he says. "Your brother the traitor is married now and they say he has a girlchild whom he named Mary, but his wife will be a widow soon and the child fatherless. And you brotherless. I am going to hunt him down whether it takes a month or a year or five years. And you shall hang there, my dear niece. You will never know the outcome. That is what I have decreed, that you wait and always wonder. That will be your reward for your treason toward me."

He turns, triumphant, still laughing, and rides away. His army follows him and the clouds of dust that mark their passing are visible long into the day. My voice has vanished. It has fled, along with my reason. Oh, God. Oh, God.

Seven years.

Why fight any more? How can I go on?

How did it get to be night so soon? For it is night, or night coming on. It is twilight, the quarter moon hanging low in the sky, soon to set.

The gates are closing and the last traffic of the day quickens to gain entry before night falls. I sit slumped on the bench, staring. Just staring. Why fight any more? How can I go on? How can my brother defeat such an army? How can he defeat a king who is so rich and so cunning? Why bother to go on? I am so weary. I am mad and lost and a hundred years old. I stare at the stars above, but I see no patterns in their spray of light; I only see the campfires of my uncle's army.

Shadows stir and fragment and coalesce along the roadway. A man—or is it a woman?—emerges briefly from the shadows onto the road and, unable to pass up a last chance on this awful day to insult me, throws a big stone. It bangs against the slats and falls inside to land with a thunk on one of the splintering planks.

But it is no stone. Suddenly I sway forward and grab the thing lying there. My hand touches a small rectangular package of cloth, concealing something hard. I open it, surprised. By the dim light of the quarter moon I see what lies inside: a pack of painted cards.

I look up, but there is no trace on the roadway of that person, half glimpsed, who threw these up here. I see only shadows as twilight fades to full night.

I handle the cards for a long, long time that night, though it is too dark to see them. I feel them, I trace the film of paint on each card and I remember what each one is, for the twilight mage, in his month at my brother's hall, taught me the meaning of each card. I only learned this knowledge then to pass the time while I waited for Duncan to return. I never dreamed I would be glad, someday, to remember it all.

Near dawn, I bind them up again and tuck them into my filthy bodice. Should anyone suspect I had them, they would be taken from me.

I hoard them for seven nights as the moon waxes. I hoard them until there is light enough to see for eyes trained in darkness, as mine are now. The mobs come every day while I wait, but I think only of the cards. I do not hear their voices.

I wait until the watchmen meet and turn on the parapet below and head away from my cage before I shuffle the cards and set them down. I have already picked a Significator: The Knight of Swords.

I lay it down and ask my question: "Where will my brother be next year?" It is the only question I know how to ask.

Placed atop it, the current situation. I turn the next card over. Seven of Swords. It is hard to remember,

but here in my cage, memory is all I have. Thievery.
Something stolen. I turn another card and lay it
athwart the first two. Crossed by—I turn another
card—the Wheel. Fate. His situation is going to
change.

I pick up another card and set it down below the
first three. At the base of matters, Strength. The
woman holding the lion. Tears sting me and I brush
them back impatiently. Have I not always been
strong? Will it still, and always, be demanded of me?
Next, what is passing away. The card I turn over now
shows a heart pierced by three swords. Three of
Swords. Sorrow.

For the first time in many years—years whose count
I have lost track of—I feel hope stirring in my heart.
Hope is so painful.

The watchmen return on their round, and I must
wait in stillness while they pause, stare at the sky, hiss
a joke one to the other and laugh boisterously, then
at last spin and head back each on their separate slow
walk of the parapet.

But I am used to waiting.

What crowns the matter. When I think of crowns,
I can only think of my uncle in his crown-embroidered
houpelande, condemning me to this cage; I can only
think of my father's crown resting on the usurper's
head. I can only think of his victory and our defeat,
our escape as children into the summer's night that
led me at the last to this cage.

But memory is a strange thing, like a fish in the
shallows, darting suddenly into view when before it
was invisible to the eye. All at once I remember what
the magician said, that what crowns the matter is how
the situation appears now, what seems to be coming
in the near future but which may not be true. I turn
the card to see a man standing with his hoe, eyeing
a verdant bush now blooming with seven pentangles:

reaping the rewards of hard work. Is it for naught? Will my brother's rebellion, now more than seven years old, be fruitless?

Once begun, a reading must be ended.

I turn the next card. What is coming into being. The Hanged Man.

Almost I weep with frustration. But the magician told me that the Hanged Man represents waiting, not defeat. "Bide your time," I whisper to myself, and that voice—*my* voice—gives me the strength to go on.

Now I draw the last four cards.

First, I turn the card which represents my brother, his inner being. A man battles with a staff, six more below him. Seven of Staves: success against the odds.

What influences him. I gasp, for now, appearing in the pale light of the waxing moon on the warped plank floor before me stands the Magician.

His wishes and fears. An angel blows the horn as the dead arise: Judgment. Is judgment not all my brother ever wished for?

But I hesitate before I turn the last card, because it signifies the outcome. I wait so long, trembling, that the watchmen return on their round. One spits over the parapet as the other gossips, and then they turn about and each goes on his way before I gather enough courage to turn that card.

Only the gullible believe in fortunetellers and magicians. But I have nothing left, nothing but this. I close my eyes and turn over the card, fingering the patterns in the paint. At last I look.

The World. Utter success.

My breath comes in bursts and I feel dizzy.

God help me. Let me not fall into madness.

I slide the cards roughly together and shuffle them again, violently. I will read the cards again. I cannot trust myself, my eyes in this moonlight, my terrible hope. I saw the king my uncle ride out with his great army, and I know that as seven years passed without my knowledge, it could take another seven for this struggle to end.

I search through the pack and take out the Knight of Swords, but then I remember what the twilight magician said, that the same question must not be asked a second time on the same day. I am shaking now so hard I drop the card and almost lose it between the warping planks. A cloud covers the moon and I weep in silence—I must never let the watchmen know I weep. It is so hard. Hope is not enough to live on.

But I can ask another question. I can ask a different question.

The moon emerges at last from the clouds. The watchmen meet and move away again. I root through the cards and draw him out, the king my uncle, King of Swords—the little emperor. I place the card firmly in the center place, the Significator.

"Where will my uncle be next year?" I ask.

"Covered by." I flip a card. "The Five of Staves. Conflict." Crossing it, I set down . . . "The Knight of Swords." The whispered words are like a second voice in my ear. Surely this is no coincidence, though I shuffled the cards very very well, too well, too violently in my anger and terror and pain, bending some, chipping off a few flecks of paint on others, before this second reading.

At the base of matters, the Devil. Malevolence. What is passing away, the Emperor.

I glance at the road, visible in the moonlight, but although there are shadows nothing lurks there. No person waits, watching me read. Yet I feel his—her—gaze on me. I feel her—his—presence beside me, even though I know it is impossible. I am alone, as the king my uncle decreed.

What crowns the matter, Eight of Staves. Quick success.

What is coming into being, Seven of Cups. Illusory success.

Yet I saw him march out on that road with a huge army. I heard him, in his confidence, abuse me and promise victory for himself and death for my brother.

There are four cards left to turn. The watchmen come, and gossip, and leave. The moon rides higher in the sky, which is bleached almost gray by its light.

I turn the next card.

His inner being. A man sits with each foot on a pentangle, a pentangle resting on his head, and a fourth gripped in his arms: Four of Pentangles. The hoarder. The usurper.

What influences him. Here, now, floats a hand in the air, cupping a Pentangle, the Ace. Material wealth and success.

His wishes and fears. When I turn over the card, I stare at first, thinking I am only remembering and not actually seeing what lies before me right now. Memory, like a fish, can quickly dart out of view and leave you grasping at shadows. Then I blink. The angel with his trumpet still plays as the dead rise.

Judgment.

So, too, in this reading, does Judgment lead to the outcome.

I turn the last, the final, card to see a dead man pinned to the ground by ten swords.

"Ten of Swords," the mage taught me so long ago, seven years ago and more, I now know. "Complete and utter defeat."

I look at this card for a long time. Then, quietly, carefully, I gather up the cards, bind them in cloth, and hide them away.

Now, for the first time in seven years, I weep as loud and long as I wish. I do not care if the watchmen hear me. I do not care if they curse me, or gloat, or report to my jailers that I have, at long last, broken.

At dawn a messenger rides in at a gallop even before the gate are open. He shouts, jumps off his horse to pound at the gates, and finally they swing open and he hurries inside.

Later, I hear the sounds of celebration.

The woman who brings my porridge makes sure to spit in it first before she hands it to me. "There's come news, hasn't there?" she says, smirking. "There's been a battle and the traitor's folk have retreated up into the hills."

But I only smile, take the bowl from her, and eat the food that is spiced with hatred. The cards nestle, hidden, inside my bodice.

I will be patient. I will wait. I know the usurper is fated to fail and that my brother will triumph in the end. I can endure whatever they throw at me until the day I am freed.

That is my strength, is it not? That I will never give in. That I will never give up.

TOWER OF BRASS
by *Teresa Edgerton*

Teresa Edgerton's books include *Goblin Moon, The Gnome's Engine, The Moon and The Thorn, The Castle of The Silver Wheel,* and *The Grail and the Ring,* among others. In leaner times, she made a living giving tarot readings at festivals. She lives with her family in California.

The Tower is a card that symbolizes change. Blending a Victorian gothic sensibility with elements from Shakespeare, "Tower of Brass" examines a world so utterly and maniacally controlled, until a stranger washes up on the tower's shore, bringing with him inexorable change.

It was a sky without birds, a sea without fishes. From the top of the tower of brass, so far as Rosamund could see, there was only water and air, those two elements and a narrow strip of sand encircling the tower itself. No ship had ever appeared on the horizon. Yet sometimes, after a storm, flotsam and jetsam arrived on the beach, and whenever the waters receded, crabs and other small creatures came out of a ring of tide pools and scuttled across the beach.

Sometimes that vast blankness of sea and sky surrounding the tower preyed on Rosamund's mind. At such times, she wished for a companion her own age to beguile the weary hours. But no such companion ever appeared. On the island, there was only herself, her magician father, and the clockwork slaves.

*Iron, Silver, Tin, Copper—so the magician had
named his creations, and so they were made, automatons powered by a fiery animating fluid principle. They
were always courteous, always discreet, ever punctilious
in the performance of their duties. What thoughts, if
any, they concealed behind their polished metal faces,
Rosamund never knew, but the actions they performed
were at once more complex and more various than the
activities of the crabs and the sand fleas; in her more
fanciful moments, she believed they must be alive and
self-aware. Her father, however, always dismissed that
notion with an impatient wave of his hand, and as he
had invented them as well as created them, she supposed that he ought to know. In any case, they were
slaves, by several degrees more degraded by virtue of
their inhumanity than even the most abject human bond
servants, and what they thought, how they viewed themselves, could not truly matter to anyone, not even the
curious Rosamund.*

*Life in the tower of brass was comfortable, but te-
dious. Rosamund had only to ask for a thing and it
was provided her: gowns, slippers, jewels, wines, sweet-
meats, books, paintings. She had everything she wanted,
that is, except for the two things she was always wishing
for: a living pet, or a pretty youth or maiden to act as
her servant and friend.*

*Once, when she was still very young, her father gave
her a mischievous clockwork monkey. At first the delicate metal creature delighted her with its antics. But as
it soon became evident the monkey was even more limited than the automatons—its seemingly madcap capers,
at first so engaging, confined to a handful of tricks
endlessly repeated—Rosamund declared she was bored
after only a fortnight, and her father dissected the re-
jected pet, creating a music box and a clock out of
the parts.*

The music box stood on a shelf in Rosamund's

*chamber. It was very beautiful and intricately wrought,
and it played a number of different tunes, but sometimes—when the echoing halls of the tower of brass
seemed to ring most hollow, when she was most particularly tormented by the thought of the emptiness outside—Rosamund wished she had not been so swift to
criticize her father's gift, and that she still had the monkey to distract her thoughts instead of the music box.*

Nick awoke with a dull ache in his head and the
taste of salt in his mouth. This, and the fact that his
hair and clothes were damp and sandy, puzzled him.
His last memory—and it was a confused one—was of
a dim inner chamber crowded with furniture, and layers and layers of dust. So why did he wake now with
this dazzle of light in his eyes and an echo of crashing
waves sounding all around him?

With a groan, he levered himself up into a sitting
position. His hair brushed his shoulders, lank and drip-
ping; it seemed that he was even wetter than he had
first supposed. As his eyes adjusted to the glare, he
gradually took in his surroundings.

It was a bare cell-like chamber, like no room he
had ever seen or imagined before: walls, ceiling, floor,
all were made of polished metal, dully reflective, mag-
nifying the light of a single branched candlestick almost past bearing.

Brass, he thought incredulously, and the walls of
the room, already claustrophobically small, seemed to
press more closely around him. *By what bizarre turn
of events have I been imprisoned in a cell made of
brass?*

Seeking some means of escape, his eyes wandered
from one corner to the next, and finally located a single arched window to one side of his pallet. White
spray dashed against panes of leaded glass and there
was a roaring and a fury outside like a storm on the

ocean. *And how came I so near the sea? The house
where I was visiting* . . . (here there was a momentary
confusion, as he could not remember whose house or
why he had been staying there) . . . *I'll swear the house
was* miles *inland.*

"I feared you were dead, you looked so pale," said
a sweet, girlish voice, the source of which he could
not immediately locate. "Yet in truth, I know not how
a dead man should look, never having met one." The
voice went from confiding to considering. "Indeed,
that *might* be interesting . . . yet on the whole, I fancy
you'll prove more diverting alive than dead. You do
intend to stay that way?"

His confusion receded. A door had opened in one
wall and a young woman—surely *not* his jailer?—in a
jeweled velvet gown, had entered the cell-like
chamber.

"Why should I not intend to live?"

She gave a brittle laugh, not quite convincing. "How
should I know what you intend? I've never met a live
man either, except for my father, and you're little like
him, that I can tell you." She moved a little closer,
her wide skirts swaying awkwardly, as if she wore an
old-fashioned farthingale like his grandmother's under
her gaudily bejeweled gown.

Nick shook his head. Surely even the ancient dames
of his grandmother's day had never worn anything like
that gown, so stiff and unnatural. And she had
brushed her dark hair up off her snowy forehead, in
a style that hadn't been seen since Good Queen Bess.
She was pretty enough, Nick decided, but her un-
wieldy garments rendered her slightly ridiculous.

She moved even closer, leaned over his pallet, evi-
dently as curious about his appearance as he was
about hers. "Why do you wear your hair so long?
And why are your cheeks so smooth? By my father's
beard!—were it not for your broad shoulders and your

pitiful lack of breasts and hips, I might have mistaken you for a girl."

His eyes opened wide at this unmaidenly speech. "And why, My Lady Tongue, are *you* dressed up like an overpainted doll in a Punch and Judy show?"

Her dark eyebrows descended in a sharp line, a faint blush appeared beneath the pale skin. "It is for me to ask the questions, and for you to answer them," she said, drawing back. "I am the mistress here, and you are to be my servant. Nor should you speak to me in that saucy way, or I'll have you beaten."

He felt a rising panic, not knowing where he was or what sort of people he had fallen in with—or what kind of power they might have over him. Yet he was not the man to give over mastery without a struggle. "And how if I don't choose to be your servant?" he asked sharply.

"Then I will ask the metal slaves to throw you back into the sea," she answered, with a show of even white teeth. "Out beyond the tide-line, where the Chaos begins, and you're certain to drown."

As she turned toward the door, the white teeth flashed again. "Then you *will* be dead, and perhaps of more use then than you are now."

The magician lived near the top of the tower, in rooms littered with books and maps and alchemical apparatus. Though for his daughter's sake Magnus had furnished the lower rooms with every imaginable luxury, his own was an austere existence, for he took no delight in anything but Philosophy.

He was an inventor who derived no pleasure from his inventions; as soon as he created a thing, he was ready to cast it aside, his restless mind already eager to devise something new. Rosamund alone of all his creations—and she was the only one which had not emerged from his laboratory—continued to command

*his interest. That interest was only sporadic, and his
love for the girl, when he troubled to think of her, was
fierce, cold, and utterly selfish.*

*Greeted with the news of Nick's arrival on the tide,
and of his subsequent awakening, Magnus frowned.
For himself, he could see no better use for the boy than
to reduce his body to its component elements and fashion something new. Rosamund, however, had other
ideas.*

*"Thou hast chosen a dangerous plaything," said the
magician. "Take care, lest it grow sharp and cut thee."*

*His daughter tossed her head, for she had inherited
something of his stubborn will. " 'Tis a pretty youth,
and like to prove more entertaining than my golden
monkey. Though he is insolent now, I make no doubt
that he'll grow docile. Why should he not? He came
here like a beggar, with nothing of his own but the
clothes on his back. He'll have no choice but to earn
his bread by doing whatever I tell him."*

*Magnus shrugged. After all, the matter concerned
him not at all, except as it affected Rosamund.*

Or unless it disturbed his peaceful solitude.

*"It may be so, exactly as thou sayst," he told his
daughter. "Yet if this creature of thine should prove
recalcitrant . . . call on me."*

Nick's shoulders ached horribly and the cramp in his
fingers grew worse with every passing minute. Dangling
from a dizzying height, awkwardly suspended by some
fiendish contrivance of the magician's art between
earth and sky, he was drenched in sweat, his mouth
was dry, and his grip on the iron bar which was his
only hope of survival was not nearly so strong as it
had been earlier. Soon, he knew, his strength would
utterly fail him, there would be a long, terrifying drop,
and he would shatter his bones on the glittering sand
some fifty or sixty feet below.

Even if he could hold on, the iron bar might suddenly lose substance, simply dissolve into mist as things sometimes did on the magician's island. If that happened, Nick thought ruefully, it would be too much to hope that the earth toward which he plummeted would also lose substance at the moment of impact.

He hung for what seemed like hours, baking in the reflected sunlight radiating off the tower wall. Thirst was the worst of his torment, and the heat which struck hammerlike at his skull.

Why not simply let go? he wondered. Yes, why not allow himself to fall and end this torture? Yet something inside him continued to resist the idea, as it had resisted so much else since he first arrived on the island.

Magnus is an ingenious man . . . at least when it comes to devising punishments.

But was he a man at all? Was not the magician some figment of Nick's own imagination, the product (along with all his inventive cruelty) of a sick brain wandering in a delirium? These were but a few of the questions that continually circled in Nick's mind, even at moments like this when he had more immediate problems to occupy him. Put quite simply, this place should not exist, and rather more to the point, there was no reason that Nick could see for him to be there.

How came I to be shipwrecked when I was not aboard any ship? His last memories before waking inside the tower remained a jumble: a flight from the University, a manor house located deep in the country where a convivial circle of free spirits had gathered . . . to do what? The voice of his friend Fulke echoed faintly in his mind. *"I've finally come into my inheritance; it was a devil of a long time coming. We'll spend a month or two at Crowhaven while the fuss dies down,*

*and then it's off to London to view the Coronation and
sample the city's wicked pleasures."*

But how had any of that brought him to *this*?

A casement creaked open a yard or two in front of
him, more or less on a level with his dangling feet,
and Rosamund appeared, in one of her gaudy fantastical gowns, seated on the window ledge.

"Are you not hungry? Are you not thirsty?" Her
mocking smile made him wish more than ever that he
might reach out, take her neck between his hands, and
throttle her. "Why do you continue to be so foolish?
You've only to agree to do as I tell you, and my father
will bring you back inside the tower. Then you can
have everything you wish—food and wine and a soft
bed to lie on."

Nick ground his teeth audibly. Her question was a
good one. Why *had* he balked at such a simple order,
even knowing the likely consequences? He could tol-
erate Rosamund's infernal superiority, her whimsical
decrees, up to a point, play the part of the obedient
servant solely for the sake of peace and quiet . . . and
then something inside him would snap, some trivial
command would stir up his rebellion, and a harsh punishment, devised and administered by Magnus, would
surely follow. *But what makes me do it?* Nick wondered. The nearest he could come to an answer was
that—in whatever fever dream or illusion he was presently wandering—his only hope of regaining sanity
was to maintain what self-determination he could,
even if that determination continued to yield such di-
sastrous results.

Momentarily distracted by Rosamund's presence,
his grip relaxed for a fraction of a second, his left
hand slid off the bar. For several terrifying seconds he
dangled there one-handed, cursing under his breath.

Then, with a supreme effort and much protesting of
his weary muscles, he swung himself around, stretched

out his arm, and caught the iron bar again. But as the skin of his palm touched the sun-heated metal in this new place, he cried out in pain.

"Is it awful . . . this pain?" To his surprise, Rosamund no longer sounded spiteful. He detected genuine curiosity in her voice. "Indeed, my books tell me 'tis a dreadful thing, but you seem to desire it."

"Stand on the ledge and place one of your fingers between my teeth," he suggested, even though he knew the distance was too great, that he swung just beyond her reach. "Then you will find out."

She colored up at his insolent tone, but she actually appeared to be considering. "You mean to bite me, I suppose," she said at last. "Yet I think I'd still not know this pain of yours. Last night I thrust my hand into the flame of a candle—a thing I had never done before, believing it must harm me—and I was not burned. I do not think that I'm made as you are."

Either that, or you have been exiled on this unnatural island too long, thought Nick. It did seem at times that his own capacity to feel pain was diminishing, even at times such as this, as though his sensations, as uncomfortable as they were, were nevertheless somehow muted, less intense than they ought to be.

And perhaps that was another reason he courted the pain. To remind himself that he was not a part of this place, and to maintain a link, no matter how tenuous, with his own place, his own world.

He continued to dangle, wondering what would really happen if he did lose his grip on the iron bar and fell from this giddy height. Would he die swiftly and cleanly, or would the magician's clockwork men take him up alive and carry him back inside the tower, more of a prisoner than ever within his shattered body?

Gazing up into his flushed, determined face, Rosamund surprised him by coming to a sudden decision.

"I'll call Silver and Tin to take you down," she said, and ducked out of his sight behind the window frame.

Her voice, retreating, sounded faintly from inside the tower. "In truth, I believe you've suffered enough."

The waves of the empty ocean beat upon the shore, the tide rose and fell at regular intervals. There was no other way to mark the passage of time, because the sun never set and the moon never rose, and the storms that occasionally battered the island blew in and out at random.

In the glare of sunlight between two storms, three figures appeared on the wet sand just above the tide-line: Nick and Rosamund, walking side by side, with one of the clockwork men pacing behind.

Nick gazed out across the bright water, trying to make sense of this place where the laws of nature were suspended, where iron never rusted and brass never turned green, no matter how long you exposed them to seawater.

"What lies beyond the tide-line?" he asked Rosamund, as he had asked her so many times before.

This time, she was disposed to answer. "An invisible barrier which you cannot pass. Nothing comes ashore, nothing leaves the island, unless my father wills it."

"And beyond the barrier?"

"Chaos. Then a great Void where the emptiness itself might almost crush you. Do not think of it," she said with a shudder, and he thought he saw some fear, some deep uneasiness come and go behind her eyes.

"But beyond the Void," he persisted impatiently. "Are there other islands . . . continents?" He struggled to fit the magician's island somewhere on the map he knew, somewhere, perhaps, among the newly discovered lands. "Are we near the Bermudas? Patagonia? Virginia?"

"I know nothing of any of those places," said Rosamund. "In truth, I wonder if they even exist. They don't appear in any of my books, and my father would never neglect my education."

No, Nick thought, Magnus would not—*had* not neglected his daughter's education. In Poetry, Religion, Mathematics, and Magic, Nick had never met a woman so thoroughly educated. But in History, Geography, and Natural Philosophy he had discovered some curious gaps in her knowledge, as though that knowledge, complete up to a point, was many, many years out of date. She knew nothing, for instance, of Oliver Cromwell or of the new King so recently restored.

And she was given to quaint speeches, which reminded Nick of his older relations—although that might only be the result of living alone with her father.

"But you know of England, France, Spain. . . ."

"I was born in England," she said. "But of that place and how I lived there I remember nothing. My father tells me that he owned a great house, that he was a great man whom many admired, yet there were jealousies, politics . . . danger. He knew of this island and thought we might live here, far from the schemes of envious men. And so, by his art, we made safe passage through the Chaos and the Void."

Nick strained to remember what Fulke had told him about the house at Crowhaven. *"A distant uncle of mine . . . a man rumored to be fearfully acquainted with the blackest arts. Some talk there was of a warrant for his arrest, but certain powerful men grew impatient waiting for the wheels of justice to grind to their conclusion. They say there were attempts on his life. Then the magician . . . simply disappeared . . . along with his infant daughter, a little maid of three or four summers. The lawyers and the courts have been arguing all of this time how to dispose of the property, but the house is mine now."*

Nick wished that he could remember more, more about his own visit to Crowhaven, but it only came back to him in jagged fragments. *Too much drinking and debauchery—what fools we were!* he thought, for it seemed to him that many days or weeks had passed in a blur of drunken revelry. And then there had been a night when he and his friends had penetrated into the magician's inner sanctum, a room which had been locked and the door boarded over for many years. They had discovered—what?

A series of bright images like playing cards danced in his brain. There *had* been cards, he suddenly remembered, but not the ordinary kind, with Kings and Queens and Knaves. These had been painted with bizarre pictures: a wheel, a pagan temple, a tower . . . but there the memory faded.

"There must be something out there," he said to Rosamund. He shaded his eyes with one hand as he gazed out across the watery expanse. "There must be ships. Else why should things wash ashore—canvas and spars and bales—as they sometimes do?"

"My father makes storms in order to draw these things to him," said Rosamund. "Where they come from I cannot guess. Yet without this matter there'd be nothing here but the tower and the sand. All else that we require or wish for—food, drink, raiment—he transmutes by his art out of the flotsam and jetsam."

Storm clouds were gathering on the horizon as they turned back toward the tower, ascended the gentle slope of the beach, and crossed the sand just below the gates of brass.

Suddenly, the earth lost substance under Nick's feet; mist and void boiled beneath him. He felt an unreasoning panic take hold of him, his stomach knotted

queasily, though he knew from experience that he
would not fall—there was nowhere for him to fall.

Then Rosamund's hand reached out and pulled him
toward solid ground. "Do not think of it," she said.
" 'Tis an ill thing for you to think of, and you're better
not to do so."

Nick swallowed hard and nodded his agreement. Of
all the queer things he had seen and experienced on
the island, only this one made his limbs go weak and
his mind grow sick.

Released from his latest punishment, Nick found
that the endless day moved with agonizing slowness.
Almost, he could have yielded to Rosamund's wishes,
if only to pass the time.

On a sudden impulse, he went in search of her.
Much to his surprise, he found her weeping, kneeling
disconsolate in a welter of whale-boned petticoats and
stiff brocade skirts, on the Persian carpet in the center
of her bedchamber. Curiously moved by her distress—
for all the distress she had caused him—he dropped
to his knees beside her.

Rosamund looked up, her dark lashes wet with
tears. "Teach me to feel as you do," she begged him.
"I care not whether it be pain or pleasure . . . for I
am dead and would be alive."

Nick shook his head uncomprehendingly. "You
must feel something . . . some pleasurable sensations,"
he said. "You eat, you drink. You must smell the food
on your plate, taste the wine in your cup."

Rosamund continued to weep. "I eat because it is
my habit to do so; I drink for the same reason. Once,
it seems to me, there was a savor to the meat, a perfume in the wine, but that was long ago."

Nick took her hand and held it to his cheek. Her
fingers moved tentatively across his face.

"What do you feel now?"

She did not answer immediately. "The heat of your skin, the prickles of your beard," she said at last. "But when I touch my own face, it is as cold and insubstantial as mist."

Moving their joined hands from his face to hers, he made the experiment. "You lie," he said quietly. "Your skin is soft but warm to the touch. Put by this play-acting, Rosamund, it does not become you."

He might have said more, but the creak of a door, either opening or closing, drew his attention. He glanced back over his shoulder, just in time to catch a brief glimpse of a stern white face, the retreating edge of a dark velvet cloak.

Magnus, thought Nick. *And perhaps not best pleased to see his daughter on such intimate footing with his would-be slave.*

In his tower laboratory, Magnus brooded. This budding friendship—and perhaps a bit more—between his beloved Rosamund and the inconvenient Nicholas displeased him mightily. Long years had Magnus and his daughter lived content on the island, but now it seemed, with the advent of Nick, that Rosamund's world had both expanded and contracted—there could be no other outcome than bitter discontent.

Magnus scowled as he moved among his retorts and alembics. Not without good reason had he long denied Rosamund's request for a human companion; he had foreseen precisely this outcome. And yet . . . perhaps he himself was in part to blame, for populating the island so thinly. The many-legged scuttling things that lived in the tide pools were of his own creation, illusions meant to give the island an air of reality, of completeness it might have otherwise lacked, but he had created the island in haste, under pressure of circumstance, had not seen the need, then, for birds or for four-footed beasts. And weary of his own kind, he had purposely excluded human creatures.

Perhaps that had been the worst mistake of all. Had Rosamund been provided since childhood with phantom playmates, illusory suitors, she might never have craved a companion more substantial. But it was too late now to so deceive her, now that she had met with the real thing.

The magician paused in his work, struck by a sudden inspiration. At the time that he created the metallic slaves, he had mastered only the grosser elements; of late he had worked with subtler stuff. In truth, he had progressed so far that—

Once an idea took hold of his mind, Magnus never rested until his efforts were either rewarded with complete success or else failed utterly. Acting, as usual, with great decision, the magician moved toward the shelves where he kept the most esoteric volumes of his magic art. He took down a weighty tome and began to leaf through the pages.

"I'll give thee a brave new companion, Rosamund," he said aloud. "More fit for thy love than this vile, jangling boy."

At midday, which was the only time that existed on the island, Rosamund came to Nick in his tiny bedchamber under the stairs. She found him stretched out on his pallet, neither sleeping nor waking, but an uneasy somewhere in between, for the continual sunlight made him restless. It took but a word for her to rouse him.

"Nick, Nick, I have something to show you. Make haste and dress yourself and follow me."

Her tone was so urgent he never thought of disobeying her. As he was already clad in a baggy linen shirt and buff-colored breeches, he had nothing to do once he rose from his pallet but to slip into his doublet, lace it up, and put on his buckled shoes.

Curious, he followed her up the winding stairs to the upper reaches of the tower. As they ascended, their footsteps rang out on the metal steps. But just outside the door to the magician's chambers, Rosamund paused and put a cautious finger to her lips.

"Come quietly now," she whispered. "He is meditating in his bedchamber, brewing up a storm, and he'll not be easily distracted. But if we should somehow gain his attention, I dare not think of the consequences."

She opened the door slowly and slipped through, and Nick followed after her.

In the magician's laboratory, something man-sized was lying under a sheet on a long table. Rosamund, moving as quietly as possible in her jeweled high-heeled slippers, crossed the room and stripped off the covering on the table.

At first, Nick thought it was a only a corpse lying there, another unfortunate washed in by the tide, the figure was so cold and still. But as he gazed longer a chill crept down his spine. The features were so finely, so nobly molded, and the limbs were so straight and heroically proportioned, it was not to be supposed that this creature had been formed of any common clay.

"Magnus has created him," said Nick.

"Magnus has created him," echoed Rosamund, "to be my friend, my lover, my consort. I know not how long he has labored over this creature, but though it is outwardly perfect in every respect, it remains inanimate. And, Nick, I fear the animating principle must come from you. My father means to sacrifice you that his creation may live."

Nick set his jaw, balled up one fist. "I'll not go easily, Rosamund, for all your father's magical arts. I'll resist while there is breath left in my body."

Rosamund replaced the sheet. "But how if I should tell you a way to avoid this fate, and neither you nor my father harmed by it?" She turned and moved toward the door, Nick following after her. But out on the landing he took her roughly by one arm and spun her around, the better to study her face.

Rosamund sighed. "Will you not trust me, Nick, and do as I tell you, for your own sake?"

He weighed the situation before he spoke. Rosamund had softened, lately, had even seemed to be growing fond of him—and there was no denying the attraction which sparked between them. Besides, what other choice *had* he but to do as she bade him, if he wanted to survive? "Aye, I'll trust you, up to a point," he finally decided. "But if I begin to suspect treachery . . ."

Rosamund nodded, accepting this conditional surrender. "There are things that I never told you before, having no wish to lose you. Yet there is a way for you to escape the island. The invisible barrier beyond the tide-line ceases to exist during the Fading."

"I'm not the fool you mistake me for," said Nick. "I guessed as much long before this. When the Fading begins, it's a sign that Magnus is pouring all of his power into making one of his storms."

There were no windows on the landing where they stood, yet Nick knew that the waves were booming on the shore with unwonted fury; the whole tower reverberated with their violence. "But I am not a strong swimmer, and the waves are dangerous out in the Chaos, particularly during a storm. Without a boat I'll surely drown."

"There is a boat," said Rosamund quietly. "Come and I'll show you."

Calling the iron man to accompany them, she led Nick down the stairs, through the gates of brass, and out to the beach. In a deep patch of shadow cast by

the tower, she fell to her knees and, careless of any
damage to her fine gown, began to dig in the sand.
Nick watched, incredulously. After only a few minutes' work, she uncovered some boards which, on
closer inspection, proved to be a section of the hull
of a boat.

"It's been buried here all these years. Did you never
guess, Nick, that such a boat must have existed?"

Her words, spoken down by the tide-line echoed in
his mind. *"By his art, we made safe passage through
the Chaos and the Void."* And Nick realized that for
all the magician's spells and incantations to quell the
elements, a boat had still been necessary.

There was little fear, even after so many years, that
the boat would have deteriorated, the planks rotted,
here where the laws of nature were suspended. Nick
knelt in the sand and began to dig furiously, and Rosamund instructed the iron man to do likewise. But the
clockwork slave worked so swiftly, the other two soon
moved aside to avoid obstructing him. In a short time,
the skiff was uncovered and carried down to the
tide-line.

By then, clouds boiled overhead, and the wind had
been whipped into a fine rage. Nick hesitated before
climbing aboard. To attempt to launch the boat before
he was certain the barrier had fallen would be too
dangerous, for he ran the risk of attracting the magician's attention when it was not wholly absorbed in
the storm. Yet if he waited too long, he might miss
his chance.

"Nick," said Rosamund, "take me with you. You'll
not be so cruel as to leave me behind?"

He turned to face her. "Would you leave your
home, leave your father, all for my sake? I cannot
believe that you care for me so much as that. And
besides . . . the sacrifice may prove to be greater than
you know."

She reached out and took his hand, clinging to him desperately. "I guess far more than you imagine. Do you suppose that I have lived here so long and never marked the passage of time? When we arrive in England, I'll be older than you are. How much older, I cannot guess . . . perhaps old enough to be your mother. But I vow I'll put no claim on you. I'll ask neither your love nor your pity."

He shook his head. "Your age matters nothing to me," he said kindly, though in his heart he was not so certain. "But for a woman to give up even the *illusion* of youth and beauty . . ."

The wind had torn her hair out of its bindings; it streamed around her in a dark cloud, making her appearance more fantastic than ever. "I'm not so vain as you think me. You called me an overpainted doll, but in truth, Nick, what is there here to occupy me but gauds and finery? I'll be more sober in England, and wiser, too."

Still he hesitated. "It is perilous out among the waves, I dare not take you on so dangerous a passage. And I know how you fear the Void."

Rosamund's hold on his fingers tightened. She raised her voice in order to be heard over the roar of the elements. "The Void is here, Nick. All is illusion— the tower, the sand, the sea—and we stand on nothing. I never guessed before you came here, made of solider stuff than anything I knew, but the knowledge has been growing within me with every passing day."

So that was the fear, Nick realized, that he had seen behind her eyes.

"If you leave me here, Nick, I will certainly go mad."

In the end, he could not deny her. "Then come with me, sweetheart," he said as he helped her into the skiff. "And together we'll make the passage . . . else die together in the attempt."

*   *   *

The wind howled and waves crashed violently against the hull of the boat. Sometimes, it seemed inevitable to Rosamund that they must be swamped or overturned, for the vessel was a light one and Nick appeared to know little about the use of the oars. It was, as they had both expected, a bitter passage.

Yet at last there came a time when they emerged from the stormy darkness and seemed to be floating on nothing at all, drawn on by some invisible force that it was impossible to fathom. But the Void was not empty as Rosamund had feared: All about her there was brilliant light, peopled, it seemed to her, by the souls of men and women who had passed on to some higher existence. Nick had stopped rowing and sat on the bench holding Rosamund's hand, as if for reassurance, but she needed no such comfort. She was happy now and strangely at peace, for she had faced her worst nightmare and discovered that it held no terrors.

Until Nick's hand suddenly turned to mist in her grasp, and the boat as quickly dissolved beneath her.

Rosamund cried out in protest, tried to catch hold of Nick . . . the boat . . . something . . . but there was nothing there. Then there was something . . . cold, irresistible, and cruelly familiar—which caught hold of her despite her struggles, picked her up, and hurled her back through Chaos and darkness.

Nick woke with a pounding in his head and the sound of his friends' voices clattering in his ears. "I believe he's about to wake at last. Nick . . . Nicholas . . . Nicky, my lad, can you hear me?"

With an effort, he opened his eyes. They were all crowded around his bed, all the familiar faces: Fulke, Christian, Ned, Nathaniel, Will. Beyond them, he recognized the paneled walls of the room he had slept in at Crowhaven.

"Where is she?" he managed to croak. "Rosamund . . . never tell me that I lost her in the Void?"

They were all silent, gazing down on him, all so pale and concerned. Or maybe just pale and dissipated, if they had gone on in the same rackety fashion he remembered before he left them.

It was Fulke who finally spoke up. "My dear fellow, you've been horribly ill. I have no idea who this Rosamund is, but there's been no one but ourselves next or nigh you these six days, and you've never once opened your eyes in all of that time. Are you certain you didn't dream her?"

For a moment it seemed that he *must* have dreamed her. "Six days . . . could it have been so brief a period as six days? I thought weeks must have passed since we broke into that room and I opened the cabinet and took out that devilish pack of cards."

His friends stirred uneasily, exchanging glances. This time it was Will who spoke up. "More than a month did pass. You disappeared—went out like a candle. Or so it seemed to us. We must have been mad-drunk, and never saw you wander off. We waited and waited for you to return, missed all the festivities in London, and had almost despaired of you. Then we heard a great thump upstairs one night, and Ned and I ran up to investigate. You were sprawled on the floor unconscious, where that pack of cards still lay scattered, the way we had left them when you disappeared, for we all felt inexplicably queer about moving them."

Fulke sat down at the foot of Nick's bed. "You've been ill ever since the night we found you. But where were you all of those weeks—or do you mean to tell us you don't remember?"

"I dare not tell you," said Nick wearily. "The story

is too fantastic and I doubt that you would believe me."

But he did tell Fulke the story, privately, two days later. There were things that he needed to know and he could only learn them by taking Fulke into his confidence. Lying in bed with his head raised only a little by the pillows (for he was still very weak) he told it all, and his friend listened carefully and without interruption.

"Either you've had the most rare and amazing dream, or a miraculous experience. I can't say which, Nicky. And perhaps we'll never know."

"But this uncle of yours," said Nick. "What was his name?"

"My *grandsire's* uncle, Magnus Catesby. You had the first name right and I don't recall telling you. And his daughter, little Rosamund." Fulke thought deeply. "You seem to know quite a lot about things we never speak of outside the family. Old Magnus has been our guilty secret these eighty years."

"Eighty years?" Nick scowled up at him. "You tell me that Magnus and his daughter have lived on that island for *eighty* years?"

Fulke reached out and patted Nick's hand consolingly. "So you see, if it really is true, this story of yours, it's just as well that you lost the girl. She would be an old, old woman now. She might even have dropped down dead the moment she set foot in England, having already outlasted her natural life span. I don't mean to sound cruel, and I expect that your heart was severely wounded if she was as pretty as you say, but perhaps it was all for the best."

Nick stared up at him. "All for the best . . . to lose her there between the worlds? I can't say whether my own heart was wounded or not, but it seems to me that you've no heart at all!"

"But you see, her father must have *known*," said Fulke. "How much time had passed and what would befall her if she left the island. You say that he was fond of her; he must have been watchful for her safety. It seems to me that he must have used his magic arts to draw her all the way back to the tower of brass, and that's how you lost her."

Nick tried to believe that it was true. It was an idea easier to live with than the thought of Rosamund cast adrift in the Void. He sighed and shook his head. Perhaps it only required time for him to accept the truth of it. For now, he was unutterably weary.

"I've kept you awake and talking far too long," said Fulke, seeing how gray he had gone around the mouth and the eyes. "Rest now, if you can, and we'll speak of this later."

Nick nodded and closed his eyes. "Now that I've told you my story, I feel as though I've shed some burden."

His friend crept silently out of the room, extinguishing the candles as he did so, and it was not long before Nick drifted off.

But his dreams were haunted, as they would be for years to come, by a dark-haired damsel with a haughty manner, who appeared before him in a series of gaudy fantastical gowns.

THE SIXTEENTH CARD
by Susan Wade

Susan Wade is the author of the novel *Walking Rain*, a magical realist thriller about a woman's confrontation with her past when she returns to her grandfather's New Mexico farm. Her short stories have appeared in *The Magazine of Fantasy & Science Fiction, Realms of Fantasy,* and *Amazing Stories,* among other periodicals, and in the anthologies *Snow White, Blood Red; Black Thorn, White Rose; Ruby Slippers, Golden Tears; Off Limits;* and others. She is at work on her next novel, *Burn Pattern,* about a woman firefighter who gets caught up in a serial arson case. She lives in Austin, Texas.

Based on a true event, "The Sixteenth Card" is a powerful story about the changes one particular Tower has wreaked upon a woman's life, as she returns to it many years later and confronts her past.

Towers are measured by their shadows . . .
—Chinese proverb

Of the Major Arcana of the tarot, the sixteenth is called the Tower. Or sometimes, "The Lightning-Struck Tower" or "The House of God." The traditional illustration for this card is of a tall, tapering crenellated tower set on a rocky island amid a stormy sea. Lightning is striking the tower's crown, and small human figures are tumbling from it to the jagged rocks below, terror clear on their tiny faces.

The Major Arcana are also known as the trumps or keys of the tarot. Their divinatory significance in any reading is far greater than that of the lesser cards, the Minor Arcana, which have four suits and are thought to be the forebears of the modern deck of playing cards. Of the trumps, only the Joker—key zero, the Fool—remains in the modern deck. I believe it is because the others were too powerful and could not be safely put in play. Remember, they represent the irresistible psychic forces that shape our lives.

The sixteenth of these powers is the Tower, a construct of human endeavor, struck by the elemental force of lightning, which tumbles the lives of its inhabitants awry. In divination, it signifies radical disruption to the life of the Seeker, a complete separation from all that has gone before. A forced rebirth, precipitated by drastic loss.

I consider the sixteenth card to be my personal crest. Although, in my case, the lightning struck not from the elements but from the tower itself.

On July 26th, 1966, in Austin, Texas, Donny Ray Deidrich killed his sister and his mother before climbing to the observation deck of the U.T. tower with his hunting rifle. He established a sniper's position and, in the course of one blazing hot Texas summer afternoon, shot forty-nine people. He was a military-trained marksman just back from Vietnam, and he made his shots count. Four people were permanently disabled; thirty-two died.

One of the people he killed was my mother.

It was strange, returning to Austin the summer I was thirty-two. I came to research a new book—a specialized art history based on paintings of the tarot—at U.T., which has one of the finest library systems in the southwest. I arrived in August and found a room for the semester at a women's cooperative that was within walking distance of the campus. I would be dividing my time between the PCL and the arts library, about ten blocks away.

The terrain had changed substantially; the campus had metastasized, a surreal growth overlaying the other, simpler landscape I remembered. The tower no longer dominated everything, and I found it possible to move through my days undisturbed by its shadow.

The overall sensation of summer in Austin was shockingly familiar—the cicadas droning like small airplanes in the huge old oaks, the hot-sugar scent of the mimosas flowering, the stark relief a breeze in a shaded spot brought. It reminded me of things so long forgotten that, even recalled, they seemed to have happened to someone else. Like the memory of my friend Kerry Brazell, sitting in my hideout in the vacant lot behind our house—a hollow cave formed by the drooping boughs of abelia bushes. I remembered the sweet smell of their leaves, and the sweeter secrets of our conversation. I remembered the deep clear blue of Kerry's favorite blouse and my own skinny brown legs, their scrapes and mosquito bites painted dark red with merthiolate. I remembered the tiny frogs, no longer than a fingernail, that had populated the biology pond on campus. My brother Timmy and I bloodthirstily wanted to feed them to the fish. Fortunately, the fish weren't particularly interested.

Our grammar school—Kerry's and Tim's and mine—had been swallowed by the university the year after Mom was killed, becoming Wooldridge Hall instead of Wooldridge Elementary School. Then Kerry's mother remarried suddenly, and they moved to New York, out of reach of even our rare visits back home to Austin. The following spring, the parks department built a senior center on the vacant lot where my hideout had been.

It was as if that single July afternoon tilted the first

domino, the one which caused all the other aspects of
my life to totter and then collapse. After that day,
everything changed. I often felt as if I were living
someone else's life, by default. As if my own had been
stolen, and some other little girl had taken it over,
living in that small jewel of a white house, with Kerry
for her best friend and aubelia bushes for a hideout.

While I was stuck in this stranger's life in Houston,
going to a school where I knew no one, suddenly
needing to wear glasses, and being labeled "studious"
instead of "a tomboy."

Returning to Austin brought it all back to me. I
suppose I'd coped with the trauma of my own disloca-
tion by forgetting. By letting my past—the sense of
my true life—slip away. But walking through the campus, with its shadow of that other campus I had known
so well, brought it all clear again: That was the building where my father had done his graduate research;
this was where I took viola lessons as part of the university's String Project; over there was the theater lab
where Kerry and I did a children's drama workshop
together.

I felt as if I were moving in slow motion, against
the pressure of the ocean of memories swimming
around me. It was an eerie, potent time, and I walked
through it in an oddly hyper-aware trance.

But none of these auspices prepared me for seeing
her.

I was eight years old when it happened. Timmy and
I were visiting our father in Houston, so Mom had
taken the chance to go back for summer session to
finish the degree she had abandoned—six hours shy
of completion—to marry Dad. Now that they were
divorced, she regretted the decision. I'd been relieved
when she went back to school; it seemed she was ral-

lying from the gloom and bitterness that had gripped her since the marriage ended.

We were all in my father's and stepmother's big bedroom—where the TV was—watching the evening news. My brother and I were sprawled on the plush gray carpet, Dad and Annabel were sitting on the edge of their bed. The national news came on first, and there was Austin, in the top news story of the day. A sniper on the U.T. tower was killing people. Police were trying to get him down, but the scope on his rifle was so powerful that it made movement anywhere on campus dangerous. It was impossible even to help some of the people who'd been shot. They lay where they'd fallen, bleeding to death in the sunshine.

The stark, black-and-white images of crumpled bodies on the street held us frozen, stunned. Then my father turned to me and said, in the voice of a stranger, "Miranda, is your mother on campus today?"

I nodded, unable to speak. Timmy started to cry. He was only six.

The lightning had struck.

My research was going extremely well, almost doing itself. Looking back, it seems as if the book was merely a lure to bring me home; once I came, the forces that had brought me back didn't want me distracted by work.

My publisher had contracted before with an artist who was doing graduate work at U.T., and they had commissioned him to reproduce the paintings from the tarot decks I selected for the book. We met to discuss the project a week or so after I returned to Austin.

Dave Breubacher was a burly man with brown hair that tumbled wildly to his shoulders. He wore granny glasses and smoked a lot, which made him something of a pariah. It was hard for him to find a restaurant that would let him in, he told me with a self-conscious laugh. Would I mind going to the Tavern? It was an old place, sometimes a little noisy, but the food was good. Could I drive? Did I know where it was?

I remembered the Tavern from when I was a kid. Its neon sign with the cold blue words "Air-Conditioned!" along the bottom and its Alpine chalet styling had made a vivid impression on me. And my mother would often sing a particular song when we passed it: *"There is a tavern in the town, in the town—and there my true love sits him down, sits him down . . ."*

I didn't remember the rest of the song, but I found the place easily. Dave and I were seated in the front room downstairs. He ordered a cheeseburger; I asked for a gallon of iced tea.

Dave sketched designs in the air with his nicotine- and paint-stained fingers. He was right on my wavelength about the book project. Oils on wood, he said, that was the way to go, for the sake of authenticity. And he didn't want to enlarge the paintings too much—just enough to allow for top-notch reproduction. What did I think of 10" by 4" dimensions?

"Sounds great," I said. "Now, about the different painting styles—"

Then I heard her laugh, and all the years stripped away. The sound was so familiar. I was out of the booth instantly, scanning the back half of the restaurant. There was such a roaring in my ears I couldn't hear her any more.

She wasn't there. But *I* was. A little girl with skinny brown legs, wearing shorts and a red-striped T-shirt I remembered very well. My stepmother had thrown it out when we moved to Houston, saying it was getting too small for me. I had cried and appealed to Dad, but he said Annabel knew more about kids' clothes and I should mind her. She bought me dresses instead.

The little girl—Miranda-the-child—sat at a tall table

on a bar stool, her brown legs dangling. She was drinking a vanilla milkshake, and had a creamy mustache. There was no one at the table with her. I was next to her without realizing I'd moved.

"Where is she?" I asked. "Where's your mother?"

"She had to go," she said. "I get to ride the bus downtown and see a movie. By my*self*." She beamed. Two of her front teeth were missing.

"Aren't you too young for that?" The question was automatic.

She scowled. "I'm *al*-most *nine*. I rode the bus all the way home from Houston by myself. Well, my brother came too, but he's only six, so that doesn't count."

I sank against the other bar stool and gripped the table. An abandoned straw leaked melting ice cream across the dark, scarred surface. Miranda picked up her glass in both hands and slurped.

"When did you ride the bus back from Houston?" I was having a hard time catching my breath.

She drummed her feet against the metal rungs of the bar stool and looked thoughtful. "Um, a while ago. I think ten or eleven days. My brother got homesick, so we came back early."

"Timmy? And you're Miranda, right?"

She scowled. "No!"

For an instant, I thought I'd made an error, mistaking some random child for myself when I was that age.

Then she said, "*Randy*. I'm called Randy. Whoever heard of a name like Miranda anyway?"

I'd forgotten my own nickname. How much else had I left behind here? Dave came up next to me and touched my shoulder. "Miranda?" he said. "Is something wrong?"

I'd forgotten about him, too. "Uh, no—I just thought I heard a familiar voice. Someone I used to know—I wanted to talk to her."

"A kid?" he said.

"No, her mother." I glanced around, realizing I should ask Randy where her mother had gone. But the other bar stool was empty. "Where'd she get to?"

Dave shrugged.

Her glass was still on the table. I reached over and touched it, to reassure myself it was really there, that I hadn't imagined the whole thing.

The glass was solid and cold under my fingers. I shivered.

Moving to Houston was a misery. It was astonishing how much we missed our mother when she was no longer a phone call away. I missed the clear skies and sun-drenched heat of Austin summers almost as much. Although those qualities may have been more emblematic of a beloved past than precious in themselves.

I abandoned the tomboyishness that enraged my stepmother, instead retreating to my room to read at every opportunity. My reward was the offer of a scholarship to a private school in Conroe, which my father promptly accepted. I was glad to leave behind the constant reminders of all that was absent from my life. At school, I could pretend my mother was at home waiting for me, at least most of the time.

Timmy was the only one who missed me. He seemed more lost each time I went back. I did my best to comfort him while I was there, but there is no substitute for consistency when you're a child. And no substitute for your own mother either. But Annabel didn't even try.

After the meeting at the Tavern, I was in a daze. Later, I could hardly remember what Dave and I had agreed to about the paintings for the book. Worse, I hardly cared.

All I could think of was hearing my mother laugh, and about what would have happened if I'd been a little quicker to reach their table. Without intending to the next morning, I detoured on my walk to the arts library. I found myself standing outside Wooldridge Hall, staring at the tall sashed windows of my first grade classroom. Canna lilies still grew high beside the chain-link fence, their fiery colors brilliant in the sun.

I went up the walk. When I was a child, it had been cracked, with seams of grass running through it. Now it was smooth and broad, and led to a ramp built on one side of the front steps.

I slipped around to the side yard, where the bicycle racks and pull-up bars had been set in messy glops of cement. As I pushed through the overgrown line of oleanders, I heard children's voices, shrieking in fun.

They were playing dodge ball on the playground, just beyond the dusty side yard. I recognized the dark red textured ball. The kids circled and skipped aside as it came their way. She was there, wearing shorts and tennis shoes with no socks, and a red-striped T-shirt that fit her perfectly. Mom must have bought her a new one when she outgrew her old favorite.

The kids were screaming, "Get Randy! Get Randy!" and she laughed, dancing out of the way easily when a bigger boy slammed the ball at her. They couldn't put her out. A woman's voice called from down the street. "Steee-ven! Lunchtime!"

After a short consultation, they crowded around Randy and held her arms so one of the boys could tap her lightly on the forehead with the ball.

She was grinning as she wriggled free of their web. "Sissies!" she called over her shoulder in a good-natured way. "Ganging up on me like that."

The kids laughed and called a few friendly insults

back before heading off in different directions. She was coming past me, toward Rio Grande Street.

"Randy?" I said softly.

She glanced over at me. Her teeth had grown in, and looked large in her little-girl mouth.

"Do you remember me?"

She shook her head. "Not really."

"I'm—a friend of your mother."

"Oh?" She seemed a little puzzled, but not at all nervous. A different world, I realized, one where kids didn't have to mistrust all strangers. "Well, I've got to go—Tuesdays and Thursdays are swimming lessons."

"What about Mondays, Wednesdays, and Fridays?" I asked, fascinated.

"Tennis and volleyball!" she shouted as she dashed off down the street. She leaped over a flower bed with a whoop, then turned to wave before she disappeared around the corner.

I walked on to the library, and was stunned to realize how late it was. Past lunchtime. No wonder Steven's mother had called him.

The research was going smoothly. I had already located a number of interesting tarot decks from different periods, which illustrated clearly my points about shifts in painting style, symbolism, and pigmentation. The text would take time to write, but I wanted Dave to begin work on the reproductions as soon as possible. All I had to do was finalize which sixteen decks would appear in the book, and which card from each deck should be reproduced.

Easier said than done. It didn't help that my concentration was shot. I had wanted to see Randy again; I wanted to follow her home and talk to my mother. Even if I only saw Mom for a moment or two, I'd convinced myself it would be enough. At the same time, these encounters had unsettled me badly. I could scarcely think of anything else.

The pile of books I'd accumulated was too large for a study carrel, so I was working at a long table near the wide glass wall of the arts library. I shoved both hands through my hair and squeezed, tugging at my scalp as if that would straighten my thoughts out. It didn't. When I looked up, I saw the tower.

It looked nothing like the painted towers shown in the books spread out before me. It's a creamy limestone building, a straight-sided square rising high above the broader base of the administration building. At the top is a large clock-face, surmounted by a Neo-classical pediment. But it was here, on the observation deck of this tower, that Donny Ray Deidrich had tumbled my life awry.

The solution was obvious. What better way to illustrate the changing trends of art than to show sixteen different representations of the same card? I would have Dave paint the Tower from each deck.

He wasn't as quick to see the opportunities as I would have liked, but the contract required him to paint whichever cards I selected. And I'll give him this: He didn't procrastinate. He started work the next afternoon, as soon as I brought him the pictures.

I spent the next day at the PCL, studying its massive collection on the tower shootings. I had no idea what I was looking for until I found it.

A black-and-white photograph of a crumpled body, short skirt twisted around slim brown legs, one arm flung wide with the hand turned palm upward as if in supplication. Dark glistening blood pooled around her.

I didn't recognize her body. What I recognized was the brightly patterned scarf tied to the strap of her straw bag.

It had been blue and red, with swirls of white. I had

given it to her for her birthday, just before Timmy
and I left for Houston.

It took me four more days to pump up the courage
to go home. The place I always thought of as home:
my mother's house. A small but beautiful white clapboard house with blue shutters on Shoal Crest Drive,
shaded by tall oaks and elms. The backyard had sloped
steeply down to a stone wall. My hideout in the vacant
lot had been on the other side of that wall.

I walked over, following the same route I'd always
taken home from school—down Rio Grande to 29th
Street. The walk was like a ritual. It seemed if I could
saturate myself in that time and place, I could find my
way back to it. To my mother.

The house looked very much the same, as pris-
tinely white and neat as ever. There was a new
safety railing at the end of the front porch next to
the driveway, which slanted down to the free-standing garage. Timmy had ridden his new bike off the
end of the porch and split his lip just before we'd
left for Houston. I guess Mom decided a railing was
in order.

The street was quiet except for the buzz of the cicadas and the soft hum of air conditioners. I stood across
the street for ten minutes, under the influence of a
strange cocktail of hope and terror.

I crossed the street and went up the walk. There
was the scar on the tallest oak tree, which I'd forgotten. It had lost a big limb during Hurricane Carla.
English ivy was still thick along the side yard, the rusty
green smell of it instantly familiar.

It frightened me to come up to that door, to knock
at it like a stranger. Which I was, now. I did it anyway.
The screen door was new.

The house was very still. Was anyone home?

Then the inner door swung open. The girl's face was

familiar—mine again—but she was older. Twelve maybe.

"Can I help you?" she said.

I wet my lips. "A friend of mine used to live here—I was hoping to see her. Elizabeth Johnson?"

She hesitated, then swung the screen door open a crack. I think she wanted to see my face more clearly. A big gray cat snaked through her legs toward the gap. She pounced lightning-fast, and scooped him up. "No you don't, Trav."

The cat gave one discontented yowl, then settled into the curve of her arm. She propped the door open with her shoulder and started scratching his chin.

"Traveler," I said. "I'd forgotten." I reached out to touch the soft fur, listening to his purr. Dad had made us give Trav to a neighbor when it turned out Annabel was allergic to cats.

The girl looked up, and her face lost any caution it may have had. "Sorry, Mom's not here right now." She tilted her head, frankly examining me. "You look kind of hot. Would you like to come in, have some iced tea? You could leave her a note."

I nodded, not trusting my voice. I pulled the door open the rest of the way and went inside.

After I went away to school, Tim seemed to shrink into himself, getting thinner and more pale each time I saw him. He grew his hair long. I knew he sometimes skipped school to hang out in the park. I didn't know what he was doing there. I tell myself that often: I didn't know.

He died of a heroin overdose three weeks after his sixteenth birthday.

She took me into the small dining room at the back of the house and offered me a chair at the table. My great-grandmother's claw-footed mahogany table. I'd forgotten it. I'd lost track of so much through the years. I looked through the door to the kitchen. On the black-and-white diamond tiles stood a tall glass with the melting remains of iced coffee in it. My mother always drank iced coffee in the summertime. I turned away, eyes burning, and looked out the window to steady myself. Beyond the slope of the back yard was the vacant lot. No senior center had come yet to uproot the tangled trees and brush.

I was back, I was home, where I had longed to be so many times through the years after she died. A sudden wild hope clotted my throat. What if I didn't leave? Could I stay here and have my real life after all?

The screen door banged shut behind me, and I jumped.

Miranda set a glass of iced tea and a teaspoon on a paper napkin in front of me.

"Don't mind the brat," she said. "He always slams the door. Boys love to make noise. I'll get the sugar and lemons." She went back to the kitchen.

I turned. Timmy dumped a baseball bat in the corner of the living room and dropped his fielder's mitt on top of it. He was taller and stronger-looking than I expected, with at least a zillion freckles. He grinned at me. "Who're you? You look kind of familiar." Then without waiting for an answer, he whirled past me into the kitchen. "Randy, will you make me some lemonade? Please? I'm so-o thirsty."

"Can't you see we have company? You can have milk or ice water now. I'll make lemonade later."

"Aww, Randy—"

"You can have some graham crackers, if you want." A big-sister concession.

He heaved a long-suffering sigh, then went to the pantry.

Randy came and joined me, bringing a blue sugar bowl and a small dish of lemons. "Here you are."

"Thank you. You take care of your brother in the summer?"

She nodded. "And after school. Mom works since she and Dad split up, so we have to manage on our own. But Mrs. Seymour is always here to help in case of an emergency—she's right next door."

And she's nearly eighty years old, I thought. But it didn't matter. They were safe; you could feel it in the very walls of the house. Nothing could hurt them here.

Timmy came out of the kitchen with a plate of graham crackers and glass of milk. He already had a milk mustache. I realized I couldn't even remember him at this age; I had been away at school too much.

"You look kind of sad," he said around a mouthful of cookie. "Everything okay?"

I blinked and turned to look out the window at the vacant lot. My hideout was just over there, through that grove of trees, in the undergrowth.

"Everything is just perfect," I said.

In the end, I didn't leave a note for my mother because I couldn't think of anything to say. *Hi, I'm your grown-up daughter from another reality, where you died years ago. But don't worry. I just want to come and live with you and be your little girl again?* Somehow I didn't think that would cut it.

Randy and Tim were sweet, but it would have been awkward—and probably would have worried them—for me to stay much longer. I finished my tea, thanked them for their hospitality, and left.

But I couldn't go back to my room at the co-op, to my here-and-now life. I couldn't face that. Besides, if I went, turned the wrong corner, how could I be sure of ever finding this place again? This life, where my mother was alive and Wooldridge was still an elementary school?

So I slipped along the far side of the garage and over the back wall. The stubble of Johnson grass poked at my thin sandals and scratched my legs, but I didn't care. I jogged over to the grove of trees and curved sharply right, then dropped to my knees and crept into my hideout.

The hollowed-out space between the abelia bushes was still there, smaller than I remembered, but screened completely by long whippy branches.

I huddled in the soft brown dust and cried. For everything I had lost, all I had been, before—I wept for it all. I cried until I couldn't think of anything more to miss or be sad for, until I was spent.

Then I fell asleep, sheltered by the abelias.

I dreamed of being in my own bed, the twin bunk-beds Tim and I had shared as children. The pale blue walls of the room were cool and mysterious in the summer twilight, and I could hear Mom humming as she folded laundry in the other room. A song about a tavern.

I've never felt safer.

When I woke, it was dark and I was stiff from lying on the ground. I couldn't face my barren little room at the co-op. I staggered up the hill to the north and hiked along Lamar to Dave Breubacher's studio. It was a ratty little place over a garage just off 32nd Street, but the upper half of each wall was solid windows, so the light was good for painting. The big trees surrounding the place made it feel secluded, almost pastoral, except for the strong smell of turpentine that permeated the apartment.

It was one large room that had been converted, with a free-standing wall that divided about half of the space. Paint-spattered muslin on a long rod was hung at right angles to that wall, carving out a studio. One corner of the remaining space served as a bedroom, the other as the living area. Plus a kitchenette and a bathroom, and that was all.

Dave didn't seem surprised to see me, but he was shocked at the condition of my legs.

"Jesus! You're scratched to bits. Come in and let me put something on those. What've you been doing?"

"Crawling through bushes," I said. I flopped down on his futon sofa and pushed off my sandals.

He went to the bathroom and brought out a bottle of rubbing alcohol and some cotton balls. "Want to tell me why?" he asked as he settled by my feet and soaked the cotton.

"I'm not sure I can explain it. It doesn't really make sense."

He nodded, said, "This'll sting," and pressed the alcohol-soaked cotton on my shin.

I leaned back and let him wash the scratches on my legs, not even trying to help. His fingers were blunt and rough-skinned, dry from all the paint and turpentine, I suppose. But his touch was gentle.

"Do you have any alcohol suitable for internal application?" I asked when he was done.

He stood up, and blinked at me from behind his granny glasses. "I think we might find something."

The "something" was tequila, which tasted a lot like turpentine to me, but it got the job done.

By the time it was dark, I no longer heard voices whispering from the swaying branches outside the windows. I no longer heard much at all except the ringing in my ears. More important, the image of Tim's pale, thin face on the blue satin pillow of his coffin no longer hovered, ready to loom the instant I closed my eyes.

Dave's messy studio was a home; my room at the co-op was not. And homes have a special magic that keeps you safe, stops the dominos of your life from being spilled and scattered until its pattern is lost.

So I stayed the night.

His hands were just fine, I decided blurrily, much later. Like tequila, they did the job.

He was kind enough to let down the shades before leaving for the nine-thirty class he was teaching the next morning. And I'm not sure I would have survived the hangover without the water and aspirins he left on the floor next to the futon.

After the pounding head and nausea subsided a little, I risked a glance at my watch. Almost noon.

I let the aspirin catch up a little more, then dragged myself to the shower. My clothes were dusty, but not too disgusting, considering. I borrowed Dave's toothbrush and comb. The result was bearable.

I didn't feel quite up to braving the midday sun yet, so I went into the curtained-off space Dave used for a studio.

He had finished the sixteen Towers. I could tell they hadn't been varnished yet, but the paint was dry when I tested an inconspicuous corner. He had used thin, laminated board, which gave the paint an extra depth. The oldest known deck—which dated to the late fourteenth century—was highly stylized and rather crudely rendered, but the colors were brilliant and the design bold. The others I had selected varied widely, from the Botticelli-like delicacy and elegance of line of the Fruehr to the orange-and-black Cubist terror of the Thoth.

They would have made a magnificent book, truly.

I felt no remorse at stealing them.

*   *   *

The tree branches tossed in the wind, strobing the shadows around my feet. Clouds scudded overhead, carrying the smell of rain on a hot day.

There was nothing to mark the spot except memory, but I found it. The place where my mother had been killed. The line of sight from there to the tower was unimpeded, even by tree branches. Some things are fated.

The reproductions were in my backpack. As I removed the linen packet I'd wrapped them in, the wind blew harder. I knelt on the hot cement and began laying out the paintings in chronological order, beginning with the one from the oldest deck. Tower after tower, each tossed in its own storm. How many people's lives had they upended through the long years?

I placed them in a pattern like the shape of her body, here the crumpled torso, there the twisted skirt, these two sketching out the pooling shape of her blood.

The shadows moved restlessly around me as the wind grew, but the cards never stirred. Their towers had taken root in the pavement. Where they belonged, here at the heart of the cataclysm they had turned loose on my life.

Thirteen, fourteen, fifteen. I laid the cards down, and the wind ripped and screamed at me. Surely sixteen keys would be enough to open the doorway I had been brought here to find.

As I placed the sixteenth card, a little apart from the others, where her reaching hand had fallen, the shadows closed around me. Randy, Tim, Kerry—their voices whispered as they pressed into me, melted through me. The sensation was of being buffeted by hot summer winds, and brought a burst of cotton-candy sweetness on the tongue, quickly gone.

If I went back, would I corrupt their other, safer

world? Would my presence call the sniper's bullet down? To her, or to me? To little Timmy?

Curtains of storm cloud rippled beyond the tower. I waited, held my breath, drawing the image from my dream in front of me like a shield. A snug bed in soft summer twilight; my mother's voice humming a familiar tune.

A "Y" of lightning flashed, huge and brilliant, cracking the sky in two as it lashed down. It struck the tower.

A darkly glimmering hollow shaped itself above the spot where her body had fallen. Beyond its insubstantial frame, I caught the echo of her laugh and saw the flutter of a red-and-blue scarf.

"Mom?" I whispered. "I'm home."

I stepped through.

ABOUT THE EDITORS

Martin H. Greenberg is the most prolific anthologist in publishing history, with most of his collections in the science fiction and fantasy genres. He is the winner of the Milford Award for Lifetime Achievement in Science Fiction Editing and was Editor Guest of Honor at the 1992 World Science Fiction Convention. He lives with his wife, daughter, and two cats in Green Bay, Wisconsin.

Lawrence Schimel is the editor of over a dozen anthologies, including *The Fortune-Teller* (with Martin H. Greenberg); *Food for Life and Other Dish; Switch Hitters* (with Carol Queen); and *Two Hearts Desire* (with Michael Lassell). His own writings have appeared in numerous periodicals, including *The Wall Street Journal, The Saturday Evening Post, The Tampa Tribune, Physics Today, Isaac Asimov's SF Magazine, Marion Zimmer Bradley's Fantasy Magazine,* and *Cricket,* and in over ninety anthologies, including *Weird Tales From Shakespeare, The Time of the Vampires, Return to Avalon, Phantoms of the Night, Fantastic Alice, Excalibur, Werewolves, Cat Fantastic III, Dragon Fantastic, Enchanted Forests, The Random House Treasury of Light Verse,* and the *Sword & Sorceress* series. He has translated graphic novels from the Spanish, and his own writings have been published abroad in Dutch,

Finnish, German, Italian, Japanese, Mandarin, and Polish translations. He is the publisher and editor of A Midsummer Night's Press, which has produced limited editions of works by Jane Yolen, Nancy Willard, Joe Haldeman, and others. Twenty-five years old, he lives in Manhattan, where he writes and edits full-time.

A feline lovers' fantasy come true . . .

CATFANTASTIC

☐ **CATFANTASTIC** UE2355—$5.99
☐ **CATFANTASTIC II** UE2461—$5.99
☐ **CATFANTASTIC III** UE2591—$4.99
☐ **CATFANTASTIC IV** UE2711—$5.99
    edited by Andre Norton and Martin H. Greenberg

Unique collections of fantastical cat tales, some set in the distant future on as yet unknown worlds, some set in our own world but not quite our dimension, some recounting what happens when beings from the ancient past and creatures out of myth collide with modern-day felines.

☐ **OUTWORLD CATS** UE2596—$4.99
    by Jack Lovejoy

When agents of industrial mogul Benton Ingles seize a goverment space station, the two cats aboard are captured and brought to Earth. But these are not Earth cats—they are fully sentient telepaths from another planet. And these cats might just prove to be the only hope for saving Earth from enslavement to one man's greed.

☐ **TAILCHASER'S SONG** UE2374—$5.99
    by Tad Williams

This best-selling feline fantasy epic tells the adventures of Fritti Tail-chaser, a young ginger cat who sets out, with boundless enthusiasm, on a dangerous quest which leads him into the underground realm of an evil cat-god—a nightmare world from which only his own resources can deliver him.

Science Fiction Anthologies

☐ **FUTURE NET** UE2723—$5.99
Martin H. Greenberg & Larry Segriff, editors

From a chat room romance gone awry ... to an alien monitoring the Net as an advance scout for interstellar invasion ... to a grief-stricken man given the chance to access life after death ... here are sixteen original tales that you must read before you venture online again, stories from such top visionaries as Gregory Benford, Josepha Sherman, Mickey Zucker Reichert, Daniel Ransom, Jody Lynn Nye, and Jane Lindskold.

☐ **FUTURE EARTHS: UNDER SOUTH AMERICAN SKIES** UE2581—$4.99
Mike Resnick & Gardner Dozois, editors

From a plane crash that lands its passengers in a survival situation completely alien to anything they've ever experienced, to a close encounter of the insect kind, to a woman who has journeyed unimaginably far from home—here are stories from the rich culture of South America, with its mysteriously vanished ancient civilizations and magnificent artifacts, its modern-day contrasts between sophisticated city dwellers and impoverished villagers.

☐ **MICROCOSMIC TALES** UE2532—$4.99
Isaac Asimov, Martin H. Greenberg, & Joseph D. Olander, eds.

Here are 100 wondrous science fiction short-short stories, including contributions by such acclaimed writers as Arthur C. Clarke, Robert Silverberg, Isaac Asimov, and Larry Niven. Discover a superman who lives in a *real* world of nuclear threat ... an android who dreams of electric love ... and a host of other tales that will take you instantly out of this world.

☐ **SHERLOCK HOLMES IN ORBIT** UE2636—$5.50
Mike Resnick & Martin H. Greenberg, editors
Authorized by Dame Jean Conan Doyle

Not even time can defeat the master sleuth in this intriguing anthology about the most famous detective in the annals of literature. From confrontations with Fu Manchu and Moriarity, to a commission Holmes undertakes for a vampire, here are 26 new stories all of which remain true to the spirit and personality of Sir Arthur Conan Doyle's most enduring creation.

Welcome to DAW's Gallery of Ghoulish Delights!

☐ **DRACULA: PRINCE OF DARKNESS**
Martin H. Greenberg, editor
A blood-draining collection of all-original Dracula stories. From Dracula's traditional stalking grounds to the heart of modern-day cities, the Prince of Darkness casts his spell over his prey in a private blood drive from which there is no escape!   UE2531—$4.99

☐ **THE TIME OF THE VAMPIRES**   May 1996
P.N. Elrod & Martin H. Greenberg, editors
From a vampire blessed by Christ to the truth about the notorious Oscar Wilde to a tale of vampirism and the Bow Street Runners, here are 18 original tales of vampires from Tanya Huff, P.N. Elrod, Lois Tilton, and others.
                                                                UE2693—$5.50

☐ **WEREWOLVES**
Martin H. Greenberg, editor
Here is a brand-new anthology of original stories about the third member of the classic horror cinema triumvirate—the werewolf, a shapeshifter who prowls the darkness, the beast within humankind unleashed to prey upon its own.
                                                                UE2654—$5.50

☐ **WHITE HOUSE HORRORS**
Martin H. Greenberg, editor
The White House has seen many extraordinary events unforld within its well-guarded walls. Sixteen top writers such as Brian Hodge, Grant Masterton, Bill Crider, Billie Sue Mosiman, and Edward Lee relate of some of the more unforgettable.   UE2659—$5.99

☐ **MISKATONIC UNIVERSITY**
Martin H. Greenberg & Robert Weinberg, editors
Miskatonic U is a unique institution, made famous by the master of the horrific, H.P. Lovecraft. Thirteen original stories will introduce you to the dark side of education, and prove once and for all that a little arcane knowledge can be a very dangerous thing, especially in the little Yankee college town of Arkham.
                                                                UE2722—$5.99

From time immemorial, they have stalked the night . . .

TALES OF THE UNDEAD

☐ **CELEBRITY VAMPIRES** UE2667—$4.99
   Martin H. Greenberg, editor

From a Catskill song and dance team, to an act of kindness by Marilyn Monroe, to a mysterious admirer of Tallulah Bankhead, here are 20 original tales about those who thirst to drink the rich, dark wine of fame.

☐ **DRACULA: PRINCE OF DARKNESS** UE2531—$4.99
   Martin H. Greenberg, editor

A blood-draining collection of all-original Dracula stories. From Dracula's traditional stalking grounds to the heart of modern-day cities, the Prince of Darkness casts his spell over his prey in a private blood drive from which there is no escape!

☐ **THE TIME OF THE VAMPIRES** UE2693—$5.50
   P.N. Elrod & Martin H. Greenberg, editors

Creatures of legend—or something all too real? From a vampire blessed by Christ to the truth about the notorious Oscar Wilde to a tale of vampirism and the Bow Street Runners, here are 18 original tales of vampires from Tanya Huff, P.N. Elrod, Lois Tilton, and others.

☐ **VAMPIRE DETECTIVES** UE2626—$4.99
   Martin H. Greenberg, editor

From newly-made vampire detective Victory Nelson who must defend Toronto against one of her own, to a cop on the trail of an international serial killer with a bloodlust that just won't quit, here are blood-chilling new tales of vampires who stalk the night in search of crimes to commit or criminals to be stopped.

Elizabeth Forrest

☐ **PHOENIX FIRE** UE2515—$4.99
As the legendary Phoenix awoke, so too did an ancient Chinese demon—and Los Angeles was destined to become the final battleground in their millenia-old war.

☐ **DARK TIDE** UE2560—$4.99
The survivor of an accident at an amusement pier is forced to return to the town where it happened. And slowly, long buried memories start to resurface, and all his nightmares begin to come true . . .

☐ **DEATH WATCH** UE2648—$5.99
McKenzie Smith has been targeted by a mastermind of evil who can make virtual reality into the ultimate tool of destructive power. Stalked in both the real and virtual worlds, can McKenzie defeat an assassin who can strike out anywhere, at any time?

☐ **KILLJOY** UE2695—$5.99
Given experimental VR treatments, Brand must fight a constant battle against the persona of a serial killer now implanted in his brain. But Brand would soon learn that there were even worse things in the world—like the unstoppable force of evil and destruction called KillJoy.

Camille Bacon-Smith

☐ **THE FACE OF TIME**   UE2707—$5.99

Tracking down a serial killer in the town of Thorgill, two New Scotland Yard officers are about to enter a whole new territory of police investigation. And though one of the detectives and the townspeople know what is really going on, no one's willing to let his partner in on the secret. But as ancient rituals begin to be fulfilled, the two officers find themselves drawn into an unholy war—facing an enemy more powerful than death itself. . . .

☐ **EYE OF THE DAEMON**   UE2673—$5.50

All the wealthy Mrs. Simpson knew was that her half brother Paul was missing, and the ad she was responding to had been lying on top of the ransom note she found in her dining room. But these were private investigators of the immortal kind—and this kidnapping was about to lure them into the heart of a demonic war. . . .
